EAGLE STATION

"Think, shithead," he yelled to himself. "Think."
Our Father; who art in heaven, hallowed be . . .
the radio. That PJ talked into the radio. He had
one of his own, he knew he did. He reached
down with slow deliberate hands and pulled
his spare RT-10 from his right cargo pocket
and extended the antenna.

"Jolly Green, this is Wolf," he said into the
dime-sized microphone embedded in the radio
face. When he put the radio to his ear to
listen for a reply, he realised the noise from
the hovering helicopter was too loud to hear
anything. He saw the man in the open door
point to his helmet and give him a thumbs-up.
The man also pointed to his wrist and held
up two fingers. A spate of rain drummed on
Wolf's face and he suddenly knew what he had
to do. There was no time to check either of the
other two men for wounds. They might even
be dead, he thought, but he would get them
out of there.

**Also by the same author,
and available from Coronet:**

PHANTOM LEADER

About the Author

Mark Berent served in the Air Force for more than twenty years, first as an enlisted man and then as an officer. He has logged 4,350 hours of flying time, over 1,000 of them in combat. During his three Vietnam tours, Berent earned not only the Silver Star but two Distinguished Flying Crosses, air medals, a Bronze Star, a Vietnamese Cross of Gallantry, and a Legion of Merit. Now a pilot-reporter and the aviation editor for a defense journal, he lives on a farm in Virginia, where he is writing the sequel to *Eagle Station*.

"Berent pulls off the impossible trick of conveying in words what it truly feels like to be a fighter pilot. His books grip your stomach like a 'g' suit."

Group Captain Ian Madelin, RAF (Ret)

"The action scenes are first-rate throughout, displaying the command of detail Berent's readers have come to expect."

Publishers Weekly

EAGLE STATION

MARK BERENT

CORONET BOOKS
Hodder and Stoughton

This book is dedicated to the KIA, MIA, and POW aircrew from Air America, the US Air Force, the US Army, the US Coast Guard, Continental Air Service, the US Marine Corps, the US Navy, the Royal Australian Air Force, and to the men of the US Army Special Forces.

While this is a highly fictionalized account of the action at Lima Site 85 in northeastern Laos, the dedication to the USAF and CIA men at the site is no less real and heartfelt.

"We stand to our glasses ready."

And to MB.

I give special thanks to combat Jolly Green pilot Dr. John Guilmartin, Lt. Col. USAF (Ret); Ed Kobernik M/Fgt USAF (Ret), the man who kept the Jollies flying; and to CMSgt Don Boudreaux, Spectre Gunner and Vice President of the Spectre Association. Any errors, of course, in their area of expertise are mine.

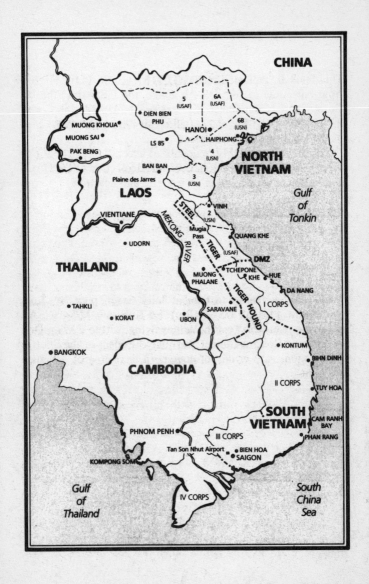

Prologue

The young men stood at positions of exaggerated attention on the grass field in front of the cadet barracks at Lowry Air Force Base. The morning breeze ruffled their new khaki uniforms, all stiff and creased. It was the cadets' first Sunday at the Academy, and as the officers called out religions one by one, they broke ranks to go where they were told: Lutherans here, Protestants over there, Catholics, Jews, Baptists, LDS. Re-form in columns of twos. Cover down. Prepare for mandatory chapel. The mint-fresh Air Force cadets hustled to line up correctly and not incur the wrath of their upperclassmen. There were 465 new cadets, and 461 of them fell into one of the religious formations. When asked why they had not, three of the four remaining said they were agnostics.

Agnostics? They were told they were *Other* and to snap to and form up off to one side.

The fourth man, eighteen-year-old cadet Fourth Class Kenichi Tanaka, didn't move. He stood five foot seven, weighed a stocky 150 pounds, and displayed a square jaw. His billed cadet hat pulled low over his dark Asian eyes concealed his black crew-cut hair. His skin was a consistent brown, as if he had a well-established summer tan.

Cadet Second Class Jerome Powers detached himself from the group of upperclassmen, walked over and stared disdainfully from his six-foot height down into the face of the lone

9

cadet. Powers's eyebrows and eyelashes were white-blond, his eyes icy blue.

"And what are you, Mister" – he glanced at the name tag – "Tanaka . . . a Confucianist?' Powers, a sometimes-Baptist from Mississippi, smirked at his little joke.

"No, sir. Buddhist."

Powers tilted his chin toward the "others." "Fall in with those three."

Tanaka stared straight ahead as he had been taught. "Sir," he said in a low voice, "those are 'others.' I am not an 'other.' "

"What?" Powers yelled into Tanaka's face. "What did you say, dumbsmack?" Whereas Marine drill instructors could use inventive scatological terms for their boots in training, upperclassmen at the United States Air Force Academy could not, hence the term "smack" had surfaced, and was used when an upperclassman really wanted to get after a doolie.

"Sir, I am not an 'other.' I am a Buddhist," Tanaka said.

"You trying to get smart with me? We don't have any *Buddhist*" – Powers spat the word out – "around here. You're a Protestant or a Jew or something. We have services for all of them. Or maybe you don't believe in any God. In that case you go to the library during chapel. But we don't have any *Buddhist*. So you are an *'other.' "* He said the words slowly and with theatrical emphasis. "You got that, Mister?"

Tanaka did not remove his eyes from the horizon. "Sir," he began, "this is chapel formation. Every cadet has mandatory church services every Sunday in the church of his faith. You called out all the religions except mine. My faith is Buddhism. I don't want to go to the library. I don't want to go to Christian or Jewish services. I want to attend a ceremony by a Buddhist monk in a temple." Tanaka's voice remained low and without inflection. He had the faint broad "a" accent of those from the Napa Valley in California.

Jerome Powers put his hands on his hips and looked around at his classmates, who were watching him in silence. Behind them, Jerome Powers saw a commissioned Tac officer headed toward him. Powers turned back to Tanaka.

"Now you're in for it. Here comes our Tac officer and he's

10

going to have your ass, Mister." Tactical officers – captains and majors – were assigned to each cadet squadron and wing to teach proper military life to the future Air Force officers.

Powers saluted as Captain Tom Dudley approached.

"What's the problem?" Dudley asked as he returned the salute. Dudley, an Annapolis graduate from Miles City, Montana, who had chosen the Air Force, had been selected from his F-86 fighter squadron to be a Tac officer. He had dark brown hair and stood just under six feet.

"Sir, this doolie won't obey orders," Powers said.

Dudley raised an eyebrow.

"He won't fall in with the group I've assigned him to," Powers continued. "I think he is trying to run a number on me."

"A number, Mister Powers?"

"Yes, sir. I think he's trying to take advantage of the system. He refuses to fall in with any of the formations set up for chapel. Says he's a Buddhist."

Dudley eyed Tanaka. "Do you doubt his word?" he asked Powers.

Powers stiffened. "Well, ah . . . you see, we have no Buddhists around here, so I . . ."

"Over here," Dudley said. He walked to one side. The morning sun warmed the air. "Look," he said to Powers. "One of the duties of a Tac officer is not to interfere with the proper duties of the cadets. You upperclassmen run your own wings and squadrons. We supervise, correct your mistakes, nudge you toward correct leadership solutions. We do not solve your problems for you."

"Sir, I don't have a problem," Powers said in a belligerent tone. "Mister Tanaka does."

"Are you going to write him up?"

Powers pursed his lips. "Yes, sir."

"On what charge?"

"Failure to obey a lawful order."

"If true, that could probably get him expelled."

Powers grinned. "Yes, sir."

"What exactly was your lawful order, Mister Powers?"

11

"Sir, I told him to fall in with that detail over there." He pointed to the three cadets who had said they were agnostics.

"What exactly is that detail for, Mister Powers?"

"Sir, it's the library detail."

Dudley didn't speak and continued looking at Powers.

"Sir, it's what we call 'others.' They're, uhm, cadets who have no religion at all. They don't believe in God or anything."

"Didn't Mister Tanaka say he was a Buddhist?"

"Yes, sir.

"Don't Buddhists believe in God?"

"Well, no God like *we* believe in," Powers snapped, then belatedly added, "sir."

"You didn't answer my question."

"Sir, I guess they believe in a God."

"Then he is a member of a recognized religion, isn't he?"

"Sir, he belongs to a religion we don't have."

Dudley drew himself up. "Powers, I'm getting mighty tired of our conversation. This is a cadet situation that I want you to solve. Solve it. Any questions?"

"Sir, no sir," Powers said, and saluted. He did an about-face and walked back to Tanaka. He was seething inside.

"All right, Tanaka," he spit out. "Suppose you tell me how you go to church, or temple, or whatever you call it."

"Sir," Tanaka said in a wary voice, "there is a Buddhist temple in Denver. I could either go there or the Academy could bring the monk out here."

"Monk, hunh?" Powers leaned down and placed his face two inches in front of Tanaka's. He spoke slowly, with great deliberation and menace. "All right, *Mister* Tanaka. You'll get your monk. But I'll tell you right now, I'll get *you*. You'll never graduate from here and I'll tell you why. My father was killed on the *Arizona* on a Sunday morning . . . just . . . like . . . today. Sunday, December 7th, 1941, *Mister* Tanaka. Killed by the sneak Jap attack. Killed by one of *you* Jap Buddhists. That's why you'll never graduate. You don't belong in *my* Air Force."

12

It was toward the end of Basic Cadet Training (shortened to BCT and pronounced "Beast"), the six-weeks period of time before the rigors of the academic year began. The time when the new cadets of the fourth class, referred to as basic cadets, were indoctrinated into Air Force life in general, and Academy life in particular. The fourthclassmen were on a five-mile run along a trail marked out on the Lowry bomb range. They wore fatigues, black boots, helmets, and carried the eleven-pound M-1 Garand rifle. On their backs were ten-pound packs. The afternoon sun shone hot through the thin Colorado air on the dry dust kicked up by their pounding heels. The elevation was over 5,000 feet. The upperclassmen, clad only in tee-shirts, gym shorts, and tennis shoes, ran alongside and continually harassed the fatigued cadets. This was their last chance to weed out the physically unfit, the laggards, and those who lacked the will to finish under adverse conditions.

Kenichi Tanaka ran easily, breathing slowly and evenly. He had lettered all four of his high school years in cross-country track, and his last two years as an offensive end in varsity football. The members of his unit, C Flight, were scattered along the last half mile of the run. Tanaka and a fellow fourthclassman, Joseph C. Kelly, had slowly assumed the lead of their flight as their mates had fallen back. Kelly was slightly taller and much broader than Tanaka and had a naturally ruddy face. Neither spoke as their boots slammed in unison on the hard path. Ahead, upperclassmen were ticking off finishers on clip boards as the stragglers from the flight in front staggered across the line. The flight that got all its members across the line before the others won the right to eat their meal "at ease" that night instead of at attention. The new cadets were assigned to twelve flights comprising four squadrons.

Tanaka looked back over his shoulder and saw that C Flight

13

was doing very well, except for a lone, limping straggler. Without saying anything to Kelly, Tanaka slowed to a walk and slung his rifle on his back as the squadron ran past. He waited for the straggler, who was grimacing with effort while favoring his right leg. His helmet was bumping his nose, his fatigues were black with sweat, and he was trying not to trail his rifle in the dust. His name tag said his name was Dominguez. Tanaka grabbed his rifle, slung it next to his own, then put the cadet's arm around his shoulder.

"Hey, man . . ." the cadet tried to speak. He was a slender fellow with large dark eyes.

"Come on, Dominguez," Tanaka said in a quiet voice, "move it and we'll catch up to the others. You can do it."

"It's my damn ankle," Dominguez gritted. "Twisted the stupid thing."

Dominguez moved his legs faster as Tanaka half-carried him in a loping run. They were within fifty feet of the rear ranks of their squadron when Jerome Powers came up alongside. He looked rested and relaxed in his white gym clothes.

"Get away from him, Tanaka," Powers snarled. He jogged along with the two men. "Give his rifle back."

Dominguez began to lag. "Maybe you better . . ." he began.

"Keep moving," Tanaka said. "We're almost there." He picked up the pace.

"Tanaka, I told you let him alone. Now BACK OFF. That's an order. "

Tanaka ignored Powers's commands and stepped up the pace even more. In seconds he and Dominguez would be even with the rear rank of the cadets, which would allow the squadron to set the record for the doolie run.

Powers jogged ahead, whirled, and planted himself on the path, fists on hips. "All right, you two, stop right where you are," he roared. Tanaka and Dominguez ground to a halt facing the upperclassman. "Drop down and give me twenty loud ones right now. Call 'em out," Powers screamed in their faces. Tanaka let go of Dominguez and they both stretched out on the ground to begin twenty push-ups. Both rifles were still slung on Tanaka's back.

14

"One . . . two . . . three . . ." the two cadets counted cadence with each push-up.

"Louder, I can't hear you," Powers yelled. "Start over." Engrossed in his work, he wasn't aware of the activity of the cadets behind him.

"ONE . . . TWO . . . THREE . . . Tanaka and Dominguez yelled out. Tanaka was pumping up and down easily, rifles sliding back and forth on his shoulders. Nor was Dominguez having any difficulty.

"You happy now, Tanaka?" Powers yelled down at the two struggling men. "You're responsible for the whole flight being last in the competition. Just wait till your buddies find out about that. You'll be in a world of trouble."

A chorus of loud cadence counts came from behind Powers. He whirled around. Joe Kelly was flat on the ground, doing push-ups and yelling cadence as loud as he could. "ONE . . . TWO . . . THREE . . ." Beyond him, other cadets from C Flight who knew what had happened were dropping down to do the same. As they did, they called up to those ahead, who passed the word on to the front-runners. They had all seen Kenichi Tanaka drop back, followed by Joe Kelly. Those closest had heard Powers's order to let Dominguez run by himself, then Powers's scream for push-ups.

Joe Kelly had organized them to action by saying, "C'mon, guys, let's hang together on this. He who fucketh with one of us, fucketh with all of us." The dipping and bobbing of the fatigue-clad cadets so close to each other made the trail look like an undulating river of olive drab.

Startled at the squadron's cohesion, Powers drew back to the side of the trail. The cadets yelled louder and louder as their cadence count finally totaled twenty. "All right," Kelly boomed out. "Everybody on your feet. Let's move it. We all go in together."

Catalyzed and hyper by their first self-organized endeavor and seeming disobedience to authority, the cadets jumped to their feet and began to double-time toward the end of the run. Then Kelly started a well-known chant that quickly swelled through the ranks. By the time the thirty members of the flight ran through the finish-line goal posts, they were in perfect formation, their boot heels slamming the ground in a forceful double-time pace, their young voices booming out their pride in the words of the song: *HERE COMES C FLIGHT FORTY-TWO, BETTER WATCH OUT, WE'RE COMING THROUGH. WE ARE C FLIGHT FORTY-TWO. FORTY-TWO, WHO THE HELL ARE YOU?*

"Not bad, Dudley," said another Tac officer, J. T. Neddle, as they jogged together behind the exultant cadets. "Quite a mover you got there. What's his name?" Each man had studied for days the background and pictures of the basic cadets assigned to their squadron. Those that stood out – on paper, anyhow – were known as boomers. Joe Kelly was thought to be a boomer.

"Joe Kelly. Iowa All-State high school tackle and president of his class."

"What about the cadet with the bad leg?" Neddle asked.

"Manuel Dominguez. Eagle Scout, wrestler, played guard on his high school basketball team. League champions. Lots of hustle. At the beginning of the run he tripped and dinged his ankle. Refused to fall out with the puny squad."

"How about the other guy?"

"The Oriental?"

"Yeah."

"Tanaka," Dudley replied. "Grass Valley, California. Good grades, good track runner and offensive end. Nothing special. No boomer . . . but maybe a sleeper. Gave up his number one position in this trek to help a guy in the rear."

"Looks like he took some heat from that upperclassman, what's his name, Powers? Happen often?"

"Saw it once before."

"Going to do anything about it?"

"We'll see," Dudley said.

The two men jogged onto the athletic field together, then separated to head toward their squadrons.

The lighted halls were teeming with cadets returning to their rooms in the new dormitories for CQ, the academic call to quarters, the beginning of the mandatory time for each cadet to study in his room until lights out at 2300 hours. The move from the temporary cadet facilities at Lowry Air Force Base to the grounds of the new Air Force Academy had been completed five months before. The fourthclassmen had marched in full field gear with rifles from the main gate to their sparkling multistoried new dormitories.

C4C (Cadet Fourth Class) Kenichi Tanaka marched down the hall of his squadron area in the dormitory and made a squared right turn into the three-man room he shared with C4C Joseph C. Kelly from Storm Lake, Iowa, and C4C Manuel J. Dominguez from Godley, Texas. He relaxed his rigid posture as he entered the door, threw his books on his desk, and slumped into his desk chair. Then he pushed his hat back on his head and slowly unbuttoned his tunic. The black cold of the night crouched just beyond the storm windows. Snow lay heavy on the mountains and hills around the Academy grounds. It was that time of year the cadets called the dark ages, when the after-Christmas slump was compounded by short daylight hours, and when the countdown of the time to the joys of spring was somewhat longer than eternity.

Both Kelly and Dominguez looked up from their desks.

"Powers again?" Kelly asked.

Tanaka nodded.

"Insoles again?" Dominguez asked.

Tanaka nodded.

When C2C Jerome Powers of Meridian, Mississippi, had exhausted all the means to find fault with C4C Kenichi Tanaka of Grass Valley, California, he had to fall back on the insole fault.

17

It was standard for upperclassmen to brace fourthclassmen and ask them a myriad of questions ranging from the height of a Thor missile to the full-up gross weight of a B-47 bomber, or any other information contained in *Contrails,* the book of basic cadet knowledge each doolie was required to memorize. It was standard for fourth-class cadets to be braced for dirty rifles, messy uniforms, unshined shoes, or bad personal grooming. And it was standard for fourth-class cadets to stand exacting and strict inspections both in their rooms and out on the fields. Lack of cadet knowledge, excess linseed oil on the M-1 Garand rifle, need of a haircut, failure to perform the parade ground march required in the halls by all doolies, an unpolished floor in their rooms, or a million other items not up to snuff could bring upon the hapless cadet punishment, ranging from a filled-out Form 10A that reported serious offenses resulting in demerits, to the command "Drive around to my room after dinner, dumbsmack," from an uupperclassman who was displeased with some aspect of the cadet's demeanor or dress.

Once in the clutches of the upperclassman in his room, Mister Dumbsmack could – at best – receive a little corrective lecture, or – at worst – be made to perform various physical fitness exercises. In between were a variety of inventive instructional harassments, ranging from singing the upperclassman's favorite college fight song at the top of his voice to reciting the first three paragraphs of Air Force Manual 1-1, which spelled out Air Force Doctrine.

In other words, the hazing (that term was never officially used) of Mister Dumbsmack was a part of underclass cadet life. The only restriction on the inventiveness of the upperclassman was that Mister Dumbsmack could not perform personal services for him. He could not shine his shoes, carry his laundry, bring a pizza, perform research, or any other personal task.

For the first several weeks, Powers had either caught Tanaka short on obscure *Contrails* knowledge or possessed of cables. Cables were the little threads that peeked out from behind buttons and collars on new clothes. Searching for cables, while considered pretty chicken-shit, was a perfectly legal method for upperclassmen to dump on a doolie.

With amazing swiftness, Tanaka had memorized all the requirements, meticulously clipped and shaved his uniforms to virgin cloth, and maintained a military bearing and carriage while outside of his room that would have impressed SAC General Curt LeMay.

Now all Powers could fault Tanaka for was dirty insoles, those little strips of black leather that lay on the bottom of the shoe between the heel and the ball of the foot. Though Tanaka would polish and wipe them at every opportunity, a walk on the path in snow or a fleck of mud would soon dull the luster, and that was what Powers waited for.

"Shoes up, Mister Tanaka," Powers would order.

"Yes, sir," Kenichi Tanaka would respond, then lift one foot after the other behind him while Powers checked each insole.

"Gross, Mister Tanaka, very gross," Powers would say in a disgusted voice.

"Yes, sir," Tanaka would respond in a clear but noncommittal voice.

"Better drive around my room after evening meal, Mister Tanaka," Powers would say in the ritual, and Tanaka was once again set up for an uncomfortable session in Mister Powers's room.

"It's no sweat. I can take it," Tanaka said as he opened his locker. "After all, it is written that the peacock crows just once before its tail feathers fall out." He shed his gear, donned his red bathrobe, and headed for the showers.

"Him and his goofy sayings," Manuel "Little Cat" Dominguez said. He wore his sweatsuit over his athletic gear. He had just come in from wrestling practice.

"Makes 'em up as he needs 'em," Joe Kelly chuckled, and returned to his books. He, too, wore a red bathrobe.

Each cadet class had a color to distinguish them from the other classes, even at a distance. Red was for the class of '62. Even their name tags were red. After the field run when Kelly had had the whole squadron doing push-ups to support

19

Tanaka and Dominguez, he had coined the phrase "Red-Tagged Bastards Hang Together; fucketh with one, you fucketh with all." It had caught on and the phrase was shortened to RBHT when one cadet needed to whisper it to another for support in the ranks or in a classroom.

Kelly looked up from his books and across at Dominguez. "How come your nickname is Little Cat?"

"Aw, it came from a basketball game." He tried to keep studying, but Kelly was persistent.

"Whadduya mean? Come on, give," the burly cadet said.

Manuel Dominguez put a pencil between the pages and put his book down. "It was a basketball game with Grandview in my junior year at Godley High – they're our big enemy, you understand. I, well, I ran around as a guard and scored a few points in the last quarter."

"Winning points?"

"Well, yeah, I guess they were."

"So why you called Little Cat?"

"Well, a sportswriter for the *Fort Worth Star-Telegram* said I ran around those big guys like a little cat."

"Easier to call you Dom. RBHT," Kelly said and returned to his books.

"RBHT," Dom Dominguez said and opened his book.

1545 HOURS LOCAL, SATURDAY 9 MAY 1959
UNITED STATES AIR FORCE ACADEMY
COLORADO SPRINGS, COLORADO

Cadet Fourth Class Dom Dominguez marched, as all fourth-class cadets were required to do even when by themselves, down the sidewalk parallel to the road behind Vandenberg Hall, the new cadet dormitory. He wore his billed cap and summer khaki uniform and carried his athletic bag in his left hand. On the opposite side of the road were long rows of parking places for the cars owned by second- and first-class (junior and senior) cadets, a privilege fourth- and third-class cadets (freshmen and sophomores) were not allowed. It was an unusually warm day.

A black 1958 Thunderbird convertible with the top down turned left on the road toward Dominguez. The car drew near, slowed to a crawl, then stopped. Sitting in the passenger seat was a young girl with long brown hair flowing down the back of her yellow dress. A young man in a white polo shirt was driving. He stopped the car across from Dominguez. The driver was Cadet Second Class Jerome Powers. He said something to the girl, who giggled. Dominguez, eyes straight ahead, took it all in with his peripheral vision.

"You, man, come here!" Powers yelled.

Dominguez did a sharp right turn, approached the car, stopped, and saluted. "Sir, Cadet Fourth Class Dominguez reporting as ordered, sir."

Powers casually touched his forehead in return. "Pretty sloppy bag you're carrying there, dumbsmack," he said in a sarcastic tone.

"Yes, sir," Dominguez barked.

"Let's see your haircut, dumbwad."

Dominguez lifted his billed cap, bent forward, and slowly rotated his head.

"Hmmm," Powers said. "Pretty long. Best get a haircut by the next time I see you." Powers had not only been riding Kenichi Tanaka since the push-ups on the run last fall, he had also gone out of his way to make life tough for Tanaka's roommates as, apparently, cadets equally unworthy of remaining at the Academy.

"Yes, sir," Dominguez barked.

"Isn't your name tag a little crooked, Mister Dominguez?"

"No excuse, sir." Eyes straight ahead, jaw set.

Powers glanced at his girlfriend and smiled. She looked merely thoughtful and did not return the smile. Manuel Dominguez was fairly certain she was the eighteen-year-old daughter of a big car-dealer in Colorado Springs, one

21

Barbara Westin. He had seen her picture several times in the society section of the *Colorado Springs Gazette* and thought she was the most beautiful girl he had ever seen. He wondered what she was doing with this rat-faced creep. Powers turned back to Dominguez.

"Pretty raunchy, Mister Dominguez. You're dismissed. I don't ever want to see this again, you understand?"

"Yes, sir," Dominguez barked, then asked: "Sir, permission to ask a question, sir."

After a tiny pause, Powers said, "Go ahead."

"Sir, are you signed out on privileges?" If a cadet kept his nose clean and was not on probation, he could sign out on an ODP, Off-Duty Privilege. That meant he could don civilian clothes and leave the confines of the Air Force Academy. But, before each ODP, he had to sign a statement that he would not take drugs, violate the limits set by the Commandant to the areas he could visit, drink in uniform in a public place, or haze an underclassman. Penalties for breaking these limits could result in dismissal, for drinking (and especially drunkenness) in a public place in uniform, to two months' restriction to the room and immediate cadet area, for hazing fourthclassmen.

"Yes, Mister Dominguez. I am signed out on privileges. Why do you ask the obvious?"

"Sir, you'll have to write yourself up for hazing."

Powers's eyes bulged slightly as his face grew red, and the girl with the brown hair, Barbara Westin, hid a smile behind her hand.

Under the code, Jerome Powers was honor-bound to write himself up for punishment for violating an ODP restriction. Hazing was not an honor violation; Powers's *failure* to write himself up once it was called to his attention would be. An honor violation would have a cadet out of the Academy in less than three hours. Powers's eyes narrowed, as he realized that two months' restriction meant no more seeing Miss Barbara Westin until this academic class year was completed in June.

Manuel "Dom" Dominguez kept the smile from his face as he marched away. *RBHT, asshole,* he thought to himself. *RBHT.*

22

A year later, Cadet Third Class Manuel J. "Dom" Dominguez sat next to Miss Barbara Westin at a table in the Kachina Lounge of the Antlers Hotel in Colorado Springs. The Kachina Lounge was a popular hangout for cadets and students of CC – Colorado College. With them were Cadet Third Class Joe Kelly and Cadet Third Class Kenichi Tanaka. The table was littered with sandwich pieces, barren french fry plates, and empty soda cans.

The three roommates were doing very well as the end of their second year at the Academy drew near. Each wore embroidered stars on the right cuffs of their uniforms, to show they were on the Commandant's List for military accomplishments, and embroidered wreaths, to show they were on the Dean's list for maintaining a 3.0 grade average. All three had pilot training slots and would soon be spending time at a pilot training base, where they would receive many hours of initial flight training in the T-37 jet.

Barbara wore a Mexican jumper, flowing skirt, and sandals. Her brown hair was shoulder-length. She was, Manuel Dominguez thought again, the most beautiful girl in the world. Twelve months had passed since he had first seen her with Jerome Powers. Twelve months in which she had all but chased Dom, who at first had had a difficult time believing she was really interested in him. Twelve months in which she had become the most important event in Dom's life.

Jerome Powers had not been idle during that time. It was true he had been growing indifferent to Barbara Westin and had started stepping out on her. Then when he had seen she was throwing herself at a dumbsmack, he had become infuriated and written her off. At first he had sought out and dated many girls, almost always with success – so much so, he was known by the sobriquet of Power Stud at most of the sororities. But,

23

as the months and days wound down before his graduation, he had realized he wanted Barbara Westin as his wife. The other girls, while earthy and fun, were not suitable to be an officer's lady. Barbara Westin was. She was attractive, would make a good presentation to his superior officers, and she was rich. He had begun an active pursuit to regain her attention. He was beginning to think he had a chance. Just two days ago they had had a heavy petting session.

Because public display of affection was against cadet rules – and Dom Dominguez was in his khakis – the best he could do was gaze deeply into Barbara's eyes. She appeared flattered by the attention.

"Like a lovesick marmoset," Cadet Third Class Joe Kelly said. "Disgusting."

"The marmoset, having eaten, looks for dice," Ken Tanaka said. He sat between Kelly and Dominguez.

"How long you guys been dating now?" Kelly asked.

"Off and on since June Week one year ago," Manuel Dominguez answered "Well, actually, it started after June Week."

The scene had been the most pleasant of the three cadets' doolie year. Just before June Week, when they had been officially recognized and didn't have to put up with any more fourth-class Mickey Mouse customs, Barbara Westin had come driving into the cadet visitor area in a black Thunderbird convertible, a perfectly legal thing to do. Sightseers from all over the country did it frequently.

"Well, hello," she had said as Manuel Dominguez had marched by. "I thought you didn't have to march in public anymore."

Manuel had swung around. *Oh my God. The Most Beautiful Girl in the World.* "I wasn't marching, I was walking."

"Like you had a board up the back of your shirt."

"You looking for Powers?" Dominguez loved being able to refer to the nemesis by his last name.

"Oh my, no. Why would I be looking for him?"

"You're driving his car."

She had made a tart face. "I most certainly am *not*. This car is *mine*. I just let him drive it that one time."

I'll bet it's her daddy's T-Bird. He had walked closer to the car, which sat very low to the ground from his position on the high curb. She had worn blue jeans and a man's shirt with several top buttons open. He had meant to examine the interior of the car when he found himself staring right down the front of Miss Barbara Westin's shirt at her cute little B-cup breasts. Startled at the magnificent view, he had looked up, face flaming, and caught her looking intently at him with her deep brown eyes. *Ohmygod, ohmygod. Now I've done it. She's going to drive right home and tell Daddy all about these lecherous cadets and he's going to call my Tac Officer and . . . and . . .*

"Want to go for a ride, zoomie?" she had asked in a husky voice.

"Oh yeah, you had been dating that Powers creep," Joe Kelly said to Barbara in the snack bar.

"As a matter of fact we owe a lot to him," Dom said, convinced that "that Powers creep" had made it possible for him to date the most beautiful girl in the world by being the biggest creep in the world. In a way quite different from what he thought, however, he was correct.

Barbara smiled sweetly and said nothing.

Dom saw Tanaka's normally cheerful face darken when Powers's name was mentioned. "Still on your case, isn't he?" he asked.

Tanaka nodded. Powers was still treating him like a fourth-classman by jamming him for the slightest infraction at the SAMIs, the Saturday AM inspections, at which he would find fault with such trivia as not liking the way Tanaka folded his laundry or, in Powers's role as a cadet flight commander, complaining of his gig line at noon meal inspections.

Dom's eyes turned hard. "I'd like to get him someday."

Tanaka, cheerful again, nodded wisely. "It is said the shallowest fish has the broadest tail."

Barbara touched his hand. "Oh Ken, you say the sweetest, most clever things. Whatever do they mean?" They laughed as Tanaka made an exaggerated face of inscrutability.

"Well," Dom said, "your dad might have something to say about our going together . . . all of it negative."

Mister George Hadley Westin indeed had something to say about his one and only daughter, nineteen going on twenty, even dating a . . . "Well," he had said, "someone of a *different race*." Since her mother had died five years before, Miss Barbara Westin had little difficulty getting her way with her grief-torn and highly protective father. She had talked him out of sending her east for college, so she could attend Colorado College and play the local scene, where she knew her way around. Out east was too alien, she thought; here she was in control and could do as she pleased, especially when it came to playing the field with all the boys.

"Don't you worry about Daddy," Barbara said. "I play him like a pinball machine that never says tilt."

"One more picture," Dom said and raised his Brownie flash camera, which he carried on a strap around his neck. They all groaned, but smiled, as he held the camera up and pressed the button. Barbara's smile was heart-melting, he knew, and he hoped he had captured her sweet warmth. He checked his watch. "Time to make my Sunday duty call." Each of the three cadets had acquired the habit of calling home on Sunday afternoons from the bank of pay phones at the Antlers Hotel. Dom patted his pocket for change and departed.

He whistled as he went down the hall toward the phones, but stopped abruptly as a door to one of the small private dining rooms opened in front of him and a youngish man Dom recognized as one of the local rowdies stepped out, pulling a very drunk Jerome Powers in a vomit-stained uniform after him.

"And stay the fuck out, punk. This is a man's game." Before he slammed the door, leaving Powers swaying in the hall, Dom saw several men sitting around a poker table littered with chips and beer bottles.

"Fucking game," Powers slurred, and tried to walk down the hall. He caromed off a wall and fell to his knees, then toppled against the wall and slid to a sitting position, eyes bleary and unfocused.

Manuel Dominguez whipped his camera in front of him and snapped three photos as fast as he could wind the film and change the bulbs.

"Here, let me help you," he said when he was done, and grasped Powers's arm.

And that was his mistake. For because of that gesture and what it led to, what Dominguez had seen and what he would do, Powers would finally get his wish to get back at Tanaka through this young cadet, though neither of them knew it at the moment.

A week later, on a dark afternoon, Manuel J. Dominguez was ushered out of the United States Air Force Academy for a violation of the cadet honor code.

EAGLE STATION

1

"Mayday, Mayday, Mayday," the frantic call sounded over the radio. Every pilot in the night sky and every radar controller on the ground within a 200-mile radius of the transmitter heard the terse voice of the man in trouble. "Mayday, Mayday, Mayday. This is Beercan Two Two. We're hit bad. My frontseater is wounded. I need a vector to the nearest friendly base. Anybody copy Beercan?" The voice was thin and desperate.

A controller at a clandestine radar site in northeastern Laos leaned close to his scope and keyed his microphone. "Roger, Beercan Two Two, this is Eagle. We copy you loud and clear. What is your location from Channel 97?"

"Beercan is a Romeo Fox-Four Charley, ah, east of Channel 97 at, ah, 15,000 feet."

The Eagle controller spotted a blip at that location and marked it with his grease pencil. "I think I have you. Squawk 53 on your parrot to make sure." Squawk 53 was the command for the man in the RF-4C Phantom jet, call sign Beercan Two Two, to turn dials on a device to send a special coded burst of energy to the radar screen at Eagle Station. Beercan was a reconnaissance version of the Phantom jet. It carried cameras instead of cannons, photo flash cartridges instead of bombs. "Beercan, you copy Eagle?"

"Ah, rodge, Eagle, I copy you loud and clear. I'm in the backseat. Negative parrot back here and my pilot is

31

unconscious. I need a vector to the nearest base and you'd better get somebody up here. My pilot can't fly, and I don't know how. All I can do is keep it straight and level . . . sort of." The RF-4C had full flight controls in the backseat.

"Uh oh," said Staff Sergeant Al Verbell, the Eagle controller working Beercan, to his senior controller, Lieutenant Bob Pearson. "I've got a problem here, Lieutenant. You working any F-4s out there tonight? I need one to intercept Beercan." He carefully watched the screen as he used the grease pencil to mark the progress of the blip. "Beercan," he transmitted through the boom mike at his lips, "turn right forty-five degrees then immediately back to a westerly heading." He watched the blip follow his instructions. "I've got you, Beercan Two Two. Maintain 270 degrees heading while I get a vector for you. What is your fuel state?"

"I, uh, think I've only got twenty minutes or so, Eagle. I need help fast." The voice was that of a young man who was doing his best to remain calm.

Lieutenant Pearson leaned over Verbell's shoulder and studied the scope. Verbell pointed out the lone blip fifty miles east of their station. The two men were in a small gray van on a plateau atop a sharp piece of karst rising 5,000 feet almost straight up from the surrounding jungle floor. Outside their van were the radio antennae and domes containing their radar dishes. They were in Laos, very close to the border of North Vietnam.

"I think I can get someone to him," Pearson told Verbell. "Meanwhile, give him a steer to Green Anchor." Verbell did as he was told, telling Beercan to turn south toward the anchor point for the orbiting KC-135 aerial tanker, call sign Green Tanker.

Pearson went back to his own scope. He wore a walk-around headset and boom mike. He switched range on his scope, keyed the mike switch clipped to his shirtfront, and called Alley Cat, an Airborne Command and Control Center (ABCCC, spoken as Aye Bee Triple Cee).

"Alley Cat, Eagle, how read?"

"Eagle, Alley Cat, loud and clear. Go ahead."

"Alley Cat, we have Beercan Two Two, a shot-up recce

Fox-Four Charley, fifty miles east. The frontseater is wounded. The backseater is flying the bird and he's a navigator, not a pilot. You got any Fox-Fours under your control we can vector up there to lead the guy in?"

After a short pause Alley Cat answered. "Eagle, go 325.4 and we'll see what we can do with an F-4 we are monitoring." Pearson switched his radio to the new frequency in time to hear Alley Cat make a call.

"Phantom Zero One, Alley Cat. We've got a little problem and we need your help. You on to anything right now?"

"Alley Cat, Phantom Zero One. We're not stirring up a thing out here tonight. All the bad guys are hiding from us. What can we do for you?"

Phantom Zero One was an F-4 on night patrol over the Ho Chi Minh Trail in Laos, looking for trucks and guns. The pilot was Major Court Bannister and the backseater was Captain Ken Tanaka, an aircraft commander being checked out as a night IP (Instructor Pilot). Bannister was the commander of the unit – the Phantom FACs from Ubon Royal Thai Air Force Base – in which they flew. In less than a minute, Alley Cat had Bannister in touch with Eagle and they switched radio frequencies to that of the crippled F-4.

"Phantom Zero One, steer 345 for an intercept with Beercan. Make angels base plus six." Eagle had just told Bannister to take up the northwesterly heading of 345 degrees toward Beercan and to use whatever it took to get to 14,000 feet. The coded base altitude for the twenty-four-hour period was 8,000 feet. Coding the altitude each day was an attempt to fool enemy radio intercepts.

Thirteen minutes later Bannister was approaching the intercept point. He was at a head-on angle to Beercan, who was one thousand feet above. Bannister needed directions from Eagle to begin a long sweeping cutoff turn that would place him on Beercan's wing.

Pearson listened as Verbell transmitted to Bannister. "We'll start your cutoff in a few seconds, Phantom. How's the weather up there?"

"Getting pretty rough. We're in what remains of a big thunderstorm.

"Get over here fast, Phantom," the frantic voice from Beercan interrupted. "We're in clouds now and I can't hold this thing much longer."

Verbell keyed his mike. "Phantom, start a left cutoff turn to . . ." A savage boom rocked the van, the lights flickered and went off.

Court Bannister heard the start of the explosion a split second before the transmission from Eagle went dead. He rolled his big Phantom fighter into a left turn.

"Eagle," he called. "Eagle, you read Phantom Zero One?" There was no answer. He tried again, then called Alley Cat for an alternate frequency to contact Eagle.

"Stand by," Alley Cat said. He called back after a pause. "Negative response, Phantom. We've tried all frequencies. They're off the air. Can you continue your intercept of Beercan?" Alley Cat, the ABCCC, was a C-130 full of radios and controllers but no radar with which to vector Bannister.

"We'll try," Court Bannister replied. He spoke to Ken Tanaka in the backseat. "You got him, Ken?" The F-4 carried its own on-board radar.

"Yes, sir. Keep turning. Tighten it up, he's thirty degrees port for six miles." Tanaka refined the image on his radarscope in the backseat.

"Phantom, Phantom, this is Beercan, Beercan. Help me, help me. I'm losing it . . ." The sound of heavy and rapid breathing filled the headsets of those listening as the backseater in his rising panic kept his thumb on the mike switch, making it impossible for anyone else to transmit. If they tried, the air filled with squeals and howls. The man who has left his mike open hears none of that. Finally the backseater said, "Oh shit," and the mike was unkeyed.

"Take it easy, Beercan," Court Bannister transmitted. He rapidly cross-checked his own instruments and small radar screen as he closed on the F-4. "Take it easy," he said again. "I've got good radar contact with you. Just keep those needles centered."

"Roll out, boss," Ken Tanaka said from Court's backseat. "We're in trail with him. He's twelve o'clock for six miles, one thou high, we have a fifty-knot overtake. You can start your climb. I'm locked on."

Court advanced the throttles a few percent and, using the radar, began to climb and jockey into position behind Beercan. After a few terse minutes he was 600 feet directly behind Beercan, thirty feet low, and closing.

"See anything?" Ken Tanaka asked.

"Negative," Court said as he alternated his scan up from the instruments in the cockpit to the windscreen and the black night outside.

Tanaka read from his gauges. "We have zero overtake, we're about fifty feet low and two hundred behind."

Court inched forward a few more feet. Still nothing. Then he slid to the right a few feet and continued his overtake. He didn't want to overrun Beercan. If he missed, he wanted to pass to one side, not ram into him. He scanned the gauges, then looked through the windscreen again. Still nothing.

"Beercan, are your nav lights on?"

"Shit no. We just came from bad-guy country. They were off when we got hit. I can't put them on from back here."

"Hell, boss," Ken Tanaka said. "No way we can intercept a blackout in night weather." Tanaka was correct. Radar could get them within 100 or even 50 feet, but was not discriminate enough to show a pilot how to join up within three feet of another airplane's wing in the black of night and in heavy clouds.

"Beercan," Court transmitted, "turn up your cockpit lights to full bright, put on your thunderstorm lamp, and twist your utility lamp to shine out the right side of the canopy."

The navigator in the backseat of the Beercan F-4 did as he was told, and Court saw a dim glow illuminate the black clouds off to his left. He quickly eased his airplane in that direction until he had the shot-up Phantom in view. The glow from the rear cockpit gave him enough reference to fly a few feet aft of the right wing of Beercan. The plane was wobbling.

"Hold her steady, Beercan," Court transmitted. "I'm off your right wing and I'm going to talk you to the tanker for some fuel, then to Udorn for landing. You've refueled before, haven't you?"

"Uh, yes sir," the backseater transmitted, his relief evident. Most F-4 aircraft commanders (or A/C, as the USAF designates the pilots in the front seat) allow, even encourage, their backseaters to learn how to refuel from the KC-135 aerial tankers. The backseat was a real pit, with limited visibility, and the practice improves the morale of the navigators (or the luckless young pilots directly assigned from flying training who have to take a tour in the backseat) and is a bit of insurance for the frontseater, should he be incapacitated and unable to perform the delicate flying. Refueling required the pilot to position the Phantom under the belly of the tanker, and hold still while the boomer flew the long thin probe to the receptacle on the upper fuselage a few feet behind the rear cockpit of the F-4. The KC-135s were the military version of the Boeing 707 airliner. Instead of passengers, the big silver airplanes carried 200,000 pounds of JP4 jet fuel, which they dispensed through the probe, called a boom, that hung underneath the rear fuselage and pointed to the rear. It was controlled – *flown* was the word – by the boomer, who lay on his belly facing aft; the compartment in which he lay had a thick rear window that would have been a perfect place for a tail gunner if the airplane had had one.

The young backseater transmitted again, his voice quavering with concern. "But I've never *landed* this airplane."

"Not to worry," Court radioed. "I'll talk you through it. It's simple once you're lined up, and I'll get you in position."

"Yeah, simple," Ken Tanaka said from Court's backseat on the intercom. "About as simple as steering a runaway race car through an obstacle course while blindfolded."

Tanaka knew, as did Court, that the view forward from the backseat was nil. Instruments and the big metal shroud curving over the instrument panel meant the person in back had no forward visibility whatsoever. Until they had the ground clues out the side windows down cold, most instructor pilots had to skid the Phantom the last quarter mile or so on final approach, in order to keep the touchdown point on the runway in view, then straighten it out at the last minute before the main gear slammed onto the concrete.

"Hell, the Navy sets up flight attitude and just lets them crash down on carrier decks," Court said. "I'm going to do the same thing for this guy. He's got to get his frontseater to come around long enough to put the hook down for him. He can't do it from the backseat. I'll have the tower prepare the runway for an approach end barrier engagement."

The hook saved many an aircraft. The pilots of shot-up F-4s, or pilots trying to land in a heavy rain (where out-of-control skidding due to hydroplaning on rainwater was common), lowered a hook attached underneath the fuselage. Like carrier airplanes, the hook caught a cable stretched across the runway a few feet from the touchdown point. The cable was attached to huge brake drums on each side of the runway that absorbed the incredible energy and braked the aircraft to a halt in less than 1,000 feet.

Court pushed the transmit button on his throttle. "Alley Cat, Phantom Zero One," he called.

"Phantom, Alley Cat, go."

"I've got Beercan. Would you have Green Tanker come up on this frequency?"

"They're already here, Phantom. I brought them up just in case."

"Nicely done, Alley Cat. Green Tanker, do you read Phantom Zero One?"

"Loud and clear, Phantom. This is your friendly tank. You call, we haul. We have you on radar. Steer 220 for an intercept. We are at 15,500 feet. You copy?"

The man transmitting was the Green Tanker navigator who had been in contact with Alley Cat on another frequency. With the Alley Cat controller's help, he had located Phantom and Beercan on his own radarscope, and was able to give them an immediate heading to his location. He had also asked his pilot to descend to an altitude 500 feet above the two Phantoms to make the final approach to the hook-up easier for them.

"Roger, copy Green. We are at 15,000," Court said. Then

he called Beercan. "Beercan, do like the man says and turn right to 220. Can you do that?"

"Uh, hell. Look, I'm not a pilot. I do have some time flying back here, but it was all *practice.*"

"Flying is flying," Court said. "Whatever you do, keep the ball in the center. Make your turn now. Bank to the right. Ease into it and I'll tell you when to roll out." Court had his own gauges and Ken Tanaka's instructions to keep him aware of what heading they had.

Court could barely make out the details of the Phantom. There were some black streaks below the front canopy and what looked like torn metal, as if a shell had penetrated the skin and exploded there. He couldn't be sure and saw no point in quizzing the man in the backseat, who had enough worries of his own.

"Okay," Beercan said and started a shaky right turn. It gradually became steeper.

"Don't let your wing down so far," Court said. The navigator brought the wing up with a jerk that nearly flung Court off to one side. "Easy now," he said. "Take it easy and we'll all get a beer at the O'Club pretty soon."

"Contact," Ken Tanaka said, "dead ahead for twenty miles. Looks like he's turning." At a head-on closure rate over 1,000 miles per hour, the tanker had to time his turn away from the Phantoms precisely. Too late and he would overrun the two Phantoms, too early and the two Phantoms would waste a lot of fuel trying to catch up. The Green Tanker navigator had given his pilot good instructions. Two minutes later, Beercan, with Court on his wing, was one mile in trail to the tanker.

"Going Bright Flash," Court said, and moved his navigation light switch to that position.

"You're one mile in trail, Phantom Zero One," Green Tanker said. The radar in the KC-135 tanker was sharp enough to allow the navigator to direct the two Phantoms into refueling position.

"Roger," Court replied. "Hold it steady, Beercan," he said. Court alternated his eyes from the Phantom next to him to his instruments in the cockpit, then up to search the night sky in front. Soon he spotted the glow from the indicator lights under the belly of the huge KC-135 tanker. The twin row of lights, called captain's bars, were manipulated by the boomer to tell the receiving aircraft to move up or down, fore or aft, left or right. That way a refueling could be performed while maintaining radio silence.

"Beercan, the tanker is dead ahead," Court said. "Can you see him?" The dim glow in the clouds was eerie, as if a lamp were immersed in a dark substance.

"Uh, yeah, ah . . . I see him . . ." The Phantom started to wobble as the backseater took his eyes from the instruments.

"Hold it steady, now," Court said. The wobbling increased. "Easy now. Let's move on up to the tanker. You said you've refueled before."

"NOT AT NIGHT," the young man yelled. His airplane started to pitch up and down in the black clouds.

"Steady, steady," Court said.

"I'M LOSING IT. I'VE GOT VERTIGO . . ."

Slowly, the Phantom fell off on a wing to the left. Court followed and tried to fly formation on the airplane in the black sky.

"You're in a left bank. Center your needle and ball," Court transmitted in as calm a voice as he could muster. "Roll out to the right and raise the nose. Make the little airplane on your attitude indicator align with the horizon bar. You're in a left bank, roll out, roll to the right. Bring the nose up."

"I CAN'T TELL . . . I CAN'T TELL," the man in the backseat transmitted in great confusion.

"Roll right, bring the nose up," Court said once more.

"Better break it off, boss," Tanaka said. "We're passing through ten thou."

The Phantom continued the slow left roll as the nose sliced lower. Court felt the G-load and the airspeed increase as he tried to stay with the airplane that was rapidly going out of control. Seconds later they were in a diving spiral and he had to break away. He leveled off and began a left-hand orbit just below the base of the clouds. He saw his altitude was 8,000 feet, barely 3,000 feet above the surrounding karst

39

ridges that he could not see in the inky blackness. There were no lights below to provide any horizontal reference. Court heard the backseater key his mike.

"I'M DIVING . . . I'M DIVING . . . I'VE GOT TO PULL OUT . . ."

"Level your wings, then pull out," Court commanded. He knew the young man was in what civilian pilots called a death spiral. A pilot who was not trained to fly instruments in bad weather invariably wound up in a sharply descending spiral, but his kinetic cues – the seat of his pants – told him he was straight and level, or maybe diving, because he saw the airspeed was rapidly rising. Then they would try to pull back on the stick without leveling the wings. Pulling back on the stick merely tightened the turn and made the nose fall more, until the airplane smashed into the ground. In the old days of wire and cloth, the pilot might even have pulled the wings off in his desperate attempt to live. Court knew the Beercan Phantom was doomed.

"Beercan, bail out, bail out now. Beercan, get out," he ordered.

He heard the carrier wave come on as the backseater pressed the mike button on the throttle, then go off, then come back on. "Can't," he said in a very calm voice. "Can't do it. Fred is still alive. I hear him moaning. Got to pull thi—"

He was cut off in midsentence and Court and Ken Tanaka saw below them a sharp white light that quickly expanded into a red mushroom.

"Ah shit," Tanaka said from the backseat, his voice thick with despair.

"Alley Cat," Court transmitted, his voice impersonal. "Beercan has gone in. No chutes. I don't think anybody got out." He leveled and began the climb back to altitude. "Alley Cat, you copy?"

"Phantom Zero One, Alley Cat copies. Give us a position of the crash site." From the backseat, Tanaka read off the coordinates provided by a device called the INS, the Inertial Navigation System.

"Hey," Tanaka said abruptly on the intercom, the death of

the two Beercan pilots put out of his mind. "We've got about ten minutes of juice left before we make a nylon letdown."

"Green Tanker," Court called, "you still on this freq? We're bingo minus a bunch."

"Roger, Phantom Zero One. Green Tanker still on orbit ready to pass gas. We have you six miles in trail." The Green Tanker navigator paused, then said: "Ah, sorry 'bout your buddy, Phantom. Tough way to go."

Within five minutes, Court had found the tanker and was being refueled through the boom at the rate of 600 gallons per minute when the ABCCC called.

"Phantom Zero One, Alley Cat."

"Phantom, go," Court answered.

"How you guys feeling? We need someone to recce Channel 97, find out what happened. Other assets, slow assets, will be there later in the morning but need some advance idea of what they will find."

"No problem, Alley Cat, we'd be glad to check it out," Court said without conferring with Tanaka, who he knew would agree.

"Are you Winchester?" Alley Cat used the code word asking if Court had any ammunition or weaponry remaining on his aircraft. As night fast FACs (Forward Air Controllers) whose job it was to locate trucks and guns on the Ho Chi Minh Trail in Laos, the Phantom FACs carried 2.75-inch marking rockets, a 20mm cannon slung under the belly, and a load of parachute flares to illuminate the ground below.

"Negative," Court replied. "We had a dry night. Just popped a few flares. We'll go take a look." His airplane was full of fuel now and he disconnected from the tanker. "Give me a steer, Ken," he asked. Tanaka gave him a heading for the radar site.

Still in the clouds, Court thanked Green Tanker, backed off, and turned back to the northeast toward Tacan Channel 97. Tacan was a navigation device which, when tuned in, would show the distance and heading to the transmitting station. They were sometimes referred to by their location, sometimes by the numbers dialed into the receiving Tacan set to pick up the continuously transmitted navigation signal.

Channel 97, known as Eagle Station by the fighter pilots and tanker drivers, was known by another name to those who controlled and flew the "slow" assets. Those men, who flew helicopters and small propeller-driven airplanes, called it Lima Site 85. Those men wore civilian clothes and worked for or were controlled by the Central Intelligence Agency.

By 0545 hours Bannister and Tanaka were ten miles out, traveling at 600 miles per hour and still descending. The jungle before the karst looked like a thick green rug in the early-morning light.

The whole area was composed of jutting limestone karst ridges and steep peaks rising above thick jungle, sinkholes, and disappearing streams. The radar and van complex at the radar site was on top of a rectangular piece of karst that jutted up from the surrounding jungle to over one mile in the air. The layered texture of its steep sides resembled buttes and mesas rising in the American Southwest. The top formed a sloping rectangle, about two kilometers by one kilometer, and held jungle and small hills of its own, as if it were a portion of the surrounding floor that had suddenly been elevated into the sky. It was oriented northwest to southeast and was only twenty-five kilometers from the North Vietnamese border. The village on the site, Poo Pah Tee, had been an important guerrilla base in northeastern Laos, but soon became viewed by the USAF as an excellent spot to put a navigational aid and, later, a radar station, both of which helped US strike aircraft find their way around North Vietnam and portions of the Ho Chi Minh Trail in Laos.

The radar at Eagle Station was the TSQ-81, a modified Strategic Air Command (SAC) radar bomb scoring system (RBS). But instead of computing B-52 electronic bomb drop accuracy, it worked in reverse. When firepower was needed in the daylight or at night, but the weather was rotten and down to the deck, airplanes equipped with special beacons could drop bombs by radar vectors from Eagle Station. The operator would key into his computer fixed information, such as target distance and direction from his site, height above sea level, and type of bomb, for which the computer already knew the aerodynamics and fall rate. Then the operator would add the weather variables: temperature aloft, air density, high and low winds. The computer would then give out a range of aircraft headings, altitudes, and airspeeds to complete the bombing equation.

The operator would have the ground target fixed on his radar screen, and then would "paint" the incoming aircraft blip with sharp resolution by receiving a pulse of energy from the beacon mounted in the aircraft. Similar systems, called the MSQ-77, were in use in South Vietnam, but this was the only facility for North Vietnam and northern Laos. The method was called Skyspot and had proved of great worth in sections of North Vietnam unprotected by SAMs (surface-to-air missiles) and Laos (pilots did not find it healthy to fly in or above clouds that obscured SAMs that might be fired at them).

What made the Laotian radar site unique from its counterparts in South Vietnam was that those that ran it were classified as "technicians," not military personnel. This situation had arisen because the US did not want to violate the 1962 Geneva Conventions by maintaining American military troops in Laos. As a result, the sixteen USAF radar controllers and maintenance men at Eagle Station, both officers and enlisted men, had become "sheep-dipped." The process entailed having the men supposedly leave the USAF to become field representatives and technicians for major American radar manufacturing companies, such as Hughes and General Electric. For this reason, Lieutenant Bob Pearson and Staff Sergeant Al Verbell were known as Mister Pearson and Mister Verbell.

A shrewd analyst of military nomenclature might have figured out the purpose behind Eagle Station by studying the nomenclature of the radar set and how it differed from those in South Vietnam. The RBS sites in South Vietnam had the designation MSQ-77. Under the DoD joint electronics type designation system JETDS), each letter in sequence had a meaning. T meant transportable, M meant mobile, S meant Special type, and Q meant Special purpose. The two numbers, 77 and 81, were model numbers. The "T" in the TSQ-81 for Eagle Station meant that the entire apparatus – scopes,

43

power, antennae – could be broken down into packages that were easily transportable by air.

Court threw the left wing down as they zoomed over the site at 500 feet. "Look at that," Tanaka breathed into the intercom. They saw the vans and a few huts, one smoking, and some large radio and radar antennas that had crashed to the ground. A small American flag flew from a rod stuck in the ground.

Mister Bob Pearson heard the roar of the Phantom as it flashed by. He grinned and started the portable generator for his Mark 28 radio pallet.

"Fox-Four doing a bubble check at Channel 97, how do you read Eagle One Four?"

"Loud and very clear, Eagle One Four," replied a surprised Court Bannister. "This is Phantom Zero One. How you gentlemen down there this morning? Thought we lost you last night."

"We took a few mortar rounds, knocked our antennas out. No one hurt. Tell Alley Cat to ask homeplate for the entire backup gear I pre-positioned with them. They'll know what you mean."

Court called the Hillsboro ABCCC, who replaced Alley Cat in the daytime, and relayed the message. Hillsboro told Phantom Zero One that it would be done and that he was to tell Eagle One Four that some special people would be on the ground at their location within the hour, and to keep a listening watch on the standard Eagle Station frequency.

Court relayed the message, then asked, "You got any more bad guys out there? We can get some strike birds in here right away."

"Negative, Zero One, but thanks. It was a small group and a probe, I think. Very professional. Worse to come, I'll bet."

44

It was in the pre-dawn dark when USAF Staff Sergeant Manuel J. "Little Cat" Dominguez entered the crowded GI snack bar at the end of the 8th Aerial Port Squadron's military air terminal at Saigon's Tan Son Nhut Air Base. Military shift workers mixed with arriving and departing passengers. Most were dressed in fatigues or flight suits.

Dominguez wore khakis (Tan, shade 1505) with the pants bloused over glossy spit-shined black (imported cowhide) paratrooper boots (the men called them jump boots). He removed his maroon beret with the silver Aerospace Rescue and Recovery Service badge. The crease in his tailored uniform shirt and pants was knife-sharp. On his left breast were two rows of ribbons under the paratrooper wings won by Air Force Pararescue men. The wings had a star and wreath over them, showing he had made at least sixty-five jumps and was classified as a master parachutist (master blaster). The jump wings were Army issue. The USAF had tried to introduce a fruity-looking enameled device depicting the wearer as jump-qualified, but no one would wear them, so the supply types had given up. The ribbons revealed he had eight years in the Air Force, was qualified in small arms as a marksman, was a graduate of the NCO Academy, had logged time in Vietnam, and had been awarded the Good Conduct Medal and three Air Medals. In the top-left position of honor (facing the ribbons), next to the Air Medal (with two Oak Leaf Clusters), was the Distinguished Flying Cross.

Dominguez carried a small blue satchel known as an AWOL bag, barely big enough to hold a pair of shoes, a shaving kit, and a shirt or two. Just enough to go AWOL, it was said. The bag was fabricated of canvas and cost $2.80 in the Base Exchange. In his AWOL bag, Dominguez carried his shaving kit and a small survival kit he had assembled, including a small RT-10 aviator's survival radio he had obtained from a pilot he had picked up from North Vietnam. "Shit, man," the grateful pilot had cried, "tell me what else you want. It's all a write-off, I lost it in the ejection, right?" Dominguez never flew anywhere in Vietnam as a passenger without this kit. For further safety, he wished he could wear a parachute, even when he flew as a passenger.

He followed the line, poured a cup of coffee into a mug from the big silver urn, disregarded the greasy bacon and yellow scrambled eggs that smelled like burnt rubber, passed up the chicken and tuna fish sandwiches because they looked like a ptomaine preserve, and finally grabbed a bag of Fritos out of desperation for something to munch on. At the cashier's position he pulled out a wad of MPC (Military Payment Certificates, used in lieu of real money) and paid his bill. He saw the latest *Pacific Stars and Stripes* on a stack at the end of the line, put a paper dime in the open mason jar, and picked up a copy.

Looking across the crowded snack bar, he saw two men leave a small table, made for it, sat down, and spread out his paper to read. He sipped his coffee as he turned the pages.

Sergeant Dominguez had just come from Headquarters, 3rd Aerospace Rescue and Recovery Group (ARRGp), and was whiling away a few minutes waiting to catch a C-130 flight to Da Nang, his home base. Dominguez had so far been in Vietnam four months. Previously, he had been stationed at Cape Canaveral, performing satellite rescue duty, and had had a standing volunteer statement for Vietnam in the Personnel Office ever since 1965. At least once a week, he'd bugged the tech sergeant in charge for action on his request. Five months ago he'd finally gotten it. Thirty days later he was in Vietnam.

Staff Sergeant Manuel J. Dominguez (soon to be a technical sergeant, he'd found out the day before) was a man who stepped out of airborne helicopters while riding on a cable. He usually practiced this insanity in territory where people were trying to kill him. He could, if the occasion demanded, make a parachute jump under the same conditions. On the personnel books, he was carried as a Pararescue Jumper (later as a Pararescue Specialist), Air Force Specialty Code 89451. They were sometimes known as Parajumpers, but always referred to as PJs.

Being a PJ was a source of great pride to the individual. A PJ was a product of intense screening and intense training powered by intense motivation. When everybody else was running around trying to kill somebody, a PJ was running around trying to save lives – usually those of shot-down aircrewmen. Of course, if a PJ had to kill somebody to save somebody, they were quite capable of doing it in any number of ways.

Every PJ was a volunteer. Once selected for his maturity, physical condition, and potential, the would-be PJ was sent to jump training at Fort Benning, then off to scuba training. From there he was sent to Gunter Air Force Base in Alabama to be certified as a medical technician. After that, he went through four types of survival schools: desert in the Mohave Desert, swamp in the Florida Everglades, jungle on an island near Key West, and Arctic not too far from McCall, Idaho. Finally, each PJ was trained to be an expert in small arms and hand-to-hand combat. When Little Cat had volunteered, so had 2,600 other young airmen. Sixteen had been selected, ten had won their maroon berets.

Manuel Dominguez had accomplished all these things since he had enlisted in the Air Force eight years ago in the early fall of 1960, four months after he had been dismissed from the United States Air Force Academy. He had returned to the small dairy farm his family owned two miles west of Godley, Texas. For three months he had labored on the farm, tackling any task he could find and throwing himself into the chores with silent fierceness. He had refused to sleep in the house and used a corner of the tack room next to the barn in which to live. His parents and older brother had been concerned, but left him alone to work out whatever burden was on his mind.

As Manuel Dominguez thumbed through the sports section, he noticed the Air Force Academy had narrowly beaten Colorado in baseball. He was almost over feeling a twinge every time he thought of his two years as a cadet. What hurt more than anything, and he had buried it as deep as pain would permit, was never again seeing the girl with the brown hair, Barbara

Westin. He could almost get through a whole week without seeing in his mind the most beautiful girl in the world. When he did, he would pull her picture from his wallet and study her face until his chest hurt.

As for the reason for his dismissal from the Academy . . . *no, cut it out,* he told himself. He'd promised himself not to go over all that again. Why dig up the worst memories a man could have?

He was saved from further thought when a bulky man wearing jungle fatigues and carrying a tray sat across from him. The man had a tough-looking, almost simian face, and was an Army lieutenant colonel. He had the CIB (Combat Infantryman Badge) and master parachute wings sewn in black thread on his left breast. On his right breast was the name LOCHERT, also sewn in black thread. Dominguez remembered now: Colonel Lochert was the man who had been hounded in the press about a so-called murder of a North Vietnamese double agent. There had been a lot of bad publicity calling it an atrocity and demanding his head – until the defense had proven conclusively at the court-martial that Lochert had only been acting in self-defense.

After a curious appraisal of his tablemate, Little Cat Dominguez went back to his paper and decided it was time for some Fritos. He picked up the bag, opened it, and took out a few to munch absently. Head bent over the page, he became aware that the burly Lochert seemed to be sitting motionless and glaring at him over his own tray.

Maybe I'm munching too loud for him, Dominguez thought, and tried to chew softly. It was not an easy or satisfactory thing to do. *Hell with it. This is a place to eat, I'm eating, at least I chew with my mouth closed.* He grabbed a few more Fritos and continued chewing.

Then, to Dominguez's great surprise, Lochert reached into the Frito bag, took out some Frito chips and, glowering at Dominguez as if daring him to do anything, popped them into his mouth and started chewing.

Startled, only by exercising great control did Manuel Dominguez keep from making some smart-ass remark about

Army lieutenant colonels who were too cheap to buy their own Fritos and had to steal them from Air Force enlisted men. *This guy is really goofy. Maybe he stood next to the cannon too many times.* Instead, he stared Lochert in the eye, reached over, grabbed a handful of the chips, stuffed them in *his* mouth, and chewed as loudly as he could.

Lochert's face appeared to swell and his eyes bulged dangerously. He seemed about to speak, then did not. He reached for the Frito bag with both hands, ripped it open with a savage motion, crammed what was left of the chips in his mouth, and chewed with what Manuel Dominguez thought was a triumphal gleam in his eye. Still chewing, Lochert snatched up his empty tray and stomped away from the table.

Shaking his head, Dominguez watched him walk out of the snack bar and disappear into the crowd outside. *God, but there are some weird ones in Vietnam,* he thought. He bent back to his paper, read for another twenty minutes, checked his watch, and decided it was time to go. Standing up, he picked up his AWOL bag, put it on the chair he had just vacated, and reached for his spread-out paper to fold it. There, underneath, was the unopened bag of Fritos he had bought.

2

"So you're the famous Wolf Lochert," the man in civilian clothing at the desk said. "Baddest guy north of the Mekong River, hey? And you're going to check our Lima Sites, hey? Well, I'll tell you, 85 is a real pisser." Another man in casual civilian dress sat in a chair by the desk. They were in an office belonging to the RRO, Regional Reporting Office, the name which had been selected as a cover for the large CIA contingent stationed in Laos and attached to the embassy.

Wolfgang Xavier Lochert, a lieutenant colonel in the United States Army Special Forces, wore civilian clothes – *almost* all civilian clothes; his white guayabera shirt hung loose over his dark trousers, which didn't quite hide the Army issue jungle boots on his feet.

The man who spoke was not smiling. He was the CIA deputy chief of logistics for Military Region Two (coded as MR II, pronounced Em Are Two, it included a big wedge of Laos that jutted into North Vietnam). Blue eyes from his blunt Nordic face regarded Lochert steadily. He had never liked Army men, especially Special Forces, since his days as an Air Force lieutenant when he had had the shit beat out of him and some of his men in a joint field exercise in South Carolina. He and four others had been on an escape and evasion training mission, when they had walked into a night ambush by a Special Forces team that had left them all hanging upside down by their belts around their ankles from pine trees. Now he was one of the scores of former military men on contract to the CIA. He wore a thick gold ID bracelet straight from Vilay Phone's, in downtown Vientiane. His name was Jerome Powers.

Powers had graduated from the Air Force Academy on time in 1961 and gone into pilot training. He had lasted through the propeller portion, but run headlong into trouble in the jet phase. He simply could not get his mind ahead of the T-33 jet trainer. Unlike a propeller aircraft, which has instant power when the throttle is pushed forward, the T-33 gas turbine engine required several seconds to spool up to develop thrust. After nearly driving his T-33 into the ground several times on go-arounds in landing practice, because he could not plan ahead for the required thrust, Powers had been washed out. Because of the education the USAF had provided Powers at the Academy, however, he owed the Air Force five years of active duty service. He'd performed in various capacities and wound up his last two years as an aide de camp to a lieutenant general in the intelligence service in Washington, DC. Contacts from that job had led to an interview with the Central Intelligence Agency at Langley, Virginia. His background and the background of his wife had checked out, he'd passed the lie detector tests about his life-style (no hidden homosexuality, pederasty, money problems, drug taking, pot smoking, or rampant adultery), and had quickly been hired to fill the gaping maw of the Indochina/Southeast Asia region.

Contract men like Powers were not merely out of military uniform and detached from their service to work with the Agency, like the sheep-dipped men at Eagle Station. They were fully and legally discharged from whatever civilian or military job they had ever held and had gone through almost-normal hiring procedures to work for the CIA. They differed from career CIA officers in that they were on contract for a specific job for a specific period of time and were not in competition for higher rank within the Agency. In this case, military-*trained* men were hired to help the friendly forces in

Laos. The US had set this scheme in motion to help maintain the fiction that, since Laos was neutral, no US military forces were in that war-ravaged country running around the hills and mountains training the locals to fight the thousands of North Vietnamese soldiers who were also quite illegally in Laos. The North Vietnamese communists, of course, helped maintain the fiction by denying *their* soldiers were in neutralist Laos.

The CIA also had a contract with two flying companies called Air America and Continental Air Service Incorporated (CASI). Each day, dozens of American civilian pilots flew light STOL (short takeoff and landing) aircraft and twin-engine cargo planes to resupply the Lima Sites where the friendlies maintained bases whose functions varied from that of large base camp to forward observation post. When the Air America and CASI crews delivered food, it was mostly bags of rice. The weapons and ammunition they delivered daily was called hard rice. The sites frequently came under attack.

There were, however, many Americans stationed in Laos who *were* military men: they worked in or for the US Embassy and were either members of the DAO (the Defense Attaché Office) or were Ravens, a flying unit. DAO members worked for the Defense Intelligence Agency (DIA), whose mission was overtly to collect military intelligence (as opposed to the CIA, who operated *covertly* to collect military, political, economic, or any other kind of intelligence they were tasked to acquire). The DAO men, known as military attachés, in fact helped run the war in Laos. This was not what attachés did in other countries.

Ravens were Air Force lieutenants and captains, and the odd major or two, who flew light spotter planes, using the call sign Raven. Neither they nor the DAO personnel wore uniforms. The Ravens, in fact, living a sort of Terry-and-the-Pirates existence, went out of their way to look anything but military. Nobody really questioned the use of civilian clothes. It seemed the thing to do, some guessed, mostly to confound the newsies who found their way into Laos to "expose" this not-so-tiny-war in this tiny kingdom. Certainly, civvies would not confound the scores of Russians from the Soviet Embassy who also ran around in civvies and maintained dossiers on all the Americans. If nothing else, Laos was a hodgepodge of intrigue involving democracy versus communism.

On the map, the outline of Laos could be loosely compared to a frying pan with the handle pointed south. The pan portion bordered Burma to the west, China to the north, Thailand to the south, and North Vietnam to the east. The bulk of the pan was called the PDJ, which stood for the French words *Plaine des Jarres* (so named because ancient tribesmen buried their dead in giant above-ground earthen jars). The handle of the pan bordered North and South Vietnam to the east, Thailand to the west, and ended embedded in Cambodia to the south.

"Let me tell you about Laos," Powers said. "There are three Laotian factions here: the Royal Lao Government, which we call the RLG – these are the guys we are trying to help – the Neutralists; and the communists, who are called PL, which stands for Pathet Lao. Currently, the PL and the North Vietnamese Army occupy the north-east corner next to North Vietnam and are supplied by Hanoi. And, currently, the NVA occupies eastern Laos all the way down to Cambodia. In 1961, the PL, the Neuts, and the Royalists were fighting. North Vietnam decided it was a good time to put 6,000 of their soldiers in-country, so in 1962 President Kennedy sent 5,000 U.S. Marines to Thailand, which forced the commies to sign the Geneva Agreements. We signed, and so did Russia and North Vietnam. The idea was to stop the fighting, make Laos neutral, and all foreigners were to haul ass. After the Marines left, we shipped all 666 of our people out. The commies only shipped out forty of their thousands. In April '63 the fighting started again because the commies were using eastern Laos as a giant supply route into South Vietnam. A route that bypassed the demilitarized zone which cut Vietnam in half. That supply route is called the Ho Chi Minh Trail."

What a Scheisskopf, Wolf thought. He had been running teams of Special Forces men up and down the Trail for years. Further, as a Special Forces major he had been in Laos in the early sixties with Project White Star, training Hmoung tribesmen who lived in the Laotian highlands. He looked at the

53

man sitting quietly in the corner who, on catching his glance, winked. He and Wolf knew each other from an operation earlier that year. He was Jim Polter, a slender, gray-eyed man with short-cropped dark hair, whose strong but pleasant face gave crinkly evidence of formidable experience coupled with humor.

"Yup, the Ho Chi Minh Trail is important to the commies," Powers continued. "On any given day they have about 200 tons of supplies moving south, and they have about 300,000 road repair crews and gunners to keep things moving. In the northern part of Laos, the war is different. It's the reverse of what's going on in South Vietnam. Up here the PL and the NVA operate pretty much as a conventional force just like we do in South Vietnam. Like us, they control the population centers and get resupplied by road. Like the VC are in the south, up here the friendlies are the guerrillas. The friendlies are our little guys, the Meo under General Vang Pao. They fight the commies." The "little guys" that Powers referred to were the Hmoung tribesmen formed up by their leader, Vang Pao, to fight the North Vietnamese and the Pathet Lao. The US Government totally supported them with training, weaponry, food, and money.

"That's *Hmoung*, not Meo, Powers," Wolf said. "Meo is a Laotian word, means barbarian. The French used it. We don't. Got it? They're Hmoung, that's their word for 'the people.'"

With a look of infinite distaste at the lecture which he had just received, Jerome Powers rose and flung up a drop cloth revealing a military map of Laos. Scores of colored pins dotted the surface. He waved his hand at the black pins. "We have 187 Lima Sites, 110 of which have airstrips. Most of them are bare-bones sites, but some are full-sized military bases for Vang Pao – we call him VP – and his army. His base is here at Long Tieng. And some" – he pointed to Eagle Station in the northeast portion of the Laotian pan – "have special gear on them for the flyboys." He winked. "You know, the ones who fly north and east of here."

"Didn't one of those sites get overrun?" Wolf asked Powers.

"Yeah," Polter answered. "Site 61 at Ban Tha Si. It was a Tacan site, no bombing radar."

Wolf shook his head and looked at Powers. "How come you didn't mention that to me?"

"Not in my area. It's in a different MR."

Wolf fixed Powers with a hard stare. "What exactly is your job here?"

Powers put his hands on his hips. "My job is to run the war in MR II." Jim Polter coughed lightly. "That is," Powers said without looking at Polter, "my job is to recruit and to supply our guys and the little guys in MR II. Without me, no war. And" – he made a leering smile – "the chief of MR II is on leave in Bangkok, so I'm in charge now."

"And that's why you're in this office, Wolf," Jim Polter said. "You were sent up here to tour the eastern Lima Sites and to inspect the defenses, particularly Lima Site 85, Eagle Station. It's one of our most important sites. We want you to make sure VP and his men are putting into practice some of the stuff the SF has been teaching them down in Thailand."

"Why me?" Wolf asked.

Polter laughed. "My request. Hope you don't mind."

"Mind?" Wolf said. "No, I don't mind. Happy to get out of Saigon. More than you know."

"I expect so," Polter said dryly. He knew all about the court-martial. There were other soldiers that could have performed the on-site inspections, but Polter figured, quite correctly, that Wolf Lochert needed a break from the United States Army and MACV (Military Advisory Command, Vietnam).

"Here's the latest report on Lima Site 85," Powers said and handed Wolf a file. "Just a minor affair, really."

For several minutes Wolf studied the papers and the attached map. He looked up. "I think it was a probe, and that there will be a full-scale attack very soon." He put the file back on Powers's desk.

"And I say it was an errant local PL commander who hadn't gotten the word to stay away from the site," Powers said.

"What do you mean?" Wolf asked. "Stay away from the site?"

"There's a lot out there you don't know about, Lochert, and Site 85 is one of them. They stay away – "

"Who are 'they'?" Lochert interrupted.

"The PL, the Pathet Lao. They stay away for a couple of reasons. One is they probably get paid off from the opium poppy farmers, and secondly, they know the site is well defended and we can have as many of VP's troops and all the air strikes we want up there in less than a day."

"Paid off? Less than a day? I'm here to check Lima Site defenses and this one sounds like a real Maginot Line and you sound like Maginot himself. What if the NVA replace the PL? And what if the site is overrun, what kind of an evacuation plan do you have for the men?"

"We have a plan not only to pull the men out, but to bring the equipment out if there is time or destroy it if there isn't. But none of that will be necessary. We consider the site well defended by VP's troops."

"Would they fight to the last man?"

"Well, no. Why should they? This isn't a piece of real estate we need to hold forever."

Wolf tapped the file. "You consider it vital, yet you don't think it worth holding? Sounds like you don't know what you want or how important that place really is."

Powers frowned. "Well, maybe you'd just better get on out there, then."

"That's exactly what I intend to do. I think there are NVA around that site, not just PL." Wolf stood up. "Tell me," he asked in a pleasant voice, "where do you fit into my inspections, Mister Powers?"

"The reason you are checking in with Powers," Polter broke in, "is that he is the assistant to the guy who has a handle on who is doing what out there, who you should see once you're out there – "

"And the man on Lima Site 85 is Mister Sam," Powers broke in. "He runs the CP and the Meo . . . unh, Hmoung garrison. Counting wives and kids, there are about 200. But he'll just tell you the same thing I am."

"Which is?" Wolf said.

56

"Goddammit, that there is no real problem up there."

"Swear one more time, *Scheisskopf,* and I'll break your arm," Wolf flared.

"He doesn't like swearing," Polter said to Powers in a conciliatory voice.

Polter turned to Wolf and changed the subject. "Jerome will rig you up with whatever gear you need as well as transportation to the Lima Sites."

"I've got my own rig," Wolf growled. It was an implied insult that he didn't carry enough of his own gear at any given time to be ready to go into the field.

Still riled, Powers opened a door to a supply room next to his office. "I'll bet you don't have one of these," he said, and held up a metal object about the size of a half-carton of cigarettes. It was an RT-10 aircrew survival radio.

"I've got *two,* " Wolf barked.

"Or one of these," Powers said, pointing to a PRC-25 FM field radio.

"Yeah, one of those too. What is this, some sort of a one-up game show?"

"How about a weapon?" Powers asked.

Polter laughed. "Give up, Jerome. Wolf Lochert was snapping caps in combat before you knew which end of the gun the bullet came out."

In point of fact, Wolf Lochert carried his Randall stiletto in one ankle holster and his 7.63 Mauser "social" weapon in the other. He had two bags with him on this trip: a duffel bag with field gear, harnesses, and fatigues, and a parachute bag with his USAF backpack T-10 parachute modified with a four-line cut for better steering control. He also carried a 7.62 AK-47 assault rifle.

"Well, I know he doesn't have one of these," Powers said and handed Wolf a small booklet.

Wolf took it. "No, I don't," he said, and thumbed through it. It was titled *Airfield Site List, Laos,* dated October 1968. It listed all 187 Lima Sites and broke out the 110 with airstrips. The index gave all the codes for radio beacons, fuel available, runway headings, slope, elevation, length and width, and the

UTM coordinates of each site. It also gave status codes such as OPN meaning *open* for all aircraft, or UNF meaning it was in *unfriendly* hands. The primary VHF frequency was 119.1 for each site. The company radio was 118.1, with 121.5 for emergencies. For really long distance, the HF radio was used on frequency 5568 at night, 8765 during the day.

"Keep that," Powers said. "It may come in handy." He dug out a paper from a folder and handed it to Wolf. "Here is your schedule for today."

Wolf scanned the list of meetings. Political/Military . . . Military Assistance Advisory Group . . . Consular . . . Defense Attaché . . . Aid for International Development . . . Raven Ops . . . Air America OPS . . . *Scheiss,* this would take all day.

And it did. It was late in the afternoon by the time Polter and Lochert finished the round of briefings. Polter drove Wolf in the jeep to Wattay airport. En route they passed the famous Vertical Runway, a tall Arc de Triomphe structure made from concrete that had been given to the RLG by the United States to expand the runway at Wattay. The King kept the monument under constant construction because a soothsayer in his court had told him that to stop would be the end of his life.

At Wattay, they walked out to one of Air America's C-46s shimmering in the sun on the concrete ramp. Three men stood in the shade under the left wing and watched them approach. A fourth man busied himself preflighting the twin-engined cargo airplane with the tail number 715.

Polter introduced Wolf to the pilot, the copilot, and to a young Lao he called a bundle-kicker, whose job, he explained, was to toss out the cargo as the ships made low passes over the Lima Sites.

"We've got to kick out some rice up in the hills at Xieng Khoung, then we'll get you to Lima 85," the pilot said. He wore dark gray trousers and a short-sleeved gray sport shirt with the four stripes of a captain on his shoulder epaulets.

The Lao, about five-two, Wolf judged, made a toothy grin at Wolf, thumbed his own chest, and said, "Is Tewa."

Wolf thumbed his own chest and said, "Is Wolf." The two men shook hands.

The crew chief signaled the airplane was ready, and they all walked to the metal steps hanging from slots at the cargo door in the left fuselage. Wolf put his two bags down and unzipped the parachute bag, then pulled out his T-10 backpack parachute and a set of rumpled jungle fatigues. He put the fatigues on over his civilian clothes, filled the cargo pockets with survival equipment, strapped the two RT-10 radios into the leg pockets, then threw the T-10 parachute to his back and shrugged into the harness. Then he pulled the AK from the parachute bag and strapped it to his leg. The pilot watched with some amusement as Wolf squatted and tightened the leg straps for the parachute.

"You always fly like that, buddy?" he asked.

"Always," Wolf growled. Except for combat assaults from helicopters, Wolf Lochert wore a parachute anytime he was in an airplane in a combat zone. If pressed, he would say it had been years before he was comfortable as a chuteless passenger on a civilian airliner. Wolf Lochert had logged 1,247 jumps since he began jumping twenty years earlier.

"Some guys," the pilot muttered, shaking his head as he climbed the small ladder and disappeared inside the ship.

"See you in a couple days," Polter said, shaking Wolf's hand. "Keep in touch on the HF net. Let me know if there is anything really gross that needs immediate attention. I don't think there is, but you never know what you'll find out there."

Thirty minutes later the C-46 was level at 8,000 feet and beginning its first run. The airplane was cargo-rigged; there were no seats, neither airliner-type nor canvas pulldowns. Even the big cargo door had been removed. Tewa had hooked a net over the opening. Wolf sat on a pallet of rice strapped down just behind the pilot's compartment. In his ears were rubber plugs he had inserted just before takeoff. He had taken them from a small tube he always carried. Special Forces men, as with any men who spent their lives in the bush, valued their hearing as much as their weapons to keep them alive. He studied the map, a 1:250,000 Aerial Navigation Chart he had pulled from his bag to keep track of the approximate position of the C-46. He felt the pilot set the throttles and slow the airplane to drop speed.

He climbed down when he saw Tewa the bundle-kicker start pulling bags of rice toward the cargo door. Because they were going into range of ground fire and Wolf wanted all his senses alert, he stowed his earplugs, then stuffed the map under his harness. Due to the tightness of his parachute straps, he had to walk slightly crouched. Tewa grinned as Wolf helped drag rice bags to the door. The Lao wore neither a parachute nor a harness and safety belt binding him to the aircraft. Earlier, Wolf had noticed four parachutes stacked haphazardly in a cargo bin on the left side behind the pilot's compartment.

The pilot made a steep left descending turn toward the tiny encampment. Out the gaping door Wolf could see the steep green hills and tall trees that made up the Laotian countryside. The pilot leveled at what Wolf estimated was two hundred feet above the terrain and began his run. In the doorway Tewa watched three small light bulbs next to the door. When the red went off and the green lit up, he began flinging sacks of rice out the door as fast as he could. The rice was double-bagged to handle any loose rice in case the inner bag burst upon impact, which it usually did. Wolf helped pitch them out. Tewa held up his hand after seven bags. They were past the short drop zone. "Is all," Tewa mouthed. Wolf nodded and put his plugs back in his ears.

The drop zone was the village itself, situated in the only clear space along the top of a small row of green hills. The pilot had tried to align the left door with the edge of the clearing so the bags wouldn't crash through the roofs of the thatched huts surrounding the longhouse of the chief.

After the pilot had pulled away to the north and climbed, the door to the pilot's compartment opened and a man wearing the three stripes of a copilot on his epaulets came back to Wolf.

"That was X-ray Kilo," he said, shouting above the noise of the engines and the wind passing by the open cargo door. Wolf reached to his right ear and pulled out a rubber plug.

"Say again," he said to the copilot.

"That was Xieng Khoung. The Company just called on HF. We have a divert. We have to go to a camp near Ban Ban and drop some hard rice. Be there in about twenty minutes, then we'll get you to Lima 85."

Wolf pulled his map out and had the copilot show him where they were going. It was a spot in the northeast corner of the PDJ. After the copilot told Tewa what he wanted and went back up front, Wolf replaced the earplug and climbed back on the rice pallet. He watched Tewa rig parachutes to the straps and hooks on three heavy wooden crates. Within minutes Wolf felt the pilot lower the nose and throttle back for the next run. Again, he carefully stowed both earplugs. As before, the pilot leveled a few hundred feet above the ground. Wolf made his way, hand over hand in the now swaying fuselage, to help Tewa. Wind swirled through the fuselage, fluttering loose corners of canvas covers.

Wolf heard the anti-aircraft fire before he saw or felt anything. Above the wind and engine noise, he heard the sharp *pam-pam-pam-pam* of what he recognized as a 12.7mm (.51 caliber) Russian anti-aircraft gun.

Immediately, the engines roared as the pilot slammed the throttles forward and the big plane tilted left in a sharp turn away, Wolf hoped, from the sudden ground fire. In the abrupt turn, Tewa started to slide toward the yawning door, eyes wide with alarm. Wolf quickly grabbed a crate strap with one hand and the tiny Lao with the other and hauled him back to safety. Then Wolf gave him a mighty shove toward the parachute bin. Before the startled Lao could protest, Wolf had a chute strapped on him, and had him started back to the cargo door.

As they reached the door, a spray of bullets drummed through the underside of the aircraft, slamming into cargo pallets and zinging through the skin of the curved top of the cargo compartment. Every fifth round was a tracer that left smoke in its path. A cargo box started to smolder. Wolf pulled Tewa down to the floor behind one of the crates. Another bullet spray hammered the aircraft closer to the front of the ship as the gunner took more lead on his target. Wolf thought he heard a shout from the cockpit as the aircraft abruptly nosed down. At the same time he saw a trail of white smoke and red flame issue from the left engine. The flames were long and hot and almost reached the open cargo door. Wolf could smell burning oil. The plane started to turn and fall into that side as the engine's propeller began to unwind. The bailout alarm, a huge bell mounted above the door, started a strident ringing that galvanized Wolf into instinctive action. Without a glance forward, he slammed Tewa's hand onto the ripcord of his chute and threw him out the door and tumbled out immediately after him.

"Wolf had never gone out the door in such an awkward position, much less at such a low altitude without a static line to open his parachute automatically. He did the best he could to roll to a spread-eagle facedown position and pulled the ripcord. For an instant he was struck by the incredible silence, then he heard and felt his parachute pop open. He looked up, checked his canopy was fully deployed, and saw the stricken C-46 crash into a hillside with a muted roar. He realized there were bare seconds remaining before he would hit the ground. He took a quick glance around to orient himself to the terrain, saw Tewa with a full canopy go into the trees south of his position, saw furtive movements heading toward where the Lao would land, then looked down to prepare for his own landing. He had instinctively grabbed the two risers that allowed him to steer his parachute and had just as instinctively turned into the wind. He saw a small clearing below and pulled a riser to steer toward it. When he saw he had it made, he assumed the landing position and slammed into the ground.

Lochert hit, feet together, knees slightly bent, arms straight up with hands on the risers, eyes on the horizon. It was to be a classic PLF – Parachute Landing Fall. As soon as his feet touched, he pulled the risers to his chest as hard and as fast as he could, tucked, and rolled down on one shoulder. But at the end of the maneuver, as the landing energy was dissipated, his head struck a rock and he knew nothing more.

"Sor, sor, is dead? Is sor dead?" The tiny Lao spoke in liquid syllables. He was crouched over Lochert's inert form, shaking his torso. "Sor, if sor not dead, sor must move. Bad fucker come, bad fucker come." He had gathered up Wolf's parachute and piled the silk near his body. The late afternoon was steamy hot and there was no breeze. The jungle, still quiet after the hammering of guns and the crash of the C-46, seemed to be waiting for the next crescendo.

Wolf opened an eye. "Sir not dead," he said softly. "What compass bad fucker?"

Years before, during White Star, Wolf had helped develop the 100-word vocabulary taught to the Lao tribesman to make the rudiments of combat conversation. A few nouns, some basic single-tense verbs, names of weapons and directions made up the pidgin English. Like spice, flavor was added by whichever additional words the Special Forces teacher felt appropriate. The basic word denoting the reproductive act, and its many wondrous and colorful variations, was by far the most popular and common.

Tewa pointed south, down the hill from the small clearing.

"What kilometer?" Wolf asked, still lying flat, head throbbing.

"Maybe one, maybe two kilometer."

"Where Tewa parachute?"

The Lao pointed down the hill. "Fucking tree. Bad fucker see sure."

Wolf sat up and felt the back of his head. He fingered a lump, but brought forth no blood when he looked at his fingers. *Scheiss,* he said to himself, *if I'd worn a pot, that wouldn't have happened.* He felt a dull throb and a momentary dizziness but nothing else.

"Okay," he said, "make weapons check." Still seated, Wolf unbuckled his parachute harness, then unstrapped the AK-47, checked it for damage, pulled a magazine from a thigh pocket and inserted it into the weapon, then jacked a round into the chamber. He checked his stiletto and Mauser secure in their holsters. He inventoried the rest of his gear and put one of the RT-10 radios in a chest pocket. He pulled two 5-grain aspirins from a waterproof pack, punctured a pint tin of water, and swallowed the pills along with half the water. He gave the tin to Tewa, who took it with a wide grin and emptied the tin with thirsty gulps.

"Okay," Wolf said to Tewa, "let's move over there." He

63

pointed to the north edge of the clearing away from the direction Tewa said the "bad fuckers" were. Once away from the open space, Wolf buried the water tin, then pointed up a tall tree and said to Tewa, "Go up, look, find bad fuckers." The Lao seemed savvy enough to Wolf to be able to give a dependable report.

As Tewa started shinnying up the tree, Wolf knelt down, quickly cut cloth from his camouflaged parachute, buried the rest, and smoothed out the disturbed brush. Then he eased to the ground next to a fallen log and concealed himself behind branches and leaves, yet leaving enough space so he could see across the clearing.

From a pocket, he took out his map and fixed what he was fairly certain was their position. He pulled the RT-10 radio from his chest pocket and extended the antenna, debating whether to use the international distress call of Mayday. Mayday, from the French *M'aidez* (help me), was a powerful attention-getter in that it meant an airplane was in imminent danger of crashing or had already crashed. The call was usually heard on what was called Guard Channel, which was 243.0 megacycles on UHF (Ultra High Frequency) radio, and 121.5 on VHF (Very High Frequency).

All aircraft had a spare receiver permanently tuned to Guard Channel, so that regardless of what frequency the pilot was using on his main receiver, he would also hear it. Sometimes Guard became too crowded with frantic voices in uncontrolled SAR or combat situations when a lot of planes were going down. When that happened, the pilot would temporarily turn his Guard receiver to Standby so as to better concentrate on whatever he was doing on his own tactical frequency.

Since the RT-10 transmitted and received only on Guard, and an airplane had crashed, Mayday seemed the obvious way to go. Yet Wolf felt reluctant to use the distress call. I'm *not in any distress,* he reasoned, *only temporarily inconvenienced.* He decided not to use the call and instead pushed the button on the small radio and began to transmit.

"Any aircraft reading Wolf on Guard Channel, give me a call." He repeated the transmission twice more and received no reply. Tewa sprang down from the tree.

"Bad fucker is halb kilometer," he said in a rushed voice.

"How many?"

"Many. *Mak-mak,*" Tewa said, using Thai slang for very many, which, Wolf realized, could be anywhere from four or five to twenty or who knows.

"This many?" Wolf asked, opening and closing his right hand twice to count ten fingers.

"*Mak-mak,*" Tewa repeated, and opened and closed both hands three times.

"Maybe thirty?" Wolf said.

"Bad fucker look us. Halb Tewa parachute."

Wolf pulled out his map. "You know map?" he asked.

"Is know," Tewa said, and patted a back pocket as if that were where his knowledge was stored. Wolf showed him where he thought they were on his big 1:250,000 Aerial Navigation Chart.

Tewa made a big grin and reached into his rear pocket for a worn Army 1:50,000 map of the region. "Is know," he repeated, and pointed to a spot on the map. Happily surprised at this man's ability to plan ahead, Wolf looked where he pointed and agreed that Tewa had accurately found their position. The surrounding countryside was shown in much greater detail on the Lao's map. Wolf had a moment in which he had trouble focusing and had to blink several times to clear his vision.

"Tewa is good man," Wolf said in a low voice. He took out his *Airfield/Site List, Laos,* and checked the coordinates in the local area for the closest Lima site in the opposite direction from the approaching Pathet Lao "bad fuckers." To the north, twenty-one miles away, he found Lima Site 36 at Na Khang. The route to the site would take them up and down several ridgelines of karst that pushed up in rows like the Appalachian Mountains in the United States. The karst punched up in bizarre forms and shapes caused by wind working on the limestone for millions of years. Wolf took out his lensatic compass, checked bearings, sliced his hand toward Na Khang, and said quietly to Tewa, "We go now." He put a finger to his lips to emphasize silence and Tewa nodded.

The direction Wolf had chosen was uphill through scrub

brush and karst outcroppings. They started to climb. At first the going was easy. The single-canopy jungle was formed of broad leaves which kept the late-afternoon sun from their backs. The slope was not too steep and the jungle floor was soft from rotted foliage but not slippery. The humidity was high. Several times Wolf stopped Tewa with a motion of his hand and they listened for pursuers. So far they had heard nothing. Once Wolf stopped and cut a plug from the base of a banana tree for the pure water it contained and they both drank their fill. Wolf pulled two prophylactics from his pocket, gave one to Tewa, then they filled the thin membranes with water and carefully put them in their front cargo pockets. Wolf put the plug back in the tree, then painstakingly concealed the spot with branches.

Soon they were working their way up through karst, the rocky limestone outcropping so common in northeastern Laos. There was no canopy over the karst; the soil would not support big trees. Some of the slope was covered with a mixture of tall elephant grass and low scrub vegetation.

It was close to darkness when Wolf signaled to stop and conceal themselves for the night. He pointed to one of many small cave openings in the porous rock. It was easily defensible and gave a good view down the slope, but was difficult to reach. They climbed the steep rock face as high as they could, then switched to a narrow vertical fissure that rose up a dozen feet and passed next to the cave opening. They ascended by bracing their feet and backs against opposite walls. Wolf used parachute cloth to make a sling for his AK to dangle under him. Halfway up, Wolf saw where his right boot had scraped a white streak in the rock. Balancing himself with both legs, he spit onto his fingers, slowly stretched his hand forward, and made mud from the surrounding wall dirt to cover the offending scratch. Below him, Tewa stayed wedged in watchful silence.

Wolf climbed the remaining five feet and levered himself onto the narrow ledge at the top of the chimney, pulled his gun after himself, and reached down to help Tewa out of the fissure. Upon Wolf's instructions, Tewa backed into the cave.

Wolf had to lie flat, then inch his way backwards through the cave opening, which was a jagged slice two feet high by four feet wide. He pulled in his AK, then, still on his stomach, looked out over the surrounding terrain from his vantage point. The rough karst, slate-colored and crumbling through the green growth, fell away steeply to the single-canopy jungle twenty feet below. He could see down onto the strip of elephant grass that lay between the jungle and the base of the karst. He saw no movement in the grass and none through the dense jungle canopy. He watched silently for several long minutes and finally noted birds take sudden flight along a line pointing fairly close to their position in the karst. He figured their panic was caused by approaching Pathet Lao troops less than a kilometer from the bottom of the karst. He inched back into the cave to where it was wider and he could sit up. What little light there was came from the darkening sky outside. His eyes soon became accustomed to the vague outline of Tewa in the cave.

"I doubt if they found our trail," he said in a near-whisper to Tewa, forgetting for the moment the Lao's abbreviated English vocabulary.

"They probably figured we would climb to the closest high point in the region. We will bivouac here. Rest. Sleep."

"Yes, yes," Tewa said in the dimness, obviously not comprehending exactly what Wolf had said but aware enough of the situation to get the general idea. The Lao drank some of his water and busied himself laying out his meager equipment.

Wolf passed him some parachute cloth and used his own to fashion a pillow, then began to pull survival items from his pocket. He drank half of the water, then positioned the thin bladder where he could get at it, put one RT-10 radio next to the water and left the second in his pocket along with a day-night smoke flare. He didn't want to take anything else from his pockets in case they had to make a hurried departure from the cave in the middle of the night. He crawled forward to position the AK near the cave opening and looked out over the jungle below. Daylight was ending and the sky was a thick violet laced with golden rays from the setting sun. He began to feel nauseated and had trouble seeing clearly in the dim light that seemed to grow more dim then become bright again. He rested on his elbows and felt himself sway.

"Is sor okay?" Tewa asked from behind.

Wolf pushed back. He knew what was happening. "Going into shock," he said. "Delayed reaction to the bash on the head. Need water, aspirin, warmth, feet up." He knew the Lao didn't understand. He fought against the increasing nausea and dizziness to drink water and take four aspirin. Finally he wrapped himself in the parachute cloth and lay back with his feet propped up on a ledge higher than his head.

"Sir is sick," he whispered to Tewa.

3

1845 HOURS LOCAL, THURSDAY 10 OCTOBER 1968
AIRBORNE IN AN HH-53B HELICOPTER
NORTHEASTERN PLAINE DES JARRES
ROYALTY OF LAOS

"Did you hear that?" Captain Joe Kelly asked the pilot sitting to his right in the cockpit of the HH-53B helicopter.

"Did I hear what?" the pilot, an older lieutenant colonel, responded.

The big camouflaged HH-53B helicopter thrashed its way north-east to Lima Site 36 at Na Khang from their home base of Udorn Royal Thai Air Force Base (RTAFB) in Thailand. The noise from the six blades of its massive rotor system and the howl of the two T-64 turbo engines would have sounded to someone on the ground like a cross between the whine of a giant sewing machine and the thrum of whirling scimitars. Only the ubiquitous Hueys made the *whop-whop, blat-blat* blade sounds. The ship weighed over seventeen tons and was cruising at 9,000 feet, with a true airspeed of 155 knots. The autopilot was engaged, freeing the pilots from the exacting job of keeping the helicopter on course. They were deploying to Lima Site 36, a secret advanced base in Laos, to spend the night. Very early the following morning they were to take off and set up an orbit by the North Vietnamese border in support of a large fighter strike in North Vietnam.

Kelly turned the volume up on the UHF radio and pressed the

sides of his olive drab helmet close to his ears. Head cocked, he listened intently.

"There. Hear that?"

"No, dammit," the pilot, Paul Shilleto, replied with some disgust, "I didn't." He was a forty-seven-year-old lieutenant colonel with eleven years in grade and hearing that had deteriorated badly due to twenty years of flying C-124s (between helicopter tours) and noisy helicopters. He sat with his hands in his lap and had been watching the countryside slip by underneath. He was at the end of his tour and didn't really want this overnight deployment . . . particularly with Joe Kelly, the squadron's youngest instructor pilot and rescue crew commander. Joe Kelly was known as a wild man. Kelly had not endeared himself to the rescue community when he had added the phrase *We Die* to the rescue motto, *That Others May Live.* Kelly, a 1962 Air Force Academy graduate, was known as a pre-Rucker pilot. That meant he had graduated from the complete fixed-wing USAF pilot training and received his wings. Then he had gone to helicopter training. Later on, USAF helicopter pilots went only to the Army's Fort Rucker for helicopter training.

"I've got it now," Kelly said. He was a man of broad shoulders made even bulkier by the survival vest and flak jacket he wore. Shilleto listened. Together they heard the faint voice.

"Hello, hello. Is Tewa. Is Tewa. Sor is sick. Sor is sick. You come please. Come now." The voice stopped with a static hiss as the talker released the transmit button. It hissed on for a second, then back off as if the talker kept pressing the button but didn't know what to say.

"Heavy accent, bad English, sounds like a flak trap," Shilleto said. He checked his watch. "We don't have much time." He put his hands back in his lap. *Christ,* he thought to himself *twelve months of this, eleven pickups, shot up dozens of times, I'm ready to hang it up. Should have retired five years ago.* He turned to Kelly. "It's a flak trap. Got sucked into one of these at Hue. When I was TDY at Da Nang, we lost a bird on a phony call from the survival radio of a dead Thud driver."

70

"Maybe so," Kelly answered, "but I'll see what I can find out. It sounds different than someone trying to sucker us in. Kind of plaintive."

"Suit yourself," the older man said, "just stay on course for Lima 36."

Kelly spoke into the boom mike attached to his helmet. "Station calling on Guard Channel, this is Jolly Green 22, over." There was no answer. "Station calling, this is Jolly Green, do you read?" Still no answer. Joe Kelly thought for a moment about what the person transmitting said, then called again. "Hello, Tewa, this is Jolly Green. Tewa, this is Jolly Green. Talk to me." He activated the radio direction finding (RDF) gear and waited for the voice to call back. The RDF needle would swing and point to the direction of the transmission.

He heard the carrier wave, then some tentative sounds, then the voice.

"Hello, is Tewa. Sor is sick. You come please. You come please."

Kelly got a good bearing, about 20 degrees port. "Yes, Tewa, I hear you. Put sir on the radio. Give the radio to sir, Tewa." Joe spoke as if to a child.

"Listen, Kelly," Shilleto said on the intercom, "we've got to get to 36 tonight and in one piece. If this were a legitimate shootdown, we would have been told by King to monitor the area and listen for a specific call sign. Even if it was an old shootdown, we would have known the approximate area and would have a handle on this call. Let's get on with our deployment." Shilleto stared straight ahead through the plexiglass of the big helicopter as if willing the craft suddenly to be past this unpleasantness and somehow be over its destination.

The normal crew complement of an HH-53B Jolly Green helicopter was five: pilot and copilot, a flight mechanic, and two PJs. The big helicopter, known as a Super Jolly Green, had three 7.62mm (.30 cal) miniguns that could fire up to 4,000 rounds per minute.

In addition to the Air Force crew were four Hmoung soldiers returning to Vang Pao's army after some special training by American forces in Thailand. They had been warned that there

71

might be a diversion in case of an emergency to pick up a newly downed pilot. They had smiled nervously and didn't seem to understand a word. None looked to be more than fifteen years old.

"Colonel," Kelly said, "for Christ's sake, it won't take any time from our flight plan to talk to this guy on the radio. You act as if every time I depress the mike button I'm changing course 90 degrees. I'm only talking to him. If he's a phony, it will be the first of a kind in this area and worth alerting the others about. If he is for real, well, then, we've got to do something."

"He's not for real, you can bet on that," Shilleto said, more on hope than conviction.

Kelly keyed his mike again. "Tewa, do you read, ah, do you hear me? I am Jolly Green. Tewa, answer Jolly Green. Push button on radio. Answer Jolly Green, Tewa."

"GET THE FUCK OFF GUARD CHANNEL," a voice boomed through their headsets.

"Cool it," Kelly said on Guard to the unknown complainer. "We may have an emergency here. Tewa, Tewa, talk to Jolly Green."

"Chollie Gleen, Chollie Gleen, is Tewa. Sor is sick. You come Chollie Gleen. You come."

"Tewa, give the radio to sore. Give the radio to sore."

Inside the cave, Wolf was fighting a wave of drowsiness. He heard as if from a great distance the halting conversation between Tewa and somebody on the small survival radio.

"Oh, sor," Tewa said and held the radio out to Wolf, "is Chollie Gleen. You talk."

With an effort Wolf pulled the radio close to his mouth and transmitted. "Jolly Green – this is Wolf. We bailed out of a Company aircraft. Hiding in cave in karst. Need pickup. Pretty sick. Hit on head."

"Understand, Wolf," Kelly returned. "Will you authenticate Romeo Alpha, please?" Rescue helicopter personnel and FAC pilots carried a code wheel that was reset to a new code each day. To verify that the person they were talking to on the radio was not an enemy, they would call out letters of the phonetic alphabet and the responder was to give the letters lying opposite them on the small cardboard wheel.

Wolf grimaced with the effort to pull his thoughts together. "Unable to authenticate. Airplane was Air America C-46 number 715. The first three of my serial number are 470. You can verify that at Victor Tango. There are two of us. Approximate location three miles north of Ban Ban." He hated to give the location in the clear but had no choice.

Captain Joe Kelly turned to look at Lieutenant Colonel Paul Shilleto. "I think we've got two legitimate survivors from an airplane based at Vientiane. If we hustle we may be able to make a pickup before dark."

"Nothing doing," Shilleto said. "That's not enough information to go on. We've got to verify there is a 715 missing from Victor Tango. Even at that, these could be phonies. They could have picked up the tail number from the crash site, same with his serial number. Could come from a dog tag. No, I think we should stay on course for Lima 36."

"Oh, bullshit, Colonel," Kelly exploded. "No way the PL could just happen to have an English speaker at a random crash site. I say let's go for them."

"And I say not until we have verification from Vientiane through Queen, and then get Queen's permission to go to the site." Queen was the call sign for the rescue command post at the Tan Son Nhut ARRS headquarters.

"It's getting dark fast, that will take too long." Kelly took the controls, snapped the helicopter off autopilot, and turned to a heading of 345, the course the direction-finding needle last pointed.

"What the hell . . ." Shilleto began.

"Colonel, I appreciate your concern," Kelly said in a conciliatory tone, "but I am on flight orders as aircraft commander for the entire deployment, and as an instructor pilot as well, and that places me in command of this flight. I'm going to check with the crew and see what they think."

A Jolly Green pilot did not arbitrarily decide to make a pickup attempt without talking it over with the two PJs and the flight mech. Too much rode not only on each man's

73

performance but on his evaluation of the rescue situation as well. What might look fine to the pilot might be clearly undoable to the flight mech or PJ. All of the men had to be up and ready to fly into what could be a true valley of death.

Kelly switched the intercom jack box by his left thigh to talk to the flight mechanic and the two PJs in the rear. He gave the backend crew a quick rundown of what he had heard and what he thought, then said: "Okay, crew. It sounds legitimate to me, but we don't have much time to screw around, so sound off. Flight mech?"

"Sir, I'm with you, but let's not hang it out too far," said the flight mech.

"PJ One?"

"Ho, let's go," PJ One said in an eager voice.

"Ditto," said PJ Two without being asked.

"All right, then," Kelly said in a light tone, "we're going down to see what's up."

He rolled the helicopter out of the turn and transmitted on Guard.

"Wolf, give me a long count."

Lying in the cave, Wolf Lochert heard the request and held the transmit button down for a mental count of ten. He was too exhausted and fuzzy-minded to count out loud. Tewa hovered nearby in the gloom.

On board the helicopter the direction needle pointed straight ahead toward the signal from the survival radio. Kelly switched the intercom jack box by his left thigh to talk to the flight mechanic and the two PJs in the rear.

"Okay, guys," Kelly said, "listen up. We're talking to two possible survivors on Guard Channel. I'm DF-ing to them now. Flight mech, make sure the passengers are seated and strapped in. PJs, be ready with the hoist if we have to go down." The two PJs and the flight mech rogered the call. Then Kelly switched over to his High Frequency radio and called Queen. He gave Queen the information about a crashed C-46 and the survivor's serial number, and where he was going to investigate further. Then he asked that a backup

Jolly Green be scrambled from alert to cover them in case they had to go in for a pickup.

"Negative backup available, Jolly Green 22. Alert birds are airborne, so are their backups. Use pilot's discretion."

Rescue procedures called for two Jolly Greens to be present for all pickups in high-threat areas; one was called the high bird, the other the low bird. The high bird would orbit high and safe from enemy guns to act as backup while the low bird went in for the pickup. There was usually an on-scene commander present controlling the entire rescue effort. He would coordinate the rescue helicopters and the big prop-driven A-1 fighters, which were used both to suppress the anti-aircraft guns trying to shoot down the rescue force and to stop enemy troops trying to capture the downed crewman.

Now, in October of 1968, over 2,200 fixed-wing and helicopter pilots had been shot down over North and South Vietnam and Laos. Over 1,300 had been successfully picked up. The ARRS crewman and support pilots had learned how best to pull a man from the ground under heavy fire. Unfortunately, the communist forces had also learned how to use crash sites, radios, and fake crewmen as flak traps. More than once a perfectly accented American voice had come up on the survival radio saying the way was clear. Usually, unmilitary phraseology or unfamiliarity with the rescue procedures that every crewman was taught in a variety of survival schools gave the fakers away before the rescue force was in gun range.

The phrase "use pilot's discretion" meant Queen had put the ball in Kelly's court. If all went well, it could be said he had used excellent discretion. If it went badly, it would be said he had used poor judgment and, at best, would probably have his IP orders revoked and a rather derogatory statement entered into his efficiency report; at worst, he and his crewmen would be dead or captured.

Kelly didn't really give two-thirds of a purple fuck for any of that. He cared only for the man on the ground and the crew in the helicopter behind him. There was a very thin line as to how far he could hang out the lives of the flight mech and PJs who depended on his skill and judgment not only to get the job done but to get it done without reckless risk.

Not every flight mech went along with Joe Kelly's *We Die That Others May Live* philosophy. Many preferred that the "others" include themselves, a reasonable request. Many pilots felt the same way.

Flight mechs were generally of a different mold from the PJs. Flight mechs started life as a General Aviation Mechanic, Helicopter (slanged to GAMs and referred to as Greasy-Assed Mechanics). Some helicopter mechanics decided they wanted to fly aboard their birds for fun and excitement, not to mention the extra flight pay added to the monthly salary and the silver wings of an aircrewman. When they had enough experience to apply (up to a five-level in USAF terminology) and were good enough as rated by their line chief and maintenance officer, they could go to school to become a flight mechanic in a specific helicopter. Others who had experience in the unit helicopter could be upgraded locally.

PJs, on the other hand, usually were quite satisfied with Captain Kelly's decisions about hairy pickups. PJs were there to rescue people, PJs were in combat so that others might live, and Captain Kelly gave them great opportunities to do just that. Ergo, Captain Kelly made good decisions, they said. The PJs remembered Kelly's reaction when a staff weinie in Headquarters had suggested that the Jolly Greens paint big red crosses on their helicopters and remove all the guns. "Hell, no!" Kelly had exploded. "As far as that goes, in addition to the guns I want a chin turret with a grenade launcher." PJs frequently traded flights among themselves to fly with Joe Kelly. An aggressive Jolly Green crew was self-selective.

PJs, who almost always were younger than the flight mechs, came in two categories: those that had become PJs purely because of their desire to get down in the weeds to help their fellow man, and those who – in addition to that reason – wanted to live the daredevil existence of a combat PJ. A PJ was either a Florence Nightingale or a knife-fighting Florence Nightingale. To a downed crewman, often injured, it made no difference whatsoever what the motivation of the man was who came to rescue him, the man was there and that was all that mattered. Most PJs felt that the helicopter and the pilot that flew it was merely a PJ delivery system. When fighter pilots and backseaters would gather and talk about air rescue people in general, and PJs in particular, they would frequently be seen to make cupping motions with their hands well apart as if describing giant three-foot globes, and the words they used would include "balls this big."

After Kelly had told them of the upcoming rescue attempt, the three men in the cabin of Jolly Green 22 set about their tasks. The flight mechanic scanned each of the four Hmoung soldiers and told them the flight was diverting to check on some downed crewman. They were to remain strapped in at all times and keep their feet out of the way when any crew member had to move about the cabin. The four Vang Pao soldiers smiled and bobbed their heads and didn't seem to understand a word the flight mech said.

The two PJs checked all their provisions, their rescue equipment, their medical gear, and the three 7.62mm miniguns mounted in a left window, the rear ramp, and the right door. The right-door gun had to be swung forward to clear the doorway so the flight mech could get to the hoist that was mounted just above the door on the outside. The hoist was a heavy hydraulic unit that raised and lowered the penetrator. The penetrator was a heavy metallic device shaped like a big arrowhead, with three paddle seats that unfolded down from it like petals from a flower. It was lowered on a 280-foot steel cable from the hoist, which was controlled by the flight mechanic. Except when the PJ rode it down, the penetrator was closed and its weight forced it through the jungle canopy. A PJ descended if the survivor was unable to strap himself onto one of the seats. The flight mech stood in the door, raised, lowered, and guided the cable while telling the pilot using hot mike on the intercom just what was happening and where he should move the helicopter to position the penetrator. If the flight mech did not guide the cable with a gloved hand, particularly when it was winding up, it would usually jump the track on the reel and snarl into a mess called a birdcage.

"Okay, pilot," the flight mech said, "all is squared away back here."

"Roger," Kelly said. "We'll try for a visual in a few minutes." Outside the speeding helicopter, the sun had just touched the horizon. "Give me one more hold-down, Wolf," Kelly transmitted.

Wolf lay flat on his back, the radio in his hand resting on his chest. He barely made sense of the request. When he finally knew what was needed, he pressed the transmit button for a few seconds and released it.

"Got a strong signal, Wolf," Kelly transmitted, "now get ready to pop some smoke and we'll see what we can do about getting you back for supper."

An involuntary groan escaped Wolfs lips. He mouthed a faint whisper. "Tewa, get smoke my pocket. Pull when I tell you." He made a feeble attempt to pull a day-night smoke flare from his leg pocket. Tewa looked confused, so Wolf tapped the bulging flare in his pocket. "Get," he said. "Get." Tewa moved to comply. The tinny voice on the RT-10 spoke again.

"We're coming up on some karsty stuff now, Wolf. Be ready with the smoke."

Wolf motioned toward the cave mouth with his thumb. "Tewa make smoke outside when I say." Tewa shrugged helplessly and pointed to the flare that lay in his hand. It was like a thick baton, six inches long by two inches in diameter. Each end had a pull tab that ignited either an orange smoke generator or a flare that would make a glowing red light. Wolf pointed to the tab on the smooth end of the baton. "That make smoke," he said. The flare end had a knobby collar for identification at night by touch alone.

Tewa became very animated and cupped his ear toward the door. "Chollie Gleen, Chollie Gleen," he said. Wolf listened but all he heard was roaring in his ears that told him he didn't have much time of useful consciousness remaining.

In the helicopter, Kelly pointed a gloved finger at the karst field rising from the jungle dead ahead. "In there someplace," he told Shilleto. Kelly punched the transmit button. "Okay,

Wolf, now's as good a time as any. Pop your smoke. Let's be quick. Almost dark."

Wolf heard the beginning of the transmission, the "Okay, Wolf" portion, then the voice faded quickly on his tiny radio. At the same time, Wolf heard the distinct sound of a helicopter overflying the cave. He thought the whirring noise sounded like the wings of a giant angel. It was peaceful and maybe he should just sleep for a while. Let the angel take care of things.

He jerked as his subconscious triggered an alarm. The radio, the smoke . . . "The antenna," Wolf said, and motioned toward the mouth of the cave. "Get the radio antenna out of the cave." Tewa looked bewildered, then cocked his head at the sudden noise that swelled in from the cave entrance. It was the sound of many guns firing, big ones and little ones, in a racketing *bam-bam-bam* of sound that mingled and boomed inside the cave.

"Holy shit," Joe Kelly said as a heavy stream of tracers seemed to converge on the helicopter from all directions. In a reflexive movement he added power, lifted and banked away from the heaviest stream. Then he heard the hammering of the three miniguns from the backend.

"That's it," Shilleto said as he involuntarily hunkered down in his armored seat. "Let's get out of here."

What the hell do you think I'm doing? "Yes, sir. We're gone." He scanned the engine and flight instruments. They appeared to be operating correctly and were not reflecting any engine damage. He took up a heading for Site 36.

"Sir, we've taken hits and we've two wounded Lao back here," the flight mech called on the intercom.

"How bad?" Shilleto asked.

"Pretty bad. The PJs are working on them. They say we got to get them on the ground ASAP."

"We're ten minutes from 36," Kelly said. "VP has a pretty good field hospital there. How's the airplane, chief? Leaking anything?"

"Not that I can see," the flight mech responded.

"Okay, we'll be at 36 toot sweet." Kelly looked at Shilleto. "See any smoke from the survivors?"

79

"Smoke, hell!" Paul Shilleto said. "There was no smoke from them. The only smoke I saw was from the ground fire. I told you it was a goddamn flak trap."

Kelly switched his intercom jack box to Guard Channel. "Wolf, Wolf," he said, "this is Jolly Green 22, you copy?" There was no answer. He repeated the call twice more as they topped another karst ridge eight miles north of the cave where Wolf and Tewa were hidden. There was no answer. He switched his main VHF receiver to the Air America operator at Site 36 and told them he would be there in ten minutes and that he had two wounded on board.

Joe Kelly set the HH-53B helicopter on the helipad at Lima Site 36 as the last ray of sunlight faded and the lavender sky turned black. They had taxied to park next to the other Jolly Green alert helicopter. Nearly a dozen people were gathered to meet the ship. They appeared little more than shadows in the soft glow from two small kerosene lanterns set on the ground at each side of the pad. Several men approached even before the big blades swished to a halt. The two PJs jumped out and chocked the wheels. Then each stepped to a side of the fuselage and pulled from their brackets the 1 × 2-foot boards with the USAF stars and bars painted on them, reversed the boards to their blank sides, and reinserted them in the slots once again, proving no American combat forces were on the ground in little old neutral Laos.

Four soldiers from Vang Pao's army bore two stretchers up to the door while three men in safari suits stood on the edge of the pad and watched. The entire crew of the second-alert Jolly Green crowded around the door and watched the Lao stretcher bearers off-load the wounded and head for the infirmary.

Joe Kelly and Paul Shilleto finished the cockpit postflight and unstrapped. They took their flashlights and walked into the aft cabin and stepped out the door. They were greeted with cold beers from the other crew, each of whom carried a flashlight. Then the two crews walked about the helicopter, shining their flashlights, trying to count the holes. The PJs were doing most of the talking about what had happened. They counted eight nickel-sized holes from the 12.7mm (.51

cal) gun that had fired on them. The night air was cool and damp.

"Probably find more in the morning, sir," the flight mech said to the two officers.

"Hopefully no leaks," Lieutenant Colonel Shilleto said. "We'll have to call back to Udorn for a replacement bird for tomorrow. No way we can fly a mission with this airplane."

"I already called Udorn on the HF," the pilot of the second helicopter said. "Nothing available. They want you to call them as soon as you land. They said they'll tell you to use your own discretion, but get on station tomorrow if you can. If you don't go, I can't go it alone, so . . ."

"We'll see in the morning when we have some light," Shilleto said with some sharpness. "But don't count on us getting airborne."

All of the men pitched in to hook up the hand pumps and hoses from fifty-five-gallon gas drums to refuel Jolly Green 22. Flight mechs were known to brag about their strong right arms from rotating the pump handle.

When they were finished, the two crews walked to the large main tent that covered their messing facility (a long wooden table made of old ammo crates with cases of C-rations underneath), their combined Officer-NCO recreational club facility (a long wooden table with cases of beer underneath), their operations facilities (a narrow wooden table with a battery-operated PRC-47 high-frequency Single Sideband radio on top), and their NCO and officer quarters (rows of metal GI cots along both sides of one end of the big tent). A 5kw generator supplied electricity for the lights. The Jolly Green crewmen would bum ice from the Air America operations hut to cool the beer if they weren't flying too early the next morning.

Bathing facilities were primitive; there weren't any. Bathroom facilities were practical; four halves of fifty-five-gallon gas drums planted in the ground. To use one, a crewman would take a board with a hole cut in it from the crew tent and a small jar of JP-4 jet fuel. He would walk out to the waste place (shit city, as some called it) being on the lookout for cobras and leeches (hard to do at night), and was careful not to overshoot because the outer perimeter had a variety of mines placed by the Japanese in World War II, the French in their Indochina war, and, currently, the defending Hmoung tribesmen. At the waste place, he would place the board across the rough edges of the hacksawn-in-two barrels, perform his business, arise, pull up his pants, sprinkle the JP-4 into the barrel, and throw in some flaming paper. *Whoosh-whump,* "toilet" "flushed." Crewmen usually preferred a recently vacated barrel, still warm from the previous flush, because said flames were sure to have incinerated the saucer-sized black spiders that found the barrels to be marvelous pieces of real estate in which to inhabit, cohabit, and replicate thousands more of themselves. Unless it was a diarrhetic emergency, no one wanted to be first to use shit city. Any anachroid tickling of a seated helicopter crewman's balls at night by searching little hairy feet not only sent him seven feet straight up while piercing the night air with a heartrending shriek, it also ruined his sex life for weeks, or whatever time it took to coax his shriveled testicles back down from someplace north of his lungs.

Joe Kelly sat in the chair in front of the HF radio and made contact with ARRS rescue control center, call sign Compress, at Nakhon Phanom. He made his report of their battle damage and noted that they wouldn't know until sometime after dawn if they would be able to fly the scheduled mission orbit, but that probably they would not.

"Roger Jolly Green 22, Compress copies your transmission. We have no standby aircraft. Use pilot's discretion."

"Yeah, right," Kelly said, then depressed the transmit key on the base of the microphone stand. "What have you got on that survivor? Does he check out?" he asked.

"We confirm an Air America Charley 46, tail number 715, is many hours overdue and there was a passenger with the nickname and numbers you gave us. But from your report it sounds like he's been scarfed up and his crash location turned into one big flak trap. Copy?"

Kelly looked up and saw Shilleto and the rest of the crew standing behind him watching and listening with consummate attention. "Understand," he said and signed off.

Although Joe Kelly was on orders as the rescue crew commander for the entire flight, as a captain, he did defer to some of the housekeeping orders Shilleto, the lieutenant colonel, was issuing. Kelly liked and respected Shilleto, who had flown rescue helicopters in Korea when the dynamics of the machines were barely understood. There had been a big phase-down after the war, until the early sixties, when the rescue mission had again been given serious attention. During the slack period, Shilleto had been flying Old Shaky, the giant C-124 prop-driven, double-decked cargo plane. Last year Shilleto had been recertified in helicopters and, because of his rank, made a detachment commander at Udorn. But, as Kelly and some of the others had said, great guy but his day is past. He paved the way but we have the controls now.

"All right," Shilleto said, "let's go check the weather." He indicated Kelly and the two pilots from the second HH-53B. "The rest of you men settle down. I don't think we are going anyplace in the morning. Turn in if you want."

The four pilots walked out of the big tent and down the dark path to the Air America operations shack.

"Ready for the weather?" the civilian inside greeted them. It was a nightly occurrence for the USAF rescue crewmen to stop by for a briefing from the Air America operations people, who in fact had a composite of the weather forecasts from all the USAF bases. They used their extensive HF radio net and teletypes to gather and collate the information. The man scanned his reports and wall chart.

"Although this is the dry season in Laos," he said, "it's toward the end of the northeast monsoon season and we're starting to get some associated weather here. I think we're going to get some low clouds and rain from the north because of a low-pressure area sitting over Hanoi. Should clear up by noon. If it doesn't rain, there may be haze due to rice paddy burning." Lao peasants fertilized their rice paddies by burning the stubble after a harvest. He went on about surface temperature, gradients, and winds aloft. When he concluded, the Air Force men thanked him and trooped back to their tent.

"Well, that cinches it," Shilleto said to the flight mechs and PJs who were lying back on their cots, talking. "We won't be flying tomorrow, what with the battle damage and the bad weather."

"Sir, does that mean we can drink some more beer?" a flight mech asked.

"Well," Shilleto said, caught offguard, "I, unh, suppose so."

"Look, guys," one of the PJs from the second ship said. "You never know what can happen in the morning. Let's lay off." The PJ was a staff sergeant and not the ranking NCO. But he was already a legend in his own time as a man who, when he went down the hoist, would not come up without a survivor, alive or dead. The men usually followed his lead; they mumbled assent.

"Furthermore," the PJ said to the number-one PJ on Kelly and Shilleto's helicopter, Jolly Green 22, "I'd like to swap with you, Stu, for whatever flight we might have tomorrow."

"Sure thing, El Cee," the second PJ said.

The first PJ turned to Lieutenant Colonel Shilleto. "That is, if it's okay with you, Colonel."

Grateful that the PJ had taken him off the hook by putting down the beer-drinking idea, Paul Shilleto gave his approval.

The PJ winked at Kelly. "Okay with you, sir?"

"Absolutely," Captain Joe Kelly said to Staff Sergeant Manuel "Little Cat" Dominguez.

4

0445 HOURS LOCAL, FRIDAY 11 OCTOBER 1968
COORDINATES UH 512480
ROYALTY OF LAOS

Wolf Lochert made a thrashing movement in his sleep, then made a powerful kick with his leg at an enemy in his feverish dream. The sudden motion woke him and he lay in bewildered silence while he tried to reckon where he was. His head throbbed and he had trouble concentrating. He finally figured out that his left hand was lying on his chest and his right hand was . . . resting at his side on something . . . something hard, with a cool and gritty surface. He arched his back slightly and felt his hips contact something rock hard. Rock . . . yes. Then he knew. He blinked the fuzziness from his eyes and turned his head to the right, toward the rectangle of gray that marked the cave entrance in the false dawn. Full awareness returned.

"Tewa," he called out in a scratchy whisper.

"Oh, sor, Tewa is here." He started as he heard the Lao whisper in his left ear.

"Where bad fuckers? You hear bad fuckers?"

"No hear bad fuckers. See smoke bad fuckers. Sor no sick?"

"Sor not sure, must move first." Wolf Lochert raised himself on both elbows. He ran his tongue around his dry lips and felt suddenly parched. "Water," he whispered.

"Sor fucked," Tewa said. "Water gone-gone." He muttered something in Lao as he searched for the words. "Bag fucked. Sor sleep bag. Water gone-gone." He handed Wolf a limp condom. In the dark, Wolf stretched it and felt the tear with his fingers, then the damp cave floor underneath. He had somehow rolled over and broken the thin bladder during the night.

"Scheiss," he muttered (Wolf; an ex-seminarian, was not one to use the Lord's name in vain). He continued his self-examination. Outside of a throbbing head, a growling stomach, a dry mouth that smelled bad, an odd feeling in his right leg, and the beginning of a terrible thirst, he counted himself fit for duty. He crawled toward the cave entrance, then slowly inched forward until he could see the horizon over the jungle in the dim light, but not so far that he could see the trees below – or be seen from below.

There was an overcast of low clouds that hung gloomy and oppressive over the jungle. Wolf blinked and rubbed his eyes and saw a thin column of smoke enter his view from below the mouth of the cave. *Odd,* he said to himself. *They usually build smokeless fires.* Then he realized they were being chased by Pathet Lao, not North Vietnamese Army (NVA) regulars, who were better disciplined and well-trained in jungle warfare. Then he remembered the sound of the anti-aircraft fire he had heard the evening before as the helicopter swept over.

The helicopter. He pushed himself back into the cave and felt around until he found the small radio, and crawled forward to the cave entrance. He turned the radio on and listened to the soft hiss that revealed no voices. He clicked the mike button twice but got no response. He made sure the antenna was exposed to the upper air but not to the jungle below and tried a call in a quiet voice.

"This is Wolf on Guard, anybody read give me a call." He tried twice more with no response. He felt dizzy as he pushed back into the cave. The light from outside was increasing and he made out the dim form of Tewa and crawled next to him.

"Go there." Wolf pointed to the cave mouth. "Stay low. Listen for airplane. Listen airplane. You hear airplane, call me. You hear bad fuckers, you call me. *Chow cow chi baw?* Do you understand?"

"Sor, Tewa understand," Tewa replied in what sounded like a hurt voice. He crawled to the mouth and lay flat, eyes alert to whatever lay outside. Wolf lowered himself down on his side, then rolled over on his back. He felt confusion again, and dizziness. When he rolled over he noticed again that his right leg did not function as it should. In seconds he was in a whirling doze that threatened to overcome him with dizziness.

0500 HOURS LOCAL, FRIDAY 11 OCTOBER 1968
NA KHANG, LIMA SITE 36
ROYALTY OF LAOS

The soft *ding-ding* from his Seiko alarm watch awoke Little Cat Dominguez from a light sleep. It was dark inside the heavy tent, and humid from the night air. The sleep sounds and old-clothes smell of ten sleeping men assailed his nostrils. He sat up on his cot, swung his legs over the side, and stretched, then reached down, picked up his boots and jacket, and carefully walked to the cot of Hiram Bakke, the other PJ on Jolly Green 22, and gently shook him awake.

"Time to go," he whispered. While Bakke got up, Dominguez awoke Tech Sergeant Dan Bernick, the flight mech for 22. Minutes later the three men stood by their seventeen-ton helicopter and started an exacting inspection with their flashlights while the overcast above them slowly brightened. They had agreed the night before that, regardless of Shilleto's pronouncements, they wanted 22 to be airworthy and ready for today's mission to support the air strikes in North Vietnam. Takeoff time was less than two hours away.

After thirty minutes of close inspection, the three men found eleven holes, three more than spotted the night before. Bernick pulled a ball of twine from his tool kit and they did what crewmen on a shot-up airplane do: they ran string from hole to hole, marking trajectories, seeing who and what – but mostly *who* – had come closest to being hit. Most holes were in the boom and aft portion of the helicopter cabin,

87

meaning the enemy gunners had been relatively inexperienced and had not led the moving craft enough when they pulled the trigger. Bernick removed the left engine cowling when he discovered a hole in it. He found pieces of the spent slug inside, but no engine damage.

"Okay," Bernick said, "let's crank it up." Bakke, wearing a helmet with boom mike and a long cord to the intercom system, positioned himself outside with an extinguisher as fire guard, while Dominguez was to assist in the cockpit, then roam the interior with a portable extinguisher. In seconds Bernick had the engines rumbling and whining into life. Dominguez scrambled into the cabin and checked for fire and hydraulic for fuel leaks.

"Holy shit, Bernick," Bakke yelled over the intercom, "shut down number two, she's smoking like a bitch."

"And we've got hydraulic fluid spraying all over the place in here," Dominguez said from the cabin. Bernick shut down both engines, checked there was no fire, and climbed from the front seat. In the cabin he looked at the hole in the hydraulic line Dominguez pointed out. "I can tape that easy," he said, then went outside to climb up and check the number two engine. "Come on up, give me a hand," he yelled. The cloud layer-filtered dawn light. A light mist had begun to envelop them with feathers of wispy dampness. The three men were on the right side wrestling with the cowling when Captain Joe Kelly walked up.

"Masochists," he said. "Didn't your mothers give you enough sense to come in out of the rain? Gather 'round, I have some news. Just talked to Compress, the Hanoi air strike is scrubbed for weather. The alternate targets are in the south and the boys from Da Nang will cover them." He looked up at the helicopter looming large and menacing in the gray dawn. "It ain't beautiful but it shore does the job. Let's fix it for the flight back to Udorn. We've got to hustle, because later on we'll get some of that same bad weather in here."

It took another twenty minutes, but with Kelly at the controls and the three men topside, Bernick found and fixed the oil leak feeding into the hot section of the engine which had caused the white smoke.

"Now we fix bullet holes," Bernick said. "You guys get me a half-dozen beer cans and make sure they're not Black Label. They rust so much I swear they're tin, not aluminum." He fished around in his big tool kit as the two PJs brought the beer cans from the tent. "Cut 'em and smooth 'em out," he said. "Give me eleven two-inch-square pieces." The mist turned to a light rain, so the men moved onto the rear ramp under the shelter of the tail boom. They cut with the shears Bernick provided and tap-tapped the cans flat, then cut out the small pieces he wanted. While they were doing that, the flight mech took from his kit a medium-sized can and pried open the top and began to stir a gooey, silvery substance within. "Good old Scotch-weld," he said. "Good for what ails a shot-up helio."

An hour later, using a makeshift ladder and much boosting up and holding each other in place and sweating, they had all the holes patched with pieces of Budweiser beer cans held in place by Scotch-weld.

"Now it won't sound like a whistling shit house," Bernick proclaimed as he wiped the goop from his hands. He took some wire and ninety-mile (duct) tape to the punctured hydraulic line and soon pronounced it secure.

Kelly cut in the air under pressure from the accumulator to start the auxiliary power plant. Once the APP was wound up and screaming (it was a small turbine engine), he tapped its electrical power and hydraulic pressure to start the engines. HH-53Bs did not make battery-powered starts for the simple reason that they had no batteries. And if the accumulator air pressure was too low to start the APP, some crewman had to man the air pump to bring the accumulator back up to its proper pressure of 3,000 psi.

Kelly ran the engines up, pulled pitch to get light on the wheels, cut the lift, and said he thought Jolly Green 22 to be flightworthy.

"Two burning and ten turning," said Bernick. "She's ready." Dan Bernick just agreed to the readiness of Jolly Green 22 by declaring both jet engines healthy (two burning), the tail rotor blades (four) turning properly, and the main rotors (six) rotating in balance (ten turning).

Kelly shut down the engines and secured the switches, then sat in the cockpit with Staff Sergeant Manuel Dominguez while the other two men went to grab a bit of crackers and jam from the breakfast C-rats.

"Together again," Kelly said. "Red-Tagged Bastards Hang Together, right?"

Dominguez was silent.

"Right, Dom?" Kelly asked. "Red-Tagged Bastards Hang Together."

"Hey, Joe, I told you. Never call me Dom."

"Yeah, sorry 'bout that. Old habits die hard."

Ever since Academy days, when Miss Barbara Westin's favorite nickname for Manuel had been Dom, Dominguez could no longer tolerate the sound of it.

"Just can't work up to 'Little Cat,' though," Joe Kelly said. "Too much of a mouthful. What's the matter with 'Manuel,' anyway?"

"Nothing. I just haven't responded to it in years."

"There are other things you haven't responded to either, you know."

Kelly and Dominguez had both been in rescue squadrons for years, but only in the last three months had they been in the same unit. Kelly had tried without success to get Dominguez to answer his concerned questions about their days at the Academy. At first Dominguez wouldn't even respond to Kelly's overtures of friendliness.

"Let's go into town and get a beer," Kelly had said to him when they first saw each other at Udorn, where their rescue squadron was based.

"No, sir, thank you, sir," Dominguez had responded, face and body stiff.

"Goddamn, Dom, come off it. It's me — Joe, the old Red-Tagged Bastard."

"Sir, don't call me Dom." He had continued to stare off in the distance, his face devoid of expression.

"Well, fuck you very much, old buddy," Kelly had said and grinned. "I'm just going to bug you until you turn back into the neat guy who was once my roomie. Don't you even want to hear what happened to Tanaka?"

After a few missions and more urging by Kelly, Dominguez had unbuttoned enough to go drink beer with Joe, always in downtown Udorn. They couldn't go to each other's military clubs on the air base. Officers did not go to NCO clubs and vice versa. Dominguez had seemed genuinely interested in Tanaka's career as a fighter pilot, happy to hear he was at Ubon, and had been quite surprised that Joe Kelly had selected helicopters. "I'll tell you why someday," Kelly had replied.

"So I don't respond," Dominguez said to Kelly now as they sat in the cockpit. "Don't make a federal case out of it. Manuel's okay, or even El C does just fine."

"So I noticed," Kelly said. He stared out the cockpit window for a few seconds, then leaned back and put his elbow on the back of his seat. "Barbara called me at the Academy once after you left. Did you know that? She wanted to know if I heard from you, how you were. Said she was sorry you were gone, but her dad was delighted. Said she might go east for school, Vassar. Or she might get married."

Dominguez was silent.

"What the fuck, Dom," Kelly said, his exasperation clear. "You could at least be civilized about this shit. You seemed so much in love with her. She finally got married, you know." He looked over at his friend. "Did you know she got married?"

Dominguez spoke in harsh tones. "Look, Joe, we've been through this before and each time you ask more questions. I told you, I don't want to hear about her, I don't want to talk about her."

"For Christ's sake, Dom—"

"And I told you not to call me Dom."

"Well, hell, it's the only time I get a rise out of you. Why won't you even tell me what the honor violation thing was all about? We found out you went to the honor representative, told him something so that he convened a board on you, and blooie – you were gone."

"Dammit, Joe, you've got to get off my back. Okay, maybe we're friends again, but if you want to keep it that way, then don't ask me about the Academy. You copy?" Dominguez's dark eyes looked even darker and more unfathomable with each word that he spoke.

Kelly threw up his hands. "God, you Texans. Bite the bullet and all that shit." He sighed and made a small smile. "Tell me, how many missions will this make, the two of us together?"

"Twenty-two."

"And how many saves?"

"You know, dumbshit." Dominguez tried to smile.

"Yeah," Kelly said with obvious contentment in his voice, "I know. Seven." He looked at Dominguez. "Want to make it eight?"

"Try me."

"Well, we gotta flimflam Colonel Shilleto a bit, but I'd like to see if we can get that fellow with the Wolf call sign to come up on Guard. I know just about where it was that we lost him. The signal loss was so fast, without any fade at all, that it had to be an obstruction like a mountain crest—"

"Or a cave," Dominguez said.

"Exactly. And I've got a pretty good fix on the map and in my head where it all took place. We were headed almost due north when we lost the signal. I remember the karst shapes in front of me at the time, they had sort of a triple peak and an odd-shaped valley. If I can find that headed south, there is a good chance we can raise them when we pass over the ridge to the south of the peaks. We'll make a little racket up there and call him on Guard. See if we can get an answer."

"Do you think Colonel Shilleto will keep his cool if we, you know, kind of get into it?"

"Actually, in a nutshell, to be perfectly honest, no . . . well, hell, that's not right. Maybe he . . . shit, I dunno. He is ready to DEROS."

DEROS was the acronym for Date Eligible to Return from Overseas. The date was the last day a military man served overseas and would be used to count the time until his next tour. In the Vietnam war, each man and woman counted down the twelve months – except Marines, who had a thirteen-month tour – to their DEROS.

"And a man ready to DEROS runs cautious," Kelly said. "In his case, real cautious."

"I flew with him earlier," Dominguez said. "He used to be okay."

"I know. But after a couple hairy ones in North Vietnam and that helo that was shot from under him, he's ready to hang it up. Shit, he's been in Rescue off and on since Korea. Got more saves than Billy Graham. We'll work something out. When I say 'look at the view,' you say you saw something and want permission to fire. I'll make sure I'm flying and will do a quick 360. Hose off a few more rounds and we'll see who the noise brings up on the radio. Let's try to ease into this thing, keep the pulse rate low and steady."

"What about that 12.7 that hosed us yesterday? We go too low, we'll raise more than some guy on a radio. That gun's effective as hell up to 3,300 feet."

"Trust me, Dom. Trust me." Kelly laughed. "Listen, I'm due some time off pretty soon. What say we make it to Bangkok together?"

"Fraternizing with enlisted is still off-limits, Joe."

"Come off it, El C. You want to go or not?"

"Sure." Dominguez turned to look at his friend. "Red-Tagged Bastards Hang Together," he said.

5

The rain had let up. At eight-thirty, Lieutenant Colonel Paul Shilleto strode through the steamy mist to Jolly Green 22. He had Bakke and Bernick with him. Kelly sat on the back ramp, munching the last of his crackers and peanut butter and washing them down with water from his canteen. Dominguez had gone to get his flight gear from the other helicopter.

"I hear she'll fly," Shilleto said in a cheerful voice to Kelly. "What say we crank up and take her home? I checked and the weather is just fine once we get to Udorn. Got thunderstorms due in here by noon, though. Sergeant Bernick talked to the Maintenance Officer and convinced him we have an airworthy airplane. We have one-time permission to fly it back for repair."

"Sure thing, Colonel," Kelly said and got to his feet. The two officers walked forward to begin the preflight with Bernick. Shilleto personally inspected each of the eleven patch jobs.

"Excellent, excellent," he said to Bernick. "That should get us home."

Dominguez walked up, carrying two C-ration boxes stacked on top of each other. They seemed very heavy and he was sweating from the load.

"You sure must like to eat that Army stuff," Shilleto said, smiling at his little witticism.

"Ah, yes, sir," Dominguez said and hurried into the cabin

94

through the side door, where Bakke was preflighting his equipment.

After the preflight, and while Shilleto was still outside talking to Bernick, Kelly walked up the ramp to where Dominguez had stowed the two boxes in the cabin.

"Look," he said, "I know better. Those aren't C-rats. What you got in those boxes, El C?"

Dominguez made a wry grin and opened the top box. It was packed with a dozen of the Mason jars HH-53 helicopter crew chiefs use to take fuel samples.

"You plan on doing a lot of samples or something? What the hell are these for?" Kelly asked.

"These," Dominguez said, and opened the second box, which had twelve M26 hand grenades and several bandoliers of 7.62 ammunition. "Pull the pin on the grenade, hold the handle in place, stuff it in the jar, screw on the cap, and you have a little something to drop on the bad guys." He touched the ammo. "I always carry a couple hundred extra rounds. You never know."

Kelly clapped him on the shoulder. "Shit hot. You're right, you never know." He went to the cockpit and was surprised to see Lieutenant Colonel Paul Shilleto sitting in the right seat of the machine. He put on his parachute and eased into the left seat. Just the opposite with fixed-wing aircraft, the pilot in command sits in the right seat in helicopters, the co-pilot in the left. All crew members wore parachutes, but only the PJs and the flight mech had any real chance of a successful bailout in an emergency.

"Joe," Shilleto said, "since this is my last flight, I'd like to be the AC. I'd like to handle everything – the radios, the navigation. No autopilot, just hand-fly the whole route."

"Hand-fly?" Kelly interrupted. "You must be some kind of a masochist, Colonel. The HH-53B was a notoriously difficult helicopter to hand-fly. Pilots on cross-country flights engaged the automatic flight control system that provided heading, altitude, and roll stability. It was simply too fatiguing to spend long hours at the controls. Best to save your energy and freshness for ingress, pickup, and egress from high-threat areas.

"Yes, hand-fly," Shilleto said. "I'm going to some Pentagon staff job, and who knows how long it will be before I ever fly a helicopter again. Maybe never." He knew Kelly was on orders for the whole deployment and that Kelly could designate who flew what position.

Kelly knew and understood what was going on in Shilleto's mind. "Sure, Colonel, go ahead. It would be my pleasure to fly as your copilot."

Shilleto looked relieved, then bent to his duties. He spread out the chart he had made on his kneeboard.

Kelly looked over at Shilleto's map and could see the direct line he had drawn to Udorn without any deviation. The area he felt sure held the survivors, though only ten minutes south of their takeoff location at Lima 36, was several miles to the east of the line.

The two pilots and Bernick the flight mech went through the ENGINE START and BEFORE TAKEOFF procedures.

"Number two oil temp is a little high, but everything else looks good to me," Shilleto said. "Let's launch."

Kelly and Bernick agreed, Shilleto got a release from Air America ops on the radio, and they were airborne.

Shilleto followed the Air America instrument departure plan for helicopters, and at 5,000 feet above the ground they broke through the clouds that clustered over Lima Site 36. Their altimeter registered 8,000 feet. Beneath them and to the south were scattered small puffy white clouds.

"Beautiful day," Shilleto hummed and fixed course for Udorn. In minutes they were almost abeam the point where Kelly was sure the survivors were hiding.

"Ah, sir," he began, "maybe we could just swing a bit east. Quite a view over there. Maybe we might hear something from those guys who called us yesterday." He had surreptitiously switched the intercom so that the two PJs and the flight mech could hear the conversation.

"No," Shilleto said. "I specifically asked Compress about that. We are to bring this airplane straight back, no deviations. They said they'd have somebody up there to check the whole thing out." Maybe Paul Shilleto wasn't Rescue Crew

Commander for this flight, but he was a lieutenant colonel who knew an order when he heard one.

"Well, they don't know quite where to look," Kelly said, "and we do." He hoped Dominguez would get the drift and act accordingly. Since he wasn't flying, Kelly couldn't make the 360-degree turn he had promised.

"Not with this bird, we don't. You forget, we got shot up yesterday. We've got patched-up holes and a damaged engine. And who knows, they probably have even more guns there now. Besides, if you don't get a shootdown off the ground right away, he's as good as captured. No, we're pressing on for the home drome."

They whirred on for thirty more seconds, then both pilots jerked at the sound of a 7.62mm Gatling gun as it spun up and made a deep-throated moan.

"For Christ's sake," Shilleto cried over the intercom. "What was that for?"

"Left gun, sir. I wanted to test-fire my weapon. Make sure it was clear. Thought I had a problem yesterday, sir," Dominguez responded. Then the right gun and the aft gun opened up for a split second.

"Yes, sir," Bakke said on the intercom. "Thought we'd check them all out."

"Okay," Shilleto responded, "but you should have informed me first."

Kelly looked down and saw they were now due west of where he thought the survivors were. He recognized the triple peaks and the odd-shaped valley. The small white clouds looked like low flak bursts he thought. In a few seconds they would be past the karst ridge, and if the survivors were still alive and free, their radio should be in range.

He verified he was receiving Guard Channel, then decided to hell with what Paul Shilleto thought and switched his transmitter to Guard.

"Wolf, Wolf, if you read Jolly Green Two Two, come up on voice or beeper. Wolf come up on voice or beeper."

"That won't do you any good," Shilleto said. "No one will answer, and if they do, we can't do anything about it anyhow." At those words, all three guns fired a quick burst.

"Sor, sor, is shoot, is shoot," Tewa said as he shook Wolf Lochert. "Shoot?" Lochert said as if from a great distance. "Who's shooting at us?"

"Sky gun is shoot. Sky gun is shoot," Tewa said and pointed his finger to the entrance of the cave.

Wolf blinked and through force of will brought his mind to bear on the subject at hand, a sky gun. The two words sounded melodic to his ear, they had a nice rhythm and rolled off the tongue well, but what on earth did they mean? Then he heard the muted roar of the minigun and knew what it meant: there was an American airplane of some kind in the local area and he had to get their attention immediately.

"Radio," he said to Tewa. "Give radio." His thirst was nearly unbearable. His tongue felt thick and he had trouble speaking.

Tewa placed the radio in Wolf's hand. Wolf extended the antenna, placed the transmit switch from OFF through VOICE to BEACON. Instead of transmitting words when the button was pushed, the little radio now sent out a distinctive and continuous whooping sound over Guard Channel. The signal both drained the battery quickly and prevented other transmissions on Guard. To receive, Wolf would have to turn the switch to VOICE. He placed the radio on the floor of the cave by his side and pushed it toward the entrance so the antenna was pointing out of the opening. He felt woozy and had to get the attention of the Americans, and the automatic beeper was the fastest method until he could get his thoughts collected.

The eerie *whoop-whooping* sound of the beacon in their headsets caused Kelly and Shilleto to swing their heads and look sharply at each other. Kelly had been alert for just that sort of signal while Shilleto piloted the helicopter, and quickly switched on the direction-finding equipment. The needle swung to their eight o'clock position.

"Sir," he said over the sound of the loud signal, "turn port." They were still at 8,000 feet.

"Nothing doing." Shilleto stared straight ahead.

"Sir, it's a clear signal. We've got to check it out."

"Not after what happened yesterday." Shilleto reached down and switched off Guard Channel. The abrupt silence after the unearthly sound was startling. "Anybody can switch to beacon on those radios," he said. "They have captured a lot of them. It's a flak trap, I tell you. We didn't get those eleven holes from friendly fire. We're not going back. This is a one-time ferry flight to get this bird home. We are *not* authorized to participate in any rescue."

"At least I can verify the signal and take a fix," Kelly said as he switched Guard Channel back on. He cut the volume control so he could barely hear the beacon. The needle pointed unwaveringly back left to the seven-thirty position. *Nuts,* he said to himself. *Maybe the gomers have captured the poor bastard and are using his radio. He's got to come up voice and prove he's okay.* He remembered the American's voice and his call sign from the day before, and tried again. He transmitted on Guard.

"Wolf, Wolf, this is Jolly Green Two Two, come up voice. Talk to me, man."

It was no good. Guard Channel was blocked by the whooping beacon transmitted by Wolf's radio.

"We're not going to do anything about it, I promise you," Shilleto said.

It was quiet and peaceful in the cave. Wolf barely registered the sound of the receding helicopter. Something tugged at a corner of his mind. There was something he should do. The helicopter faded from his hearing, and with it the insistent nagging. He dozed, fitful and restless.

Tewa knew he had to do something. The helicopter was going away, headed south, and would never, never come back. He crawled over to the radio that lay inert on the rough floor of the cave near the entrance. He knew if you spoke into it, someone would answer. That is how it worked before. He carefully pressed the button and called many times for Chollie Gleen, with no response. He had seen Wolf work one of the switches, so he fingered it back and forth and tried again. No answer. He didn't understand why it had worked yesterday and not today. He studied the switch positions, and next to each the incomprehensible chicken scratches the Americans said were words. He decided to work the switch from *sei* to *qwa*, left to the right, and stop and call from each position, then wait for an answer. Nothing happened for him at the full left position, which was "off." He would go to the next and try again.

In the helicopter, when Kelly heard the beeper signal stop, he immediately pressed his transmit button and called Wolf.

Tewa turned the switch to the second position from the left and heard the last part of the call.

". . . talk to me, Wolf."

Tewa jammed his finger onto the transmit button. "Oh, Chollie Gleen, you come now. Sor sick. You come now."

"Let me talk to sor," Kelly transmitted on the radio.

"I'm telling you, we are not going back," Shilleto said on the intercom. "I don't care what he says."

"Make sore talk," Kelly transmitted again.

Tewa pushed back to Wolf Lochert and shook him. "Sor, you talk. Is Chollie Gleen. You talk Chollie Gleen." He shook Wolf again and tried to hand him the radio. Wolf barely stirred.

"We must talk to the American," Kelly said with urgency. "Put the American on. Put . . . the . . . American . . . on . . . the radio." He unkeyed and waited. *Double-damn, triple-shit,* he said to himself, then tried again. "Wolf, Wolf – talk to me, Wolf."

Through a haze, Wolf heard the tinny American voice. When he rolled his head toward the sound, Tewa held the radio to Wolf's lips and said, "Sor talk. Sor talk now." He pressed the transmit button.

"Anyone read Wolf, give me a call," Wolf said with difficulty.

Kelly was overjoyed. "Wolf, Wolf," he said, "this is Jolly Two Two. Got you three by. Give me a hold-down." Kelly was telling Wolf he heard his transmission clear but not loud. Five by five for clarity and volume was best; one by one was worst.

Wolf blinked several times in the gloom of the cave. Hold-down, what was . . . then he remembered. "Tewa," he said. "Press button. Press button."

Tewa grinned and bobbed his head several times and pushed in the transmit button and released it.

"Hold the button," Kelly said. "Hold the button down, count to ten."

"You don't really believe that's an American survivor down there, do you?" Shilleto asked. "He wouldn't have all this much trouble talking."

"He might if he were injured or wounded," Kelly said. Shilleto flew straight ahead and didn't answer.

"Look," Kelly said, "at least can't we do a 360 turn? If not, we'll be out of range soon and never get a good fix. Just a 360. It won't cause us any trouble."

"One turn," Shilleto rumbled and put the helicopter into a left-hand turn.

"Wolf, give me a long count," Kelly said, and looked with anxious eyes at the direction-finding equipment.

"Tewa." Wolf's whisper was raspy. "Hold button down, keep pressing. Talk to Jolly Green. Talk to them, Tewa."

"Ah, Chollie Gleen, sor say talk you. Tewa talk you. Tewa is talk. You talk Tewa?" He released the button.

As Shilleto turned the HH-53B through north, the homing needle pointed straight ahead and Kelly could see the area where he was sure Wolf and Tewa were hiding.

"Smoke, Tewa, give me smoke," he said. "You have smoke grenade? You have smoke flare, Tewa? Jolly Green must have smoke."

"The smoke won't do you any good, Kelly, we're *not* going in," Shilleto said in a loud voice.

"Sir, it's your last flight. Why not end it with a rescue? Think of how much publicity you'd receive."

"Kelly, you're insulting. All the years I've been in Rescue, I've *never* done it for publicity."

"Sir, that's a human being down there. You said yourself if a shootdown isn't picked up right away, his chances are shit. This guy has hung on. He's all screwed-up but he's hung on.

Maybe Compress can't get someone here in time. Maybe we're his last chance."

In the cave, Wolf heard the voice on the radio ask for smoke. Still lying flat, he pushed the day/night flare from his cargo pocket. He rolled it toward the Hmoung. "Tewa, make smoke. Cannot make smoke."

Tewa picked it up and edged to the opening of the cave. He remembered the one-hour course he had had when he became a bundle-kicker for Air America on the rudiments of emergency rescue procedures and how to generate smoke by pulling the proper tab on the cylinder. He put his finger through the ring tab, then looked back at Wolf with a worried frown. "If smoke, bad fucker shoot smoke."

Wolf digested the news and tried to clear his brain. His tongue felt terribly swollen in his mouth and his thoughts ran away from him like scattering leaves in a wind. He knew Tewa should release the smoke because . . . because someone should know where they were. If there was too much ground fire for a pickup, well, he would just have to sleep on that. Maybe they would die. That was all right, too. He was so tired, and his head felt so funny. He started drifting. From the far reaches of his mind a small voice said maybe they would be captured.

CAPTURED. An alarm as real and as loud as a firehouse gong sounded in Wolf's brain, and all his fleeing thoughts returned. He knew exactly where they were and exactly what the problem was. He gathered his energy and rolled over to lie next to Tewa.

"No smoke," he said. "Tewa right. No smoke." He picked up the radio and punched the transmit button.

"Jolly Green, this is Wolf. We can't give you smoke. There are enemy forces deployed about a klick south of our position. If we pop smoke, they'll get a fix on us and . . . and they will be ready to hose you down if you come in for a pickup. They can probably hear you right now just like we can. I don't see how we can do this today." He unkeyed. "*Scheiss,* Tewa, we can't let that helicopter in here. We don't know what's out there." Tewa looked wide-eyed and uncomprehending.

"Wolf, this is Jolly Green, *we'll* make the decision whether or not we can make the pickup," the strong voice of Lieutenant Colonel Paul Shilleto sounded over the radio. He unkeyed and switched to intercom. "Flight mech? PJs? You got any problem with our going in?"

"No, sir, not at all," they assured him. Rescue men were up there to do just that, rescue, not pass up perfectly good opportunities. PJs actually flipped coins to see who would be *first* down the hoist.

"What made you change your mind, boss?" Kelly asked in surprise.

"Hell, since he was going to turn down a pickup because *we* might be in danger, I figured he was not only a real American but a brave one, one we should see what we can do about." He kept the nose of the helicopter pointed toward the source of the signal. "And look up there." He pointed northeast at a line of thunderstorms. "They're coming this way, may be here for days. We've got to move now." Shilleto punched his radio button. "Wolf," he transmitted, "we are homing in on your signal. Hold your smoke. Tell us when we pass over your position."

Shilleto unkeyed and said to Kelly, "Call Cricket, see if there are any A-1s in the area, we may have a full-blown SAR on our hands." Kelly saw the light of challenge in Shilleto's eyes, and he seemed ten years younger.

Buoyed by the confident voice and the possibility they might be rescued, Wolf rogered the transmission. His brain cleared and a new thought occurred to him.

"Jolly Green," he said. "I *will* go ahead and release some smoke. If they shoot at us, okay. But I don't think they will. I think they know where we are and don't want to give themselves away and are waiting for you to come closer to start shooting. Either way, we'd be no worse off than before and you'd get a positive fix on us. You copy?"

"Roger, copy," Shilleto said. "We're ready. Pop your smoke." Shilleto glanced at Kelly. "What does Cricket have for us?"

"A ration of shit," Kelly replied. "They say we are to proceed as planned and they will handle this whole thing."

Shilleto set his jaw. "We'll see about that." His eyes flashed and his haggard face looked joyfully animated. He punched his mike button

"Cricket, Jolly Green Two Two. We found a target of enemy troops. I need some A-1s, and I'm damn well going to stay right here until you provide them. Either you provide them or we run out of gas and you got to run a SAR on us. You copy, Cricket?"

"Why, sure, Jolly Green," the Cricket controller said from his position in a large radio capsule loaded in the back end of a C-130. Thirteen other men were in there with them at consoles, running the airborne command post. "I think we can get something up for you." He was a young ROTC first lieutenant and was pretty sure he knew what Jolly Green Two Two had in mind. He had been required earlier to pass on the order for 22 to go home, but now he decided to go along with what he was sure was a bit of a charade. Laos was a fucked-up place, and anytime you had the opportunity to unfuck it, he believed, particularly when it might save an American, then he'd go along.

"Okay, Wolf," Shilleto said, "you hang on to that smoke until I tell you. We'll get a couple Sandys or Hobos in here and then we'll see what we'll see."

"Roger," Wolf said, aware that the Jolly Green wanted the A-1 firepower handy in case his smoke provoked any return fire.

Sandy and Hobo were the USAF call signs of the giant prop-driven Douglas A-1 aircraft that carried four tons of ordnance under their wings (on fifteen hardpoints – seven under each wing and one under the centerline of the fuselage), had four forward-firing 20mm cannons, and enough gas to stay on station for hours. Though certainly not in the jet fighter class, the A-1 was preferred over the faster jets for close air support because of its delivery accuracy and endurance. US Navy pilots still cackled over the shootdown of a MiG-17 in June 1965 by two A-1s from the *Midway*. They called the A-1s Spads. The USAF had acquired fifty A-1s – from the Navy in the early sixties, expressly for use in Vietnam. The TAC jet fighter boys had gritted their teeth, but had had to give in to the request from the Air Commandos for the versatile prop aircraft.

Joe Kelly pointed out to Shilleto the half-mile-wide karst cliff where he thought the two men were hiding. There were too many crevices and outcroppings on the cliff face for him to know which was the exact spot. They orbited two miles south. Eight minutes later two Sandys checked in. Shilleto brought them overhead, steered their eyes in the general direction of the cliff, and had them orbit above them at 9,000 feet.

"Here's how it is, guys," Shilleto said to his crew. *If* we get a good smoke, and *if* we can get the bad guys to reveal their position, and *if* we can get the Sandys to wipe out the bad guys, we may have a pickup on our hands. You guys game to try?"

"Shit hot, Colonel," said the flight mech, Dan Bernick.

"Press on, sir," said PJ Two, Hiram Bakke.

"Let's get 'em," said PJ One, Manuel Dominguez.

Joe Kelly nodded his head in pleased assent.

"Pop the smoke, Wolf. We're ready," Shilleto said.

Wolf Lochert did as he was told and flipped the belching baton out on the ledge at the cave mouth. Within seconds, thick red smoke billowed up and away from the cliff, then became torn sheets in the shearing vertical wind currents.

"I've got a good tally on your position, Wolf. Hear anything?" Kelly asked.

Wolf lay silent for a few minutes. "Nothing," he said. "Nothing at all, but I know they're out there."

"Sandy, you ready to do your famous troll trick?" Shilleto asked Sandy One, the leader of the flight.

"Roger that. Two, orbit west and see what I stir up. Lead's in west to east, off south." He pulled up, hung on his prop for a second, then lazily wheeled over and down, gaining airspeed, then pulled out to zoom in on his run. He made a long, low pass over the jungle parallel to the cliff face.

"See anything, Two?" he asked as he pulled off short of the approaching storms, the powerful 2,700-horsepower Wright radial engine roaring out over the muted jungle.

"Negative," came the laconic reply. "Want me to try it?"

"Rodge, go ahead," Sandy Lead said. "Make it from the opposite direction."

"Wolf, you hear any shooting?" Shilleto asked.

"Not a round."

"Two's in, east to west." He dodged in front of the approaching rainsquall and dove in on his run.

"Gotcha covered," Sandy Lead said.

Sandy Two made his pass as directed, and no one reported seeing or hearing any groundfire.

"Nothing for it, gang," Shilleto said on the intercom. "Let's give it the old cathouse try." He would have to fly the big helicopter down to less than two hundred feet above Wolf and Tewa, then have Bernick let the penetrator down from the hoist to the ledge at the cave mouth so the two men could strap themselves onto the device. Then the Jolly had to wait while the flight mech winched the two men up high enough to clear the surrounding terrain before they could fly away. Depending on penetrator ground time, the entire sequence required the Jolly Green helicopter to hover in one position as a perfectly still aerial target for at least three minutes. Shilleto punched up the UHF radio.

"Sandy, Jolly Green Two Two is going in. Give me hover cover. Wolf be ready. I'll have the penetrator at your front door in about four minutes. If anybody shoots at us first time around, we'll pull off and have the Sandys prep the area."

"Jolly Green, Wolf. I think you should prep the area first. There are enemy troops one klick due south of my location. I saw the campfire smoke at dawn."

"Wolf, they didn't shoot today, they may have moved. Besides, weather is moving in. Running out of time. We've got to try a pickup. Coming down."

Lieutenant Colonel Paul Shilleto started the first move in an intricate aerial ballet that required perfect timing from himself and the two Sandy pilots. Each Sandy A-1 had to weave a protective cover over the moving helicopter, a protective cover that allowed them to keep the helicopter in view while simultaneously scanning the terrain beneath the helicopter, the prospective pickup site, and the surrounding region for probable anti-aircraft guns. If one or more guns came up, the Sandys had to crisscross each other's path and that of the Jolly Green helicopter to suppress the fire. Normally, the force was doubled: two helicopters and four Sandys.

"Jolly Green Two Two, this is Cricket. Ah, sir, Crown just called and said you are not to attempt the pickup. You are to show Sandy Lead where the survivor is located, then depart the area. Jolly, you copy Cricket?" The young controller's voice was thick with dismay.

Shilleto looked at Kelly. "You hear anything?" he asked.

SouthEast Asian (SEA) theater regulations prescribed that no ARRS helicopter could attempt a rescue without full backup. As courageous as the rescue crews were, some early spectacular failures and losses had caused the clamping-down by higher headquarters of just what constituted a rescue package. To break the regulations was to invite a grounding. Occasionally, hard feelings had occurred over a situation just like this, when a rescue by a USAF helicopter was theoretically possible but had not been attempted. In a couple of cases, while a Jolly Green had hung back on orders, a lone Air America Huey helicopter had sped in and rescued the downed crewmen.

"Did I hear anything?" Kelly said. "No, I didn't hear anything. Damn radio is acting up again."

"Sandy, you hear anything?" Shilleto asked.

"Ah, negative, Jolly. Not unless you did." Sandy pilots had big ones, great big ones, and were never eager to give up a mission. The Cricket controller wisely remained silent.

"All right, gentlemen, we are in to see what we can see," Shilleto told his crew and started down. In the rear, PJ One, Dominguez, manned the left gun, PJ Two, Bakke, manned the ramp gun, and Bernick, the flight mech, took the right door gun. Over their flight suits they wore a harness attached to what was called a gunner's strap, which could be clipped onto one of many anchor spots within the cabin. Each man wore an olive-drab flight helmet with boom mike swung up to their lips. And each man was equipped with a .38 in a shoulder holster and a bandolier of ammunition.

Shilleto flew the HH-53B from east to west, barely ahead of the rain, while the Sandys crisscrossed the area, searching and trolling for ground fire. As the helicopter went into hover, Bernick swung his minigun back from the doorway to its stowed position against the forward wall and started the penetrator down from its hoist above and outside the door. Facing the door, the hydraulic control handle to start and stop the hoist was on the fuselage wall to the right. The handle pointed down like the large hand of a clock pointed at six. Swinging the handle up to nine o'clock lowered the penetrator, back to three o'clock raised it. The cable raised and lowered at 200 feet per minute except for an automatic slowdown just before the full raised position. Bernick pulled the handle forward with his right hand, hung partially out the door, and put his gloved left hand on the cable to guide it. He wore a heavy linesman's glove.

Because the HH-53B hovered in a 5-degree nose-high attitude and the pilot could not see the cable or the penetrator under him, the man at the hoist had to guide the pilot on the intercom on where he should position himself.

"Forward five, left five, forward two, that's it, that's it. Hold. Hold," Bernick said as he moved the hoist handle to keep the penetrator moving. Bernick had to yell because the rotor noise picked up by his boom mike was nearly overpowering.

Because the ship was directly above his cave, Wolf could no longer see it. He eased forward on his elbows until his head cleared the mouth of the cave, then rolled onto his back. He looked up through a rush of downwash air and saw the wide bottom of the rescue helicopter. The noise was deafening. He saw the descending penetrator. "Out here, come out," he yelled to Tewa. He started to crawl further out of the cave, and his right leg was numb. *Must have gone to sleep,* he told himself as his thoughts focused on the imminent rescue. He pulled himself forward with his elbows and pushed with his left foot until he was clear of the cave mouth and flat on the ledge.

Behind him, Tewa squeezed out of the cave and half-sat on the ledge as the penetrator, looking like a giant plumb bob, came closer. He crouched as it came within reach, and reached out. As he put his hands up to grasp the device, he jerked backwards and slammed up against the cliff face and started to slide down, as lifeless as a rag doll.

Wolf, lying on his back with his feet toward Tewa and the cave mouth, could see the tiny Lao was going to slide off the ledge into the jungle below. He rolled toward the cliff, raised his good leg and, hooking the toes of his boot around Tewa's waist, pulled his body crashing down on his own. He had to thrash his arms to keep the two of them from rolling off the ledge. At the same time, above the sound of the helicopter blades and engines, he heard the popping and *blam-blam* of many guns and saw chips and pieces of rock fly away from the cliff face. One round spanged off the metal penetrator.

"Abort, Abort, Abort," Bernick in the right door, guiding the cable, yelled over the intercom. At the same time, both Dominguez and Bakke opened up with their miniguns at the jungle below. "The penetrator is clear," Bernick said. "Abort."

"Jolly, they're shooting at you," Sandy Lead called.

"Haul ass," Kelly ordered, but Shilleto didn't need any further words. An "abort" call from any crew member was heeded instantly. He was lifting straight up to clear the penetrator from the cliff and to get over the opposite side of the karst ridge away from the guns. "Get that penetrator up, check for damage," Kelly ordered the flight mech. Bernick rotated the handle to up.

Sandy Two again spoke urgently over the UHF radio. "Jolly, they're shooting at you."

"Roger, roger, don't we know it," Kelly replied. "You see where they are, Sandy?"

"That's affirmative," Sandy Lead said. "I'm rolling in on them east to west, will pull off south. I have you in sight, Jolly." He paused for a second to see if anybody had anything else to say, then said, "Sandy Two, set up random, use both sides of the ridge. Keep Jolly in sight and watch the thunderstorms." He was telling his wingman he could roll in from any heading he wanted to confuse the gunners, but had to keep everyone in sight. "You going to try again, Jolly?"

Kelly looked over to Shilleto. "What say?"

Shilleto was busy checking the stick, collective lever, RPM, rudder pedals, and the engine instruments for damage. He nodded his head. "Probably. Depends on what the Sandys bring up and how well they do. Get a damage report."

"How does it look back there, Sergeant Bernick?" Kelly asked the flight mech. "Everybody okay?" He scanned the engine and system gauges. They appeared normal.

"No problems, sir. Hook is up and stowed. Ship and crew fit and ready to go."

"Jolly will hold north of the ridgeline," Shilleto told the Sandys. He turned to parallel the ridge for a last look before they dropped behind it. Sandy Two was in the middle of his run. Two glistening cans of napalm detached from beneath his wings and tumbled into the brush between the karst and the jungle almost directly beneath the cave entrance. A wave of burning gel splashed down on the tiny blue-clad figures running through the brush in the direction of the cliff.

Sandy Two pulled off sharply to the south as Lead rolled in from the west. "They're in the open," Two said, "trying to get to the cliff. About twenty or thirty."

"Any big guns?" Kelly asked. "Yesterday there was a 12.7 here."

"How do you know?" Sandy Lead asked.

"By the size of the holes in our bird," Kelly said.

"Ha ha," Lead said as he pickled off two 500-pound bombs into the trees where the running men had retreated. He hazarded a quick glance at the ledge.

Kelly switched to Guard Channel. "Wolf, do you read Jolly Two Two? What's your status?" There was no answer. Kelly switched back to rescue frequency. "Sandy Lead," he called, "do you see anything around the mouth of that cave?"

The A-1 jinked south, then pulled off to the northeast and passed east of the karst as he climbed through 3,000 feet. "Two guys on a ledge," he said. "One seems to be moving, but not very well."

Wolf Lochert groaned in effort as he tried to slide feet first into the cave, clutching Tewa's body to his own. He had a hard time steering his numb right leg. His elbows

110

felt raw and torn. Bullets continued to hit the face of the cliff above his head, but because he was flat on the ledge, the lip prevented the PL from getting a clear shot. *Soon,* he thought, *they'll be close enough to lob a grenade up here or fire a rocket-propelled grenade into the cave.*

He felt a pain from his back and realized he had strapped on his AK-47 and it was digging into him and holding back his progress into the cave. There was nothing he could do about it, he slowly reasoned with fragmented thoughts. He had to get Tewa and himself into the cave. His tongue grew more thick and the throb in his head increased. He stopped moving and didn't notice Tewa's blood trickling onto his torn and dirty shirt.

He heard the roaring of the first A-1 as it swept by, then he felt the heat of the dropped napalm sweep over him like a wave of warm water. He thought he heard cries and screams from below. Then came the concussive bomb blasts.

Sandy Lead rolled in and released two more bombs in a line from those dropped by Sandy Two. The four bombs and the two napalm had blunted the attack. The Sandys had a dozen more bombs and napalm and hundreds of rounds of 20mm cannon shells remaining.

"Wolf, Wolf, this is Jolly Two Two on Guard. Do you read?" Kelly tried again. Still no answer. "What do you see, Sandy Lead?" he asked. Shilleto kept the helicopter a mile above the ground north of the ridge.

"They're still on the ledge but not moving. I don't think they were hit but can't tell for sure."

"How about the guns? How about that 12.7? Anybody still shooting?"

"I'll make a pass," Sandy Lead said. "Two, cover me. See if anybody shoots." Sandy Lead rolled in and flew from west to east at 500 feet above the ground. He saw bodies on the torn earth and jungle where the bombs had hit, and he saw shrunken black figures where the napalm fire still smoldered. He looked down to his left at the karst ledge and saw one of the two figures feebly kicking his leg. Then he had to pull up abruptly to avoid flying into the wall of rain enveloping the eastern end of the karst ridge.

111

"Nobody shot at you as far as I can see," Sandy Two said.

"Okay, good," Sandy Lead transmitted. "About the guys on the ledge. One is still alive. But I got to tell you something, Jolly. They both seem to be wearing civilian clothes and one could be Asian."

"Okay, that's okay," Kelly said to Shilleto, "that would square with people on board an Air America airplane. They run around in civvies all the time."

Shilleto nodded. He looked at the heavy squall line east of the cave. It was moving in rapidly. "Okay, Sandy, we'll try again," he said. "Coming around for another pass, north to south." He took the big helicopter due south toward the ridgeline and started down. "Okay, gang," he said on the intercom, "we've only got one shot at this. I'll pop over the ridgeline and go into a hover facing west. PJ One, stand by to go down the hoist. Watch yourself. Get a positive ID from those guys. We don't want to be sucked in by any of those Russian advisers we hear about."

Dominguez rogered and took off his parachute. He checked his equipment. He wore a green mesh survival vest, two canteens of water and a knife on a webbed belt, a .45 caliber automatic in a shoulder holster, and a slung CAR15. Normally, there was no way to communicate with the helicopter except by hand signals to the man on the hoist. Kelly always made sure his PJs had a survival radio so that in emergencies the PJ on the ground could communicate directly with the pilot. Although the PJ could talk into the tiny radio, he could never hear the pilot speak because of the roar of the rotor downwash.

Kelly stood in the door next to Bernick and looked down. They were about eighty feet above the ridgeline and barely south of it. Twenty feet down the cliff face from the ridgeline was the ledge where the two survivors lay. Dominguez pulled the penetrator to himself, opened a seat and mounted it, and gave the signal for Bernick to start the hoist motor and let him down.

Bernick kept up a steady chatter to Shilleto about where to position the HH-53B. "PJ on the hoist, PJ started down, you're drifting back, forward one, forward one, that's it, that's it. Hold, hold. PJ halfway down. Hold steady."

Dominguez sat on one of the unfolded petals, with one arm around the shank of the penetrator. He swept his eyes first to the survivors, then to the surrounding territory for probable enemy positions. He had the best view of anybody on the helicopter, for he could see in all directions plus up and down. Although this was his twenty-fifth time down the hoist, his pulse rate was high and he was breathing rapidly. He almost regretted wearing a helmet so he could hear the slightest popping noise above the sound of the helicopter that meant someone was shooting at him. He motioned with his free hand to be let down further. He didn't sense he was being shot at, and riveted his eyes on the survivors below on the ledge. He saw two men, both in civilian clothes, both very dirty and covered with blood, one lying on top of the other.

Dominguez had heard the conversation about the civilian clothes and the Asian. He took the .45 from his shoulder holster and held it in his right hand, pointed straight down at the head of the man on the bottom. Ten feet above the two men, he called out.

"Hey, you guys hear me? Hey, you guys okay? You understand English? Talk to me. Move your hand. Give me a signal." The penetrator swayed slightly as he shifted his position and signaled for Bernick to put him on the ledge a few feet away from the two men. A sudden wind current splattered raindrops on him. He disengaged from the penetrator and used both hands to keep the .45 pointed into the face of the bottom man as he approached. The man on top was definitely Asian.

"Hey," Dominguez said as he stood directly over the two men, the gun muzzle two feet away from the nose of the dirty and unshaven face of the Caucasian. "Hey, I'm not touching anybody until I'm sure what's happening here. We gotta move. Hey, you alive? You American? Talk to me."

Wolf Lochert heard the voice and felt the first raindrops on his parched lips. He forced open his eyes and looked up at the figure looming over him. His eyes focused on the gun and a great surge of adrenaline charged his brain and cleared his mind. He looked at the man holding the gun.

"Hey, yourself. You're the *Scheisskopf* that ate all my Fritos."

With relief, Dominguez holstered his gun and took out his radio. He tried to keep his hands from trembling. "It's okay down here. One is American military," he told his helicopter. He knelt by the two men. The penetrator lay on the ledge, the vibrating cable snaking in the wind up to the hovering ship.

"Anybody still shooting down here?" he asked Wolf. He had to shout to overcome the noise of the helicopter.

"Not after those A-1s made their attacks. Get this guy off me. He's unconscious and wounded. I don't know how bad. I need water." He spoke with effort against the downwash of air and sound.

The ledge was too narrow for Dominguez to get to the side of the two men. He remained at Wolf's head, handed him a canteen, and slid backwards toward the penetrator pulling Tewa off Wolf. Freed, Wolf drank heavily from the canteen, then rolled onto his belly and crawled after them. Dominguez stopped at the penetrator and signaled Bernick to pull it up two feet from the ground. He unfolded the remaining two petal-shaped seats and pulled a Velcro fastener that opened a canvas collar around the shank of the penetrator. Three attached safety belts dropped out, one for each seat.

"Can you make it on your own?" Dominguez called to Wolf Lochert. He wondered how long it would be before someone shot at them again.

"Yeah," Lochert said, and grimaced as he tried to push forward with his legs, and found the right one still numb and lifeless. He looked past the struggling men and saw the rain mass moving closer. He stopped moving, exhausted.

Dominguez turned and checked Tewa for the severity of his wounds. He found a hole in his left arm and chest where a bullet had gone through the fleshy part of his upper arm and buried itself in his chest muscles. Messy, but he saw no evidence of severed veins or arteries. He could dress them properly once on board the helicopter and clear of the area. He rose to his knees and started to lug Tewa onto the penetrator.

114

The second he rose up and was above the lip of the ledge, chips and dust rose from the cliff wall, something tugged at his pant leg, then he felt a smashing jolt to his head, as if struck with a hammer, and fell into blackness, his body limp as an empty gunnysack.

6

"PJ's down, the PJ is down," Bernick yelled into his boom mike.

"Whaddya mean, down?" Kelly asked. "I thought he already went down the hoist to the surface."

"He's hit, the PJ's hit," Bernick said quickly in a calmer voice.

"Oh shit," Kelly said. "Can you tell how bad?"

"Forward two, forward two, steady, hold," Bernick commanded Shilleto. "No, I can't. He's not moving. One of the survivors has crawled to him. I think he's checking him out."

The helicopter was facing west to place the hoist and penetrator on the south side of the ridge. Neither pilot could see the approaching rain to their rear. Shilleto fought the controls of the big ship as the advance gusts from the storm buffeted the ship back and forth, trying to weathervane the tail first one way then the other.

"PJ Two," Kelly called to Bakke. "See anything? Are we being shot at?"

Bakke answered from the ramp gun. "Can't see any fire from here, but I tell you that storm is going to eat us in about five minutes."

"Roger, understand," Kelly said. "Get on the left gun and tell me what you see from there."

"Pilot, they're shooting plenty down there," Bernick said.

116

"I see dust puffs and chips coming off the wall just over their heads."

The left gun opened up with a throaty roar as the Gatling-style minigun spewed out thirty-three rounds of high-speed 7.62mm (.30 caliber) slugs per second. "Yeah, they're shooting," Bakke said on the intercom. "I can see the smoke and muzzle flashes. I'm returning fire."

"Sandy, we got a problem," Kelly transmitted on the UHF. "They're shooting bad."

"Got a tally, Jolly," Sandy Lead said in a deep, measured voice. As the rescue attempt progressed, his voice had deepened and his cadence had slowed. This was his forty-second rescue sortie. "I'm in east to west, just south of you, with CBU. Two, set up for the same pass. Make it fast. That rain is as good as here."

Four slugs tore through the left side of the helicopter cabin and out the right. "Goddammit, we just took a few rounds," Bakke, at the left gun, said. He swung the barrel back and let loose a stream of bullets in the direction from which he thought the burst had come.

Slant range between the guns on the ground and the guns in the air was 800 feet. The wind was gusting from the east up to thirty-five knots. Fourteen PL soldiers on the ground who had advanced into the napalmed area closest to the ledge were shooting AK-47 assault rifles at the hovering helicopter. They were not aiming high enough to counter bullet drop, nor were they compensating sufficiently for the wind. Three other PL soldiers were wrestling with a large 12.7 (.51 cal) gun that had been blown down the hill by one of the bombs. Two PLs carrying rocket-propelled grenade launchers, and their two helpers, were fighting their way up the hill, past their dead and wounded comrades. Between the four of them, they had forty-four rounds of the high-explosive grenades. They had made their plans. When they were within twenty meters of the cliff they would blast the wall with grenades that would shower metal fragments on the men lying on the ledge below.

Bakke saw the advancing AK-47 gunners and triggered over 100 rounds their way in a three-second burst. One bullet took

117

a man in the stomach, sitting him down as if slugged with a baseball bat. He went down still firing and involuntarily raised the muzzle of his gun. Two rounds tore through the side of the helicopter. One smoked up into the roof and scattered pieces of lead as it splintered on a crosspiece. The other hit Bakke. He went down hard, his left leg blown backwards with the sledgehammer blow as the bullet entered his left thigh and severed an artery. Bernick saw him go down.

"Bakke's hit," he shouted. "We're taking fire back here."

"Hold on," Kelly yelled back. "How bad is he hit? What's happening to Dominguez? Are they on the hoist yet? Can we start up? There ain't no second chance."

"Sir, too many questions. You gotta come back here. Things are turning to shit and I need help." Bernick's voice was hurried and high-pitched.

"Go ahead," Shilleto said to Kelly and nodded his head toward the aft cabin.

"Be right there," Kelly told Bernick. He unstrapped, pulled out his intercom plug, and prepared to climb from his seat when he looked over at Shilleto. The colonel was soaking wet. Sweat was dripping from under his helmet into his eyes. Kelly pulled a sweat rag from a leg pocket and wiped his brow the best he could. "Thanks," Shilleto mouthed. His lips looked thin and blue.

Kelly went into the cabin and plugged into an intercom line. He bent over Bakke's body, which lay in a widening puddle of blood. He knelt down, turned Bakke faceup, and saw bright red blood pumping rhythmically from under the left leg of his flight suit. Bakke's eyes were partially open and dazed. His moan was lost in the roar of the engines and the rotor blast. Kelly pulled his K-Bar knife from its scabbard and cut open the cloth around the wound, then tore the material down to Bakke's knee. The wound was half-dollar size and jagged. Kelly stood and opened the latches on a first aid box strapped to the side of the helicopter. Moving quickly, he ripped open two compress packages and took out the tourniquet kit. He scrambled back to Bakke, pressed the compresses to the wound, fastened the tourniquet over the compresses, and tugged it tight.

He twitched but did not look up as an AK-47 slug impacted the ceiling above his head. He pulled Bakke back to a litter, took off his helmet, and strapped him in. Bakke's eyes focused on him and he attempted a smile. Kelly squeezed his hand and moved over to the left gun.

He pointed the barrel down and fired three two-second bursts into the general target area to let them know the gun was still active. Then he ran to the open ramp, trailing his black intercom cord like an umbilical to the ship, and fired a quick burst with the ramp gun. After that, he ran to the open door by Bernick. He waited until the flight mech gave more maneuver instructions to Shilleto. It was becoming increasingly difficult to hold the hover in the path of the approaching storm.

"How is it down there?" he asked on the intercom when Bernick was finished. He had to hold the doorframe to keep his balance as the helicopter dipped and swayed in the gusts.

"We got about three minutes, then we gotta GO," Bernick panted. Kelly braced himself in the doorway and looked down.

Below, Wolf Lochert groaned not with pain but with the mental energy required to perform the tasks he had to perform or die. Everything seemed too large and unwieldy and the air was filled with blasting sounds and was thick and stinging from the downrush of rotor wash and the rainstorm was going to blow them off the ledge and he had to get everyone attached to that thing and get out of there and he didn't know if he could do it at all.

He stopped moving and lay flat on his back. Looking up, he saw a man waving frantically from the helicopter door 100 feet above. He blinked and wondered what was happening. Four bullets tore into the stone over his head, showering his face with stinging fragments. The shock caused a wave of clarity to wash over his mind.

"Think, shithead," he yelled to himself "Think." *Our Father, who art in heaven, hallowed be . . .* the radio. That PJ talked into the radio. He had one of his own, he knew he did. He reached down with slow deliberate hands and pulled his spare RT-10 from his right cargo pocket and extended the antenna.

"Jolly Green, this is Wolf," he said into the dime-sized microphone embedded in the radio face. When he put the radio to his ear to listen for a reply, he realized the noise from the hovering helicopter was too loud to hear anything. He saw the man in the open door point to his helmet and give him a thumbs-up. The man also pointed to his wrist and held up two fingers. A spate of rain drummed on Wolf's face and he suddenly knew what he had to do. There was no time to check either of the other two men for wounds. They might even be dead, he thought, but he would get them out of there.

"Okay," he said into the radio. "Okay, now. Here's what we do. Can't stand up, heavy fire from below. Leave the plumb bob flat on the ground. I'll get all three of us strapped on and give you a signal. Then it's up to you. Give me two thumbs-up if you understand."

Kelly leaned out and gave Wolf two exaggerated thumbs-up signals. "Get the penetrator to lay flat," he said to Bernick.

Bernick toggled out several feet of line. The helicopter drifted. "Forward one, steady, steady. Hold," Bernick said on the intercom to Shilleto. When he was finished, the penetrator lay next to Dominguez's body.

Kelly wanted to watch but knew he had to get on the guns. He ran back to the ramp gun and fired a burst, then to the left window gun and began searching for targets. He saw three men by a splintered tree, holding AK-47s to their shoulders and firing so rapidly the smoke from the gun muzzles made a white swirling ribbon. He swung the barrel toward them and depressed the trigger even before he had them in his sights. He saw the bullets impact in the charred grass and walked them to the three men. One fell down and the other two ducked behind a fallen tree. He saw two others kneel down with some kind of a long shoulder weapon. An RPG, he guessed.

"Paul, tell the Sandys we need more bombs and CBUs. The PL are all over the place," Kelly cried over the intercom. From the aft cabin, Kelly could talk on the intercom but not on the radio. Shilleto relayed the request on the UHF radio.

"Jolly, you're too close for me to drop bombs," Sandy Lead said. "You'd get hit by fragments. We'll try CBU and strafe.

120

But that storm is *here*. We'll maybe get two passes max. Lead's in."

Summoning all his will, Wolf crawled to the penetrator. It lay like a three-pronged anchor on its side. He shoved and pushed Dominguez, then Tewa, over the extended seat petals and fumbled the safety belts about them. Both of the inert bodies were awkwardly draped over the penetrator. Wolf pulled himself in position and gave the thumbs-up to Bernick in the door.

Bernick eased the handle back. "Hook's coming up," he said to Shilleto on the intercom. "The civilian is giving the signal. The PJ is not moving. Back one, back one. Steady. That's it. Hold." Bernick delicately moved the hoist handle. As the line tightened and took up the slack, the penetrator began to straighten from its tilted position on the ground. Bernick took up more slack and the two bodies flopped back and slid off the seats. To raise the hook further would cause the two men to fall completely off and out of the safety harnesses.

"Oh shit," he said on the intercom. "Pilot, we got a big problem. The civilian can't get Dominguez and the other guy strapped onto the seats."

Joe Kelly heard Bernick and came over to stand next to him in the door. He looked down and saw the biggest of the three men struggling without success to get the other two secure in their seats. Their bodies kept slipping out of his hands like grain sacks half-filled with buckshot. He saw the first wisp of rain sweep under the helicopter and felt the cool breeze behind it. The helicopter buffeted and rocked abruptly.

"That's it," Shilleto said on the intercom. "I've got to lift. What's their progress? We got to go. Flight mech, as soon as you hoist them clear of the ridge I'm moving this thing. I'll take them out still suspended. Then we'll bring them up as we go. Are we clear?"

Kelly could see they were not clear. He looked up at the lever on the hoist that would cut the cable and free the helicopter from its burden, allowing it to speed away. The cable cutter was there to free the rescue helicopter from a snagged cable. Such a disaster had happened. In his mind's eye he could see the long wire falling down on top of the men below, and the anguished look on the survivors' faces. He had sworn this would never happen to him, to leave a survivor behind. He licked his lips and shuddered. Kelly's hands began shaking as he knew what he should do.

When Kelly had first arrived in SEA and performed a few missions, he had thought that something like this might occur someday, and now here it was. He had never told anyone what he had in mind because he was afraid that if the occasion demanded, he wouldn't be up to it. He had secured a device called a descender from a Special Forces friend and carried it in his flight bag. The man had given him a few rudimentary instructions on how to operate it and wasn't at all sure it would work on a metal cable. ARRS was working on a strap affair called the sky-genie, but it wasn't in the field yet.

"Hold steady," Kelly cried into the intercom and ran forward to the cockpit to get the descender from his flight bag.

"What are you doing?" Shilleto asked when he saw Kelly pull out a metal mechanism that looked like a cross between a vise-grip pliers and an extra-heavy can opener with an eight-inch metal handle. A D-ring similar to a mountaineer's cara-bineer was snapped onto the middle of it.

"Okay," Kelly said on the intercom to Shilleto and Bernick. He took a deep breath, not sure he could control his voice. "I'm going down the cable and strap those guys on proper."

"You're crazy," Shilleto said. "Nobody can go down a bare cable. Your hands won't hold."

"With this, I can do it." Kelly shook the device at Shilleto, then ran back to the door. "Give me a pair of gloves," he ordered Bernick, who tossed him a heavy pair of linesman's gloves. "When I get down there I'm going to get those guys in place, then give you the pumping signal to start up. Don't worry about me. I'll still be attached with this thing. Just tell the Colonel we're clear and he'll lift up and get out of here. You can start the hoist up when you want, but get him moving us out of here immediately. I'll use my radio only if I have to."

He threw a glance over his shoulder out the left window. "Colonel, tell those Sandys to dump everything they've got in one pass. The storm is here and they won't be able to work anymore." He looked back at the taut cable. "Down two feet," he told Shilleto, who complied while telling the Sandys what was happening and what he wanted them to do with their remaining ordnance. Kelly unplugged the intercom cord from his helmet. He felt suddenly alone and cut off. He bent and snugged up his parachute harness straps. The first rain swirled through the cabin.

When the cable was slack, Kelly motioned for Bernick to pull it toward him. Bernick leaned out the door, snagged the cable, and pulled it inside. Kelly fitted the descender to the wire, closed the gripping jaws, then snapped the carabineer onto the front of his parachute harness, wishing he had just the harness and not the extra bulk of a parachute he could not possibly use.

This was the moment he had thought about: a terrifying descent using a method with which he had no experience and which had never been tried by anyone in the rescue business. He stood in the door and tried not to look down. He didn't know if the Pathet Lao were still shooting or not, he only knew he had to go down the cable. He stepped out of the door into the buffeting rotor wash, which spun him around so he was looking straight at Bernick. The two men locked eyes. The last thing Kelly saw was Dan Bernick giving him a thumbsup as he toggled the switch lowering him from view. He wrapped his legs around the cable.

The descender was stiff and slightly rusty. Kelly had difficulty opening and closing its jaws. He jerked and dropped in fits and starts as he manipulated the handle to open and close the jaws. Once he fell nearly ten feet in a free fall until he jerked to a stop that took his breath away. He resisted an almost overpowering urge just to hang there and signal Bernick to lift away. He continued and was halfway down before he mastered the descent rate. The noise and buffeting was as he remembered in training, when he had played victim to see what a pickup was like from the survivor's point of view. He was thankful the cable was anchored to the penetrator on the ground, otherwise he would probably be spinning in addition to the buffeting. Then he felt pain in his legs and thought he had been hit. He looked down and saw that the inside of his flight suit pant legs were shredded and covered with dots of blood as they flapped like so many ragged pennants. He focused in on the cable and realized it was covered with thousands of wire hairs from broken strands that were raking his legs like tiny steel claws. He unwrapped his legs and let them hang free. Behind, he heard the roar of the quad 20mm cannons as a Sandy made a firing pass.

Kelly heard a sharp explosion below and looked down to see a square-foot portion of the rock face crumble away from the cliff and fall to one side of the men on the ledge. He was twenty feet above the men now and almost touching the cliff below the ridgeline. He saw another explosion on the wall and looked down the karst slope to see two men with RPGs standing up and preparing to fire again. They looked like they were aiming directly at him. He felt a spasm in his stomach and a wild urge to stop everything and urinate. He saw one man's weapon fire and was sure he could see the missile in flight as it arced up to the cliff and detonated on the wall thirty feet west of him. The roar was deafening, and he felt his body lightly peppered with stone and metal fragments. The rotor downwash and the wind from the rainstorm had protected him from more serious impacts.

Kelly's heart leaped again as he saw the second man take aim. He had never felt so exposed and vulnerable in his life. His bladder threatened to burst. Behind the soldier, he saw the second A-1 pull up from a pass as the last of its napalm cans splashed along the base of the karst directly toward the RPG gunners and they disappeared in the red inferno. Kelly could feel the heat. Then the first of the rain was on him and the jungle and scrub karst were totally concealed, so that the A-1s could make no more passes, but the enemy could still see the cliff.

He was ten feet above the survivors when he heard the popping of small-arms fire and looked down the karst and, *Oh Jesus,* there were three soldiers shooting and preparing to throw grenades. He released the jaws in a spasm and fell heavily to the ledge below, next to the men and the penetrator. Stunned for a second, he lay still as he caught his breath. With disgust he realized his bladder had let go. He jerked as an object arced through the air from below, struck the cliff face, then bounced back over the ledge and exploded. Kelly unsnapped his carabineer from the descender. Immediately, a second object, a grenade, hit the cliff face and fell to the ledge. Kelly's whole body reacted in a blaze of motion as he rose to his knees and scrambled after the grenade and brushed it over the cliff edge, then fell flat before it exploded. As he fell, he saw several soldiers below aiming AK-47s and firing and preparing more grenades. He ducked back and pulled a 9mm Browning automatic from his shoulder holster and without looking held it over the cliff edge and pulled the trigger in rapid succession until the magazine was empty and the slide cocked back. Another grenade arced over the edge and bounced off the cliff wall but fell beyond the ledge and exploded just under the lip with a huge roar. Kelly knew it was just a matter of time until they lobbed several grenades that would come to rest on the ledge.

Kelly fumbled a new magazine into his Browning and was surprised the weapon was wet. He looked around and saw the rain was on him, then heard an increase in noise and looked up and saw the helicopter had descended to hover just above the ridgeline barely thirty feet over his head, and Bernick was tossing objects out the side door. They fell one after the other to land below the ledge. When loud booms began a regular cadence, it registered with Kelly that Bernick was dropping Dominguez's Mason jar bombs on the enemy soldiers. He didn't dare look, for exposing himself to the fire and the fragments, but there were no more grenades arcing up from below. He felt an insane desire to giggle. Then he did giggle as he realized the rain would soak his flight suit and hide the fact that he had peed in his pants.

He crawled over to the thickset American in a shredded white guayabera shirt who lay next to the penetrator. The other two, Dominguez and the Asian, were sprawled over the device.

"Can you move?" Kelly yelled to the man.

"Not well. Leg won't work," the man answered. "Gimme that CAR-15," he demanded, pointing at the weapon slung over Dominguez's back.

"No time, no time," Kelly said as he unstrapped them all and rose to his knees and righted the penetrator with one hand while motioning Bernick to take up the slack with the hoist. When it was two feet above the ground, he prepared to strap in the two unconscious men. A dozen bullets spanged the rock over his head and he dropped down.

"GIVE ME THE GUN," Wolf Lochert bellowed.

Lying flat, Kelly pulled it from Dominguez and slid it to him. Lochert rolled to the edge and pointed the barrel down.

"When I fire, you stand up and hook up," he yelled, and started pulling the trigger in short bursts.

Kelly scrambled to his feet and wrestled, first the small Asian, then Dominguez, into the saddles and strapped them securely in place. Then he flopped down. "Now you," he yelled at the other man.

Wolf Lochert back-crawled to the penetrator and rose on his good leg. "Need help," he said. He nestled up between the two bodies, but couldn't brace himself well enough to hook his strap.

Kelly boosted him the rest of the way and helped him secure his belt. The penetrator, free of the ground, swayed ponderously in the wind. Kelly looked up at Bernick and gave him the "hoist-up" sign. Bernick frantically waved "no" and pointed to his own chest.

"Oh shit," Kelly yelled out loud as he realized he had not hooked himself up and lunged for the cable but couldn't reach high enough to snap the carabineer on the descender. Without a second thought he stepped up onto the big man's left leg and snapped the ring in place. Immediately, the penetrator started up, and Kelly heard the blades change pitch and tone as the HH-53 surged to take up the strain and began to move.

For long agonizing seconds they hung in the air as they swung out beyond the karst face and over the soldiers below. Those that remained were shooting frantically at the four men on the hoist. Wolf Lochert hugged the penetrator with his left arm, leaned over and back holding the CAR-15 like a pistol in his right hand, and methodically fired short bursts into them. Then the storm swept over them and they were alone in a world of stinging rain and spinning vertigo. The buffeting and noise were appalling. There was a moment where Kelly thought it was all over, when it felt as if they were in free fall, then with a lurch they were hanging on a taut cable again. It was as if the helicopter had plunged ten feet before being recovered.

Kelly knew Shilleto was flying the helicopter on instruments in the rainstorm. A slight miscalculation either way and their swaying pendulum of humanity would hit a cliff or the treetops, and pieces of them would be ripped off, like the man whose foot had wedged in a tree during an emergency extraction and been torn from his leg. Kelly heard that the man, a Special Forces soldier, had bled to death before he had been winched into the helicopter. He held the cable and looked down at the three men seated and strapped to the penetrator. The Asian was still unconscious and slumped like empty clothes against the shank. He was held in place by the belt under his arms and around his back. The big Caucasian with the CAR-15 had slung the gun over one shoulder and was helping hold Dominguez against the shank. Dominguez seemed to be moving his head, but Kelly couldn't be sure. Then Kelly had to pull the visor in his helmet down over his eyes because movement through the rain made the drops sting like pellets from a BB gun.

Kelly sensed the penetrator was more upright, which meant they were approaching the hoist. Then the sound of the rotor was deafening and he saw the bulk of the big ship looming in the clouds above him and then he was level with the door and Bernick snapped a long safety strap onto his harness and pulled him in. Bernick toggled the penetrator up to the door and the two of them pulled the three men in one by one and stretched them out on the floor of the cabin. Bernick began checking their wounds, Dominguez first. Kelly grabbed the unattached intercom cord and plugged in.

"We're all aboard, Colonel," he said.

"You'd better . . . get up here . . . and take it, Joe," Paul Shilleto said in barely audible words.

Alarmed, Kelly got up and went forward to the cockpit and climbed into his seat on the left. He put his hands on the controls and monitored the instruments to maintain level flight band.

127

"Okay," he said, "I've got it." He was surprised his hands were so steady.

He felt Shilleto release the controls and heard a loud groaning sigh over his headset and saw from the corner of his eye that Shilleto had slumped back in his seat, head rolling back and forth with the buffeting of the helicopter. His hands rose to his chest, then fell back into his lap.

"Flight mech," Kelly said into his boom mike, "get up here soon as you can. I think the Colonel's been hit."

Kelly concentrated on turning the helicopter toward Udorn, then called Cricket and told the controller what had happened.

"Roger, Jolly Green Two Two," Hillsboro responded. "Understand you've made the pickup and have wounded on board. Where are you headed and are you declaring an emergency?"

Kelly had checked the gauges and found the number two engine was running hot. There was no transmission warning light, meaning the most critical piece of machinery to maintain flight was apparently not damaged. Then his eyes widened when he saw the failure warning light for the number two (second stage) hydraulic flight control system was glowing amber. The main system was functioning properly but if it failed without backup the helicopter would plummet out of control.

"I'm headed for Udorn. And yeah," Kelly said with reluctance, "I'm declaring an emergency." All pilots hated to declare an emergency unless the aircraft had obvious problems, like being on fire or a wing half shot off. For an HH-53B, any flight control problem was an emergency.

"Jolly Green Two Two, Udorn is closed due to severe thunderstorms. The whole area is in bad shape. We'll put you in touch with Invert Radar, they will vector you to Ubon. You got enough fuel?"

"Roger," Kelly said. "Okay on the fuel. Going to Invert." He changed frequency, identified himself to Invert, and received a vector and a promise of flight monitoring to Ubon Royal Thai Air Force Base. He settled on course. He didn't dare take his hands from the controls to check the slumped Shilleto.

Five long minutes passed before Bernick came forward to

attend to Paul Shilleto. He bent over the man, opened his straps, and unzipped his flight suit. He found no wounds nor saw signs of blood. When he took off Shilleto's helmet he noticed the blue pallor on his face and around his lips. He grabbed his wrist to feel for a pulse. After a moment he slowly straightened.

"He's dead, sir," he said on the intercom to Kelly. "Heart attack, I think."

Captain Joe Kelly didn't fly the HH-53B above 150 feet once he was clear of the battle zone, in case he had engine or control problems. Unlike fixed-wing pilots, helicopter pilots are not comfortable at high altitudes. Fixed-wing pilots love all the altitude they can get so they can trade it for distance if they need to glide to a safe area. In combat, fixed-wing pilots also like a lot of altitude between them and ground fire. While that is true of helicopter pilots also, they get nervous sometimes if they must fly too high when they are not being shot at, particularly if they have a problem. Helicopter pilots don't want to trade anything for anything; the one thing they cannot gain or lose if something goes wrong is time. They do not want the excess time necessary to descend from altitude if they have a problem. Helicopters are unique in that fashion – a problem usually means they have to get on the ground immediately before something catastrophic happens, like a rotor or gearbox failure. There is no glide whatsoever in those cases. It is a straight-down plunge. When a gearbox breaks up, a helicopter becomes a very inelegant projectile. Helicopter pilots have a saying: Never hover high when you can hover low; never hover when you can land. Kelly wanted to get on the ground *now*, even if he had to put it down in some Thai rice paddy.

The weather was clear. Invert handed him off to Lion Radar, who set him up for approach and told him to call Ubon Tower on 236.6. The Tower cleared Jolly Green Two Two for approach and landing from any direction to runway 23; altimeter 29.55, winds from the west at 5. Kelly manipulated the controls to fly forward into a rolling landing. As soon as the wheels touched, he gently lowered the collective and pulled off the power. At an intersection he turned off the runway onto a ramp. When he stopped, he was surrounded by crash-crew fire trucks who aimed their foam turrets at the helicopter like cannons in battle. Kelly shut the engines down. When cleared in by the fire chief, two blue ambulances backed up to the right side door and two flight surgeons carrying medical kits and several male nurses scrambled into the cabin. They shooed Kelly and Bernick out of the craft. In less than five minutes they had the situation in hand and motioned for litters from the ambulances.

Kelly and Bernick stood by the door and were surrounded by the colonels who commanded the fighter wing, the base, and various other organizations at Ubon. The commander of the Ubon Rescue Detachment, a sandy-haired lieutenant colonel, listened while Kelly told his story. Kelly stopped in midsentence and they watched as the medics started to remove the litters from the helicopter.

Bakke was first out. His face was slack and he wore a sleepy morphine smile. A male nurse carried an IV jar that dripped liquid into his arm through a tube. Bernick moved anxiously alongside and accompanied him into the ambulance. Manuel Dominguez was on the next litter. His helmet was off and he wore a wide gauze bandage around his head. His eyes were swollen and black and blue and his gaze was cockeyed. Joe Kelly walked over to him and took his hand.

"Hey, LC, whaddya know? How do you feel?"

"I feel terrible, like some mule done kicked me in the head."

Kelly looked up at the flight surgeon accompanying the litter. "A 5.56 slug entered his helmet from behind and slid halfway around the inside." He thumbed over his shoulder toward the helicopter. "You should get the helmet. Keep it as a souvenir for him."

"Will he be okay?" Kelly asked as they levered Dominguez into an ambulance.

"Probably, but we've got to keep him under close observation for several days. Skin line torn all the way around, but we won't know about bones until we X-ray." The flight surgeon climbed into the wagon.

Kelly turned and saw the stocky civilian on a litter. An IV tube led to his right arm. He was accompanied by a nurse and a flight surgeon whose USAF fatigues bore the name Russell.

The civilian held up his hand to stop the litter. "I hear your name is Kelly. Mine's Lochert." Wolf Lochert held up a hairy paw. "You did a great job. How'd you like to work for me?"

Kelly smiled and shook his hand. "Well, thanks, Mister Lochert, but I'm sort of employed as it is right now."

"I'm not a mister, I'm a Special Forces lieutenant colonel. Come see me in the hospital." Wolf looked over and saw the next litter being carried out with the tiny body of Tewa covered completely by a blanket. They placed the litter flat on the ramp. Wolf looked mutely at the nurse.

"Sorry, sir. He didn't make it. He's been dead a long time. Never knew what hit him. He took one right through his heart."

"Awwr," Wolf said, and motioned to his bearers to carry him away. He looked pale and his eyes didn't seem to focus well. Alarmed, Kelly looked at Doc Russell, who said, "Probably mild concussion and some dehydration confusion." He stood back as Wolf Lochert was loaded into the ambulance, which drove away.

The last litter out carried the body of Lieutenant Colonel Paul Shilleto. The bearers laid it on the ramp next to that of Tewa.

"Massive heart attack, died instantly," Doc Russell said.

Kelly remembered the lurch. Bernick had told him on the flight back to Ubon that during the rescue Colonel Shilleto had made a disturbing loud groan on the intercom and seemed to have lost control for an instant. "The bird sank a dozen feet or so," Bernick had said, "while you guys were hanging on the wire. I thought for sure he had been hit and we were going in. God, I thought we'd had it."

Kelly looked at Doc Russell. "I don't think he died instantly. He had to fly for at least another ten minutes before I was able to take over."

Doctor Conrad Russell looked thoughtful and solemn. "Then you had a dead man flying your ship."

7

"Hard day at the office?" Doctor Conrad Russell inquired of Major Court Bannister, who sat at a table in the Ubon Officer's Club dining room. Russell took a chair across from him and picked up a menu.

"Normal-normal. Excitement, terror, high blood pressure, lots of laughs." Court tried to joke while behind his eyes he saw Beercan Two Two explode on the night karst. He wore a black flight suit with his name and rank stitched in small white letters on the left breast. His hair was cut short and bleached nearly blond by the sun. His face was Nordic, eyes gray-blue.

The Phantom FACs, the sixteen-man flying unit Court Bannister commanded, flew their F-4s only at night, which meant their days were reversed by twelve hours. It was now 1830 (6:30 PM) by the Phantom's daily clock, not early morning, and their working day was over. Some of the men had gone to the bar, others were working out at the base gym. They felt elite, the Phantom FACs. They said they supposed day pilots were okay, but they really wouldn't want their daughter to *marry* one.

Court had had his daily meeting with the wing commander and all the other squadron commanders at 0730. Now he was having shrimp-fried rice for dinner. There was the usual hum

133

and buzz of conversation as aircrew ordered breakfast from the Thai waitresses and talked among themselves. Doc Russell looked up as a waitress glided up to his side. He ordered #5: Bacon (crisp), Eggs (poached), Toast (dry), Jam (raspberry), Coffee (black). The poached eggs usually arrived as hard-boiled golf balls wobbling around on a saucer.

Doc Russell was a bit overweight, rotund in fact. His round, young-looking face vaguely resembled that of Baby Huey, the cartoon character. He wore standard Shade 45 USAF blue two-piece fatigues. His name, rank, and flight surgeon wings were embossed on a piece of leather stitched to his left breast. At Ubon, Doc Russell was doing what he loved best, serving as a flight surgeon to combat fighter crews in the United States Air Force.

Court and Doc Russell had known each other since their time together at Bien Hoa, South Vietnam, in 1966. Bannister had been flying F-100s on ground support missions; Russell had been the squadron's flight surgeon. Court knew Russell was competent, hardworking, and, unlike many military doctors, not in the service merely to pay off his medical schooling tab picked up by the USAF, or for the varied experience that would take a civilian ten years of general practice to acquire. Those kind of MDs usually snickered at the servicemen they treated and could hardly wait until they could get out and earn eighty grand a year and tell funny stories about the nincompoops in uniform.

"You're not smoking anymore, I notice," Doc Russell said.

"Trying to quit. Working out a little, too. Weights, running." Court pulled a Zippo with a rubber band wound around it from his leftsleeve zippered pocket. "Kept this for old time's sake."

"Makes your old doctor's heart happy," Doc Russell said. He stared at his greasy bacon and pushed it away. "Maybe I should do a bit of the same." He looked up. "Better get over to the hospital," Doc Russell said. "Admitted an old pal of yours last night from that shot-up Jolly Green that recovered here." Court looked up in worried anticipation. "Wolf Lochert," Doc Russell said, then added hurriedly when he saw the concern on Court's face, "But he's going to be okay. No wounds, just a mild concussion. You can ride back with me after your breakfast . . . ah, dinner."

Army Lieutenant Colonel Wolf Lochert occupied a bed in a tiny two-bed room in one of the connected trailers that made up the Ubon hospital complex. The other bed was empty. An IV rack stood in one corner. It had held, one after the other, the six bottles of 5 percent saline solution that had been dripped into Wolf Lochert's veins. While Doc Russell studied Wolf's chart, Wolf smiled and shook hands as best he could with Court Bannister. They had known each other since 1966, when Lochert had been on temporary duty with the III Corps Mike Force team outside Bien Hoa Air Base. Court had seen Wolf recently at a celebration party following Wolf's court-martial acquittal.

Wolf told Court about his mission to survey the Lima Sites in Laos and what had happened during and after the C-46 shootdown. "Now I know why you pilots never let a Jolly buy a drink," he rumbled. "They're magnificent."

"So you were on your way to Eagle Station," Court said. He recounted his experience three days before with the shot-up F-4. He described his morning recce of the site after the attack as easy, all was calm.

"No one shot at you?" Wolf asked. "No big guns?"

"Didn't see a thing. That doesn't mean there weren't small arms. You can't hear them, so you can't tell about that until you get some holes, and we didn't have any holes. The controller on the ground, Lima 14, said all was quiet for the moment, but he thought that it was a probe and there was more to come."

"Yeah," Wolf said. "I read the report and I think there will be more." He looked thoughtful. "You know, there is a lot of hidden meaning behind the fact the attackers withdrew so easily and that no one shot at you. Lost radio contact, you say, at the first moment. Sounds like taking out the radio antenna was intentional, not just a lucky round. That point wasn't made in the report. No one thought to call you to see if you saw anything unusual."

135

"That's normal," Court said. "If I'd been a slow FAC, maybe they would have. Slow FACs flew propeller airplanes, not jets.

"Here's what I think," Wolf said, elbowing himself to sit up. "Eagle Station is probably the most important post in all of Laos to help hit the targets in North Vietnam. What greater coup than to knock the site out to slow down the air strikes?"

"Is what you think an official evaluation?" Court asked.

Wolf barked a deep laugh. "Not at all. It's just a supposition at this point. I need more data before I can be sure."

"How soon are you going back to Vientiane?" Court asked him.

"This afternoon."

Doc Russell looked up sharply. "Negative on that, Colonel. You are going to log a *minimum* of forty-eight hours' observation right here in this room on this air patch." Doc Russell made what he hoped was a menacing face. "What it is," he said to Court as much as to Wolf, "is a mild concussion. Pulse, respiration, and blood pressure are fine, which leads me to believe there is no hemorrhage in the brain. But there could be a slow seepage from a ruptured blood vessel or capillary. We check his vital signs every thirty minutes to see if there is any dramatic change. So he can't leave for two days."

Wolf barked a sharp laugh. "I've already been in contact with Udorn. They're sending an airplane down to pick me up at 1600 today. That will have given you" – he consulted his wristwatch – "nearly twenty-four hours to observe. I've got work to do."

Doc Russell came to his bedside. "Wolf, if you can climb out of bed, close your eyes, and stand on your right foot for one minute, I'll personally drive you to the flight line to catch that flight."

With a disdainful look, Wolf Lochert leapt from the bed, his green hospital gown flapping around his legs, closed his eyes, lifted his left leg, and promptly crashed back onto his bed.

Court and Doc Russell lifted his legs and straightened the grizzled Lochert on the bed. "What happened?" Lochert asked in a surprisingly quiet voice.

"You just bought and paid for another couple days in here, old buddy," Court said.

"I've got to get out of here. I've got to get up to that Eagle Station and see what is going on. That place is too important for me to be fooling around in some hospital."

"Is it really all that important?" Doc Russell asked Court.

"Sure, just as important as the air war in North Vietnam," Court said.

Later, when Court told the Phantom FACs about Wolf and the Jollys in the hospital, they made a unanimous decision. They would host a party for the Jolly Greens (no combat aircrew member ever let a Jolly buy a drink) and for the famous Special Forces soldier Wolf Lochert (they knew his story; great job shivving that commie double agent). Since their heroes were all to be discharged from the hospital in a few days and return to their respective units, the Phantoms decided to set up a big celebration the night before they left.

Full Lieutenant of the United States Navy Rolly Grailson was placed in charge, mainly because he was the Special Projects officer for the Phantom FACs. Grailson was on exchange duty with the USAF from the carrier USS *America*, CV 66, where he had been flying F-4JS with VF-33, the Tarsiers. Grailson said he would have a long talk about making the party memorable with Major Richard "Chef" Hostettler, the Wing Intelligence officer, who had the extra duty of Club Officer.

1230 HOURS LOCAL, SUNDAY 13 OCTOBER 1968
HANOI CITY HOSPITAL
DEMOCRATIC REPUBLIC OF VIETNAM

USAF Major Algernon A. "Flak" Apple was the first black pilot shot down over North Vietnam and captured. He was also one of the first POWs to make an escape from the Hoa

Lo Prison, known as the Hanoi Hilton. He and his partner, Ted Frederick, had gone over the wall in the dead of night in makeshift coolie clothes. Their plan had been to make it to the British Embassy and seek asylum and eventual repatriation. They had been discovered at daybreak hiding in a cemetery. Frederick had thrown away his chance of freedom by creating a diversion, allowing Flak Apple to escape capture. Flak had dashed through the streets, bowling aside the early crowd as his costume unraveled, to the doors of a Western embassy. Instead of falling into the welcoming arms of the British, however, he had been disdained and clearly unwelcome at the French Consulate. Over the protests of a French doctor, he had been tossed back to the North Vietnamese soldiers.

There were now 451 American prisoners of war held in seven prisons in North Vietnam. Only a handful were not shot-down aircrew. Non-aircrew members included Army soldiers and Marines and civilian workers captured in South Vietnam and marched along the Ho Chi Minh Trail to captivity in the North. Most died along the way.

Most of the POWs had tumbled out of the skies into the hands of a vengeful populace or searching North Vietnamese Army troops. Not all of those who reached the ground alive turned up in the prison system. Many were beaten to death where they fell, others succumbed to starvation and beatings as they were made to run the gauntlet of villagers made wild by the foaming harangues of communist political officers. Very few evaded capture for more than an hour or two, none escaped for more than a few hours. Those that did escape from a prison camp faced the severest of torture, which under the humane and lenient policy of the Democratic Republic of Vietnam was called "punishment." Some of the escapees died horribly from their "punishment." There was no attempt by the DRV to keep within any of the Geneva Convention guidelines, because the American POWs and the Thai POWs who were unlucky enough to be in Hanoi were called war criminals and any day now could face trials for their war crimes.

"After Flak Apple's recapture, without preaching or preamble they hung him from a meathook at Hoa Lo and started

138

beating on him. For three days and nights they flayed him with whippy bamboo rods and lengths of rawhide, and even a fan belt wielded by a Caucasian, a Cuban known as Fidel. Finally, when he was an unrecognizable length of raw bleeding meat, when he had voided every possible bit of waste and moisture from every orifice in his body, when he was so close to death his mouth hung open and his dried-out tongue protruded, someone near the top of the communist party hierarchy sent word down that the piece of reactionary black filth was to be spared because he might prove to be of value. They might have plans for him. In any event, they were sure the Westerners finally knew he was alive, because his name had been given in a broadcast of an interview conducted by that unmentionably ignorant American named Robert Williams, who made his home in Cuba.

Williams had said, quite contrary to the fact of Flak Apple's obvious wounds, that Apple was alive, happy, and being well-treated by the humane and lenient people of Vietnam. And, most assuredly the Party reasoned, the French would have told the American authorities that the very same man had appeared one day at their doors in Hanoi demanding asylum. However, the Americans, for some obtuse reason of their own, had not seen fit to make public the details of criminal Apple's aborted escape. The Party did not find it necessary to inform those below their level that the criminal Frederick who had accompanied Apple had been shot and severely wounded. Later that day, Frederick had died without uttering a word within minutes of the start of his beating. His body had been taken to the big mortuary in Hanoi, where the remains of hundreds of American men lay awaiting opportune usage. The Party maintained flawless records of every American aircraft shot down and the disposition of its crew. They probed every crash site and bits of wreckage for remains and pieces of map or ID cards and flight suits. They correlated their information gathered on the scene with that sent by spies from American military bases in South Vietnam and Thailand and with the extremely useful packets containing newspaper articles and, in some cases, high school and college yearbook information sent by Americans who prided themselves on doing all they could to support the just revolution by the peoples of the Democratic Republic of Vietnam against the oppressive regime in the South.

Yes, the Party spelled out, they wanted criminal Apple not only alive, but in a pliable and cooperative mood to meet with a special delegation from the United States; a delegation that would arrive in Hanoi via Bangkok very soon. If all went well, that is, if Apple were so pliable as to agree to an early release, then the prison personnel who participated and helped bring about this progressive change in heart of this black criminal would receive special treatment themselves. In the meantime, prison personnel were to provide a list of names of those criminals who were proving cooperative, and who were perhaps even in favor of the just struggle for peace against the imperialistic oppressor. In the past, he had found only two.

Flak's first awareness was a steady thrumming sound. Hearing was his first sense to transmit to his newly conscious brain. He heard before he saw. He listened to the sound for . . . hours, maybe? He didn't know. He only knew he was not going to open his eyes to see *where* he was, nor was he going to move to find out *what* he was. He didn't want to know if he was a slab of raw beef hung from a meathook or that he was a dead man whose skin had been stretched across a frame. He knew he wasn't alive, he simply couldn't be alive. Not after the centuries of pain and mindless drooling and screaming and being on fire from within. The torture straps, the ropes, the thuds, the blows, the filthy rag stuffed in his mouth. A kaleidoscope of purple and red and black pain and muscles popping and shredded nerve endings . . . no one could live through that. *Thrum, thrum.* The steady thrumming, it suddenly became clear to him, was the big tube of humanity through which all the blood flowed and the nutrients flowed as they were sucked out by . . . by. . . No, it was something else. He knew what it was, and it wasn't any big tube of humanity. It was . . . OH GOD. . . **AAAHHHHHH, AAAHHHHHH, AAAHHHHHH** he screamed, as pain and reality and terror returned in a torrent of agony and streaming hot wires running through his nerves and fire melting his nerve endings. It was rain, and he had been tortured to insanity and death in the rain.

He howled like a dog when he felt the unmistakable touch of a human hand on his arm. "NOOOOOOOOO," he howled and tried to jerk away, but the straps bound him. "NOOOOOOO, NOOOOOOOO," his scream faded as what little strength he possessed gave out. He still felt the touch. He couldn't open his eyes. He didn't *want* to open his eyes. He didn't *want* to see the sallow faces of Big Ugh and Crazy Face and the others who had tortured him into mindless screams until blessed oblivion had occurred. He had one last breath. If he screamed it out, he would be blessed and die. "NOOOOOOOOOO."

A cool hand placed itself on his brow, then a cold cloth was brushed across his sweat-soaked and torn face. A quiet voice murmured liquid tones in his ear.

It was a lie. He was dead or they were just preparing him for more torture. They did that, he knew. They had splashed buckets of water on him and fed him a banana and later, his own vomit and excrement. He was dead; or would be dead; he would die. He willed himself to die. He could not take another second of pain. They were going to torture him again. He was through. "Dear God," he sobbed, "take me, TAKE ME, **TAAAKE MEEEE.**"

The cool cloth again, and the liquid tones. The touch, soothing, the cold cloth. He refused to respond. Then blackness folded into blackness and he knew no more.

She looked at his torn face, slack in repose. She had never seen such deep brown skin or such wiry curls of hair. She traced in wonder his broad nose and lips with her fingers. He lay naked on the white bed in the hospital room the Party had assigned to him. The body that had once been big and robust was now shrunken and wasted. There was hardly a place unbruised or untorn. White stripes of adhesive tape holding the tubes in his arm and nose were his only covering. The doctors had been told to make him alive again, to make him eat and function and look presentable, and, above all, to be pliable, to be kindly disposed toward the North Vietnamese. She thought that was an odd request, but one did not question the Party. She was assigned to be his constant companion, to sleep on the bare cot in his room. There were no others, she was told, who wanted to touch him, to feel his body – this black criminal, this murderer of mothers. But she was lucky, she had been chosen to be allowed to make a contribution to the Party by making this black criminal well and pliant. She herself, the product of a Senegalese Legionnaire and a Vietnamese mother, her features so broad and her hair that refused to lie straight, she herself, who was called Co Dust, had been allowed to serve the Party when she returned from France with a nurse's license. Co Dust meant unmarried girl so useless as to be made of dust. She rinsed another cloth and mopped his brow as the thrumming of the rain on the hospital's tin roof provided a cover to the prayers in her heart of hearts.

For ten days now she had never left his side except to eat and bathe. She had scrubbed and gone with him to the operating room twice; once to repair what had been burst in his stomach, and once when they had to rebreak his left arm and try to straighten it. She marveled he was still alive after the crash he had suffered, and then after the incredibly crude surgery by a doctor who said he hated even touching this black man. She could tell the bent left arm would never be better and was worried about his intestines. The Party did not know it but she had become a Christian in France and she prayed to the Almighty to give her the strength and power to soothe and heal this man who had been through so much. He did not *look* like a murderer; he did not *act* like a murderer.

He awoke a day later, more aware and alert than ever before. Without moving or giving any indication he was conscious, he checked out his senses, one by one. The most prominent input was noise. He heard . . . movement, both far and near. Footsteps, small rattles, an occasional horn. He felt . . . pain, yes, but not electric or blinding pain, just a dull ache over most of his body. He wanted to be more specific about this. It was important. Perhaps he wasn't dead. His hand rested on something. He carefully increased pressure with his finger, not enough so that an observer would see a movement but enough to inform him of the surface upon which his hand rested. His hand was on his leg. His leg felt the pressure and so did his right forefinger. Next, smell. He sampled what was passing through his nose and palate. It was . . . sweet alcohol and . . . hospital.

142

That was all he could think of the smell – the combination of peculiar odors that spelled out hospital. Then all the hospital smell vanished as he smelled and almost tasted in the back of his throat the overlying odor of the spice and *nuoc mam* of Vietnamese food. Now all that was left to sample was sight. Did he dare open his eyes? He *reasoned* he was in a hospital and he *knew* he was in North Vietnam and he *remembered* all the details of being beaten and why he was beaten, and was all this care just to make him well enough and conscious enough to undergo further beating? Would the beating begin again once he was pronounced healed? He had better be very, very careful.

He lay for a long, long time, then, finally, he carefully lifted one eyelid a fraction of a millimeter, just enough to admit light. He decided he had to move the other eye in parallel coordination, otherwise his effort to squint would produce a pronounced muscle movement in his face and somebody might see that and punish him for it. Carefully, carefully, he eased both eyes open just a slit, wary and alert for motion that would mean pain. But he saw no motion, only light, and soon a form took shape and he concentrated and synapses closed and he recognized . . . a girl. This was not what he had expected. Maybe everything before was merely a bad dream, a nightmare.

She was so attuned to his every motion and movement and knew what his hoarse cries had meant that she remained motionless while he experimented with himself and his surroundings. She knew he had to come to terms with the situation of his injuries and capture in his own way and in his own time. She sat motionless as his brown eyes took her in, then roamed the room, then returned instantly to her for a few seconds, then roamed again like a small child wanting to explore but afraid to leave the comfort and safety of its mother. He finally fixated on her. She glanced quickly at the door, then allowed a small smile to creep to her lips and she slowly rose and walked to the bed.

He saw the smile and the movement and watched her approach his side. She looked so calm and real and . . . human.

He could see compassion in her dark eyes. A tear rolled down his cheek. He tried to speak, but she put her finger to his lips and shook her head. He spoke regardless.

"Am I home?" he said in a plaintive voice. "Am I home?"

Her own eyes suddenly glistened like black oil as she took his hand and said quietly, in an accented voice close to his ear, *"Ah, non, chéri.* I am so sorry. You are not home." She took his hand and stroked it.

"How long have I been here? What's wrong with me? Is the war over?" He struggled to get up. She pushed him back down and checked the tubes in place. She put her head close to his.

"I am sorry, the war is not over. You are in the Hanoi City Hospital. You were sick, injured, and now you are getting . . . not sick." She could not think of the English word. She had studied the language in the *lycée* in France, but had had very little practice. She did not know if the Party knew she spoke English or not. It didn't matter, she would be careful. She must keep some secrets from them. They had told her to make him happy in whatever way she could. Once he was well and happy, the Party would deal with him about their requirements. She had been told she had very little time to prepare him.

"Sleep and soon you will be strong and I will answer all your questions." Co Dust stroked his brow until he fell asleep. She looked again at his body and the bruises and tears. *He is very fortunate,* she thought, *to be alive after suffering such terrible injuries when he was shot down.*

The Thirty-Sixth President of the United States, Lyndon Baines Johnson, sat at the end of the conference table, sipping root beer from a glass tumbler. He looked up at the Air Force general standing near the table and put the heavy tumbler down with a crash.

"I'm tired," he said in an angry voice. "I'm tired of feeling rejected by the American people. I'm tired of waking up in the middle of the night worrying about the war. I'm tired of all these personal attacks on me. Do you understand?"

Johnson, a big man who wore wire-rim glasses, was dressed in a gray pin-striped suit and red tie, coat unbuttoned and hanging loose. His heavy face looked tired and worn. Scattered on the table were several files and briefing books.

Across the table from him stood USAF Major General Albert G. "Whitey" Whisenand. General Whisenand, a white-haired, portly man with burn scars on his face, wore his Class A blues with ribbons and command pilot wings. As he studied the President it seemed to him that LBJ didn't fill out his clothes as much as before.

"Well?" the President demanded.

"Yes, sir, I understand," General Whisenand said.

LBJ slapped his hand on the table. "How could you?" he roared. "You're not *President* of the United States. You're not the *leader* of the Republic. You're just another of those pissant generals who — " He stopped in midsentence to rub his face and massaged his temples.

"Sorry, Whitey, gawddammit. Didn't mean to flare up at you. Your old President is tired — mighty tired."

Whitey Whisenand felt a wave of sorrow tinged with pity. Sorrow that this vital man who had once leaped at political problems with verve and talent had reduced himself to ever-increasing isolation, and pity because his overbearing arrogance had blunted his ability to see the public as people who could not be swayed by mere bombast from a former Texas senator, even if he was sitting in the White House.

In previous discussions seven months earlier, in March, LBJ had released two bombshells to Whitey before he made them public. One was that he was going to stop all bombing north of the 20th parallel. "It has to be done," LBJ had said. "Ever since that damned Tet offensive, the American people are upset over every little thing. I *know* – if I stop this bombing up there in North Veetnam they'll be happy." The 20th parallel was a few miles north of the DMZ, in a region called Route Pack I by fliers, but considerably south of the Hanoi/Haiphong port area. Whitey had had to work hard on the President to get him to allow reconnaissance flights north of Pack I to track all the supplies entering the Ho Chi Minh Trail pipeline.

The other bombshell was when LBJ had said he was not going to run for a second term as President of the United States because he had to prosecute the war. Whitey had not been sure he had believed him. At the time, Whitey had thought LBJ was afraid he wouldn't get the nomination, that Kennedy or McCarthy would gun him down. Maybe even Humphrey. Then McCarthy had dropped out and Bobby Kennedy had been shot dead by a deranged man in Los Angeles and Humphrey had become the nominee.

LBJ slumped back and worked on his temples. "Ah, what's the use?" After a few moments he took his hands from his face and looked somewhere in the distance beyond Whitey. "Maybe you can't understand how tired I am," he said, "and how all this gawdamm war business has affected me. And the election, too. There's a tie-in, you know. There has to be. I'm not going to let that Nixon become President of the United States. He wasn't even a good *vice*-president."

A strange look came over his face. "I still have ways of having him defeated. You'll see."

They were on the back porch, the October chill held at bay by the brilliant sunlight. Bird sounds trilled and fluttered through the screened windows. Whitey Whisenand sat on a white wicker chair enhanced with dark green cushions. A matching chair, sofa, and glass-topped coffee table were in the ensemble. Whitey wore old khaki pants and a gray sweatshirt. Part of *The Washington Post* was on his lap. His wife, Sal, stood at her gardening table in a light blue blouse and blue jeans. She was tall, of regal bearing. In contrast to her husband's head of white hair, hers was a blue-black hue which she wore short, so it was more manageable. Sal was British by birth and American by marriage.

Whitey and Sal had grown used to Whitey's need to talk out his thoughts at the end of each workday. She was an astute woman, a product of the British secret intelligence service in World War II, who easily grasped the complexities of Washington politics. Her questions and comments helped her husband better formulate and organize his thoughts. Whitey had met her in the UK in 1944. They had both worked in that red-brick Victorian monstrosity, the Bletchley Park Intelligence Center in Buckinghamshire, northwest of London. At the time, he had been an Army Air Force captain trying to get back into Mustangs, and she was a Wren decoding specialist in the Royal Navy.

Sal had newspaper spread on the table and was repotting some rhododendron for the winter, although it was probably too late, as they had already suffered a hard frost. Some obscure gene from her Anglo-Saxon background forced her to plant things. She bent over to get another clay pot of wilted flowers.

"Such an awful year," she said, and stood up to face Whitey. "The killing of Martin Luther King, as barbaric an act as could

147

be imagined. And the riots afterward . . . well, I just thought the whole country was doomed. The Army having to be called out." She shuddered. "I'll never, never forget those awful nights when Washington was burning, the flames at night turning the sky red . . . smelling the smoke all the way out here."

Whitey rubbed his face. "There's a lot of confusion out there, and hatred. A lot of it directed at Johnson. All he ever wanted was to be loved and respected and he's getting just the opposite. It's all too much for him."

"Poor man," Sal said.

Whitey snorted. "Don't feel sorry for him. Feel sorry for all those American soldiers that are dead because of his waffling."

"But that hatred of LBJ doesn't mean they will vote for Nixon," Sal said.

"Don't be too sure. I think there'll be a backlash." He paused. "And I think he's got something up his sleeve."

"Like what?"

"Our air strikes. He's going to stop them all," Whitey said in a flat voice. "I'm sure of it. He was asking questions just today about the effects of no more raids north of the DMZ. How I thought the South Vietnamese would feel. What I thought the North Vietnamese would do. How the American public would react. He never asked what the military would feel, much less whether they should be in on his decision to stop the strikes."

"And what did you tell him?"

"I said I thought the South Vietnamese would feel betrayed, the North Vietnamese would celebrate a victory, and the American public would feel relieved because they never knew what was going on anyhow. He seemed to take that without too much difficulty, but when I said the American military would see it as a retreat, he became very angry and said all we generals like to do is—"

"Bomb, bomb, bomb," Sal finished for him. "That's what he always says. I don't care if he was in the Navy in World War Two, I think he hates the military." Warming up to the subject, Sal shook a trowel at Whitey as she spoke. "Call it off? Winston wouldn't have done it that way."

148

"No," Whitey said as he walked over and put his arm around his best pal, "he wouldn't. But there is more to this than that." He stood back from her. "I think he will announce his decision to stop all the raids right before the election. I think he will use the lives of all those men to get the public to vote for Humphrey."

"Oh, Whitey, I can't believe that. He wouldn't be that cynical – I'm surprised that you are."

Whitey shook his head. "Just wait, Sal. I have a plan I want him to listen to, but if he won't . . . then it's coming. I can feel it in my bones."

8

Colonel Stanley D. Bryce was the Wing Commander of the famed 8th Tactical Fighter Wing, a position that historically (with one exception) had led to promotion to brigadier general. The one exception had been a commander who had mistakenly imposed teetotalling at the Officer and NCO Clubs, in the assumption that it was *good* for men in combat. "Stan the Man" Bryce conducted a daily ("That's seven-days-a-week daily," he was quick to point out) meeting with his four squadron commanders (all lieutenant colonels) and Major Court Bannister, commander of the Phantom FACs. The purpose of the meetings was to pass information up and down the chain of command about any item that affected combat operations. Things that affected combat operations ranged from available aircraft and aircrews to morale and discipline problems.

Bryce was a well-built man who stood six feet, with smooth black hair combed flat, gray eyes, and broad shoulders. He had a square and pleasant face, his sharp eyes complementing an aggressive upthrust chin. He was a former footballer from the University of Georgia, where he had received his commission from the Air Force ROTC. He sat behind his desk, which displayed a large teak carving of command pilot wings and his name.

Colonel Al Bravord, Bryce's Director of Operations for the 8th Tactical Fighter Wing, sat quietly to one side on a red vinyl couch, smoking a pipe. He had white hair surrounding a bald pate like a monk's tonsure. A former sergeant pilot who had had many fighter kills to his credit in World War II and Korea, he had quiet and unassuming mannerisms, a steel-trap mind, and eyes like a twenty-year-old sniper.

Both colonels and the five unit commanders wore flight suits. Court's black flight suit matched that of the commander of the 497th Night Owl squadron.

The meeting was almost finished. All the happenings of the previous twenty-four hours had been gone over: who had been shot down, who had been saved, what targets had been destroyed, what targets needed to be restruck, how the maintenance, electronics, armament, and weapons people were performing. The meeting was an easy give-and-take until Bryce's final question.

"Bannister, how many trucks have your Phantom FACs killed in the last four weeks?"

Court consulted his notes. "Sir, we've killed seventeen trucks in the last four weeks." The Phantom FACs had been operational for eight months.

"And how many sorties did your men fly during that time and how many strikes did they put in?"

"We fly about thirty per week, so that's 120 in the last four weeks, sir." He calculated rapidly. "And we put in about seventy night strikes."

"Your sortie-to-truck kill ratio is not very impressive," Bryce said. "I'm getting pressure from 7th Air Force."

Seventh Air Force at Tan Son Nhut Air Base outside of Saigon in South Vietnam was in a jumbled command chain combined with 13th Air Force in the Philippines. The two Air Force commands ran the out-country (anything other than South Vietnam) air war and reported to CINCPAC (Commander in Chief, Pacific), a Navy admiral who answered to the Department of Defense.

151

Up to 31 March 1968, the Department of Defense had been under the stewardship of Robert Strange McNamara. Until he had been replaced by Clark Clifford, McNamara had run the DoD and the Vietnam war in an incredibly personal and inept manner. Whereas previous Secretaries of Defense had expended their energies and talents ensuring a good logistics base, adequate budget appropriations, and public support for the military, McNamara had taken over operations as if he were the top general of the combined armed forces.

Some said Jack Kennedy had created a monster when he had hired McNamara and his whiz kids from the Ford Motor Company in 1961 to clean up the defense procurement monolith that encouraged duplicate and costly weapons. It was a monster that maybe Kennedy could have controlled, but President Lyndon Baines Johnson could not. Only the top members of the military knew that, for one year after JFK's assassination in November 1963, President Johnson had barely inquired as to the status of the pending Vietnam conflict, much less given direction to McNamara – who had felt free to do as he wished. Ever a slave to the bottom line, McNamara had instituted a few needed reforms. They had been instituted, however, at the expense of a line of communication and trust between the military and McNamara and his boys. As one grizzled Admiral had put it, "Better cholera than McNamara."

In a few deft strokes fueled by monumental ego, McNamara had replaced the traditional steel links in the chain of command with telephone wire and radio circuits and computer paper from which he demanded bottom-line information. How many bombs and bullets expended to ensure a body count of enemy dead commensurate with good Ivy League management principles? Bannister and the others at his level knew they had to produce quantifiable results, which was given to them after each sortie as BDA, Bomb Damage Assessment. They would dutifully report their BDA to the debriefing officer, who would enter it into the big DoD computer. Not being veterans of World War II or Korea, where the position of the front line was more important than bean-counting, McNamara's men thought this was how a war was run.

"No, sir," Court responded to Bryce's comment, "the truck-kill count is not impressive. What is impressive is that truck traffic on the Trail at night has just about come to a halt. And since day strikes have stopped the traffic flow during daylight hours, that means the Trail is almost bottled up. Which fulfills one of the CINCPAC mission requirements: stop the flow of traffic down the Ho Chi Minh Trail day and night."

Al Bravord spoke up. "I'll tell you what is impressive, Stan," he said, looking at the Wing Commander. "These lads have destroyed nearly 400 guns."

Bryce nodded. "Bannister, how do you account for such a discrepancy, destroying so many more guns than trucks?"

"First off, sir, to me, stopping the traffic flow is accomplishing our mission. I compare it to fighters defending a target. Sure, they'd like to shoot down the attacking bombers, but their mission is to ensure the targets are not destroyed. If by attacking the bombers they force them to jettison their ordnance before reaching the target area, then they have saved the targets. If they can shoot down some bombers while accomplishing the mission, fine. But the original mission to protect the targets was achieved. Our original mission is to stop supply movement. We're doing it. As far as killing so many guns, we can see them when they shoot far easier than we can see trucks, so it's relatively easy to take them out."

"Do you think you can get more truck kills if you equip the Phantom FACs with harder weapons? Replace your marking rockets with bombs, for example?" Bryce asked.

"No, sir, I don't. First off, our job is to *find* the trucks, then call in strike aircraft to kill them. That's the whole mission and purpose of the Phantom FACs. We don't need bombs – the strikers carry the bombs. We need the marking rockets to show the strikers where their targets are. But there is something else I want to bring up. We can't see the trucks unless the night is exceptionally clear. We need night eyeballs. And the enemy isn't dumb. Right now they hole up off the road when they hear us coming down the Trail. But they will soon start rolling again, using more deceptive methods once they realize they aren't being hammered so much. Then the traffic will pick up and the supplies will start getting through to South Vietnam again."

Bryce dismissed the other commanders and asked Court to stay behind. Bravord remained on the couch.

"I know how hard you worked to get this unit going," Bryce said, "and now you are telling me it may become ineffective."

"Yes, sir, it may." Court paused. "I briefed exactly this subject a few weeks ago to you and to Ops and Plans at 7th."

Bryce looked exasperated. "It didn't take. It's a big war. Let's go over it again. What did you tell them? What did you tell *us*?" he corrected himself.

"I said the statistics of supplies moving down the Trail prove we have cut traffic dramatically. The flow is definitely less. Then I said that if they wanted more night truck kills, we'd have to have a way to see at night."

"Starlight scopes are too big?" Starlight scopes were electronic light-amplifying devices that looked like fat telescopes.

"Too big, too clumsy, and they restrict vision too much. Like trying to look at the Trail through a toilet paper tube."

Bryce nodded. "You're interested in the AC-130s we're getting, is that it?"

"Yes, sir. Major Hostettler worked out a plan where we could suppress flak for them as well as augment their firepower."

Dick Hostettler, as the wing intelligence officer, spent much of his time with the wing weapons and tactics officers, devising new ways to kill. The AC-130 gunships were huge four-engined (turboprops with over 4,000 horsepower each) transports under modification to carry 7.62mm, 20mm, and 40mm guns firing from the left side of the fuselage. Future plans called for a 105mm gun to be mounted in the plane. The original idea called for the big gunships to go out along the Trail and hunt trucks. They were being outfitted to carry radar, low-light-level TV, infrared heat sensors, and a unit to detect the emanations from spark plugs.

In his briefing to 7th earlier that year, Court had gotten wound up, something young majors shouldn't do when talking to full bird colonels. He had said he and his Phantom FACs were having trouble killing trucks. He said they had dropped a lot of flares, called in a lot of strike birds, dumped a lot of ordnance, caused a few secondary explosions, but had few positive truck kills, although they had wiped out plenty of guns. He had said that their airplanes humming along the Trail dropping flares gave the gomers plenty of advance warning to pull over and watch the fighter pilots make little karst rocks out of big ones. While Court had gotten his point across, 7th was chock-full of men with more experience and higher rank than Major Courtland Edm. Bannister. Men who had *their* pet ways to win the war, and fast FACs on the Ho Chi Minh Trail, day or night, wasn't one of them. The only really high-ranking man who had stopped in at Court's brief had been Major General Milton Berlin, 7th AF Director of Operations. He had done so because he had played a role in getting the Phantom FACs set up in the first place and was interested in any of their activities and their successes. With him had been his assistant, Colonel Tim Mayberry.

"I think you have a good idea there," Bryce said. "Get down to Tan Son Nhut and liaise with their advance party at 7th. Take Hostettler if you need him."

"Yes, sir," Court said and departed.

1030 HOURS LOCAL, TUESDAY 15 OCTOBER 1968
HQ. 7TH AIR FORCE
TAN SON NHUT AIR BASE, SAIGON
REPUBLIC OF VIETNAM

Court landed his F-4D Phantom, with Major Dick Hostettler in the backseat, on runway 25 Left, Tan Son Nhut Air Base. He was directed by Ground Control to park in the transient aircraft area. He did so, shut down, and was met by a blue flight-line van, which took the two men to Base Operations. From there they were picked up by a Motor Pool taxi. Both men wore black flight suits. Hostettler, standing 5'10" and weighing a muscular 220, filled his like a guard on a football team – which he had been at West Point. The taxi dropped them off at the large 7th Air Force Headquarters building.

Twenty-four hours a day, 7th AF was a droning bee-hive of activity. From the big building came the command and control of 70,000 airmen and pilots, and 1,500 air-planes on twenty bases in South Vietnam and Thailand. Additionally, 7th also had operational control over 400 more airplanes based in the Philippines, Okinawa, and Guam. Commander, 7th AF, a four-star USAF general, worked directly as the deputy for air for COMUSMACV, four-star Army General William Westmoreland.

Court and Hostettler found the small office of the advance AC-130 party, Lieutenant Colonel Jack Nailor, in charge. "I got your TWX," Nailor said, referring to the message Court had sent about their visit. He was a dark-haired man with a thin angular face. He looked tired. "I'm damn short of time but your thesis intrigues me. You two really think fighter aircraft can help a gunship kill trucks, do you? Suppose you show me how." He pointed to a small blackboard next to a map of Southeast Asia.

Hostettler took some chalk and drew a squiggly line across the board. Along the line he made several small rectangles at one-inch intervals. "These are trucks along the Trail. Show me the attack pattern your gunship would fly."

Nailor drew a series of loops crossing the road, followed by a three-quarter circle. "We have three phases," he said. "Search, detect, attack. In the search phase we use all our sensors to detect heat, movement, metal, and/or spark plugs." He pointed to the loops. "These are the search loops over the Trail. Once we detect a target, we set up for a firing pass." He pointed to the three-quarter circle and explained the basic firing geometry for a side-firing gunship.

"Unlike you fighter guys, who must align the longitudinal axis of your aircraft with the target and dive in a straight line toward the target, we set up an orbit and shoot laterally from the

156

gun ports on the left side of our C-130." He smiled and paused for a moment. "You might find it interesting to know that the original idea came from missionaries in South America trying to make contact with Indians. They made pylon turns over them and let down a bucketful of trinkets on a rope." In a pylon turn the pilot maintains a constant ground reference point off the low wing of his aircraft. "What we do, instead of letting down a bucket of goodies, we sight down the line and let down a stream of lead. The pilot looks through a gunsight out his left window and aligns crosshairs on a digital display. He tells the gunners which guns he wants and presses the button on his control wheel. He has his choice of four 7.62mm miniguns or four 20mm M-61 Vulcan Gatlings, or both at the same time. We only have one C-130 test bird in the theater – we call it Gunship Two because it's a follow-on to Spooky, the AC-47. Later birds will have 40mm cannons instead of the 7.62 and maybe someday a 105mm tube." He frowned. "You probably know we've lost several of the early Spookys on the Trail. The threat got too high and they had no night capability beyond what the pilot's eyeballs could do. That's another reason we have the C-130: besides carrying more and bigger guns, all its sensors provide night vision. And flying at night gives the airplane a great measure of security from non-radar-directed guns."

"And that's where we Phantoms come in," Court said. He drew several wide circles above those of the gunship search-and-attack patterns. "We can have one bird at a time orbiting your gunship and tuned to the same radio channel. You orbit from 8 to 10,000, we orbit from 15 to 18,000. If anybody shoots at you, we see it and give a warning as well as roll in on the gun. You move to a safer area while we either take out the gun or call in strike birds to take out the gun. Secondly, and here is the most important point, when you find a series of trucks, we augment your firepower. You shoot up a few and make some flamers, or you can mark with tracers, or you can throw out a few of those burning logs that make a good night beacon to show us where the trucks are. Same as before, we roll in or we call in strike birds to help you kill the trucks."

Nailor grinned. "You sound like you're begging, Bannister. I've heard of your Phantom FACs. New outfit, isn't it? Running out of a mission already?"

"Not exactly," Court flared. "I just think if we work together we can come up with a more efficient way to kill trucks." He tapped the map next to the blackboard and pointed to the hydra-headed black band coming from North Vietnam through the mountain passes of Mu Gia and Ban Karai into Laos, then farther south in Laos to re-emerge into South Vietnam. The areas the Ho Chi Minh Trail hydra passed through Laos were code-named Steel Tiger and Tiger Hound. "And there are going to be a lot more of them. Now that we can't hit north of the 20th parallel, the trucks are going to have it pretty easy transiting North Vietnam from Hanoi down to Laos and the Trail."

Hostettler broke in. "Preliminary intell reports and aerial recce photos show about a 50 percent increase in southbound truck traffic in North Vietnam headed toward the Lao border." He placed a staff study on a corner of Nailor's desk. "All the details and diagrams are in here."

Nailor checked a schedule board on the wall. "The gunship is on a tight test schedule. It's really a breadboard model on which we try out the new sensing equipment and guns. Right now it's working the ground support mission in II Corps. After that we are scheduled to fly out of Ubon for six weeks. Some of the time is scheduled for fire control harmonization flights on the Chandy bombing range, some of the time to fly the Trail and see what we can see, all at night, of course. I'll try to work out something with the higher-ups to let you guys fly with us and try out your plan. I can't guarantee permission on this test phase. It would be a cinch to try later this fall or early next year when we get all the birds in place. I'll let you know soonest." He picked up Hostettler's staff study. "Meantime I'll study this and pass it on to the 7th AF Directorate of Tactical Analysis."

"You have a call sign yet?" Court asked.

"Yeah – Spectre."

Court and Hostettler went back to the flight line, cranked up, and were back at Ubon by 1700 hours.

En route, Chef Hostettler said he and Grailson had had a long talk about the bash for the Jollys and Wolf Lochert that was to take place that very night. Chef said they had prepared several colorful and, they hoped, memorable events. Court would see. After they landed, Hostettler scurried off. "Gotta hustle," he yelled over his shoulder. "The party starts in two hours."

1330 HOURS LOCAL, TUESDAY 15 OCTOBER 1968
SITUATION ROOM, THE WHITE HOUSE
WASHINGTON, DC

On the first level of the White House basement, down a corridor past uniformed civilian security guards, was a crowded room with a low acoustical tile ceiling and no windows. Called the Situation Room, it was the nerve center that received all the processed communications and reports from the Pentagon and other important agencies. Clattering teletypes labeled with major wire service logos spouted news and intelligence from around the globe. There were pneumatic tubes to send and receive messages throughout the building, and a teletype hot line for Moscow that operated via the secure Pentagon communications net. On the wall were four clocks with Washington, Saigon, GMT, and what was called official Presidential time that President Lyndon Johnson kept regardless of where he was. The overhead lights were low; the information screens cast a green tinge over the military and civilian duty officers. Tiny colored action lights were sprinkled over a map of the world on the far wall. From within the main room (the command post), and down a few steps was another room with a long, highly polished oak conference table and pull drapes on the walls that covered maps of current hot spots. There was an assortment of telephones, three of which were secure connections to vital military installations. Among the telephones was a direct line to the Prime Minister of Great Britain. Others went direct to American embassies throughout the world.

The President walked in and sat at the conference table. Major General Whitey Whisenand entered behind him, carrying his battered USAAF issue briefcase. He suddenly remembered to button the top button of his tunic. He had just come from his small office and, preoccupied with the President's sudden demand to hear his plan, had forgotten to check until just now. The open top button of the four on his tunic was his way of showing he was an old-time fighter pilot. The tradition had started in World War I, when the flamboyant fighter pilots in their wood-and-cloth crates had found the high-buttoned collar of their uniforms too restricting and took to leaving them open. The tradition had been passed down to those who now wore the blue Air Force single-breasted uniform tunic whose collar ended in lapels that lay flat. Whitey had another more permanent manifestation that he had once worn the equipment of a jet pilot. During the war in Korea he had crashed on takeoff when the engine in his F-80 had failed. The resultant fire had burned his hands and the part of his face not covered by his oxygen mask. The white unburned area of his face, in contrast to the rosy red burn marks, made him look as if he had just removed his oxygen mask after a long flight.

The President sat heavily in his chair and looked up. "Just tell me something I can manage," he said in an exasperated voice, ready, finally, to hear the plan Whitey Whisenand had put together. "Like, how do I stop the flow of supplies down Ho's Trail through Laos without flattening Hanoi? Or without, as your General LeMay once said, bombing them back to the stone age? I try to be nice to Ho Chi Minh and where does it get me?"

Be nice to Ho Chi Minh? Whitey mentally shook his head, then remembered something he had studied recently. He said to LBJ, "I want to quote someone for you before I begin. Clausewitz says the following in his book *On War:* 'Kindhearted people might, of course, think there was some ingenious way to disarm or defeat an enemy without too much bloodshed, and might imagine this to be a true goal of the art of war. Pleasant as it sounds, it is a fallacy that must be exposed. War is such a dangerous business that the mistakes which come from kindness are the very worst.'"

LBJ waved his hand as if at a pesky gnat. "All right, all right. I don't need the thoughts of some long-dead German. Just tell me how I stop the flow of supplies."

"Mr. President, you have always had the entire JCS to answer that question. Not to mention your Secretary of Defense."

The President fixed Whitey with a scornful look. "Let me show you what Mister McNamara wrote about bombing just before he left office. You've never seen such a load of horseshit." He pawed through a manila file folder and handed Whitey a Department of Defense memorandum sheet.

The tragic and long drawn-out character of that conflict in South Vietnam makes very tempting the prospect of replacing it with some new kind of air campaign against North Vietnam. But however tempting, – such an alternative seems to me completely illusory. To pursue this objective would not only be futile, but would involve risk to our personnel and to our nation that I am unable to recommend.

Whitey made no comment. Instead, he walked to one of the wall drapes.

Johnson made an exaggerated sigh. "It won't do any good, but go ahead, show me your plan."

Whitey pulled aside the drape to reveal the map of Southeast Asia he had prepared. He pointed first to the rail lines from China and the seaports that funneled war matériel into the Hanoi area.

"We can stop the supplies coming into North Vietnam at these places. About 15 percent comes down the rail lines, 85 percent from Haiphong Harbor. The supplies then must be delivered into South Vietnam to the North Vietnamese Army and what is left of the Viet Cong. The US Navy and the South Vietnamese Navy under Operation Market Time have done a fine job preventing the North from resupplying by sea their troops in the South. Nothing gets through their blockades. Same thing at the DMZ, the Demilitarized Zone. US and ARVN troops in Eye Corps prevent direct overland resupply." Whitey made a small smile and said, "And of course outside of a helicopter or two, there is no air transport capability from North to South Vietnam."

"You've been telling me this for years," the President said. "I only listen to you because . . . because your sincerity always impresses me. Damn few others around here I call sincere." What could have been a grin crossed his face. "You might be repetitive, but you don't try to bullshit me." He waved his hand for Whitey to continue.

"Here is what I think we should do, Mister President. We take out the SAM sites as required, we hit the MiG bases, and we cut the rail lines and keep them cut. But rather than mine Haiphong Harbor, I say we should destroy the dredge that keeps it open. The Red River that flows into it deposits tons of silt every day. Periodically, the silt must be shifted and removed. Without dredging, the harbor would be useless in a matter of weeks. Furthermore, the sunken dredge itself would help block the harbor. This would eliminate the risks to the Navy minelaying aircraft as well as not damage ships that belong to nations that are supposed to be friends of ours."

"You mean like Sweden and Great Britain," LBJ said in disgust.

It was an interesting anomaly. British ships regularly offloaded non-war supplies for the North Vietnamese; at the same time hundreds of British males per year volunteered for the US Army to go fight in Vietnam (due to immigration laws, few were accepted). Just the opposite pertained with the Swedes: while they off-loaded supplies in North Vietnam, some American soldiers stationed in Germany with more of a predilection for pot than patriotism deserted and found refuge in that cold country which advertised itself as a warm safe-haven for Vietnam war objectors.

Of course the Soviet Union and other East Bloc countries were the biggest suppliers of North Vietnam. They shipped in millions of tons of supplies plus all the oil and petroleum products the communist North Vietnamese war machine required.

"Yes, I do," Whitey replied. "And there are three more proposals for which I need approval."

LBJ slowly nodded for him to proceed.

"First is the destruction of a portion of the dikes around Hanoi."

"Oh, no!" LBJ roared. "All those civilians would drown. You told me many times that was why we should not take out those damn dikes."

"Yes, sir, that's true. I don't want the drownings. What I do want is to take certain dikes out in the dry season a month or so before the rainy season would cause flooding."

"What the hell for?"

"Three reasons. One is that the North Vietnamese have known all along that we would not bomb the dikes, so they have put air defense centers, anti-aircraft guns, and petroleum tanks on the tops of the dikes – they are thirty and forty feet across, you know. They are military installations, hence are legitimate targets that deserve to be destroyed. Secondly, they would have to put tens of thousands of workers and soldiers on the job to repair the dikes before the rains. This would further weaken the economy and slow the war effort in the South. Thirdly, such a decisive act would show the North Vietnamese we are finally getting serious about bringing them to their knees and that maybe next time we really would take the dikes out when there is water behind them to flood Hanoi."

"You said you had three things you wanted approved. What are the other two?"

"Smash and capture the communist sanctuary camps in Cambodia while at the same time we cut the Ho Chi Minh Trail in half by sending American and Vietnamese troops straight across the Laotian panhandle to Thailand."

"Invade Cambodia and invade Laos? You're crazy. They're both neutral countries." LBJ tapped his finger on the table. "You're crazy, all right. You tell me you have a plan that not only incorporates bombing, but the invasion by American boys

163

of Cambodia and Laos as well. I don't know whether to laugh or to cry. Both those countries are neutral."

"Mister President, they are neutral in name only. Sihanouk in Cambodia is already complaining to us in secret communiqués that he is unhappy with the North Vietnamese occupation of the western part of his country. Of course, he brought it on himself by letting them use that area, in addition to his providing the port of Sihanoukville for them to run supplies from the Gulf of Siam to South Vietnam. Simultaneously, up north, the Laotian Royalists and neutralists are unhappy with the North Vietnamese occupation of the panhandle of their country – not to mention the North Vietnamese holding the northeast section of Laos while trying to capture the Plaine des Jarres."

"We have to respect their neutrality," the President interrupted. "And goddamm it, that's what I have been doing all along. We've all those damn treaties and things."

"Sir," Whitey began, "under the 1907 Hague Treaty—"

"*Another* damn treaty," LBJ interrupted.

"This is different," Whitey continued, unperturbed. "Under the 1907 Hague Treaty, a neutral is a neutral only so long as it can maintain its neutrality. Neither Cambodia nor Laos is capable of doing that. In both cases our enemy, the communist forces from North Vietnam, are using and holding territory in these so-called neutralist countries against that country's will. Under the rules of international law we have the right to pursue our enemies into those countries. It is time for us to go on the offensive."

Whitey tried hard not to recite as if speaking to a dull-witted child. He knew LBJ to be anything but dull-witted – until it came to making hard decisions that might damage his reputation at home and abroad. Then he would do his best to compromise, to satisfy both sides while obtaining some goal of his own. At home he pushed his desire for both guns *and* butter: win the Vietnam war, but don't raise taxes, while spending vast sums on his Great Society social programs. Abroad, LBJ wanted acclamation as a great US president, not as a despot hell-bent on pulverizing a small Asian nation.

"Have you talked to anyone on the JCS about this?"

"Yes, I have. They are busy trying to figure out what the new Secretary of Defense is like and right now don't want to make any waves.

The new SecDef, Clark Clifford, had queried the Department of Defense for the status of the war in Vietnam and for whatever recommendations the military might have for a conclusion. Rumor had it he was unhappy with the slowness and lack of depth in the response he was getting from military leaders.

Whitey pointed to the eastern Laotian panhandle. "South Vietnam looks like a bow and the Ho Chi Minh Trail running down eastern Laos is the bowstring. The Trail is literally the shortest distance from north to south, and it bypasses all our troops by running through the Laotian-Cambodian sanctuary." He traced the east-west line he had drawn, extending the DMZ across the thinnest part of the Laotian panhandle over to Thailand. "Here, we cut the supply trail." He pointed to the area of Cambodia called the Parrot's Beak that jutted into the portion of South Vietnam near Saigon. This was the southern end of the Ho Chi Minh Trail.

"Down here in Cambodia I suggest two days of concentrated air strikes followed by a lightning ground attack by our troops to capture high-ranking commanders and documents, to prove what Ho Chi Minh has been up to in a so-called neutral country. Maybe even send in some of our more critical journalists and TV crews to record what we find."

President Johnson leaned forward on the conference table and studied the wall map. He began tapping a pencil against a yellow legal tablet in front of him. The only other noise in the room was the soft hiss from the air vents. He put the pencil down, leaned back, and regarded Whitey Whisenand through tired, red-rimmed eyes. He rubbed his face and smoothed his forehead.

"No. I cannot agree to those actions – and I'll tell you why. But you must never tell the reason to anyone until I make it public." He looked at Whitey for agreement.

After a pause, Whitey said, "I'm not sure I can agree to stipulations. If my plan proves sound and you don't agree, I may want to—"

"You may want to NOTHING," the President thundered. "Now hear me out, dammit." He stood up abruptly, leaned forward, and rested his fists on the conference table. "I will not be here to see what you propose, this plan of yours, to conclusion. I do not want to start something I cannot finish. I do not want to start something that may go very, very badly and then have to turn it over to someone else. Do you understand?"

"Mister President, there is a good possibility that if you implement my three-pronged attack with sudden resolve and fierceness, it would bring the North Vietnamese to the negotiating table with far less intransigence than they have shown up to now. We are, after all, not out to destroy North Vietnam. We are out to prevent them from taking over South Vietnam by force. And because of these new tactics, the negotiations could lead to *our* withdrawal and *their* withdrawal from South Vietnam. It is something to think about."

Lyndon Baines Johnson looked at Whitey Whisenand and snorted. "Something to think about." He slammed his fist on the table. "SOMETHING TO THINK ABOUT." He drew himself up to his full height, thrust his chest out. "Whisenand, what in Gawd's green earth do you suppose I think about day and night? I think about THE GAWDDAMMED WAR, that's what I think about." He snorted again in derision. "And you, you pissant general, you have the nerve, THE NERVE, to tell YOUR PRESIDENT the gawddammed war is SOMETHING TO THINK ABOUT. You disgust me."

Major General Albert G. Whisenand, United States Air Force, stiffened, his face a mask of cold indignation. His two years of watching this man ruin the American military surfaced as barely controllable bile.

"Mister President, if there is any disgust in this room, it is on my part at you for your squandering of lives of our soldiers while you pursue will-o'-the-wisp, half-baked military and economic plans without having the slightest knowledge of what you are doing. You are a disaster as a Commander in

Chief of the Armed Forces of the United States. I can no longer stay in your employ. Effective immediately, I resign from this position."

Johnson smashed his fist on the table. "Whisenand, you don't know the half of what goes on around here and you don't understand politics by one piece of a sick cow's turd. You who are such a bomb-happy general . . . let me tell you, I'm STOPPING all bombing north of the DMZ. You hear me? No more strikes north of the Demilitarized Zone. Now take that to your precious Chairman, and while you're there tell him for me YOU'RE FIRED."

"Sir," Whitey spit out, "you don't understand. I'm quitting you."

"No, Whisenand," Johnson roared, "you don't understand. Nobody quits *me*. *I'm* firing *you*. Now get out of here."

9

The party was to kick off promptly at 1900 hours when the seven off-duty members of the Phantom FACs would appear at the hospital with a rented Thai baht bus to pick up the men they planned to honor. The bus was then scheduled to tour the base to allow the honored guests to receive accolades from the fighter squadrons. It would pull up to the Officer's Club promptly at 1930 and the festivities would begin.

The base commander had warned Hostettler about the huge soiree he was hosting in the Officer's Club for the visiting congressional delegation and the local Thai Ubon village dignitaries. "Keep your people on the patio and keep the noise and foul language down," the base commander had ordered. Base commanders had all the house-keeping duties on an air base, thereby relieving the wing commander for operational concerns. Base commanders in combat zones were generally known for their tactful ability to allow shenanigans in the Officer and NCO Clubs that would automatically provoke court-martial in the States.

Doc Russell, dressed in fatigues, had been prepping the honored guests with mission whiskey at the hospital in the doctor's lounge since 1700.

"Say again about this mission whiskey, Doc," Joe Kelly

asked. Because neither he nor Bernick had been wounded, they had reported back to Udorn the previous Saturday, immediately after the weather had cleared up. They had returned to Ubon two hours ago on a courier flight to attend the party and were to fly back to Udorn with Manuel Dominguez the next day. They both wore their bright-green Jolly Green Giant party suits and had brought one for Dominguez. An Air America plane would be in to get Wolf Lochert at 0800 the following morning. The number two PJ, Hiram Bakke, was no longer at the Ubon hospital. His severe leg wound had required he be medevaced to the big Army hospital in Saigon.

"Mission whiskey is, young man," said Lieutenant Colonel Conrad Russell, MD, USAF, in a stentorian tone made rich by the whiskey, "the remnants of an old Air Force tradition." He held up a tumblerful of Jack Daniel's and examined the amber liquid against the light from the window. "Not bad," he said, and took a dainty sip – his sixteenth of the past hour. "Back in the big one, the one we won, I might add, and in Korea, the one we tied, I might add, the hospital and clinics were provided whiskey to equal one shot per pilot per day. Supposed to be dispensed in the intell rooms at postmission debriefs. Help the aircrew unwind after a mission. We'd order it through the pharmacy, just like any other medicine, in accordance with Air Force Reg 160-18. Led to a lot of pleasant moments, it did. Free, of course." He reached into his black doctor's bag and pulled out the nearly empty fifth of Jack Daniel's. "Let me top you off."

Joe Kelly held out one of the white coffee mugs Doc Russell had handed out. "Looks like it's no longer free and you're buying."

"It's no longer free and I'm buying. It is my privilege and rare pleasure to top you off, sir. And you, sir, and you too, sir." Doc Russell carefully filled the mugs of Kelly, Dominguez, and Bernick. Wolf Lochert wasn't drinking. He wore a cotton sport shirt and dark pants he had purchased at the BX. His folded green beret was tucked under his belt.

"Gentlemen, a salute to warriors." Doc Russell tipped his mug.

169

"Warriors," the others said and sipped their whiskey.

"To Colonel Shilleto," Kelly said, and the men drank again.

Wolf took a deep draught from the Coca-Cola can he had in his fist. He rarely drank and was dangerous when he did. He stood up.

"I owe my life to many people. There have been other battles, other places. This time it started with a little guy named Tewa." He tilted his Coke. "To him." He didn't mention he had saved Tewa's life when the C46 had gone down. The others held their drinks up. "Tewa," they said, and drank.

Manuel "Little Cat" Dominguez looked like a disfavored sparring partner of Cassius Clay. Slitty eyes peered from an overripe eggplant face. His head had been shaved following the circular bullet path, making what hair he had remaining on top look like that of a rag doll. Next to him was his shot-up helmet Joe Kelly had brought back to him. It had a big red bow tied around it and a note saying:

> To Little Cat Dominguez
> This is your life.
> Signed,
> GOD

Wolf Lochert's grizzled face looked pale, but his voice was hearty when he said to Dominguez, "Here, this is for you." He handed him a large bag of Fritos he had purchased from the Base Exchange earlier. Attached to the bag was a note Wolf had printed on a hospital Rx memo:

> TO MANUEL DOMINGUEZ,
> I OWE YOU FRITOS FOR LIFE.
> SIGNED THIS FIFTEENTH DAY OF OCTOBER 1968,
> WOLFGANG X. LOCHERT
> LTC, USASF

"I'm overwhelmed, Colonel," Dominguez said. "Simply overwhelmed. Thank you." He popped the bag and offered Fritos all around. Soon the small lounge sounded like a herd of eight-footed elephants loose in a cracker factory.

"And I have something for you," Wolf said to Joe Kelly. He rummaged in a brown paper bag and pulled out a 105mm howitzer shell lined with glass. Brazed to the shell was a carabineer, and snapped into the carabineer was a Special Forces descender. "This is so you can drink and descend . . . or descend and drink, or whatever you want to do."

Kelly dumped his whiskey into the clanking apparatus and used both hands to hold it to his mouth. He lowered it and smacked his lips. "Ahh, good. Fits just right," he said, beaming. He tilted it toward Wolf and took another swig. "You sure know how to do it up right, Colonel. Thanks." Kelly put the 105mm shell down and reached into his leg pocket and pulled out something folded and held it up. "For you," he said to Tech Sergeant Dan Bernick and handed it over. "For outstanding work on the hoist, I present you with the award of the golden glove."

Dan Bernick unfolded a left-hand electrical linesman's glove that had been painted a bright golden hue. "Well, doggone, Captain, that's right nice of you," he said and put the glove on.

Outside, raucous noise broke the serenity of the hospital area. The anemic horn from the baht bus (so named because for the one-baht coin – about 20 cents – a passenger could ride from the air base to the town of Ubon) was joined by squawking sounds that could best be likened to the slow strangling of a fat swan.

One sound, reminiscent of a flatulent duck intermixed with other less identifiable sounds, became louder until it was outside the lounge. The door flew open and Lieutenant

Rolly Grailson and Captain Donny Higgens burst into the room. Grailson tootled a child's tin horn while Higgens blew arpeggios on a black Bakelite duck call.

"Gentlemen," Grailson announced, "yon chariot awaits your most exalted and honored presence." Both men were dressed in their black party suits.

Party suits had become a widespread tradition in the Vietnam war. It was the perfect marriage between inventive fighter pilots and the plethora of starving tailors in South Vietnam and Thailand. Cut in the pattern of the K-2B flight suit of the material and color of the crewman's choice, each party suit displayed highly creative patches, emblems, labels, badges, insignia, graffiti, and other memorabilia of the wearer. Each squadron had a color and design unique unto itself. Party suits of the Phantom FACs were an unimaginative black with highly imaginative white codpieces. The overall effect was startling. The codpieces were held in place by Velcro and could be removed if the occasion demanded. Phantom FAC Captain Tom Partin had thought of the exotic costumal addition and had immediately been given the sobriquet Cod Piece Partin.

The men trooped out the door behind Grailson and Higgens. As they approached the open-sided bus, Grailson held up a hand. "Trooops . . . halt. We have for you a special surprise."

From a concealed spot on top of the bus, a barefoot figure clad in a black flight suit but wearing the full black mask of a Ninja leaped to the ground and started twirling and slicing a huge Samurai sword in ever-decreasing arcs and circles around the astounded helicopter crewmen while uttering wild "yahs" and "hahs." The Ninja singled out Dominguez and quickly cut him from the crowd, then did the same with Joe Kelly, who by now knew who was wearing the funny clothes and waving a fake sword.

"Hah, yourself, you Ninja nincompoop," Joe Kelly said and leaped out to do battle, waving a wooden pencil he plucked from his pocket. The sword whistled through the air, coming ever closer to fearless Joe Kelly, who blithely waved his pencil sword, then moved in for the kill. With a blinding slash the Ninja neatly severed the pencil exactly two inches from Kelly's outstretched fingers.

"Jesus Christ," the shaken Kelly said as he leapt back two feet in a blinding move of his own that some thought even faster than the flashing sword.

"Tanaka, you Jap bastard," Manuel Dominguez said and leapt to hug the Ninja, who had stopped his war dance and was stuffing the giant sword in its ornate curved scabbard. The startled Ninja stepped backwards and tripped over the long scabbard, tumbling the two men to the ground.

"Revenge, Tanaka, you Jap bastard," Kelly shrieked and grabbed and shook a beer and sprayed it full into the eyes of the man wearing the Ninja mask.

"I say, did someone call me?" Captain Kenichi Tanaka said in an affected English accent from behind Kelly's back.

"What the hell?" Kelly said. He swooped and pulled the mask from the Ninja's head and stared into the eyes of a man he had never seen before.

"I say, you ruffians," Tanaka said, "what are you doing spraying beer all over my dear friend and fellow Phantom FAC, Mike Steffes, who just this evening learned how to handle my authentic Samurai sword?"

"Just this evening?" Kelly gulped.

"Shit," Dominguez said and rolled over and pulled Tanaka's legs out from under him and tried to stuff dirt in his ears.

Kelly thought that a splendid idea after being so badly abused, and he helped the dirt on its journey with beer spray.

When it was all over the three men, soaked in beer and panting, stood up and linked arms in a huddle and yelled out their RED-TAGGED BASTARD calls to the cheers and applause of those watching.

When they calmed down, the men took their places on the baht bus, which had open sides and seats facing forward. The Phantom FACs handed each man a cold Budweiser from a garbage can full of ice and beer. When Wolf Lochert turned down the offer, Donny Higgens blew a startled quack, followed by ripples of duck laughter. Wolf glared at him and took a pull at his Coca-Cola.

173

Grailson took the wheel (the Thai driver sat behind him, a five-dollar bill clutched in one hand and a cold beer in the other) and steered the bus down to the flight line for a tour of the fighter squadrons. Once on the ramp, one Phantom FAC cranked up a hand siren while at the back of the bus two others popped red smoke flares. All the aircrew from the squadrons came out to applaud and whistle as the bus drove slowly by.

The sun was at the horizon as the bus pulled up to the patio behind the Officer's Club. The patio, the size of a tennis court, was a slab of concrete covered by a wooden roof attached to the main club roof and supported by wooden pillars. It was open on all sides except where it was connected to the Officer's Club, where a door opened onto the patio.

The fresh evening breeze began to cool the sweat-drenched men as they stepped down from the bus, unloaded the garbage can full of beer, and with exaggerated pig snorts fell upon the linen-covered table crowded with Thai hors d'oeuvres arranged by the club officer, Major Dick "The Chef" Hostettler. Grailson and Higgens played an unintelligible duet on their musical instruments, the tin horn and the duck call. Doc Russell beamed his beatific Baby Huey smile and nodded around at all present. He held his whiskey in an IV bottle and turned the tap when he needed more. Joe Kelly, Manuel Dominguez, and Dan Bernick were surrounded by admiring Phantom FACs who were trying to teach them the words to "Brown, Brown."

Wolf Lochert let a quarter-smile play across the right-hand corner of his mouth. He looked at the cod pieces and the bizarre flight suits, heard the cacophony, and rasped to Court Bannister and Tom Partin, "Good to see troops enjoy themselves, but you flyboys are sorta strange." It didn't occur to Wolf that the SF habit of sticking a wet thumb in a buddy's ear as a form of greeting was anything remotely considered bizarre. The two pilots laughed as they walked over to where Dick Hostettler was doing something to a large meaty object on a spit rotated by a small Thai waiter. The spit was braced over glowing charcoal in a fifty-five-gallon drum cut in half down its length.

"Suckling pig," Hostettler said by way of explanation. "All

174

112 pounds of it." He dipped a paintbrush into a #10 can and basted the pig as it twirled slowly.

Wolf took a sniff of the can and the pig. "Not bad. Garlic, pepper, oil, vinegar . . . and something else."

"Rosemary and some fine-ground chili pepper," Hostettler said.

"I should have known," Court Bannister said.

Dick "The Chef" Hostettler was well known throughout the SEA fighter pilot community as the Chili-Fart Briefer. The title came from Hostettler's deep-seated belief that hot chili made the world go around, and that the briefings he gave pilots before their missions needed to be humorous as well as point-making. He started each day downing a giant bowl of hot chili. At the daily intelligence briefing for the combat crews, when he came to the part where he had to point out where the enemy guns were, he used farts of varying intensity to signify the caliber of the guns, starting with the light 12.7mm all the way up through 37s, 57s, 85s, and the gigantic 100mm. SAMs (Surface to Air Missiles) and enemy MiG fighters were ripsnorters that caused stage curtains to ripple.

Hostettler hummed as he basted the pig. Its hooves had been cut off, the hair removed, an apple added to its mouth. The small Thai slowly turning the handle had been on duty for the last six hours. It was succulent pork at its best.

"That's a lot of pig," Hostettler said proudly to Court. "But it's not the *pièce de résistance*," he added, a sly look on his face.

"What do you mean?"

"Never you mind, you'll see soon enough."

"Not even a hint?" Partin asked.

"It's a grand tribute to the Jolly Greens is all I'll say." He squinted at the sky. "Pretty soon now," he said in a conspiratorial tone, "before it gets too dark." He slapped the brush with an extra flourish.

Kelly, Tanaka, and Dominguez stood off to one side, getting reacquainted. Each vowed they wouldn't let so much time go by.

"Say, Ken," Kelly asked. "How the hell did you know Steffes wouldn't slice our ears off?"

"I didn't. He just got that idea all by himself. Saw too many chopsocky movies, I guess."

"Why didn't you stop him?" Dominguez asked.

Tanaka took a sip of beer and burped politely. "The wise bird does not fly midst the petunia bush."

"There's no such thing as a petunia bush," Kelly said.

"Told you it was a *wise* bird, you dumb shit."

"Well, what are you doing here?" Kelly said. "Last I heard you were an IP at George and had a lodge up in ski country."

"All true," Tanaka said. "I'm here on a six-month TDY to pass on some of what we have and to learn what's new here. Particularly this night-flying stuff. We're not teaching much of that. Got to find out how the troops in the field do it, don't you know?" The three Red-Tagged Bastards drank more beer and got caught up on what each had been doing.

Music from the jukebox in by the bar was piped out to the patio. The loud twang of the Doors well into "Light My Fire" flowed and surrounded the pilots. Hostettler checked his watch. It was 1925. "Act One," he said.

Eight giggling Thai girls came running out onto the patio from the club, trailing hundreds of green balloons on strings that floated and bobbed behind them like daisies rocking in the breeze. The girls tied the tugging balloons to everything they could find: pillars, pilots' zippers, pilots' fingers, handles on the barbecue barrels, and, with the Thai equivalent of ooh-la-la's, cod pieces. Several balloons got loose and huddled nervously under the slanted roof of the patio.

"You're quite the entrepreneur," Partin said to Hostettler. The four men stood in a group at one end of the patio.

"And cook," Wolf said, nodding at the spitted pig.

"I'm kind of planning on getting out of the Air Force and putting my magnificent talents to better use," Hostettler said.

"You are?" Court said in surprise. "Whatever for?"

Dick Hostettler, USMA '54, took a long pull at his beer. "It's like this: I can no longer contribute commensurate with my talents."

176

"What do you mean?" Wolf Lochert said with a frown, eyeing Hostettler's big West Point ring. He firmly believed it was every American's privilege and duty to serve his country, *particularly* an American who had the benefit of an engineering degree from Hudson High at taxpayers' expense.

"Here's how it is," Hostettler said. "I'm a non-rated man in a rated man's Air Force. The pilots are the first-class citizens, navigators are the second-class citizens, and we non-rated pukes are in the third or worse class. Here I am with an engineering degree from West Point, a Master's in International Relations from Columbia, and my assignment out of here is to study computerized administrative procedures at a university in Texas. If I can no longer perform the mission I'm good at and the mission I love, which is the intelligence field, why stick around? Nothing doing. I'm getting out."

Court was silent.

"I think the Air Force has gotten too much into the people-product business," Hostettler continued.

"As opposed to what?" Court asked.

"As opposed to a 'mission' product. What I mean is, the USAF seems bound and determined to produce highly trained officers and airmen who have great university degrees, terrific professional and technical school certificates, and marvelous breadth of experience assignments. That's all well and good if the purpose of all that personnel management and training is to ensure that mission accomplishment is the end product. But that's not the way it is. Ever since McNamara became Secretary of Defense in '61, we're getting more and more into the concept of *producing* managers, not leaders. Managers, with the manager himself the end goal, the product spit out of the factory, when all along the end product should be successful accomplishment of the mission regardless of the college level of the doers."

"Point well made. So what will you do?" Court asked.

"I'm going to CIA."

"That makes sense," Partin said. "You do have an intelligence background."

177

"Intell has nothing to do with it," Hostettler said. "I'm going because I love to cook."

"Love to *cook*?" Wolf burst out. "Cook what, commies?"

"Cook, as in cuisine. I want to be a gourmet chef, and the Culinary Institute of America up in Hyde Park, New York, has a two-year course for just that very thing. I've been interested in cooking since I was camping out in Texas as a kid."

"Making all that chili, I'll bet," Court said.

"Yeah, and a few other things," Hostettler said. He checked his watch. "Almost time for Act Two." He motioned to two Thais by the walkway to the club. When they came over he put them to work setting up the plates and slicing the roast pig. "Chow's on," he called to the crowd and disappeared into the Officer's Club.

"This is great," Joe Kelly said to Manuel Dominguez as they took their plastic plates heaped with steaming pork and coleslaw to a picnic bench at one side of the patio. Both carried ice-cold Budweiser beer cans.

"That was a hell of a thing you did, Joe," Dominguez said. "The last I knew I was on the ledge trying to get those guys hooked up, the next thing I knew I woke up on board as we were flying back. I owe you a big one."

"Red-Tagged Bastards Hang Together." Kelly finished his beer and brought two more. "A big one, you say. Okay, I'd like to collect right now."

"Sure, anything."

Kelly looked serious. "Why in hell did you bail out of the Academy?"

Dominguez slammed his beer can down and glared at Kelly. "You're really sticking it to me."

"What do you mean? How can I be sticking it to you?"

"You're sticking it to me because . . . because it's so damn hard to talk about." He stared outside the patio area, puffy eyes suddenly glistening. "Damn hard."

Kelly punched him lightly on the shoulder. "RBHT, El C. RBHT."

Dominguez put his fork down and took a long pull at his beer. "Okay, I'll tell you." He took a long swallow of beer.

178

His mind flashed back to the scene: drunken Cadet First Class Powers sitting on the floor . . . himself taking his pictures as Powers lay drunk and helpless, then helping Powers to the bathroom and watching him become violently ill . . . then the final scene, in which he threatened Powers with exposing his public drunkenness in uniform if he didn't back off from harassing his friend and roommate, Ken Tanaka.

"Fuck you, I'll get that little Jap bastard," Powers had slurred.

Dominguez had patted his camera. "You do, and these pictures will be on the Commandant's desk in half a heartbeat."

Dominguez took another swallow of his beer and sighed. "I caught Jerome Powers drunk in uniform and took pictures of him. I thought I had a great way to get him off our backs, particularly yours, Ken."

"Jesus Christ," Kelly said in dawning awareness. "Blackmail."

"Exactly," Manuel Dominguez said. "Good old American blackmail." He shook his head. "Then I realized what I had done and turned myself in."

"But not him?" Tanaka said in surprise.

"No."

"Why not?" Kelly asked.

"I had had my chance and didn't use it at the time. I just told the committee I had seen a cadet drunk and didn't report him. When they asked me who, I couldn't tell them. I just couldn't. That did it. They voted me out." He slammed his can down on the table. "Tell you what I did do before I left. I got that asshole Powers and told him I still had the pictures as proof, and though I was leaving I could still nail him for the offense if he kept bugging you guys. He caved in. Damn near cried. Promised he'd leave you alone."

"Well, I'll be goddammed," Ken Tanaka said. "I wondered why that weasel never called me around again." He looked at Joe Kelly. "We talked about that a lot, didn't we? Never could figure it out. He seemed almost afraid of us." Kelly nodded.

"So you turned *yourself* in to the Honor Committee." Kelly

shook his head. "You are one rigid guy. You gave away a hell of a lot."

"The whole world," Dominguez said and stared out beyond the patio. After a moment he turned to Kelly. "What would you have done?"

Kelly hesitated, then threw back his head and laughed. Dominguez stiffened, a wave of hurt crossed his face. Joe Kelly reached over and tapped his wrist. "You know what Tanaka and I thought? We thought you had VD and didn't want Barbara to know."

Dominguez grinned. God, Kelly, that's rotten. He leaned forward. "Do you think it's too late?"

"For you and her?" Kelly looked at Dominguez with compassion. "Yeah, El C, I think it's too late. She's been married for five or six years.

"Who to?" He thought of her worn picture in his wallet.

"Jerome Powers."

It was nearly dark and Rolly Grailson was setting up two long tables in a row. "Gather 'round, you nuggets," he yelled. "I'm going to teach you what real carrier pilots do." He poured beer over the tables.

"Shit, Rolly, we already know how to do carrier landings," Higgens said and blew a quack at him.

Carrier landings was a glorious stunt whereby a pilot had to run directly at a long beer-soaked table, then belly-flop and slide in the beer, to be caught by a rolled-up towel held by two men on each side like a carrier deck's wire. Since he was making like an airplane, the pilot ran with his arms extended, making appropriate jet noises.

"Wait a minute, nuggets," Grailson said. "How many of you have made night carrier landings in bad weather with a damaged aircraft *and* a damaged carrier?"

The men looked at each other. *Night and bad weather? Damaged?* They became attentive and eager.

Grailson spoke to one man, who immediately disappeared on an errand, then he briefed their duties to the two men holding the "wire."

180

"Okay, Higgens," he called, "you're first. Taxi on over here." Higgens complied, and Grailson blindfolded him with a napkin, positioning him ten feet to one side of the table on what he called downwind. "Right," Grailson said. "I'm your GCA operator and LSO." Ground Controlled Approach and Landing Signal Officer. "Run like hell and I'll tell you which way to turn. When I yell 'cut,' you're in position to land. Trust me and just belly-flop on the table."

As LSO, Grailson had an important job: yelling "cut" too early would belly-flop the nugget on the floor, maybe bashing his head on the "fantail" of the "ship"; yell "cut" too late and the nugget would crash the "fantail" into his groin.

While talking, Grailson poured a shot of warm whiskey down the back of Higgens' party suit and lit it with a match. At the same time, a third man with a seltzer bottle appeared by the two "wire" holders.

"Move!" Grailson yelled.

Higgens took off at full throttle and Grailson yelled, "Turn right 90 degrees, another 90 degree right turn, okay, you're on final, left, a little more left. Slow down . . . that's too slow, you're stalling, faster, faster." A fluttering cockscomb of cheery flames trailed behind Higgens. The man with the seltzer bottle sprayed the dry portions of the table with lighter fluid and lit it off with a whoosh. When Higgens was five feet from the table edge, Grailson yelled "CUT," and Higgens launched himself in the air. He belly-flopped onto the table, slid through the beer and flames, and was braked to a halt by the "wire." The "fireman" grabbed the seltzer bottle and shot it all over Higgens' back, then on the table surface, where the lighter fluid was merrily filling the air with the smell of burnt plastic.

Higgens stood up and whipped the blindfold off. Only slightly rattled about what had happened to him, he bowed.

"Bravo . . . shit hot," the crowd yelled.

"Okay, who's next?" Grailson inquired.

"NEXT? . . . You outta your mind? . . . Shove it, squid . . . Go piss up a rope, anchor-clanker, no more." Clearly, there were no takers. Looking greatly put out, Grailson grabbed a fresh beer. The crowd returned to its food and loud talk.

"Those squids are as nuts as you zoomies," Wolf Lochert said to Court Bannister and Doc Russell. They sat at a table, eating suckling pig with greasy fingers.

"You should talk," Doc Russell said, "you who run around in the woods eating snakes and preparing your knees to keep orthopedic surgeons in clover for life." Doc Russell hoisted his IV bottle of whiskey. "To your knees."

Wolf tipped his cola can in response. "Doc, you fixed me up good, so I guess I can't complain." Wolf had unrolled his beret and put it jaunty and neat, cocked right, SF Vietnam flash to his left.

"A little rest, a little fluid, and you're ready to go pound yourself on the head with hammers again," Doc Russell said. "All you had was a mild concussion coupled with dehydration bordering on severe. But you had no fracture and no subdural bleeding. All our vital-sign checks on you indicated all was normal. Your leg problem was caused by the blow, just like a boxer who got slugged extra hard. You're in excellent shape. You fixed yourself up."

"Yah," Wolf said. "I'm still dehydrated. I need another Coke." He looked around and saw only beer and liquor being dispensed. "Going to the bar," he said over his shoulder.

"Wait – your hat – take it off," Court yelled after him, but it was too late. Wolf disappeared into the Club.

"HAT ON IN THE BAR. HAT ON IN THE BAR." The cry was caught and echoed throughout the bar as Wolf Lochert entered still wearing his green beret. He ordered a Coke from the grinning Thai bartender.

A burly lieutenant at one end of the bar clanged the big bell and, in case this Army dummy didn't know the rules, chanted out the poem on the plaque above the bell:

HE WHO ENTERS COVERED HERE
BUYS THE BAR A ROUND OF CHEER

Wolf made a sheepish grin. "Oh, yeah, right." He pulled out a wad of money and started laying bills on the bar. He

182

liked fighter pilots and was happy to buy them a drink. Many times CBU or napalm at the right time had made his life more secure.

"Oh no, dads," said the big lieutenant, who did not put together what it meant for a man in civilian clothes to be wearing a green beret. "You got to chin yourself before you have the privilege of buying us a drink." He pointed to a brand-new chinning bar the lieutenant himself had installed to show off his own substantial muscles. "Right here, dads."

"Aw, shut up, Tony," someone from the crowd shouted. Ignoring the cry, the lieutenant grabbed the bar and did 20 two-handed chin-ups in rapid succession, watching Wolf all the while.

Wolf stopped putting his money on the bar and walked over to stand under the chinning bar. While holding the lieutenant's eye, he made an effortless leap, caught the bar with his right hand and, gazing directly into the lieutenant's eyes, did 25 right-handed pull-ups, changed in midair, and did 25 left-handed pull-ups. He slowly let himself down to the floor. Still holding the lieutenant's widened eyes, he jumped back up, grabbed the bar with both hands, wrenched it from its holder, dropped to the floor, bent the bar into a horseshoe, and let it clang at the lieutenant's feet.

Cheers and laughter rocked the bar. "Shit hot . . . terrific . . . don't take that man's money . . ." Wolf got his Coke, left some money on the bar, and went back out to the patio.

"What's all the ruckus?" Court asked.

"Some guy said something funny, I guess," Wolf Lochert said.

Doc Russell studied Court for a moment and snapped his fingers. "Now I know what it is," he said, sudden enlightenment on his face.

"Now you know what?" Court asked.

"I haven't seen you smoke for . . . I don't know how long. You're doing great. You really did quit, just like you said."

"Trying to."

"Congratulations." They resumed drinking. There was a commotion to one side.

Amid appropriate gongs and cries of silence, two ancient Thai men dressed as Siamese warriors of King Mongkut's era were introduced to the crowd. They stood, tall and resplendent, armed with large knives and spears. They were soon surrounded by the Phantom FACs, who thought it only fair the two warriors be treated to some alcoholic beverages to show respect for their fellow comrades-in-arms, regardless of customs, age, or culture. After a period of uncertainty, the ancient warriors grinned and accepted all drinks. The festivities resumed.

Wolf Lochert took a swallow of a fresh Coke. "Heard from Parker lately? How is he?"

USAF Captain Toby Parker had been the man to spot Wolf Lochert's cut off patrol a few years back near Bien Hoa. His prompt actions had saved their lives. Parker had been awarded the Air Force Cross for his heroism and had been given a pilot training slot. Currently, he flew O-2 FAC aircraft out of a Da Nang squadron with the call sign Covey.

"Toby is just fine. He'll be going to F-4 upgrade soon." Court took a long pull at his beer. "You going out to Eagle Station?" he asked Wolf.

"It's my job. I want to see what sort of defense and evacuation plan they have. Want to come along?"

"Sure, if I can get away, which I doubt. Got a lot on my plate these days. What are you doing, putting together a task force?"

"That's exactly what I would like to do, but not for inspections. As a matter of fact, I'd like to put together a unit that, at all times, has components for special operations under a single commander. As it is right now, we can't pull off any Special Forces movement using Air Force people or Air Force equipment without requesting and justifying the request far in advance through Army and Air Force channels. Don't get me wrong, your Air Commandos and TAC Airlift guys are doing a great job. Same with the USAF Green Hornet helicopter people. But lining them up through the upper echelons is time-consuming. Not only does it take a long time for approval, but everybody has to add their ideas. We need a way to put a package together overnight or sooner."

184

"You're looking for a degree of interservice cooperation that we have at the operator level but not at DoD level," Court said.

He had barely finished his sentence when a series of explosions and whistling noises split the air outside the patio. Wolf Lochert hit the deck, clawing for his social weapon from his ankle holster that wasn't there; the Jolly Greens went down yelling "Incoming"; and the fighter pilots stood around asking what in hell was happening.

"Somehow I have a hunch this is Chef Hostettler's Act Two," Doc Russell said. He pointed to the back of the patio. "Check that."

Wolf crawled out from under the table, looking like a man who had just hit his thumb with a hammer. He and Court followed the Doc's gaze to look at Roman candles and pinwheels erupting from a frame set up in the adjoining open field. The two Siamese warriors, walking with the studied ponderousness of those who have had a bit too much to drink, were moving about with sticks of punk, igniting the fuzes. Skyrockets tore upwards and exploded in sonorous brilliance, cherry bombs tossed by shadowy figures punctuated the air with sharp flash-bangs, spinning firewheels sprayed sparks in a widening circle. All was noise and light.

A series of pops and bangs sounded within the patio, causing Wolf again to reflexively crouch. The partygoers had discovered that hydrogen-filled balloons made marvelous flaming air bursts when ignited with a cigarette or match.

"Nuke Hanoi . . . BLAM . . . Y-One yield . . . POP . . . Gotcha, Red Baron . . . BLAM BANG BLAM BANG BLAM . . . Hey, I just made Ace . . . I'll bet they're full of Hostettler's chili gas . . . more, more . . ."

As the last balloon burst, the crowd's attention was caught as a husky Tarzan yell split the air and there was a motion of something massive and ponderous over their heads. Something very big from high in the evening dark was plummeting their way.

Painted green, and wearing cardboard cutouts of the Jolly Green Giant's pea-vine adornment, Chef Hostettler swooped down on the crowd standing on a giant 5,000-pound lead wrecking ball swinging from the Lorain crane used by the base engineers. At the controls, happily pulling levers and pushing buttons and singing "Anchors Aweigh" at the top of his lungs, was Navy Lieutenant Rolly Grailson.

The Volkswagen-sized lead ball pendulumed massively back and forth next to the side of the patio. The Jolly Green Giant stood on it, one arm looped around the wire, waved, "Ho-Ho-Ho-ed," and bellowed the tag line of the "Valley of the Jolly Green Giant" song.

The Phantoms and the Jollys were ecstatic with pleasure over this fine tribute to a great organization. So pleased, in fact, they shook up their beer cans and followed Chef Hostettler with foaming sprays of beer that drenched the night air worse than a Milwaukee tavern when their bowling team won.

Off to one side, the one-baht bus driven by Captain Donny Higgens drew up next to the crane's control cab. Higgens sat back in the driver's seat, swilled a beer, and watched the Green Giant majestically whoosh back and forth between the patio and the bus. Inside the bus were twenty-two barefoot Thai girls covered only by a light sarong. Each girl carried a thirty-six-inch anchovy and cheese pizza – one for every member of the party. This was to be Hostettler's greatest accomplishment. It would take top honors in any Command and Staff College for planning, coordinating, directing, and controlling. Here was a culinary and entrepreneurial feat requiring great skill, cunning, coordination, and highly selective bribery.

Higgens reclined further in the driver's seat, feet up on the instrument panel, and drank more beer as he awaited the signal to bring the bus close to the patio and open the doors to let the twenty-two merry girls grab their hot pizzas and run into the crowd to dispense their favors.

The pendulum swung once again while Chef Hostettler Ho-Ho-Ho-ed and roared out that the Jolly Green Giant would now provide the second course of the meal and signaled Higgens to move the bus into position as he started on the upside of his swing. At the same time he gave an okay sign to Grailson in the cab of the crane to draw up the pendulum and turn the crane away from the patio. Grailson, tight and grinning with pleasure at his efforts and with the acclaim the Jolly Green Giant was receiving, pulled one lever too many, turned the wrong way, and lowered the pendulum by two feet.

As Higgens brought the baht bus to the side of the patio, the bottom of the giant pendulum neatly peeled back the top of it like a sardine can, causing the panicked exit of twenty-two screaming, nearly naked brown bodies jumping through windows and climbing over each other and mashing the hot pizzas. The Jolly Green Giant rode the ball to the top of its swing, where it halted briefly next to the roof of the club before starting its inexorable downswing. Chef Hostettler said, "Oh oh," and stepped smartly onto the roof. The pendulum started down and, with an unstoppable motion gathering speed, it swooshed past the screaming brown and now pizza-colored girls and removed quite precisely two of the supporting pillars of the patio roof. The wood snapped with satisfying cracks and the roof structure groaned and slowly collapsed like an elephant going to its knees with its rump still up in the air, as the end attached to the club roof creaked and acted like a hinge but did not tear loose. The terrified girls darted like a frightened school of minnows into the only refuge they could find – the front door of the Officer's Club.

"Save the booze," cried some of the pilots. "Save the pork, save the pork," cried others. "Pork who?" asked the bewildered Higgens, who staggered from the wrecked bus just in time to watch the patio roof come down around his ears. He crawled to a corner in the rubble and sat down with his beer and duck call. "Pork who?" Quaaack? "Pork who?" Quaack.

"I think that's 'whom,' old buddy," said Cod Piece Partin, taking a seat on the floor next to him. He hugged a small keg of beer, which he held up to drink directly from the tap.

The two Thai warriors appeared upset with all the confusion, and advanced shoulder to shoulder, aggressively holding their weapons in front of themselves to vanquish whatever demons or foes were causing the fracas.

The screaming girls who took refuge in the Officer's Club nearly fell over each other trying to stop as they dashed into the large room full of the American congressmen, their wives,

187

local Thai dignitaries, and the Wing Commander, Colonel Stanley D. Bryce. The girls squealed and turned and pushed back, trying to get out of such august company as fast as they could. Their thin garments were not holding up well. Two big Air Policemen came in the front door of the club, blocking that exit. The girls scampered through the rooms of the club, diving out whatever opening they could find, to the surprised delight of the Phantoms and the Jolly Greens who had gathered their composure and their beers. Delighted with this new performance, they took seats in and on the wreckage and cheered for each little shrieking and squealing pizza-covered girl-form that leapt from the windows and doors of the Ubon Officer's Club and darted off every which way into the darkness like frightened bunnies.

Faces of bug-eyed congressmen and their wives appeared in the windows, taking in the disappearing rumps of the delectables, several of whose sarongs had torn or, in one or two cases, been ripped off entirely. In scowling disbelief they surveyed the patio wreckage and the cheering pilots. They quickly jerked back as they heard the two warriors utter war cries and saw them draw back their ancient arms and throw their spears in the general direction of the huge crane looming in the dark sky.

More slender bodies hurtled out of the windows, then cries of dismay began from the audience perched on the wreckage. "Wait . . . My gawd . . . I don't believe it . . . Do you see what I see?" Sitters stood, standers peered closer. Chef Hostettler stood on the roof, fists to waist like a proper Jolly Green Giant, and stared down in green disbelief. Things were waggling where things shouldn't waggle. Odd things were skittering and jittering where there shouldn't have been odd things.

The darting brown bunnies weren't girls, they were lithe and smooth-skinned *katoys* – female impersonators

Someone had made a terrible mistake.

10

"Yes, Sir – no, Sir – no excuse, sir," were the only words Court Bannister had uttered in the last twelve minutes to Colonel Stanley D. Bryce, Commander, 8th Tactical Fighter Wing, and (hopefully, in Stanley D. Bryce's mind, anyhow) brigadier general selectee.

During that twelve minutes, Bryce had questioned Court's wisdom in allowing his troops to participate in what was now known basewide as Hostettler's Holocaust; the wisdom of the United States Air Force in even allowing an officer's commission to be placed on someone such as Court Edm. Bannister; his own wisdom in allowing Bannister into his Wing to begin with; and finally the wisdom of almighty God in saddling him with such a bunch of juvenile delinquents masquerading as F-4 aircrewmen. Stanley D. Bryce roamed his office, smacking his fist into his palm and glaring at the object of his anger.

Court Bannister was taking all these fusillades by himself. Chef Hostettler was in the hospital with a sprained ankle, suffered when he fell off the Officer's Club roof because he had laughed too hard to retain his footing. "There will, by God,"

Colonel Stanley D. Bryce had thundered, "be a line-of-duty investigation about that Hostettler and his ankle."

Nor was Lieutenant Colonel Conrad D. Russell, MD, on the line in Bryce's office to suffer the slings and arrows, since he was in jail in the town of Ubon Ratchithani, along with such exalted participants in Hostettler's Holocaust as Army Lieutenant Colonel Wolfgang X. Lochert, USAF Captain Joseph Kelly, USAF Technical Sergeant Manuel Dominguez, Technical Sergeant Dan Bernick, and various members of the Phantom FACs who had thought a midnight swim in the Mun River was just the ticket after a hard evening at the club.

It wasn't the nocturnal swim that had upset the Thai city police so much as the fact that the *farangs* (foreigners) had demolished a corner of the wall around a Buddhist *wat* as they had run the borrowed baht bus into the Mun River, where the bus had floated for eight seconds, then sunk nosedown in the mud. A *wat* is the complex containing Buddhist temples and other buildings.

The commander of the Phantom FACs, USAF Major Courtland Esclaremonde de Montségur Bannister, FV470-28-6484, was not in the Ubon Ratchithani slammer because he and Captain Thomas "Cod Piece" Partin had accompanied Major Richard "The Chef" Hostettler to the hospital rather than motor into town with the troops.

Stanley D. Bryce was a big man, almost as tall as Court Bannister and broader of shoulder. He stood at 90 degrees to Court and bellowed into his ear, "Do you know what California Congressman Nebals told me? He said I was just as culpable as the animals that wrecked the club patio, and that he held me personally responsible for the stress, mental anguish, and offended sensibilities of his wife and the wives of the other members of the congressional delegation. Further, he said the Thai Government plans a formal protest to the Department of State about the naked, ah, Thai people in the club, and about the damaged *wat* in town. This whole affair will seriously erode relations between the US and Thailand and may cause revocation of certain measures of the Status of Forces Agreement."

Bryce was breathing hard, and retreated around his desk to sit down. Court remained at rigid attention. Bryce continued.

"I should relieve you of command of the Phantoms, revoke your IP orders, and reassign you as mess hall officer at Soc Trang." Soc Trang was the tiniest of USAF bases in the steamy Delta of South Vietnam. Its mess hall was a 10 × 20-foot tent.

"But I won't . . . for now, anyhow. We're too shorthanded. But you fly straight and level or that's exactly where you will wind up. You read me, Major?"

"Yes, sir," Court said.

"My God," Bryce said. "We just had the big River Rat bash with over seventy pilots at Udorn, and except for some elephant shit in the Officer's Club they didn't get into near the trouble you and your men did."

"Yes, sir."

"Consider yourself lucky you're not getting an RBI."

"Yes, sir."

An RBI was a Reply By Indorsement letter from a commander to a miscreant, who had to indorse that he had read the contents of the letter chronicling the Indorser's misdeeds.

"What I want you to do is get the Legal Officer and go to the Thai Police. Straighten out that mess, pay the damages, get the men out of jail. There's a helicopter waiting for Kelly and his crew, and an Air America Beech for that Green Beret. Get them to their planes and get them out of here, understand?"

"Yes, sir."

Bryce looked at his watch. "Then get back here. At 1400 I want you to report to Colonel Mayberry, who is here from 7th Air Force specifically to see you. He will be in the intell office."

"Yes, sir." Court remembered Mayberry as the man who worked for the Director of Operations at 7th. *Oh shit,* he thought. *I'm really in it if I have to see* him *about all this.*

"Dismissed," Bryce said.

"Yes, sir." Court saluted smartly, did an about-face, and marched from his commander's office.

The door to Bryce's ante-office opened and Colonel Tim Mayberry stepped in. He was a thick-shouldered man with black hair, and wore Air Force fatigues with command pilot wings stitched in white thread over the left pocket, and big white colonel's eagles on the collar tips. He had a wide and amiable face and heavy wrinkles around his eyes. He was grinning.

"Good job, Stan," he said. "I'll bet Bannister's going to walk mighty softly around here for some time."

"Thought you'd find it interesting to listen in. I just wish I could hook him up with that asshole of a congressman, Nebals, and let him hear Nebals freak out about what dregs, lechers, and murderers our military men are today. That would be the worst punishment I could think of for Bannister and his crew. Thank God for that guy from Michigan who was with them, Ford. He said he heard we lost a few this week. Said he saw some combat himself in the Pacific in the Big War. He knows how guys act. He'll keep a lid on this back in DC."

"What about the Thais?" Mayberry asked.

"Yeah, well, that's another story, a bad one. If Ambassador Martin hears about the *wat*, we're dead."

"Think the Legal Officer can smooth things over? Collect money from the guys and pay remuneration or such?"

"Maybe he can with the monks from the *wat*, if we pay for the damage, and to the owners of the bus, but if the mayor and the *kha luang,* the province governor, decide to take it to Bangkok, then the Ambassador will hear about it for sure."

"No way of stopping that from the Pentagon," Mayberry said. "Then it's goodbye BG for you."

Bryce smiled.

"You don't seem all that worried."

Stan Bryce sighed. "Funny thing, Tim, I'm really not. It just doesn't seem important anymore. What's important are the guys here and the miserable war they're trying to fight." He got up and walked to the window overlooking the busy flight line. "I despise this war more than anything I've ever encountered . . ."

"The war, or the people running the war?"

"All of it. The goddammed politicians that favor or oppose the war based only on whether or not they'll get re-elected,

192

not what is best for the country. The goddammed people in this world who really believe the North Vietnamese horse-shit that they are an oppressed nation. And those are the same people who believe Ho Chi Minh is a real national-ist and patriot, not a man who spent twenty years out of his country learning how to lead it into slavery, and who killed tens of thousands of farmers and landlords to con-solidate his position to do it. And goddammit, I despise our chiefs in Washington for putting up with that mean, petty, GI-killing micro-managing son of a bitch McNamara. And that SOB Johnson who let McNamara do it." He was breathing hard.

"Easy, Stan. You're pretty wound up."

"Let me tell you I'm wound up. And any combat wing commander in this fucked-up war who isn't wound up about the stupid ways and stupid reasons for which his guys are getting killed doesn't deserve to be a commander." Stan Bryce walked back to his desk. "I'm not the same man I was when I took over this wing last fall. Yeah, I suppose I did see it as a chance to make BG. Most every other commander from here has. But now it's the troops I care about. I want to take care of them, see them through this."

Tim Mayberry coughed. "Well, there is such a thing as the mission, you know. That is supposed to come before the troops."

Bryce sat down. "I used to think I had to accomplish the mission at all costs. But you know, Tim, some of these missions are not worth the fuel they consume, much less any crewman's life. As far as I'm concerned these guys are all heroes in a war that isn't allowed to have heroes. I don't really care if they get all bent out of shape at the club. They don't get much and yet they deserve a lot. If they can blow it all off at the club, I'm all for it. You don't *get* rich in the military and you don't *learn* how to get rich in the military. Combine that with the shit these guys go through, and a bit of a drunk now and then is little enough compensation. My only worry is that I might get fired, then perhaps these guys will get some meathead as a commander who'll do anything to make BG."

Stan Bryce sat back and made a definite effort to relax. "What is it you want to see Bannister about?"

"Eagle Station."

1145 HOURS LOCAL, WEDNESDAY 16 OCTOBER 1968
POLICE HEADQUARTERS, UBON RATCHITHANI
KINGDOM OF THAILAND

Colonel Tienchai Sumisupan had a look of quiet rage on his leathery face. He wore the dark green uniform of the Thai Special Forces. Hands on hips, his upper torso thrust forward aggressively, his eyes flashing obsidian, at five foot ten inches he all but towered over the police captain standing at nervous attention in front of him. In the liquid syllables of the Thai language, Colonel Tienchai informed the captain that indeed the captain had done a superior job in apprehending the American *farangs* and that he would undoubtedly be handsomely rewarded in this life if not the next. Colonel Tienchai then told the captain that he should immediately release the prisoners and all the associated paperwork to the colonel's control and that he, the colonel, would take the matter on to proper prosecution. Court Bannister stood quietly to one side, a thin major from the JAG office next to him. Both men had prudently decided to wear civilian clothes.

With all deference, the Thai police captain politely inquired if the esteemed Colonel Tienchai had the proper authority to resolve this unfortunate occurrence.

Tienchai's liquid syllables suddenly became marbles poured on a tin roof as he informed the captain that he, Colonel Tienchai Sumisupan, was not only the head of the Thai Special Forces, he was also an aide to the King of Thailand. He pointed to the special badge on his uniform.

The police captain's face became the color of clay. He stiffened and barked commands to two other men in police uniform, who all but leaped through the door to an adjoining room used for the Thai police court.

So far, Court did not have to become involved. When he had arrived he had found Colonel Tienchai already taking up the case of the imprisoned *farangs*. He was acting on behalf of a special friend, Tienchai had said when Court had explained who he was and why he and the JAG were there.

In the courtroom, reposing in various positions on the benches and chairs set up before the dais, were the sad remnants of the nocturnal attack on the Buddhist *wat* and the Mun River. Wolf Lochert sat tilted back on one wooden chair, arms folded, feet propped on another chair. Doc Russell lay flat on three chairs placed next to each other. Some of the men were asleep on the floor, others sat up against the wall. All except Wolf Lochert looked wan, hung over, and exceedingly contrite. The two Thai police officers motioned them out and they filed into the main office, Wolf in the lead. He brightened when he saw Colonel Tienchai.

"*Sawadee,* Colonel Tienchai," Wolf said to him, and made the *wye* greeting by placing his hands together as if in prayer and inclining his head. Tienchai returned the greeting and the two men shook hands. Tienchai turned to Court.

"Your men are free to go. I want to talk to your men, but not in here. Put them on the bus. I'll talk there."

As they walked out, Court told Wolf an Air America airplane was waiting for him. He led the group out into the bright sunlight and to a blue USAF bus. They walked with small steps and were very quiet. When they were seated, Tienchai came on board and stood in front of them.

"Gentlemen," he began, "the Thai government has the legal right to declare you persona non grata and give you twenty-four hours to get out of Thailand. However, Colonel Lochert here, a witness to the whole scene, has interceded on your behalf. It is fortunate indeed for you that he and I have a long-standing acquaintance. Earlier this morning he was able to convince the police captain that it would be in the captain's best interest to contact me." He kept a straight face as he spoke. When Donny Higgens made a motion as if to tootle on his duck call, Wolf Lochert gave him a glare that could have bored through concrete.

Tienchai continued. "Each of you will yield 4,000 baht to a disbursing officer I will have at the Air Base tomorrow, to compensate for the bus being dried out and the *wat* being fixed. Whatever is left over will be considered a contribution to the monks at the *wat*." At 20 baht to the dollar, the fine for each man was $200. "Each of you will also write a short note to the monks at the Temple, apologizing for your actions. Give them to the disbursing officer tomorrow."

Several of the men looked as if they wanted to speak to Colonel Tienchai and perhaps thank him for his intervention. Doc Russell cleared his throat and stood up from his seat on the bus. "Sir," he began.

Colonel Tienchai held up his hand. "I do not wish to hear anything from you men. You have insulted Thailand. I do not wish to hear either excuses or regrets. The monks may forgive you, I do not." He motioned to Court and Wolf Lochert to follow him off the bus. "I'll drive you to the air base," he said. Court told the JAG to get the men back to the base and to see that the three Jolly Greens were delivered to base operations, where the helicopter crew to return them were waiting.

The three men climbed into Tienchai's jeep and followed the bus back to the Air Base. Court sat cramped in back. As with most Thai Army jeeps on civilian roads, the top was up to protect the occupants from the sun.

Wolf spoke as they pulled away from the police station. "You may not accept thanks from them, Tienchai, but you get mine, whether or not you want them. We spent a lot of time together at Lop Buri. You taught me many things. I thank you."

The Thai colonel drove in silence for a while. When he finally spoke, his voice was jovial. "My friend Wolfgang, we indeed go back. Not just Lop Buri. You and I did terrible things one night in Fayetteville when I was in training at Fort Bragg. And you saved me from certain arrest by the sheriff for breaking both arms of the man who insulted my skin color."

The gate guard saluted the three men as Tienchai drove onto the base. They parked under a tree next to base operations on the flight line. Tienchai rested an arm on the wheel and looked at Wolf. "I tell you this. If those men had been tourists, they would be in jail for the next five years. We do not tolerate public drunkenness, and damage to a *wat* is beyond comprehension." He sighed. "But these are difficult times. Your men are doing difficult things. Few in the world truly understand what you Americans are doing here in Asia. You are buying us time to recognize the communists for what they are, and you are buying us time to improve our economic bases. We stand with you." Thailand had been the first Asian country to send troops to support the UN in Korea in 1951. In South Vietnam they maintained the Black Panther Brigade of Thai soldiers, which fought alongside US troops.

They said their goodbyes and promised to meet under better circumstances. Tienchai drove off. Court and Wolf walked into the base operations building, where the Jollys were ready to depart. Lochert threw a headlock on Joe Kelly and Manuel Dominguez before they could move, and gently butted their heads together.

"You two men are warriors. I needed you and you came." He released them and slammed Bernick on the back. "You, too," he said with grave enthusiasm. "You, too." Then they were gone. In a great thrash of blades and turbine noise, the big Jolly Green HH-53B took off.

Court walked Wolf to the twin-engined Beech that was to fly him to Vientiane. The pilot was in the cockpit.

"So you're going back to Eagle Station," Court said.

"I have to. I've had some time to think about it and I don't like the way the defenses are set up. We have the high ground, granted, very high ground. Over a mile almost straight up. But that karst ridge is like a boat in the water. You'd have to station a man every ten feet or so all the way around just to see the boarders, much less repel them. And" – he waved a finger – "it is quite a setup for an airborne attack by parachutists or helicopters. Following that, it would be very difficult to get reinforcements up there."

"What do they have in the way of a defending force?" Court asked.

"Not much. The basic defense plan is for VP's men to see and stop them somewhere along an encircling perimeter they have set up several kilometers from the base of the karst."

"Why so far out?"

"Because there are villages out there and the defenders are from those villages."

"No place else has ever had an airborne attack?"

"No. You know, maybe it wouldn't be a parachute drop. There are increasing reports of enemy helicopters being seen in Laos. And Eagle Station is close to the North Vietnamese border, so they could get over there fairly quick."

The pilot signaled and Wolf climbed on board. In minutes the plane was over the end of the runway, then droning off to the north.

1000 HOURS LOCAL, WEDNESDAY 16 OCTOBER 1968
HANOI CITY HOSPITAL
DEMOCRATIC REPUBLIC OF VIETNAM

You do not have the luxury to tell us what to do, the man said to Co Dust in Vietnamese. His name was Thach and he was the liaison between the Party and the head of the North Vietnamese prison system. Forty years old and slight, even for a Vietnamese, his features revealed a great deal of Chinese ancestry, and his specialty was propaganda: specifically, overseeing and directing the captured Americans' English-speaking interrogators and manipulators.

Co Dust bowed her head in the proper fashion and did not answer. Moments before, she had tried to tell Thach that the criminal Apple was not well enough to talk to anybody, though she knew he was.

They sat in a small whitewashed room used by the doctors as a place to rest. There were several wooden straight-backed chairs and a long grimy hardwood bench with deep scratches. A window overlooked a courtyard full of patients in threadbare hospital garments trying to take the sun. Most were young men missing limbs, their stumps swathed in yards of gray bandages.

"I have read the reports. He is well enough." Thach switched to English: "Soon, in a matter of days, you will take me to his bed and we will talk about his release."

She kept her head bowed and gave no indication she understood his words.

"We know you speak English," Thach said. "We know all about you and your schooling in Paris. You must cooperate with us or things will go very badly." He had been picked for his liaison job because he spoke English better than any of the prison interrogators.

"I don't *care*," she said.

"Not for you, oh no. It would go very badly for the criminal Apple," he continued imperturbably. "Oh yes," he said to her when he detected a slight motion in her shoulders. "We know all about you. We know how you feel about him, how you stroke him and croon to him. All this has been reported and noted in your file. You have soiled your Vietnamese soul, but it is just possible you can redeem yourself, and maybe the criminal as well, if you cooperate." He seemed to have forgotten she had been instructed to do just that. He pulled a pack of crumpled Gaulois cigarettes from his tunic pocket and lit one with a sputtering match. He blew the smoke toward the ceiling. It was hot. The window could not be opened and the ceiling fan did not work. The few doctors who staffed the hospital never used the room.

He looked at her. "Would you like the criminal to receive his freedom?"

She shrugged, but would not meet his eyes.

"Would you like for him to go home? Would you like to see him go back to his own people and" – he tilted his head toward the shabby surroundings – "to an *American* hospital?"

She shrugged again, still looking at the floor.

"You can make this happen. Would you like to know how you can make this happen?" he said very gently.

She nodded.

"You must speak to me."

She looked up, but not directly at him. "Yes, I would like this to happen."

"And you will help?"

"Yes, I will help."

"For right now, I want you to go back to his side. Talk to him, make him laugh. I will supply you with little gifts of chocolate and bananas. Tell him you stole them. Make him dependent on you, but afraid you might get caught and severely punished."

"How can this possibly help him get to his home?"

"You must prepare him for it. And you must prepare him for a visit from some people who will help him go home. People who will take him home."

It had happened before. Through his contacts with certain people in the United States, Thach had arranged for American "peace" organizations to visit Hanoi. A few months earlier, he had arranged visas for three members of the Women's Strike for Peace. He smiled with pleasure for an instant as he remembered beating an Air Force lieutenant named Carrigan for weeks because they had pronounced him "wayward." He wrinkled his nose as he thought of the group that had come to Hanoi with Tom Hayden and Rennie Davis. The four American girls in the entourage had smelled so bad, he had had to chastise his Vietnamese serving women when they looked with contempt at them and refused to serve them tea. He almost laughed over that American novelist – what was her name? – Mary McCarthy. She had seemed so bewildered and vague about everything when she had met with American prisoners. He still puzzled over the motion that young dolt of a seaman Hegdahl had made with his middle finger at Tom Hayden.

"Do you understand me?" he asked in a harsh tone. "Will you obey me?" He had not told her that the reason the criminal Apple had been so near death when he had been brought into the hospital was from the beating he had received while in the

Hoa Lo prison. He had been evasive when she had asked why no other Americans had been brought to the hospital, by saying perhaps they had not been wounded when their airplane had been shot down, as Apple had been.

"Yes," she said, "I will do this thing." Inside, she told herself she would do it for the man himself, not for this skinny jackal.

"You must be prepared to . . . sacrifice your body if such a thing becomes necessary. You understand? You must do whatever it takes to prepare him." He thought for a moment. It would be good to have the black man's spirit so compliant that he would take advantage of a Vietnamese woman. He could be manipulated much easier if he had that on his mind. "Yes, do that. Make him interested in you."

Thach could see no expression on her face. He told her she was excused and had two whole weeks to prepare the criminal for his visitors and eventual release into their hands. After she walked out, he decided when it was over he would take the wench himself, then denounce her for having slept with the enemy.

He went down the stairs to the small Lada sedan in front of the hospital and was driven to Party Headquarters. As he filled out his report, he wondered if he would have as much success with this criminal Apple as he had had with the three men he had released in February. Black, Matheny, and Norris Overly had returned to the United States without causing any problems with the press or the people. They had been conditioned. He had seen to it they had been singled out for special treatment.

Thach was also proud of how he worked things with journalists. It had always gone well with all of them. He had arranged for selected journalists from communist countries, as well as that man from *The New York Times,* to see for themselves what damage the Yankee Air Pirates were doing to peaceful Hanoi. He was particularly fond of quoting what the *Times* man had written: "One can see that United States planes are dropping an enormous weight of explosives on purely civilian targets."

He studied Algernon A. Apple's dossier. Admittedly, it would be a coup if he could bring this big man to heel. The first black man in the North Vietnamese prison system to be released would be particularly savory, since he was also a criminal who had tried to escape. It all depended on how Co Dust did her job. Based on the negative results of the beatings, he did not think that criminal Apple was a man to give in merely to threats of more beatings. Thach snapped his tongue against his teeth in disgust. Those imbeciles at the Hoa Lo prison, particularly that cretin the American criminals called Bug, would have killed Apple like they had Frederick, out of sheer vindictiveness over his escape. Did they not know these criminals were worth more alive than dead? *Choi oi*, he shrugged, a few more or less of the white race would not make any difference. It was the Negro race that could make an enormous difference on the propaganda front. If only he could get him to perform.

He picked up the second dossier on his desk and thumbed through the articles about the Peace and Power to the People Party that Alexander Torpin and a woman named Becky Blinn had founded in San Francisco. Torpin and the Party were doing well. The Blinn woman was not. She had died of a drug overdose in an alley and her body, which had been savaged by dogs, had not been found for days. He thoughtfully tapped the picture of Torpin, a powerful black man in a dashiki. He had thought of asking him to come to Hanoi but had decided it would be too risky. Better he stay in place and work for the Party. Besides, Torpin was a pragmatic man. Were he to see how things truly were in Hanoi, he might become disenchanted. Better he stay convinced that North Vietnam was the worker's paradise and that Hanoi was being indiscriminately carpet-bombed by American pilots. He would ask too many questions and demand too many answers. He was a hard one to control. But Torpin and Blinn, before she had become so drug-dependent, had landed a big fish indeed.

He permitted a small smile to play across his lips when he opened the third dossier, the one containing information on the big fish. Now this one was not hard to control. Here was a journalist who showed promise in many ways. He picked up the photograph and studied the wide smile of Shawn

202

Bannister on the cover of an American tabloid. On the cover next to Shawn was a shot of his half-brother, Court Bannister, in full jet pilot gear. The lurid headlines screamed out, ONE KILLS THEM; ONE SPIES FOR THEM, and detailed the story of the two men.

Late the previous fall, Shawn had been apprehended by the OSI, the Office of Special Investigation of the USAF, for gathering data on the F-4s flying from Ubon. Shawn had claimed, successfully, that he was just a newsie acting as a guest writer for the *Nan Dan* newspaper published in Hanoi. Bomb loads, tail numbers, damage on return, call signs he had heard on his little radio in his room overlooking the Ubon runway were all newsworthy items, he had said. The international press had picked up the small article about the case in the *Bangkok Post,* and it had spread over the world with lurid headlines.

Other articles by Shawn Bannister as Vietnam war correspondent for the *California Sun* were in the folder. One detailed how Shawn had flown with his brother on a combat mission arranged by an Air Force Public Affairs Officer, who had thought the USAF would reap favorable prose. The opposite had happened: Shawn had said his brother was a murderer who napalmed a civilian bus (the "bus" Shawn claimed to have seen had actually been a shot-up M-113 personnel carrier captured by the Viet Cong). Another widely acclaimed article by Shawn was of his visit with a Viet Cong colonel in the tunnel system beneath Saigon. Shawn had written quite explicitly that the Viet Cong would be the victors in their civil war against the puppet Saigon government run by US imperialists. Shawn had been promised a Hanoi trip by his Saigon mentor, Nguyen Tri, if his articles reflected the truth as Hanoi saw it.

Thach sat back and mused how Shawn Bannister had been brought along nicely, not only by Torpin in San Francisco, but by Nguyen Tri in Saigon and Huynh Va Ba in Czechoslovakia and Cuba. Two other Americans had been in Czechoslovakia, too, Bernadine Dohrn and Tom Hayden, as Huynh Va Ba had told them what they could do for the revolution. And

Thach needed the help, for he knew he was part of a complicated plan that required the meshing of many schedules and the cooperation of all concerned.

One of the Americans at the Czechoslovakia meeting had explained at length about the election process in the United States. He had said the voting public was very subjective and easily swayed by events at the last minute. Therefore, incidents occurring just prior to the up-coming election on the fourth of November, if powerful enough, could possibly be very decisive and influential on the outcome. When asked what could do this and why, the American had replied that anything to put America and American troops in Vietnam in a bad light would influence the voters to vote for whichever candidate said he would immediately pull the United States out of Vietnam. Was there such a man in the election? Yes, he was told, Hubert Humphrey was the man. Richard Nixon, his opposition, could not be trusted to end the war.

Thach had been given the task to ensure cooperation from the first black American pilot POW. Coupled with something very important about to happen in Laos, Thach had heard, the American POW's actions could be influential. The plan would result in both a propaganda coup and a vital military victory.

Thach looked more closely at the photograph of Shawn Bannister, amazed that a man who looked so vacuous behind that showy smile would come to Hanoi. Nguyen Tri's promise was being kept.

The final article in the dossier was from a California magazine. Thach picked it up. The magazine had resurrected an old movie publicity photo of Court in cowboy regalia, from his brief foray into the movies, and placed it next to one of him in his uniform. Underneath was a cropped shot of a bearded man wearing a tuxedo and bow tie.

HOUNDED OUT BY JEALOUS MOVIE STAR BOSS, SAYS AIR FORCE CAPTAIN

Courtland Bannister, movie star son of famed Sam Bannister, hounded him out of the Air Force, said former Air Force captain Richard Connert at a Sacramento fund-raiser for Shawn Bannister, brother of Courtland and son of Sam. Connert, deputy campaign manager for Shawn Bannister's bid for a state assemblyman's seat, said Courtland Bannister was "a tyrannical killer who harassed and tormented me until I had to resign from the Air Force to preserve my sanity."

Air Force Major Court Bannister would not respond to queries for his side of the story. USAF public affairs officers when contacted at the Pentagon would say only that Connert had been let go "for the good of the service."

A former Air Force sergeant said that Connert "was about the weirdest officer I have ever known, and I've known some weirdies. I was in a fighter squadron at Tan Son Nhut when he was assigned as an F4 backseater right at the beginning of Tet, when all airplanes were pressed into service. According to Major Bannister – and I heard him say this to the Ops officer – that Connert did everything wrong in the backseat he could. They finally realized he wasn't a pilot. Turns out he was a non-rated F-4 simulator instructor who had dummied up orders as a pilot. That's the last I heard of the guy until he got into some sort of politics."

Thach closed the file. These Americans, he thought, they are so divided. They need a central government to tell them what to think and do, as we have here. It is so much more simple.

1400 HOURS LOCAL, WEDNESDAY 16 OCTOBER 1968

INTELLIGENCE ROOM, HEADQUARTERS, 8TH TACTICAL FIGHTER WING

UBON ROYAL THAI AIR FORCE BASE

KINGDOM OF THAILAND

"Major Bannister reporting as ordered, sir." Court Bannister stood in front of Colonel Tim Mayberry. Court wore his black flight suit, Mayberry was dressed in USAF fatigues.

Mayberry offered his hand. "Relax. Smoke?" He held out a pack of Luckys.

"No, thanks, sir. Trying to quit."

"I did, once," Mayberry said and lit up. "For a couple years. Got back on it down at 7th."

"Yes, sir."

"Quite a party you gentlemen had."

"Yes, sir."

"That's not what I'm here to talk about."

Court looked surprised.

Mayberry walked to the big map on the wall and pointed to an area in northeastern Laos. "I want to talk about Eagle Station, also known as Lima Site 85."

Court nodded, even more surprised.

"You've seen it from the air. I want you and the Phantom FACs to take a special interest in that place. We have the day FACs keeping an eye on it, but we need night coverage as well. Not everybody agrees with me, but I think Eagle Station is of special interest to the North Vietnamese. I think it's quite obvious. They need a big coup. Tet failed miserably, even though the press would have the world believe otherwise. It is my belief that General Giap wants to capture Eagle for two reasons. One is to put the radar out of business, the other is to hold up the men they capture to the world press as violators of the 1962 Geneva Conventions." He stopped and lit another cigarette. "Too bad you're not cleared for SI," he said through the smoke as he exhaled.

"No way, Colonel. I wouldn't take it if it were offered."

No combat pilot wanted a Special Intelligence (SI) clearance unless he didn't want to fly combat. Holding one meant the recipient was privy to extremely sensitive material produced by SIGINT (Signal Intelligence) systems, which normally come from ground-based and aircraft collection systems. Owning the clearance meant you were forbidden to be in any kind of a position where you might be captured by an enemy. Even visiting East Berlin was forbidden. Wing commanders, who had to know certain things their squadron people were not cleared for, always had an SSO, a Special Security Officer, who handled cryptography for him, and upon orders of his commander gave him only what he could bear as a combat pilot who might be captured and tortured.

Mayberry debated how to word his idea. "I want you to visit Eagle Station and I want to give you some, um, *information* that would be of use in your visit. Let's just classify it as speculation on my part. Understand?"

"Yes, sir," Court said. He decided to wait and see what Mayberry had to say before bringing up Wolf Lochert's connections and plans for Eagle Station.

"I think Russian special forces men are in on the deal," Mayberry said. "I think they are in Laos on training missions – training themselves, not the Pathet Lao. And I think an attack on Eagle is a natural for them, and not just for Giap's reasons to shut it down and display the prisoners. I think the Russians find this a great opportunity to capture an easily transportable, highly secret US radar station, the TSQ-81. Or at least the Klystron tube that powers the radar. We, ah, *understand* they really want this thing." He made a derisive sound. "They just haven't pieced together that the principle is the reverse of a radar bomb scoring system that's been unclassified for years." Mayberry put out his cigarette. "Here's what I want you to do at Site 85. Familiarize yourself with the entire Eagle radar complex and how to defend it from the air at night without radio communications."

"I know a system we used to defend the SF camps in South Vietnam. It's called Flaming Arrow."

"Good. I'm familiar with it. Set it up. They're all technicians there and don't know a damn thing about defensive measures."

"Colonel," Court began. "Do you know an Army LTC named Wolf Lochert? Wolfgang X. Lochert?"

Mayberry thought for a moment. "Wasn't he the man who beat a court-martial for killing that VC double agent?"

"That's the one. Know anything more about him, say in relation to what we are talking about?"

"Can't say that I do."

"I saw him off barely an hour ago on his way to Vientiane. He's on loan from MACSOG in Saigon to some spook in

AID up at the American Embassy in Laos. His job is to look into Lima Site defenses. He's taken particular interest in Eagle up there at 85. He thinks it's a natural for an airborne assault – by helicopters."

Mayberry threw back his head and laughed. "'Tis a small, small world. I've been reading our AIRA's reports of what must be Lochert's activities up there and of Lochert's conclusions. The AIRA is merely passing them on without stating whether he believes what Lochert says to be true or not. He didn't ID Lochert by name, and what you say is news to me, especially about the helicopter. The AIRA never mentioned the possibility."

"Maybe Lochert didn't think of it at the time. Maybe he did since he left there and I'm the first person he told."

"Maybe. So, can your number two man run Phantom FACs while you're gone for a few days? And do you think you can hook up with Lochert to visit the Eagle with him?"

"Yes, sir, on both counts."

"Then get with it. I'll square things with Stan Bryce."

"Yes, sir."

1430 HOURS LOCAL, FRIDAY 18 OCTOBER 1968
SUB-COMMITTEE OF THE CENTRAL
WAR PLANNING COMMITTEE
HANOI, DEMOCRATIC REPUBLIC OF VIETNAM

"Comrade Thach, what have you to report?" the Committee Chairman, an old man with a wispy beard, asked. Only those who commanded special respect grew beards in Vietnam. It was time for Thach to brief current results on his part of the plan called *Cuoc Chien Tranh Gay Gac* – Valiant Struggle. The Committee body sat at a long table in front of tall windows letting in the gray light of a low overcast day. Each man had one pencil and a thin note pad in front of him. In the center were paper drinking cups and plastic water bottles. Most of them smoked. Thach lit a People's Cigarette. It would not do for the Committee to see him smoke French Gaulois cigarettes, although he was sure every member did when they were not in public. He used to be very glad when the sky was filled with an overcast, for that meant the Air Pirates would not strike. Now, since that fool Johnson had panicked and told his pilots not to strike north of the 20th parallel, he would gladly trade the low clouds for a high sun. The city was once more learning how to relax.

Thach had been surprised when he had first entered the building to see a man he recognized to be from the Soviet Embassy. He did not know his name, only that he was with the GRU, the military intelligence office. Political people from the Embassy were frequent visitors on Party matters of one sort or another, but the GRU men were usually at the War Department, not committee meetings. Thach looked up at the Chairman and began to speak.

"Comrades, the Americans are in place in the city of Bangkok and await only our word. I have taken great pains to see that the International Control Commission is aware of the trip and has told the American Air Pirates to provide safe passage for their flight to Vientiane, thence here to Gia Lam." He shuffled his papers.

"Yes, yes, comrade," the old Chairman said in a creaking voice. "You have told us that before. We must have a positive date for them to arrive. Why do you not give us that date? Is it because you do not have results with the criminal Apple?"

"Comrades, it will be soon now. He is coming along. This is too important a thing to take a chance."

"Comrade Thach, you had better take something if you wish to continue in your post as liaison officer with Hoa Lo. There are certain perquisites that you would be reluctant to give up. And I speak not of just the sedan and driver and the condiments you are given to hand out as favors." His voice suddenly crackled like old parchment. "I speak of your very freedom, comrade. If you do not produce the criminal Apple with his desire to return to his country, you will take his place in a cell of your own. Or perhaps take a long walk to the South from which no one returns. The time is growing short. The necessary men are in position in Laos. We must have that press conference or the overall plan will fail. Timing is crucial in this."

A much-shaken Thach returned to the Hanoi Hospital and pulled Co Dust into the empty room, wrinkling the sleeve of her white uniform with his nervous grip. "It was not for nothing that you were placed in his room. So why is nothing happening?"

"He . . . he is a very strong man. He knows his own mind." She did not look at him. She sat hunched over, staring at the floor, as she thought of what to tell this man to put him off for another day. She raised her head and looked out the window. "You must tell me more."

"I don't have to tell you *anything* except what to do." He spun her around and slapped her hard twice before she could react.

She thought quickly and kept her composure. "I did not explain myself well," she said with great dignity. "He, the criminal Apple, will ask many questions. He will ask that if someone is coming who is a friend and who wishes to take him home, he must at least know who that friend is. He will say that is a reasonable request so he does not become surprised and upset to see a stranger. Please, it will be important to him to know these things."

"Will it sway him to what we want?"

She hesitated. "Yes, it might." She had gained a day, maybe two. "He would want to know who is coming, what they do. He would want to know if they are sent by his government. He would have many questions."

Thach was silent for long moments. "All right, then. I will return." He faced her with a snarl. "I will see him, and talk to him. There must be no further delay. Thach stormed out. That the pressure was on him by the Committee, there was no doubt. But why, he wondered? They knew these things took time. It was common to put an American criminal in leg irons for months or solitary confinement for years to get them to sign a statement or make a broadcast. Why the intense pressure to adhere to such a short time schedule? What did they have in mind? Did it have anything to do with the Soviet GRU man? That had to be it. They were always impatient, and setting the kind of schedules that were so alien to the Vietnamese way. If they would just supply the war matériel and technicians and dispense with the advice. And the Chairman had mentioned Laos. Thach knew it was not his to question the grand scheme of things, but secretly he could wonder. Little bits of information always helped him advance in the Party.

Co Dust went immediately to her post in Flak Apple's hospital room. His eyes lit up when she entered and moved to his side. She took his hand and felt for his pulse. It was a secret between them. She would hold his hand while pretending to take his pulse. Then they would squeeze each other in slow tempo. She had not intended to develop real feelings for him, but, unbidden, they had been creeping slowly into her consciousness.

"Hello, Princess," he said. She had been teaching him a few simple words in Vietnamese, and when he had found out she was known as Unmarried Girl of Dust, he had immediately started calling her Princess.

"Bonjour, Roi Noir," she answered and checked his body with a practiced eye. They had ceased the intubation and IVs a few days back when he had proved he could sit up and take nourishment by himself. The antibiotics and the salve that had been delivered by the Quakers from the United States to North Vietnam were performing well, and he was healing fast – externally. Internally, his intestines were sore and she was afraid there might be an infection. She took his temperature and pulse and entered them on the chart.

She called him *Roi Noir,* Black King. "If I am to be a princess, then you must be a king," she had said. "A great black king." They had talked, slowly at first because he did not believe she was anything but yet another instrument of torture. After she had calmed and cooled him many times when he had yelled and screamed in the night, Flak had become convinced she wanted to help him. Although she had carefully brought up the subject of visitors and his possible repatriation, she had not gone into any details when he pressed for more information. Thach had told her it was a move by his government to interview sick and lame POWs, with a view toward taking them home. She had kept him on just enough drugs so he wouldn't question her too deeply, because she really didn't know any details. He seemed so vulnerable, she must protect him as long as she could. Yesterday she had started easing him off the drugs. Today she would have to tell him what was really happening.

"You have wondered why you are getting special treatment?" she started, and was surprised when he rose to his elbows.

"Special treatment? What do you mean?" Flak was suddenly very concerned. Paragraph III of the Code of Conduct very specifically pointed out that no POW was to accept parole or special favors from the enemy. "You told me I was getting the same treatment as every American in this hospital was getting."

She took his hand and put her head very close to his. "I . . . I lied to you. There are no other Americans in this hospital."

"What?" His voice rose alarmingly.

"Shh, oh please, you must be quiet! I think they listen to us, maybe even *see* us. I did it for you. I lied to them, too. They think you are aware what is about to happen. That even maybe you approve."

"About to happen? *What* is about to happen?"

"Two Americans are coming to Hanoi. I do not know who they are, but I am told they want you to return to America with them. The Party here wants very much this to happen. There is a man, he will be here today to talk to you. He is very powerful in the Party. His name is Thach and he can help you go home."

Flak Apple lay back. He spoke with difficulty. "Princess, listen. You've been very good to me and I appreciate that, but you have just given me devastating news. You must understand this. I cannot accept special treatment that the others don't get. And I certainly can't go home until we all go."

"But you are badly wounded. Surely under the Geneva Convention— "

"Geneva Convention," he snorted. "Where have you been? You don't expect these monsters to torture one day and follow the Geneva Convention the next?"

She drew back. "Monsters? They are monsters, my people? That is a harsh thing to say."

He took her hand. "I am sorry to make you feel bad, but my body did not get this way falling down a flight of stairs. Those monsters in Hoa Lo tortured me and practically everybody else over there that wouldn't make broadcasts or sign statements."

"Broadcasts? Statements? Torture? I do not understand what you are telling me."

He explained to her in detail what had been done to him. He started with the straps that bent his shoulders back in a V, and his torso forward so grotesquely his toes were in his mouth; he progressed to being hung upside down and beaten with rods for three days; and ended with the water hose inserted in his rectum and his stomach beaten until something burst. She looked ill. Everything he said matched with the tears and bruises on his body.

"I . . . had heard things. I didn't want to listen, to believe." Her face was a study of anguish. "There has been talk, quiet talk behind closed doors here at the hospital. Pilots have died here. We were told their bodies were torn upon jumping from their aircraft or in the crash. But nurses experienced in these things would look strangely and say these young men were injured not from crashes but from other things. They would never go beyond that. They were afraid to say any more." She squeezed his hand. "If there was only some way I could help you." When the words came out she realized how deeply she felt toward this man and she was surprised. There had been a man in France, a Frenchman who had taught her many things that a young woman from Vietnam would not – *should* not – know.

"Help me?" His grip tightened and a strange light came into his eyes. "Yes, there is a way you can help me." He pulled her head closer. "You say they can hear us in here?" She nodded and he continued whispering into her ear. "Do you really want to help me?" She nodded again, and snuggled her face against his throat and shoulder.

"Can you hear me?" he whispered.

She nodded.

"I want to escape."

213

She struggled to sit up, but he pressed her tightly against his chest. "You cannot do that," she murmured into his throat.

"Yes, I can, and you can help me. I don't know how yet, but you can. Will you help me?"

An idea was forming in his mind, involving the two Americans that supposedly were coming to interview him. They were Americans, they would help a fellow American. That was what his country was based on. That was what his mother had always taught him. That was what he believed. One American always helped another – especially when they were overseas in some God-forsaken country and one was in trouble. God, wasn't America a great country and weren't Americans the greatest people in the world? He knew they were.

He thought for a while and tried to get his priorities straight. It wasn't easy – his mind was still fuzzy from the drugs and as bruised by the beatings as his body. The slightest sound or rattle, and he would leap and jerk almost uncontrollably. He fought to keep the torture memories from his mind, for to let even the slightest bad thought surface was to bring on trembling and acrid sweat. To keep free from unwanted thoughts, he conjured up an evenly burning candle and concentrated on the flame to the exclusion of all else, until he felt ready to continue whatever thought process he had in his mind at the time. Other times he multiplied numbers to great amounts. Finally he had a plan of sorts laid out.

"You must prepare yourself. Very soon I will need you to make some contacts for me in the prison at Hoa Lo. I will make a plan and let you know what I need." He seized her hand and spoke with deep fervor. "I will escape."

11

Court met with his operations officer, Captain Howie Joseph, and the instructor assigned to Ubon on temporary duty from George AFB, Captain Ken Tanaka, and told them he'd be away for a few days, running around the boonies in Laos.

"In civilian clothes?" Tanaka asked.

"Yup," Court answered. "No American military in Laos allowed. *Over* Laos, yes. On the ground, no."

"No problem on the schedule, boss," Joseph said. "It will be a little tight, but we can cover the missions. I'll just hold Tanaka here from his four-day R & R in Bangkok for a while. You going to tell us what's going on up there?"

Court told them what he knew and said he didn't think he'd be gone more than three days. "The reason I have you here," he said to Tanaka, "is because you have seen Eagle Station at low level in the daytime. Now I want you to get familiar with it at night. See how to get in from any direction if the weather is bad, see what the best laydown patterns are for some of our more accurate weapons like CBU, napalm, and 20 mike-mike strafe. I'll get word back to you when I'm up there, and on a frequency we can talk, and I'll show you what Flaming Arrow is."

"Flaming Arrow?" Tanaka echoed.

"I can see you haven't had a tour in South Vietnam," Court said with a grin. "Flaming Arrow is when you have a friendly camp that has lost its radios and is about to be overrun by the bad guys. The men in the camp have already rigged up a ten-foot plank and some boards shaped like a big flat arrow. It's mounted a few feet off the ground on a pipe so it can be swiveled to point in any direction. Nailed to the top of the arrow are a bunch of cans stuffed with oil-soaked rags. When the bad guys are climbing the wire and there is air support available but no way to talk to them, the guys light the arrow up and point it in the direction they want. The fighters lay down everything they have at a prearranged distance beyond the tip of the arrow."

"Simple enough. We can do that," Tanaka said.

Court looked to Joseph. "Meanwhile, Howie, I want you to start scheduling the dusk and dawn patrollers to take a look at Eagle while there is still light. Then you, Ken, start showing the guys the place at night."

"Shit oh dear," Tanaka said. "That means I have to ride in the black pit." He meant the backseat of the F-4, from which forward vision was nil in the daytime, minus nil at night.

"The very place," Court said. "You're a combat night IP now, I checked you out. Start IP-ing."

1145 HOURS LOCAL, SUNDAY 20 OCTOBER 1968
EAGLE STATION AT LIMA SITE 85
ROYALTY OF LAOS

Landing a turboprop Pilatus Porter airplane uphill is not an easy task, yet Air America pilots in Laos had reduced it to the humdrum. In weather where the mists and clouds cut off mountain tops, the pilots could snake their planes from a well-known bush to a favorite rock to a tree they knew, then finally smash onto the ground with a great roaring of reverse propeller. If the ground was dry, a great dust cloud would envelop the plane.

Court Bannister sat in the right seat as pilot Dave Little dropped the flaps and slowed the Porter to 35 knots in preparation for landing at the dirt clearing at Eagle Station. Wolf Lochert sat in the rear, wearing a new T-10 backpack parachute. If the parachute bothered Little, he made no comment. Court tried to appear nonchalant as Dave Little slammed onto the short strip, so steep and narrow it looked like a Tahoe ski run in the summertime.

Fighter pilots have a natural aversion to being in a small plane that someone else is flying close to the ground in dangerous conditions. Unless he had flown with the light-plane pilot many times before and trusted his abilities, a fighter pilot was always convinced he could fly the plane better, thereby taking his own destiny into his own hands. Most fighter pilots believed in the statement of Saint-Exupéry's friend Guy Mermoz: "It's worth it, it's worth the final smashup." But if there was to be a final smashup, they did not want it at someone else's hands.

Court was no different, but all he said to Dave Little as the dust cleared was, "Good job."

Bob Pearson waved to them from the edge of the clearing. A husky, cowlicked, blond, twenty-five-year-old with a clear face, Pearson wore old khaki trousers cut off at the knees, thongs, and no shirt. He looked like he had just come from the surf at Malibu, except that he carried an M14 carbine. Two Hmoung soldiers trailed behind him. They also carried M14s. Off to one side stood a solid dark-headed man in civilian clothes.

Court and Wolf climbed down from the Porter and reached in for their bags. Dave Little waved and said he had some rounds to make. Court looked up at the low clouds. "Good luck," he said to the pilot. "It's no sweat," Little replied and gunned the plane around and took off downhill.

Wolf unzipped his bag, pulled out an AK-47, took off his parachute and put it in the bag. He and Court picked up their gear and walked to the shade, where the USAF controller stood. (Ground scope dopes were officially called weapons controllers

217

– probably in the attempt to make them feel like steely-eyed killers.)

Both Court and Wolf wore dark cotton pants, light guayabera sport shirts, and combat boots. They had bought the clothes at the Ubon PX. Wolf's combat boots were a "gift" from a supply sergeant who said all he wanted was to be able to say, "Why sure, I know Wolf Lochert." Court wore a green mesh survival vest over his sport shirt, and a 9mm Browning automatic in a shoulder holster.

"So you're Phantom Zero One," Pearson said to Court and extended his hand. "And you're Eagle One Four." They shook and Court introduced Wolf Lochert.

"And this is Mister Sam," Pearson said as the dark-headed man walked over. He was a thin man who wore khaki pants gathered at the waist and a dark green sport shirt. They shook hands.

Pearson pointed to the two Hmoung. "These are my buddies, Lee and Loo. They're the local *kato* champs." *Kato* was a cross between volleyball and soccer. The two small men, barely as tall as their M14s, nodded shyly. They had the bodies and faces of twelve-year-olds and the wise eyes of jungle cats. They took up front and rear positions as Pearson and Mister Sam led Court and Wolf up a trail to the radar site.

As they climbed, the vegetation thinned until the path was barren as a mesa. The radar bubbles were the first things they saw of Eagle Station, then the radio antennas. Long wires, whips, blades, and log-periodic that looked like a TV antenna on any roof in a city. The first sound they heard was the muffled throaty purring from the buried exhaust of a big generator. Pearson led them into an air-conditioned van, opened a small refrigerator, pulled out a Coke for everyone, and started his brief.

"Victor Tango told me why you're here and I want to tell you, I'm damn glad to see you. I get the feeling we are, if not abandoned, at least forgotten out here. Victor Tango only *thinks* we are well defended."

"What about the Hmoung soldiers up here? The ones you met us with?" Wolf asked. "Who do they belong to?"

Pearson nodded at Mister Sam. He looked to be in his late thirties and had dark, sad eyes rimmed by many lines. Mister Sam spoke quietly.

"This peak has two layers. The one 600 feet below where the airstrip and my command post are located, and the Hmoung garrison up on this level, where the radar and Tacan equipment is situated. This level is not sawed-off and flat. It has many ups and downs and is like a piece of jungle elevated straight up, although without the triple canopy. It has many trees and a lot of bushes, vines, and huge plants. There are maybe 200 people up here, and only sixty do I consider as good fighting men. Their boss is Major Hak. If he thinks he'll win, he'll fight. Otherwise, the *phi* is bad and no one goes out. *Phi* means spirit. They are animists and believe there is a spirit in everything – rocks, trees, streams, everything. My job is to run the airstrip and keep Major Hak informed of what the big boys at Victor Tango want. I can't force him to do anything. All I can do is gently hint he might not get any more American supplies and weapons if he doesn't perform."

Pearson brought out a 1:50,000 map and handed it to Mister Sam, who spread it out. He showed them where the Site 85 karst mountain, with Major Hak's village, Poo Pah Tee, and Eagle Station, was located. He pointed to the tiny village of Muong Yat at the base of the karst. "This is where the LAD-C is," he said. "The Local Area Defense Commander, Colonel Bunth. Hak supposedly works for him. Bunth is a Hmoung who works for, after a fashion, General Vang Pao. He has about 800 people, of which maybe 200 are good fighters. He is supposed to get from one to twenty-four hours' notice of an enemy concentration or buildup, and he is supposed to tell us and Victor Tango what he sees. Then we call in air strikes under what we are told is our 'Self-Defense Plan.' If the enemy gets past him and try to climb this mountain, then it's up to Major Hak's boys to fight them off."

Mister Sam pointed to a spot on the map where a piece of the topography of Site 85 showed a graduated descent instead of the sheer cliffs that marked all the other sides. "This is the climbing side. The only way you can get up here. Bunth has the overall responsibility for this wedge of territory from the base of the climbing side out to his village and beyond. It is his job to see no enemy gets in that wedge to make an attack." He swept his hand in a wide circle around Site 85. "We want to keep the PL and the NVA out of this twelve-kilometer perimeter. That way, even if they don't attack, they can't lob mortars or use artillery. If they do, Bunth spots them and calls us for air strikes."

In a surprise move, Pearson snorted and smashed his fist down on the map. "It's a useless crock of shit! Call in air strikes? Do you know the only way we can put in an air strike is to use secure radio? Neither the strike birds nor the FACs have them. That means we have to talk to an ABCCC, who will relay to the FAC, who will talk to the fighters. Not only that, we have yet to talk to the LAD-C, Colonel Bunth. We don't even know what frequency he is on. So how the hell can he tell us there is a problem and how the hell can we call in air strikes? And these guys up here, they're kids. Kids, maybe twelve, fourteen years old. All they do is play *kato.*"

Wolf studied the maps, then spoke in a soothing tone. "I'll go down there and find out what they have going for themselves. Radios, weapons, experience, plans. I'll find out and come back up here and help you work out a plan."

"We're technicians, not soldiers. Just find me a way to know if there is going to be an attack, then we'll work out an evacuation plan," Pearson said, "because we sure as hell can't defend this place!"

"No evac plan?" Court said.

Pearson shook his head. "Not much more than walk to the nearest corner and whistle for a taxi," he said with disgust.

"Okay, we'll work on that too," Wolf said. "Let me have a couple of your kid soldiers to show me the way and I'll get going."

"When will you be back?" Court asked.

Wolf looked again at the map and at his watch. "Tomorrow before dark or I'll call in."

"We've got an inspector down there right now," Mister Sam said. "A DEA guy." DEA, the Drug Enforcement Agency, had men in the field trying to track and stop the flow of drugs through Cambodia and Laos into South Vietnam.

Wolf's eyebrows went up. "Powers never told me that."

"Powers is not too swift sometimes. Not always up on things. That's why he's an assistant."

"Well, Powers is in charge now, his boss is in Bangkok on leave," Wolf said. "Where is the DEA guy?"

"Here, at Bunth's place." Mister Sam pointed to Muong Yat, eight kilometers southwest of Site 85.

"What is he inspecting?"

"Opium traffic."

"Does he know I'm coming?" Wolf asked.

"Not yet. I'll tell him on the Agency's net," Mister Sam said.

"Did Jim Polter know he was there?" Wolf asked.

"The AID guy? No reason for him to know," Mister Sam said.

"I'll get started then," Wolf said. Jim Polter in Vientiane had helped him get new gear before this trip: jungle fatigues, a harness, and the necessary weapons and equipment for a jungle trek. Polter had also scrounged up a survival radio from the Assistant Air Attaché. Wolf stripped and, clad only in combat boots, heavy wool socks, Randall knife, and Mauser, he put on the heavy fatigues, webbed belt with two canteens he had filled in Vientiane, harness, grenades, flashlight, K-Bar knife taped upside down. Court handed him his floppy jungle hat.

"Got a Prick-25 so we can stay in touch?" Wolf asked. The battery-powered radio was about the size of five cigarette cartons stacked on top of each other. Pearson found one for him.

They established working and backup frequencies, and tactical call signs of "Wolf," "Eagle" for Pearson, and "Maple" for Mister Sam.

"What kind of a leader is Bunth?" Wolf asked Mister Sam.

"Far below what Vang Pao usually has working for him. But he has been the chief in this area a long time and refused to let any but his locals do the defending, so VP had to put him in charge. We sent him out for a lot of training. Some of it took.

221

But I think he has been on the take from smugglers and maybe even the PL. He does like his gifts of money and booze. I don't really trust him but what can you do?"

"Kill him."

Mister Sam made a dry laugh. "He has no good number two and his people would never accept a new leader supplied by VP from another tribe."

"Why haven't you found and developed a good number two?"

"I should tell you it's above my pay grade, but the fact is any young man that looks good down there sooner or later mysteriously doesn't return from a patrol."

"Anyone in particular that Bunth always sends on those types of patrols?"

"Matter of fact, yes," Mister Sam said with approval. "A shifty-eye named Touby. He's a brother of one of Bunth's wives. Big scar on left cheek. He is the village Curer." The Hmoung believed a Curer was a man or woman given magical powers by spirits living within them. Curers had the power to heal, to determine the meaning of signs, to communicate with spirits. They were paid fees by their clients.

"Does Bunth send out many patrols?"

"Not as many as I'd like."

"Pearson said you don't have radio contact with him."

"We gave him three PRC-25s, but he always says he loses the frequency card. We try to change the numbers every day but it doesn't work out. Probably sold the radios."

Wolf looked at Pearson. "Can you spare another '25? With half a dozen batteries?"

Pearson said he could and brought them out.

"I'll see what I can do," Wolf said.

"What about frequencies?" Mister Sam asked.

"I'll see what I can do there, too. What can I promise him if he cooperates? Money? Weapons?"

"No, we don't want to give him any more weapons. He doesn't deserve or use what he's got. Maybe he sells them. But I can get him more rice. Lots of rice."

"An extra ten or twenty kilos per day?"

"Sure."

They walked out and Pearson called Lee and Loo. Wolf spoke to them in pidgin Hmoung and they both made wide grins and bobbed their heads. Mister Sam nodded approvingly.

"What did you say?" Court asked.

"I said we were only going down to inspect, not to fight, and that at the appropriate time I would provide a roast pig party." Wolf said goodbye to the three men, picked up his AK, and with a nod he and the two Hmoung disappeared down the back trail. Pearson shook his head. "Hey," he said to Court, "when that Wolf changed clothes, you notice he didn't wear any underwear? How come?"

Court laughed. He remembered his few days the year before in the Laotian wilds after he had been shot down, and the incredible humidity. His own skivvies had disintegrated in less than forty-eight hours. "Because it rots off."

Mister Sam said he was going back to his CP by the runway, and walked off.

Pearson led the way back into his combination office and sleeping quarters in the van. He pulled two sodas from the tiny refrigerator. "So," he said to Court, "tell me how you and the United States Air Force are going to save the world."

It was an hour before dark when Wolf and the two Hmoung reached the bottom of the karst ridge. Going down, Wolf was glad he had had extensive mountain-climbing experience with the Special Forces. He was bulky and had trouble keeping up with the nimble Loo and Lee, who skipped from rock to rock and ledge to ledge like mountain goats. At the bottom, he stopped and looked back up the steep sides. Before they had landed, he had had the Porter pilot make a few turns around the karst, and his descent now confirmed his belief that the near-vertical sides made for a rough assault. The trail they had just descended was easy enough to booby-trap and defend. They stood at the bottom in a well-trampled clearing that extended out the length of a football field to the two-canopy jungle.

Wolf studied his map, took a bearing with his compass toward the road numbered 602 by the French two decades before, and struck out across the clearing. At the jungle edge he saw several paths, one leading in the general direction of 602. He motioned to Lee and Loo and plunged down that path.

For the rest of that day and until past noon of the next, Wolf Lochert roamed the perimeter defenses of Site 85 in general and the Eagle Station karst mountain in particular. He met several patrols, was stopped by two command posts, and radioed his location to Eagle and Maple. Then he headed toward the village of Muong Yat. As was customary, Lee and Loo went ahead to arrange the protocol of the visit with the village chieftain. He was the LAD-C that Pearson had called Colonel Bunth. Wolf was squatting under a tree, rifle at the ready, when they returned.

"Wolf not go village Yat," said Lee. *Muong* meant village in Hmoung.

Wolf stood up. "Why not?"

Lee looked uncomfortable. "Bunth he say nothing why."

"Do you know why?"

"Bangpee." Maybe.

"What bad happen Wolf go village now?"

Lee giggled nervously and dug a bare toe into the dirt. Loo spoke up.

"Mercan. Bunth say no another Mercan in village."

"The American there told Bunth to keep other Americans out? Is that it?"

Lee nodded.

Wolf sat down and turned on the PRC-25. Mister Sam had said he would maintain a listening watch, and in five minutes Wolf had contact with him. He had to be careful how he talked in the clear.

"Did you tell the inspector I would visit his location?" he asked. "Affirmative."

"He say anything about not wanting me to visit his location?"

"Negative."

"I'll be out one more night. Copy?"

"Copy."

"Maple, Wolf, thanks. Out."

Wolf stowed the radio and stood up. He pulled out a roll

of *kip* and handed several of the thin bills to Lee. "You go village Yat, buy pig, pay old woman to start roast over fire. Make peace with local *phi*. Buy palm beer. Set it all out. Tell people man who make party will arrive later. Understand?"

Both men bobbed their heads and grinned.

"Most important," Wolf continued, "listen well, ask questions. I want to know if anything unusual is happening. Not just information on Pathet Lao or North Vietnamese Army, but anything else unusual or different. Can you do that for me?"

"Can do," Loo said, proud of his English, and made a thumbs-up sign.

The two Hmoung went back up the trail to Muong Yat. When they were out of sight, Wolf found a concealed spot well off the trail and sat with his back against a tree. He loosened his gear, drank from his canteen, and reviewed what he was going to do.

That DEA dope-hunter doesn't want me in his turf. Why? If he is in the middle of delicate negotiations, why didn't he walk back and tell me? It's not that far. What is he scared of? That I might find out something he doesn't want me to know? Wolf looked at his watch. Two hours until dark. *Once the boon gets going and there is a lot of noise, I'll just recce some.* He sharpened his stiletto until he heard village sounds grow louder. The *boon* was beginning. He stood up, adjusted his gear, checked his map and compass, and began to circle the village.

He found the paths that led to water and to other villages. He saw the small open areas where the tribesman slashed, then burned the grass so they could plant crops and edible tubers. He saw no poppy fields. From a hidden vantage point he watched the village and movement of the people. Unlike Laotian villagers, who raised their houses on stilts, the Hmoung did not. He saw the village chieftain's longhouse. Next to it was what he figured to be the thatch structure used by the DEA inspector. Like a ghostly bear, he made his circle of the village and, just at dusk, returned to where he had started and made himself comfortable. He didn't expect an attack, but he did lay an almost invisible wire on a small perimeter around his spot and attach it to a finger on his left hand. He sat against a tree with his AK in his lap and programmed himself for a light nap of one hour's duration. The last he heard before he fell asleep were the soft sounds of flutes and gongs from the village, signaling readiness for the *boon*.

Thirty minutes later, when it was quite dark, a twitch on the wire jolted his body like a massive electrical charge. Adrenaline surged throughout his body and into his brain, bringing him to instant physical and mental alertness. Without making a sound, he rolled to a crouch, put his rifle down, and pulled out his Randall stiletto. He figured it was probably the advance guard or point man of a patrol, but he didn't know if the patrol was friendly or enemy. If it looked like he was to be discovered, he wanted to examine and, if necessary, kill him silently.

The faintest of moonlight filtered through the high trees, illuminating vague tree forms but no definitive shapes. He heard the lightest of movement, as if a mouse sought its burrow, then the slow compression of leaves. He cocked an ear and thought he could hear breathing. He cupped his ear and slowly moved his head, like a radar antenna homing in on the direction of the sound. Barely perceptible in the air was the smell of a human who used bug repellent. It was not, he knew from experience, an Asian. From the corner of his eye, he caught movement advancing toward his tree. His muscles tensed; almost without conscious thought or signal from his brain he curled his hand, stopped his breathing, and, when the man was in position, rose up from behind. Silently cupping the man's mouth with his left hand, he pulled the head back to stretch the throat while simultaneously placing his knee in the man's back, bending his body into a tight backward bow. In the same silent and fluid motion, he placed his blade against the exposed throat. His mouth was next to the man's ear.

"Who are you?" he whispered.

The man went slack and shook his head and made a mumbling noise deep in his throat.

"Quiet, now. Who are you?" He released the pressure of two of his fingers over the man's mouth.

"James Perrit, DEA," the man said and coughed. "Let me go. You're choking me."

Wolf pulled him back to the tree and down to a sitting position. He could barely see him in the darkness.

"Just what are you doing out here?" he asked, trying to keep his voice low.

"I was just taking a walk. I heard you were out here someplace and I thought maybe I could see you and tell you to stay out of the village while I'm there. I didn't expect you to jump me." The man spoke in a hoarse whisper. "My glasses are gone. Help me find my glasses."

"Don't run around the jungle after dark. Why didn't you want me in the village?"

"These are very skittish people. I'm having a hard time getting their attention. I didn't want anybody else around to complicate things." Perrit groped around until he found his glasses.

"I think it's dumb of your company to send you out alone."

"We don't have enough men over here."

Wolf stood up. "Let's go," he rumbled. "Regardless of how you feel, I got work to do." He padded off into the darkness without another word or gesture. Perrit stumbled through the darkness to keep up with him.

The flickering fires illuminated the figures of Wolf Lochert and James Perrit as they walked with stiff steps into the main clearing of the village Yat. Wolf stopped and studied Perrit. He looked about thirty-five, slender, brown hair, horn-rimmed glasses. He wore a dark green safari suit.

"I've got work to do too, you know," Perrit said. "I'll be in my hootch." He walked to the thatch hut next to the chief's longhouse.

Wolf caught his bearings and headed for Lee and Loo, who stood next to a fire pit where a pig was roasting. Scores of small brown men, some naked except for loincloths, others in various portions of rough military jungle fatigues, sat or stood around the clearing, chatting among themselves in the glottal stops and tones of the Hmoung language.

"Come see Colonel Bunth. He wait you," Loo said, and led the way to the opening to the longhouse. Inside, under a kerosene lantern hanging from a roof support, sat Bunth and the dozen or so members of his family on mats. Out of the corner of his eye Wolf noticed a man with a scar on his left cheek. From the yoga-like way he sat, Wolf knew him to be Touby. Thin smoke rose from a charcoal brazier. Bunth and the two older women were puffing on long pipes, sending up a sweet thick white smoke into the close air. Wolf placed his rucksack and AK-47 at his side, muzzle away from Bunth, sat on his ankles, and stared at the coals in the brazier. After a long silence, Bunth spoke.

"Why you make *boon* for the people of village Yat?" Bunth spoke the advanced English of one who had spent many months in training at the Special Forces camp at Lop Buri in Thailand.

Wolf raised his head. "I make party for the brave warriors of Bunth and their families to display my appreciation and the appreciation of my government for their fierceness and loyalty in battle."

"Who are you?"

"A soldier. A simple soldier who does what he can."

"You have a name?"

"I am called Wolf."

"I have never seen a wolf. It is said to be a cunning and dangerous animal."

Wolf lowered his eyes and did not speak.

"Are you a wolf?"

After a short pause, Wolf spoke in a low voice. "Only to my enemies."

The man with the scar rattled off a few words. Bunth nodded without answering and spoke to Wolf.

"Do you have something for me?"

Wolf nodded to Lee, who handed him the radio from his back, which he put on the earth in front of him. Wolf took the spare batteries from his ruck and placed them next to the radio. He looked at Bunth.

"Mister Sam said you are a brave man who patrols his territory well." Inside, Wolf thought fleetingly of his vow, made years before, never to lie.

Bunth nodded, pleased. He said something very quickly

to one of the women in the longhouse. She came forward with a wrist-thick tube of bamboo full of liquid. A bamboo straw stuck up from the liquid.

Wolf forced a smile to his face and murmured sounds of appreciation. He knew what was expected of him. One tube was handed to him, and he sucked and slurped loudly from the straws. He did not like to drink alcohol because it made him nearly uncontrollable and he did not like to lose control of himself. When he was finished, he smacked his lips and said, "Ahhhh," as was expected.

When Bunth sipped it was the signal for the others to be given tubes of the beer, which was made from fermented palm. Bunth, as the headman of the village Yat, was the current chief of the Yat clan that had migrated generations before down from China. When the local soil was exhausted, it was up to him to determine where to move next. Hmoung preferred to live at high altitudes. Wolf knew there had to be a good reason for Bunth to have moved his village to this low terrain.

"Your patrols are good," Wolf repeated. He patted the PRC-25 and leaned forward. "There are numbers you like?"

"Every man has numbers he live by," Bunth replied.

"That is wise." He sipped his palm beer. "Maybe if you use your numbers for this radio to talk to Mister Sam you will receive more rice." Bunth's eyes flickered. He nodded in understanding.

"You are clever man," he said.

Wolf dug a small, green-covered Army field notebook and a pencil from a pocket and handed them to him. Bunth wrote a few numbers down and handed the book back. Wolf read three sets of five numbers. He put a period after the first two digits of each set.

"Let's use the first four numbers in each set," he said. "Primary, secondary, tertiary."

Bunth nodded. He had been taught radio frequency rank order at Lop Buri.

Wolf felt he had control of the situation enough to risk a command. "Call Mister Sam when the sun goes down and when the sun comes up."

Bunth stared at the PRC-25 and did not answer. From his sitting position Wolf picked up the radio and batteries and placed them in front of Bunth.

"For every time you call twice each day, Mister Sam will add five kilos of rice to your ration."

Bunth looked up. "Not five, no. Give ten more each day. Plane drop rice maybe every ten day. Send hundred more kilo each drop."

Wolf nodded. Bunth had doubled the load but he had left room for bargaining. "Yes, that is possible. Mister Sam will add ten more kilo each day you call *two* times, once at the morning sun, once at the evening sun." It was silent in the longhouse save for the sipping noises. Wolf spoke again.

"You can tell Mister Sam of your brave patrols. He would be most interested. One patrol in the night. You can tell him of that in the morning. One patrol in the day. You can tell him of that in the evening."

"You do not like my beer?" Bunth asked, unwilling to agree.

Wolf took a long sip and the level in his bamboo tube was immediately brought to the top by a wife.

"Ahhh, good." Wolf smacked, and wiped his lips. He was beginning to feel dizziness and the onset of nausea. He knew what he had to do. He spoke with Bunth of inconsequential things for a few minutes, then excused himself and went outside into the bush and stuck his finger down his throat. While it was perfectly acceptable to be ill from the liquid, it was not acceptable to refuse more until the party was over. When he returned he was handed his tube, freshly filled with palm beer. He sipped and smacked and sipped some more. Then he spoke.

"You understand there must be something to speak of when you contact Mister Sam."

Bunth studied his beer.

"Something of consequence."

Bunth said something in rapid Hmoung, causing the others to laugh.

"Something of what your brave soldiers see on the patrols. He wants to know if there are enemy soldiers moving toward

230

Poo Pah Tee. Where they are, how many, what direction they are moving. Mister Sam is only interested in what you see, not who you kill. It is not necessary to fight yet."

"You think we cannot fight?" Bunth responded quickly in a thin voice.

"No, I do not think that. I know Bunth and his men are good fighters. But for now Bunth and his men should act as the creeping tiger stalking his prey, not being seen, not giving his position away. Report what you see twice a day and Mister Sam will give you ten kilos for each day you report two times on your radio."

The man with the scar spoke again. Bunth answered, then nodded to Wolf.

The deal was done.

Cradling his rifle Wolf walked out to the area where the *boon* was in progress. Lee and Loo fired off some rapid-fire words, and the Hmoung sitting around the fire pit made "ahh" sounds through toothy smiles. He took the offered bamboo tube of palm beer and accepted a dripping slice of pig on a banana leaf. He sat down and made a big show of eating and pretending to drink. For a while he spoke with Lee and Loo, then he went to the thatch hut next to the longhouse of Bunth and went in the open door.

The light from a kerosene lamp turned low barely illuminated the face of James Perrit, who was sitting cross-legged on a straw mat eating C-rations from a tin. Placed on the mat next to him were a .45, two caliber .38 revolvers, and a Swedish K assault rifle. A rucksack and a PRC-25 radio were in one corner. He was barefoot. A pair of combat boots with brown socks draped over them stood next to the radio. Behind the boots was a rolled-up sleeping bag. Wolf waved a hand at him.

"Do you know how many airstrips there are in Laos?" Perrit asked without preamble. His voice was thin and official, as if quizzing a subordinate.

"Over a thousand," Wolf replied, amused at the man's intensity.

"Twelve fifty-six, to be exact," Perrit said. "Can you believe that? And do you know that nearly every one of them can be used to fly dope in or out? Did you know that?"

Wolf stared at the man and did not answer. He had dealt with DEA men on other occasions and found that some were obsessed almost beyond reason with their job to stop the flow of raw opium from Asia.

Perrit snorted. "I told all this to the Air Attaché. When I asked him how much radar he had to cover all the strips, he told me there wasn't any. Can you believe that? I asked him what he was going to do about it and all he did was laugh. Can you believe that? I don't know how you people out here expect us to do our jobs if we don't get at least *minimal* cooperation from all agencies. Just minimal." He sighed and seemed to wind down. "I've got a message to send."

Wolf hazarded a guess. "About Touby?"

"Yes."

Wolf sat with his gun across his knees and did not speak. The evening air was cool and clear but humid. The soft flute and tocsin bell sounds floated on the light breeze that wafted smells of roast pig and sweet tobacco.

"How many days have you been here?" Wolf asked.

"Three."

"So what have you found?"

"I think Bunth or somebody out here is a big opium producer and transporter."

"Or somebody?"

"Touby, maybe."

"The one with the scar? The Curer?"

"Yes, that's the one. Why are *you* here?" Perrit asked.

"Didn't Mister Sam tell you? I'm here to see what level of competence Bunth and his people have in protecting Eagle Station."

"So what do *you* think?"

"Right now, not much," Wolf said. "Just a few hours ago I made a complete turn about this village and was not discovered. Bunth is supposed to protect the climbing approach side to Eagle Station out to a radius of twelve kilometers. At best, he has to find and stop attacks. At the very least he must provide

232

a warning system. I don't see how he can perform any of those missions if his people can't even find someone prowling about their village in broad daylight."

"Do you expect an attack?"

"Sure, although I'm not certain the Agency men in Vientiane think so."

"You mean the station chief?"

"No. Some minor functionary with a big head named Jerome Powers doesn't think that last attack here amounts to much. He said it was done by an errant local PL commander who hadn't gotten the word to stay away from the site. He thinks the PL leave the entire site – Eagle Station included – alone because they probably get paid off from the poppy farmers, and because they think the site is well defended and can get full troop and air support in a matter of hours. Funny, he didn't mention Bunth as one of those who might be running dope and paying bribes."

"I'll tell you what I think," Perrit said. "I think Bunth is paying off the Pathet Lao so he can move opium. Powers didn't mention it because at the time he didn't know. He's not really in my loop. Now that I'm out here, I find enough evidence to believe Bunth is doing that, but until now I haven't reported this suspicion. I am just now ready to send the message to Vientiane, telling of my suspicions of Touby and his control over Bunth and the paying off of the Pathet Lao. But I don't think that has anything to do with whether Site 85 will be climbed and Eagle Station attacked or not. It's the North Vietnamese that want the site taken out. They can't stop the PL collecting dope-smuggling fees – maybe they even encourage it – but they can probably attack anyplace they wish at any time they wish. I wonder if Bunth would let the NVA go through his sector without reporting them."

"No," Wolf said, "because that would mean he would get on the wrong side of General Vang Pao and the United States government, from which he gets funds and supplies. I think he would put up a token battle to make it look as if he were seriously fighting. But in the final analysis that's all that Eagle Station really needs, the warning. Hak's men can defend the climbing approach and air strikes can do the rest."

"What do you think of Touby?" Perrit asked. "I've told you what I thought."

"I agree with you. He's more in control of Bunth than meets the eye. Very savvy and shifty-looking to be a Curer. They usually appear more mystical and serene than he does. He has great control over Bunth, more than a Curer should have. Political control, certainly, maybe military as well. Mister Sam thinks Touby kills or causes to have killed any promising number-two man to replace Bunth."

"Why does he exercise such control? Is it just his nature or is there some other reason?" Perrit asked.

"I hope to find out," Wolf said and looked out over the village. The male villagers were sitting in an elongated oval around the big fire pit. Many had weapons and other fighting gear next to them. All were tearing into chunks of meat and drinking palm beer. A few old men played flutes and softly tapped the tocsins.

"Stay here for a while," he said. "I'll go see if the seeds I planted are bearing any fruit." He stood up and, rifle in one hand, walked to the edge of the firelight. Loo saw him and came over.

"They thank you," he said, "and want to know why you do such a good thing."

"Tell them it is because they are brave and fierce warriors." Wolf added a few more compliments as Loo translated. The men made collective "ah" sounds and nodded their heads.

"They say you are animal-man to walk always with your weapon in your hand."

"Animal-man?"

"One who has weapon a part of his body, like teeth of tiger or poison of snake. Your weapon is a part of you." He looked up at Wolf. "They like you. Come with me, they have something for you."

Wolf walked with him to the center of the oval by the fire pit. Several of the men started tying strings around his left wrist in the eternal gesture of Hmoung friendship. Each string meant good luck and happiness. They chanted as they tied the small strings in the *bacci* ceremony.

234

When it was over, and Wolf expressed his gratitude, he drew Loo aside.

"Have you any information for me?"

Loo nodded. "They say for the last many days and weeks, strange men appear like magic. The men talk and give much *kip*."

"What kind of men?"

"White-skinned men."

"American?"

"I do not know, but they do not talk as you talk."

"French?"

"Not French."

"They give *kip*. What for, *yafin*? For opium?"

Loo scratched his head. "It is difficult to know. One cannot say why they give *kip*. It is not for *yafin*. They do not take any with them when they go."

"Who do they give the *kip* to?"

"The Curer."

Wolf looked up, as a smiling Bunth stepped from the longhouse to survey the festivities in the village. He was clearly outlined in the firelight and seemed pleased with the *boon*. After a few moments a scowling Touby walked out and spoke into his ear. Bunth stopped smiling. He spoke to Touby, who responded in harsh tones. After a moment Bunth turned toward the fire and raised his hands.

"It is over," he said. *"Go to your houses."*

With barely perceptible hesitation the villagers melted into the darkness outside the firelight and returned to their houses. In minutes the square was deserted. Lee and Loo arranged themselves on the ground next to the fire pit. The light from the fire pit waned, as a woman swept dirt over the coals. Wolf sat for a while with Lee and Loo, then walked back to the DEA man's hut. *When it's over,* he thought, *like a curtain pulled down.*

The village was dark, sleep sounds came from the open thatch huts. Wolf entered Perrit's hut and saw his form on the sleeping bag, arm tucked under his head as if asleep. Wolf turned up the lamp and noticed that Perrit lay on his side in a strangely loose way. He knelt down, turned him over, and felt

235

for a pulse at his neck. Perrit's mouth was slack, his eyes half opened. There was nothing, just the cooling skin of a recently dead man. He made a cursory examination and found no blood or signs of wounds. He sat back on his heels and thought about what he had found. Maybe a heart attack. *There is nothing I can do now. It's too late, he's already cold. I'll call Mister Sam and have him get an evacuation helicopter here in the morning.* Wolf had seen death many times before and had learned not to react in any but a perfunctory manner.

He straightened out Perrit's body, opened the dead man's sleeping bag, rolled him into it, and zipped it closed. He carried the heavy sagging bag to the side and laid it next to the wall. Then he squatted by his PRC-25 radio, turned it on, picked up the handset, and called Maple several times. He knew he maintained a listening watch. There was no answer. He tried a few more times, then twisted one of the knobs to listen for the hiss of a frequency change. There was no sound, so he changed the battery. Still no sound.

He reached over for Perrit's PRC-25. When he had the same negative results, he looked at the back of each set, then pulled the batteries off. He grunted in surprise. Both radios had one of the battery contacts pinched off. With the battery in place, it would be unnoticeable. He put the radio down and snatched up Perrit's Swedish-K. The magazine was gone and no round jumped out when he pulled back the bolt. The cylinders of the revolvers and .45 were empty. Wolf pulled over his harness and rucksack. The magazine pouches were empty and his grenades were missing.

Okay, Wolf said to himself. *We have a bit of a problem here.* Someone wants me unarmed and cut off. He checked the twenty-round magazine of his AK-47 and then the Mauser 7.63 strapped to his ankle. He slapped the stiletto on the other ankle to ensure it was in place. Then he glanced over at the bulky sleeping bag. He went over and quickly unzipped the bag, stripped Perrit and examined his bare body. He found it when he lifted Perrit's left arm: a small drop of dried blood under Perrit's arm between two ribs near the top of his rib cage.

Wolf rubbed the dot away to reveal a tiny puncture mark.

He drew his breath in. Someone had punctured Perrit's heart with a hard, thin wire. It had gone through to his chest cavity and entered the heart. Wolf sat back on his heels, thinking about the old trick that fooled dull-witted coroners into believing the person had died of a heart attack or a stroke.

Let's see, Wolf thought. *They've broken the radios, taken the ammunition, and killed Perrit. I'd better get out of here – but not immediately – could stumble into all sorts of traps in the dark. For some reason they made all three incidents not easily recognizable. Perrit looked asleep and I shouldn't have noticed otherwise until morning. They could have smashed or stolen the radios, stolen the guns, killed Perrit outright and ambushed me – but they didn't.*

Wolf sat on the floor and leaned against his rucksack. The light from the lantern shadow-painted Comanche warrior designs on his face. He pondered who "they" might be. *Not Bunth or Touby – too sophisticated for them. And I don't see why the NVA would go to this much trouble – or the Chinese. They're in Laos, but as road builders and guerrilla advisers. They don't get into clever tricky stuff like this. It's got to be* Spetsnaz. *I'll bet it was a Sov team in the area, on training missions either to train themselves or to train the NVA or PL. Or for all three reasons. Everything done here could be performed by any average* Spetsnaz *team.*

But why? he asked himself. *For what reason? Whatever the reason, I found out they murdered Perrit earlier than they expected. They didn't think I would be on to his death as a murder until morning – or maybe never.* He frowned in thought. It was as if all they needed was to buy a few hours to do something.

He leaned back and shut his eyes. He thought about using the village radios but doubted that they would let him. *Bunth or Touby might not have done this,* he thought, *but I think they're in on it – it really doesn't make much sense – and maybe that's the key.* He opened his eyes and sat forward, flipped the cloth covering back, and looked at his watch. One o'clock. It will be daylight in about five and a half hours. He decided to talk to Lee and Loo.

He squatted outside the opening for several minutes to

accustom his eyes to the darkness and to listen and catalog the sounds of the village. There was no moon. Sleep murmurs from one side, a thumping of wooden boards as someone turned over on their pallet, a cough, frog sounds from the jungle. He heard the passage of jet fighters, some very close to the top of the karst. Soon, as his eyes made out distinct forms in the starlit village, he distinguished the individual sounds of relaxed breathing. He smelled the old smoke from the fire pit and the vinegary odor of palm beer. He looked around, then slowly rose to his feet and walked very carefully to the two forms sleeping by the fire pit. He quietly woke them and asked if they had heard anything from anybody about the strange men being close tonight.

Yes, they said, they'd seen a little motion in the dark they hadn't thought was normal, around the longhouse of Bunth. When Wolf asked if it could also have been near the hut of the *mei-mei*, the American, they said yes it was possible, but they could not say if the strange men were involved. Wolf brought them to the door of the hut and told them to be on guard and to keep one man awake at all times. He sat nearby against a tree.

He heard the faint clatter at three o'clock in the morning and recognized the whopping sound for what it was. Twenty minutes later he saw a shape that could have been Touby enter the longhouse.

He drifted off and woke while it was still dark, packed up his gear, and took Perrit's identification. After a healthy intake of water and some crackers, he left as the village was first stirring under a cool and vague dawn. Lee and Loo fell in with him. He noticed the absence of guards and security outposts along the way. They refilled their canteens at a small stream and added purifier tablets. At first the going was easy, the trail clear and wide, as the daylight turned from dawn gray to morning blue. He walked with an easy, distance-consuming stride. He didn't feel good about leaving Perrit back there but figured he'd send a helicopter for his body.

He was surprised he could depart the village so easily, and thought about the helicopter he had heard take off. He guessed it was a pickup for the people who had killed Perrit. *Maybe,* he thought, *they heard Perrit transmitting, weren't sure if it was about them or not, so they made a quick decision to take him out and cripple the radios and hope I wouldn't discover what had happened. Probably had to meet that helicopter or be left behind. That trick with the wire is right out of the* Spetsnaz *and KGB wetwork manual. I think they were running out of time and didn't want to get delayed. It was probably more important to get on that helicopter and get out of here than it was to kill me.* He stopped for a rest in the shade of a large limestone outcropping. Lee and Loo took up guard positions. Wolf removed his floppy-brimmed hat and wiped his brow with an olive drab bandana.

If it is *the Sovs,* Wolf continued thinking, *then it would be the first time they've been active enough in Laos to be spotted. None have ever been seen or even suspected in this part of Asia. So if they're here, it's for a special reason, a very special reason, to risk so much time in and around one small village.* He rested a few more minutes, then resumed the climb.

They passed several fighting positions filled with alert and well-armed men from Major Hak's village. He saw they had radios and were probably keeping Hak and Mister Sam advised of the American's approach up the steep path. It was shortly after the noon hour when he reached Mister Sam's hut and reported to Vientiane on the Collins HF, using the scrambler device. A helicopter was promised in three hours to extract him and go down to get Perrit's body. When he was finished, Court came down from Pearson's radar site.

Wolf told him about Perrit and his belief that *Spetsnaz* was in the area.

"*Spetsnaz?* Don't know much about them. Why not China? They supply a lot of aid to North Vietnam."

"China is not all that easy to work with. Besides, while the North Viets want Chinese war materials," Wolf said, "they don't want Chinese soldiers running around pulling off operations in Vietnam or Vietnamese-controlled territory. The people and the language the men describe to me mean Russian. And Russian means *Spetsnaz.*"

"Say again who or what they are."

"*Spetsialnoye Nazranie*. That means 'forces at designation.' "

"Strange way to put it."

"What it means," Wolf said, "is that they go in before a raid or an attack or even before a war starts so that they're there when the main force arrives. Their job is sabotage, killing important people, and generally wiping out command and control centers, all the while trying to create panic and disruption of the populace. They are trained in the customs, language, and may even wear the uniforms of the country they work in. Many members of the Soviet sporting teams that travel and compete around the world are *Spetsnaz* members."

"What are they doing in Laos?" Court asked.

"Training, I'd say," Wolf replied. "No better place to run around and teach and practice tactics than a moderately safe combat zone. Some *Spetsnaz* commander bucking for promotion probably decided taking out Eagle Station would be good for his career." Wolf stretched and yawned. "What is your impression of Pearson and the Station layout?"

"These Air Force men are not soldiers. Sure, they've qualified in M-16s and .38s on the range, but they've never been shot at, never have gone through basic infantry training. They're radar technicians and that's all. They can't be considered part of a defending force. If the place is going to fall, they must be evacuated well ahead of time. Mister Sam brought up Hak and some of his men. I taught them the Flaming Arrow trick but made the point it was last-ditch stuff. They showed me the best places and we built two. My guys checked in with F-4s and we spent most of yesterday and last night getting them familiar with the area. We lit the arrows last night and arranged the construction until they said they were just right. They're ready to go."

Wolf nodded. He told them what he had seen below in Muong Yat, how he didn't trust Bunth or Touby, and about the helicopter he had heard.

"Glad you heard that helio," Court said. "For a couple weeks my guys have been saying they had seen funny, flitting shadows down low around this area and Mu Gia Pass. When one suggested helicopters to a visiting Intell debriefer from 7th

240

Air Force, he was patted on the head and said to keep looking for guns, that no enemy helicopters had ever come into Laos since 1962."

Wolf nodded. "What I want to do now," he said to Mister Sam, "is go to Hak's village and see how his defenses are lined up."

"They are about as good as you'll find. C'mon, I'll take you there."

They returned from the inspection just before the Air America helicopter clattered into the helipad to pick them up. Wolf told Mister Sam that outside of a shortage of mortar tubes, he was satisfied Hak's plans were good, and Hak himself seemed like a true warrior, not just talk and subterfuge like Bunth and Touby. Court shook hands with Pearson. Mister Sam said he would radio VTT when they were off the ground and inbound for Vientiane. He raised a hand in farewell as the Huey helicopter lifted off.

The helicopter crew was well briefed. The pilot buzzed the Muong Yat village, while Court and the crew chief pitched out a few double-bagged sacks of rice to prepare the villagers for their unexpected arrival, then they landed in a clearing. The pilot kept the blades turning.

The crew chief, a ropy-looking Hmoung, pulled out a body bag. Wolf took a packet from his survival kit, then led the way to the hut. The villagers didn't seem as friendly as before, and most looked away as if the three men didn't exist.

"They have been told bad things about us," Wolf said.

"Maybe they don't believe what they hear, but they must act as if they do," Court said.

When they reached the hut and walked in, it was empty.

"What is it you would do now?" the Hmoung crew chief asked.

"We buy him back," Wolf said with disgust. From past experience with Lao bandits and a few undisciplined Hmoungs, he knew what to do. The bandit's way of life revolved around larceny, and deals that could be betrayed if it meant an additional profit.

He led them out and to the opening to the longhouse. In the

dim interior they could just make out Bunth and Touby sitting cross-legged on mats. Bunth was smoking a pipe, from which the thick, ropy smell of opium rose in overpowering waves.

"Help me talk, translate for me," Wolf said to the Hmoung crew chief.

Court nodded in greeting as Wolf made the appropriate salutations, then used the crew chief to ask where the body of their friend was.

"He is one with the spirits," Bunth said in a dreamlike state.

"You have buried him?" Wolf asked.

"He is one with the spirits."

"There are those who would want to have him back, to prepare him for his journey to the other side."

Bunth smoked and remained silent. Touby studied some items of magic he had in a small animal-skin bag.

"There are those who would reward you for your very excellent care of him."

Bunth looked up. "That is only to be expected. He must be a very important and rich man to send a helicopter for him."

At that point Wolf opened the negotiations. In ten minutes they settled on an ounce of gold, worth about $40. Touby spoke a few words to two men outside the rear of the longhouse. In moments they produced the sleeping bag. Touby's eyes flickered when Wolf unzipped it and steeled himself to look inside.

"There seems to be some mistake," he said, and held open the flap. The decomposed but unmistakable features of an elderly villager gaped at them.

"It is regrettable," Touby said without looking at the body. "Perhaps one could be persuaded to make a better search for that rich man."

"Perhaps the rice drops and the ammunition drops that fatten this village cannot be persuaded to continue," Wolf added in a reasonable voice.

Touby's body tightened in anger. "Go with them," he hissed, waving at the two Hmoung, who straightened up from the sleeping bag and stepped out of the longhouse.

Wolf and Court followed them out of the longhouse and to a nearby thatched hut, where they stood at each side of the opening. The crew chief stayed outside when they entered and found Perrit's body. It had been stripped bare.

12

They landed at Vientiane just before dusk. Jim Polter and two DEA men met the helicopter. The two men took Perrit's body and said they would debrief Court and Wolf at the Embassy. Jim Polter drove them there in his jeep and said to come by his office when they were finished and to plan to spend the night at his villa. He would arrange a plane to get Court back to Ubon tomorrow.

The DEA men were competent and professional. They took Wolf's statements without comment until Court told them what Wolf had had to go through and what he had had to pay to get the body back.

"We can't reimburse you, I'm afraid," the heavier of the two men said.

"The hell we can't," the younger man said and took two twenty-dollar bills from his pocket and handed them to Wolf. Unlike in South Vietnam, Americans stationed in Laos could deal in dollars, not military script. "Listen," he said, "you did a hell of a job. Most people would just have left him there. James Perrit was, well, really into his work. He could be abrasive. Thanks for the debrief and we will continue to track Bunth and Touby."

"You got anything at all on unusual activity in that area other than dope traffic and the commies?" Wolf asked.

"Like what?" the older man said.

"Like Russians."

The older man laughed. "You're nuts. Nothing like that in Laos."

"Try the Agency," the younger man said. "That's more their line of work."

"No point in seeing them," Wolf said as they strode down the hall.

"Mister Sam has told them all we know. Although I might see if the boss of that *Scheisskopf* Powers is back. He's the one I was supposed to meet in the first place." He entered the office.

A comely brown-haired woman standing by the empty desk said Mister Powers and his boss were in Bangkok for an unspecified period on Company business. She eyed Court with obvious approval and seemed about to speak as they walked out and headed for Jim Polter's office.

Polter had a visitor, a firm and sturdy blonde wearing a tan skirt and light blue blouse. Her eyes widened as she saw them. "Vulfgang," she said in surprise.

Wolf Lochert snorted in recognition. His mouth moved from a glad smile to a heavy frown. He had met Greta Sturm earlier in the year, when he had rescued her and Jim Polter from the roof of a CIA safe house that had no longer been safe in Hue, South Vietnam. She had been a nurse with the German Maltese Cross mission. At first reluctant to shoot at the attacking North Vietnamese, she had later proved to be cool and capable with an M-16. Afterward, quite taken, Wolf had talked at length with her, and revealed a reflective and gentle side of himself not seen since the days before he had left the Maryknoll Seminary to become a soldier. She had told him she would leave the mission and get a job as a nurse in Saigon to be near him, to be his girl-friend, but when Wolf had gone to her apartment shortly afterward, she had not been there, and the neighbors, who worked at the German Embassy, had not seemed to know her very well or where she had gone. He was disappointed and bitter that she hadn't tried to see him.

"Just what are you doing here?" he sputtered.

She looked like a doe trapped in a hunter's spotlight. "Not here," she said, and moved swiftly into the hall. Wolf followed her. Court eyed Polter, who winked and stayed behind.

In the hall she reached for his hand but he jerked away. "Wolfgang, I know you must be angry. You must think I lied to you." She spoke in a low, urgent voice. "I know I said we would see each other, then I was not available." Without makeup, her face looked like that of a young Teutonic boy with a firm chin.

"What are you doing here?" he repeated.

She licked her lips. "I am here on business. I work as an administrative nurse for the Agency for International Development. They sent me here with some studies." She wrung her hands. "Oh, I didn't want us to meet like this. I was afraid this would happen. Why didn't Jim tell me you were here?"

"You weren't in Saigon when I went to see you," he persisted.

"You never told me you were coming." Her gray, wide-set eyes looked worried and she seemed happy and flustered at the same time. There were dark circles under her eyes. For the first time Wolf noticed how thin she was compared to the last time he had seen her. Greta spoke. "Please – I must talk to you. I must explain."

Jim Polter walked up with Court. "C'mon, you two, quittin' time," he said with a grin. "I'm taking you over to my place for dinner." He grabbed them both by the arm and urged them out the Embassy door. No one noticed the brown-haired woman from Powers' office who watched from down the hall. She allowed a knowing smile to cross her face as she made plans to undertake a little seduction that night.

Polter drove them in a jeep to his rather sumptuous villa in the American compound called KM6.

"Yes," he said, only slightly embarrassed as they entered through wide doors into the polished, teak-floored hallway of his one-story American-style rambler, "it is like back home, isn't it?" The house was in a peaceful neighborhood with other

246

ramblers. There were manicured lawns, a few pools, concrete driveways leading up to garages, a few kids playing, bikes lying on the grass. Typical American suburbia in Vientiane, Laos. Many of the Embassy and AID people lived in these surroundings. Their younger grade-school-aged children went to the International School in Vientiane. High school-aged children went to the International School in Bangkok. Those college-aged kids who were actually in college were in Switzerland, taking advantage of the AID tuition and travel benefits. Most, however, were flitting about the world in grassy attempts to find themselves.

Polter showed the two men to the guest room. Polter offered Greta a room because, he said, they would probably be up talking well past curfew. She nodded but didn't reply.

After cleaning up, they sat in Polter's air-conditioned, teak-lined study, and were served drinks while they discussed the results of the last few days. Court was wearing a pair of Bermuda shorts, a tank top, and thongs. His tanned body was fit and trim. Wolf had put on civilian khaki pants and a short-sleeved sport shirt that accentuated the ridged muscles and dark hair of his forearms. Court and Polter had beer in thermal mugs so chilled that ice crystals had formed in the foam. Greta and Wolf had iced tea.

Wolf outlined his findings, saying he was quite sure Touby was in charge of Bunth and his men, and that he was playing both sides of the war, as well as the opium smugglers. Polter agreed and said small indicators in the past supported the theory. At dusk he brought them to the brick patio in the rear and put steaks on the gas grill while a servant hovered and replenished drinks. A large, curved pool, as fresh and immaculate as if it had just been constructed that afternoon from a picture in a garden magazine, stretched out to the tall trees and thick foliage around the patio. They settled in lawn chairs about a round white metal table with a center hole for an umbrella; muted classical music came from two waterproof speakers under the eaves on each side of the patio. They were discussing life in Laos in general and in Vientiane in particular. Jim Polter had just told them a Russian Embassy was there, and that occasional contact was made with the Russians on the streets and at the occasional functions attended by all of the diplomats in Vientiane.

"We kind of have fun with the Sovs, bait the attachés with phony stories, kiddy stuff like that. Years ago, before they stopped coming in to Wattay, we used to get drunk with the pilots who were flying stuff in for the PL." He got up to attend the grill as the sun set and a servant lit the Tiki torches. Greta looked imploringly at Wolf, who finally got the message and asked if she wanted to look at the flowers at the other end of the pool. Court sipped his beer and tried not to smile as they walked away.

They sat on a cement bench in a small flower garden that gave them partial concealment from the grill and the house. She took his big hand in hers.

"Wolfgang, if I hurt you, I am so sorry, so very sorry."

He remained quiet.

"Please," she said, "I did not handle it well. I know that. The battle, the fight, the deaths . . . you being so, so fierce and gentle at the same time . . ." She trailed off.

He shook his head. "I told you so much. You seemed so . . . defenseless. Then you shot so well. You put on quite a show. I should have known. The villa, after all, belonged to the Agency's man in Hue."

Her eyes widened. "You think I am with the CIA?"

There had been a bloody firefight during the escape. Greta Sturm had said she was a nurse and could not, *would* not, shoot a weapon, but when things had been at their worst, and a man with an M-16 had been killed next to her, she had picked up the weapon and proven to be a very good shot, quite cool under fire.

"It was quite a show."

"It wasn't a show. Oh no, I was afraid. I was very much afraid. I was not sure I could do it. I was not sure I could kill."

"All that about you being a nurse and your father not wanting you to be a doctor. And your joining the Maltese

248

Aid Society to get away from him. That wasn't true – was it?"

"Stop it," she said. "Stop it. It is true, all of it. Why don't you believe me?"

"Then why have you avoided me?"

She calmed down. "Because . . . because you are a soldier, a warrior."

"You knew that when we met and when we saw each other once at Tan Son Nhut."

"Yes, but . . . but . . . this is difficult . . . if I were to lose you . . . maybe I thought if I didn't see you ever again, then there would be no pain if . . . if—"

"If I got my tail shot off."

She wrung her hands. "Oh, I did miss you and I *am* glad to see you. So very glad."

Wolf turned to her. The torchlight framed her face. He shook his massive head. "We talked so much. I told you so many things about myself."

"Were they true?"

"Yes."

"Do you regret it?"

He thought for a moment. "I suppose not."

"Suppose? Why *suppose?*"

He inhaled a deep breath. "I have never revealed so much of myself to anyone, and when I could not find you I thought maybe . . . maybe I had scared you away."

She took his big hand in hers. "Oh, *Liebchen*, you could never scare me. You are so gentle. I am so sorry for what I did. I promise, I will not again hide."

He took her hand. "You look very nice," he said in a soft voice.

These were the most romantic words Special Forces Lieutenant Colonel Wolfgang X. Lochert had ever said to a woman in his life. Greta Sturm was the first woman seriously to attract his attention since his infatuation with a leggy dancer named Charmaine years ago. When he had watched Greta in the fierce battle at the Hue villa, calmly firing three-round bursts from an M-16, dirt smudge on her forehead, blonde

249

hair falling over the stock as she took aim, he had thought he had never seen a more attractive woman.

"No, I don't." She took her hand away. "I look terrible. I'm worried and all tired out."

"Well, you've lost weight."

"*Mein Gott*, Vulfgang. You do not know how to compliment a woman, do you? Lost weight, *ach*." She laughed and tossed her head. "*Yes*, I've lost weight. I work too hard. I can't help it."

"Tell me why you are really here in Vientiane."

She smiled. "You are only being nice to me to learn why I am here."

"Perhaps."

"I am here delivering some papers."

Wolf made a small sound in his throat, which she interpreted as a snort of derision. "You don't think a woman should be out here?"

"Hold on, there. I didn't say anything of the sort."

"You had better not. Your precious Army doesn't see fit to use women in anything but typing jobs. At least AID lets us get out in the field once in a while."

Wolf gave her what he hoped was his most sincere smile. "That they do," he said. "Delivering papers."

"You think I'm just a courier? Well, I am not. These papers are the results of my studies on health care for children in South Vietnam and Laos."

"What did you find?"

"South Vietnam – some care. Very little in Laos, outside of the Tom Dooley foundation."

They sat silently for a moment. "Wolfgang," she whispered into his ear. "Regardless of what you think about me, I *am* glad to see you. I mean it, I do want to see you in Saigon." In the darkness, she turned and kissed him lightly on the cheek.

"We will see each other," he said quietly.

Jim called that chow was about to be served. They went back and talked with Court for a few moments, when they heard the sound of the front door being opened by the houseboy, then the slap of sandals on the teak floor. The brown-haired girl from Powers' office stepped through the French doors onto the patio. She wore a brightly colored summer frock. The men rose.

Her brown eyes grew large in exaggerated surprise. "Oh, Jim, you have company," she said breathlessly. "I'll come back." She swept her eyes around and looked long at Wolf and Court. A half-smile formed on her lips. "Well," she said with a lilt, "maybe I will stay."

"Hello, Babs, drag it in and I'll wet it down with the usual," Jim Polter said and kissed her on the cheek. She curtsied in return.

"Greta, gentlemen – I present Barbara Powers. Call her Babs, but don't call her anything or talk to her until she has had at least two sips of one of my famous Vientiane coolers." Polter moved to the liquor table and quickly mixed cassis and soda over shaved ice in a tall glass. He added a cherry and handed it to her. She took two long pulls.

"Lifesaving. Absolutely lifesaving," she said. She put the drink on the table and offered her hand to Wolf, who happened to be closest.

"Hi – I'm Babs. Say, you are a brute, aren't you?" She looked at him with frank admiration.

"Wolfgang Lochert," Wolf said and shook her hand.

"Wolfgang?" She lifted an eyebrow.

Lochert cocked his head. "Wolf, then."

"Right. You look like a Wolf, all savage." She stood nearly an inch taller than the stocky man. She turned and offered her hand to the seated Greta Sturm.

"Babs," she said.

"Greta Sturm." Greta made no effort to smile or rise up from her chair. She reached up and pumped once, Continental-style. Powers' eyes swept from Greta to Wolf and back. She turned to Court and offered her hand.

"I'm Court Bannister," he said before she could give her name.

"I know," she replied. She smiled prettily, but Court noticed her eyes did not crinkle in accompaniment. Instead, they looked

251

directly into his own for just an instant longer than normal. He noticed fine lines that aged an otherwise young face. He guessed her at less than thirty, but how much he couldn't say.

"Gentlemen, please. Be seated," she said airily and sat on a metal chair next to the table. She picked up her glass and quickly drained it. Jim Polter took it from her and mixed another.

"Babs works at the Embassy," he said as he handed it to her. "Ambassador Plenipotentiary, I think."

"Powers?" Wolf said to her.

"Powers," she agreed. "Sister to Jer Powers. You know him, don't you? The great Jerome Powers?" She took a long drink of her cooler.

"You do kid, don't you, Babs," Jim Polter said with a strained smile.

"Actually, gang, Babs is *Mrs.* Barbara Powers – Jerome's wife."

"His little wifey," she said in a cloying falsetto.

Things had not gone as Barbara Westin Powers had dreamed and planned that Colorado summer nearly ten years ago. The first part had been successful – the part where she had toyed with that young Dominguez. Driving him nearly wild while she used him to tantalize Jer Powers had worked as she had anticipated. Powers had taken the bait, but the hook had been set by her father, who had been so relieved she was no longer dating out of her *race* that he would have done anything his little girl wanted. First, he'd thrown the biggest and most sumptuous coming-out party seen at the Broadmoor Hotel since gold mining days. Then, as the time had passed and Powers had seen more of her, Mister Westin had had a man-to-man talk with him and said that were he by some chance to become his son-in-law, a percentage of the dealership would be theirs to do with as they pleased and, further, a thirty-year zero-interest loan up to $100,000 would be available when it became time to buy a house. Naturally, his-and-her Ford Thunderbirds would be wedding presents. Barbara Westin became Mrs. Jerome T. Powers after her one and only year at

Vassar (she decided she could afford a year to see what it was like), where she discovered good bourbon and bad boys. It was there she adopted the nickname Babs, because Barbara sounded too provincial. She had tried to get the girls to call her Buffy, but it never took.

Sometimes now she thought, *God, what did I do to deserve this? I can't divorce that pig and still live a halfway decent life.* By a halfway decent life, Babs Westin Powers meant a life where she did not have to work, but could have enough money to enjoy a nice house, a new car every two years or so, and plenty of clothes and jewelry to wear while visiting friends and touring exotic vacation spots and meeting many different men. Daddy would cut her off. He was very old-fashioned and believed in monogamy. He could have trampy girl-friends, she thought, and he had, ever since Mommy was gone, but *she* had to be Miss Goody Two-Shoes or at least appear to be. Jerk Jerome's family had enough money to supplement his income by $500 a month, and Daddy had delivered as promised, so she hadn't lived *too* badly . . . so far. Jerk Jerome was certainly making more money with the CIA once he had cut loose from the Air Force after his service commitment had been up. And he couldn't fly – too bad: something might have happened and there was the $100,000 life insurance policy. And he had not been a good administrative officer. Couldn't take orders or something. So he had gotten out as soon as he could and found an immediate job with the Agency, which was desperately seeking young men with a college degree and military experience. Jerome had found himself the third Air Force Academy graduate hired by them and had done surprisingly well in training. After a short time in the States, they had been extremely pleased to be posted to an embassy right off. Pleased until they arrived at dusty, Oriental boomtown Vientiane. Even a nifty ranch-style house and shopping trips to Bangkok hadn't brightened the absolutely dull day-to-day existence for a bright young (I'm not even thirty and look twenty) Embassy Wife.

There had been a few men, all but one in Bangkok. A quick liaison with a CASI pilot had occurred once at Jim Polter's, but that, she had decided, was too risky. Besides, she thought maybe the other wives looked at her funny. Too risky, that is, until now – Court Bannister.

To Babs Westin Powers, Court Bannister was a catch. Handsome, rich, well-known, not married. What a pair they would make. She knew she could make the break from her dumb, dull, desultory existence married to a man who didn't know how to fuck, fight, or frolic. (She loved that phrase. The CASI pilot had taught it to her.) And Court Bannister could do all three, she was sure, because she knew about him. Her favorite reading material, the tabloids, the society pages, the Hollywood magazines, kept her well abreast of what was going on in that exciting world of what they called the jet set. She had a pretty good idea of what he was like . . . and what he liked. After all, he *was* the son of Sam Bannister and everyone knew Sam liked his women. And Court *was* a fighter pilot and everyone knew they liked *their* women.

"What do you do at the Embassy?" Greta said, studying her.

"Nothing much," she said, pulling herself back. "Just some typing in the political section. Look in at Jer's office. Keeps me busy." She took another swallow. "Keeps me off the streets and out of the bars."

"Must be *wery* tiring," Greta said, cursing herself for letting her accent slip. It happened sometimes when she was tired or upset.

"Not too," Babs said as she accepted a fresh cooler from Polter. He quickly refreshed the others' glasses and Court's Budweiser and said he had to tend to the grill. Wolf glanced over and saw there was just the right amount of steaks, as if Polter had known Babs, or someone, would be joining them.

Babs Powers turned back to Court and fixed him with her eyes. "What brings you to Vientiane, Court?"

He almost smiled at the intensity of her gaze, for he thought he knew what it meant. He had been brought up around movie stars, starlets, and sycophants all his life. He knew a come-hither gesture when he saw it.

"Tourism, ruins, Plaine des Jarres, cultural activities. The usual." He could feel the beer.

"Hmm, yes, the usual. How *were* things out there with the dear old natives?"

"Revolting. "

"Yes, I'll bet they were." She finished her cooler and looked up at him with a slight smile curved barely short of mocking. She absently thanked Jim Polter as he handed her her third cooler. Wolf and Greta walked over to the pool and sat on the diving board, talking quietly. Jim busied himself with the steaks. Babs took a sip while holding Court's eyes.

"Do you come this way often?" she asked.

"Offhand – no." Court drained the beer from his mug and was handed another by a houseboy.

"Pity," she said, her eyes admiring his body. She leaned forward and reached over to tap his bare knee. "You keep in shape, don't you?"

"I try." He couldn't help noticing her own figure, the almost too muscular calves of her legs, the smooth curve of flank under the silk.

"You obviously indulge in a lot of exercise yourself."

"Oh, I do." She made a mirthless smile, reminding Court of the cartoon cat about to devour the canary.

"Food's on, chow down," Polter sang out from the grill. "Eat now or forever hold your peace."

"How do you spell that, James?" Babs asked.

Polter guffawed and said, "Now, now, girl, be nice." He signaled the houseboy, who brought wooden platters for the steaks. Wolf and Greta came over and they sat around a picnic table under an arbor by the pool.

"Goodness, Jim," Babs said, "I didn't expect to be fed. I just popped in to say hello and see who all your charming guests were. We get so few *interesting* visitors around here. This is a *dreary,* dusty *village. "*

"I guess you'll just have to take Earthquake's steak," Polter said, and flopped the biggest of the steaks on her plate. Wolf nodded in comprehension and appreciation.

"Earthquake McGoon?" Court said.

"What on earth are you talking about?" said Babs.

Polter explained. Jim McGovern, nicknamed Earthquake McGoon, after Al Capp's character in his *Li'l Abner* cartoon strip, had been a heavyset pilot – a very heavyset pilot – from the Midwest who'd wound up flying C-119 twin-boom cargo ships for CAT or Flying Tigers in 1954. He'd been shot down air-dropping badly needed supplies to de Lattre's beleaguered French soldiers at Dien Bien Phu weeks before it had been overrun by the Viet Minh in March of 1954. He'd almost landed his crippled ship onto a sandbar in the nearby river. When he'd seen he couldn't make it, he'd calmly radioed, "Looks like this is it, son." None of his fellow pilots and friends at Vientiane really believed he was dead. He had survived one crash and was too legendary not to survive another. Someday he would emerge from the jungle and demand his steak and his drinks. "Monte Banks at the Purple Porpoise was so sure Earthquake was coming back he had his big Papasan chair mounted on sort of a stage and wouldn't let anybody sit in it," Polter finished.

Jim made the toast, "To Earthquake," and they all drank. A Bach quartet sounded from the speakers. Jim broke out a strong red Burgundy and poured for Babs, Court, and himself. Wolf and Greta stayed with iced tea. The houseboy lit Tiki torches around the pool as the purple dusk turned darker. They spoke of life in Vientiane: the influx of newsmen trying to dig up stories of the war in Laos, the latest Dooley Dollies who had come in to replace the volunteer stewardesses who had taught English and nursed for the Tom Dooley Foundation, and the antics of the Air America and Continental Air Service pilots.

"I wouldn't know about that," Babs said. "I make it a point never to date pilots. From around here," she added, swinging her eyes back to Court.

"You must have very many . . . friends," Greta said, trying to hold her eyes wide and innocent.

"Well, I do represent the American Embassy, you know. I'm paid to make friends," Babs replied with scarcely a glance in Greta's direction.

"Yes, I bet you are," Greta said in as near a snarl as possible without violating the laws of civility. "Your husband – you *are*

256

married, are you not? Your husband – what does he do?"

Jim Polter interrupted the interchange with some innocuous comments about the weather. Court and Wolf stretched out a conversation about the National Football League until dinner was over. Greta barely maintained control of her seething disposition while Babs cheerily traded remarks with Jim about Asian versus American sunsets.

It was well after nine and totally black under an overcast sky when they moved from the patio to the study. Greta said she was too weary for words and said she would take Jim up on his offer for a room. She bade goodnight. Wolf hemmed and hawed around until he too said goodnight and followed her down the long hall. Babs made a lewd grin when they heard him knock quietly on Greta's door.

"Well, how was Lima Site 85, home of your charming Eagle Station?" Babs said with a wide smile to Court.

Court looked at Jim Polter. "What did you say she did at the Embassy?"

Polter laughed.

"What makes you think I know what you're talking about?" Court said.

"Come off it, Court," she said. "Everybody knows what everybody else does around here. Nothing's classified."

"The hell you say. Maybe everybody who is anybody knows what happens to someone who is somebody – but I'm not somebody. I'm just passing through."

"You don't just pass through Vientiane. You're either going someplace in Laos or coming from someplace in Laos." She turned to Jim. "Isn't that true?"

He held his palms up. "How would I know? I just labor here." He put down his napkin and stood up. "I've got an early git-go tomorrow aye-em," he said to her, "so I'm packing it in. You know where the booze is, Court. Come to think of it, so do you, Babs. Make yourselves to home. Night."

They said goodnight in chorus as he walked out.

Court poured them both a Drambuie from Jim's well-stocked cabinet. He eyed Babs. "What makes you think I know anything about – what did you call it? Lima Bean 85?"

"Get off it, Court. I know exactly why you're here."

"Well, you are married to a man in the business. I suppose he keeps you informed. Where is he tonight?"

She ignored his question. "I specialize in interesting people. I try to find out as much as I can about them before I meet them."

"Hell of a hobby. You should be a spook." One of the houseboys cleared the table. He accidentally knocked a glass off the edge, but Court caught it before it hit the hard floor.

"Nice catch," she said. "What else can you do with your hands?"

He sat back; "Babs, if you will excuse me for asking, why do you come on so—"

"Forward?" She sipped her wine and looked at him over the rim of the crystal. "I thought all you Hollywood types liked that kind of woman.

"I'm not a Hollywood type. I haven't lived there more than five years in my life, and that was over ten years ago."

"Well, you were acting. I did see you at the movies."

"Years ago, when I was young and dumb. I was an extra for gunsmoke and horseshit, sand and sex."

"Well, maybe it was your father I saw so much." She recited: "'Silk Screen Sam, the ladies' man. If he can't get in, no one can.'" It was a rhyme that had been around since 1938, when young Sam Bannister had been the bachelor idol of young movie fans throughout the world. "Is that what they say about you, too, Court? Do you want to get in?"

Court tossed his napkin onto the table. He got up and walked out to the patio. One Tiki torch cast a faint glow over the patio and pool. He had to get away from this woman.

"You could be more friendly, you know," she said as she followed him out into the night air.

Court didn't turn around, then was startled by a splash. He turned to see the dark form of Barbara Powers stroking quietly in the dark water of the pool. He recognized her dress, lying in a careless heap on a deck chair, her shoes underneath. Something white and filmy hung from the back. He sat down in a wicker chair near the pool rim and watched her swim

258

almost to his feet. She was attractive, and it had been a long time.

"Come on in," she said in a throaty voice. "The water is, as they say, fine."

Court shook his head. "I think not." He could see the V-shaped shadow of the cleavage between her trim breasts. Her dark hair hung seal-sleek down her back. She reached out and lightly ran her fingers over the top of his bare foot. Despite himself he felt the blood rising within him. He saw himself dropping his shorts and plunging in and taking this girl underwater. He almost shivered at the thought.

"I think I'll stay out," he said, his mind finally made up.

"Cold?"

"No, chicken."

"Court Bannister? Chicken? I don't believe it." In one fluid motion, she hoisted herself out of the water, twisted in midair, and sat lightly on the edge of the pool. The torch flickered golden on her curves.

"Babs," he said. "I'm taken." He tried to talk lightly and did the best he could to keep eye contact with her, and not let his gaze roam over the secret valleys and mounds.

"Surely you're not married?"

"No, just . . . taken." He thought about the letter in his room.

She rose to her feet and sauntered over to pick up her dress, then stood hipshot and made a little sound of derision. "Well, you don't leave me much, do you? All that beautiful body simply wasting away. How utterly ridiculous." Embarrassed now, she dressed quickly and left Jim Polter's patio and rambler house without another word. Damn, she thought. Why had she come on so strong? She wondered how she could arrange to get another chance at Court Bannister.

Court watched her leave, then stripped off his tank top, dropped his Bermudas and made a running dive in the pool and let himself knife into the cool depths. He made several laps of the pool as quietly as he could, trying to tire himself. After ten minutes he emerged and walked slowly in the Asian darkness to his room. "Taken," he had said, and it was true.

Our love is here to stay, he hummed in tuneless repetition, as he thought of Sue Boyle, the one girl who had held his attention for more than a week or two. It was, let's see now, over a year since they had been together. Court had met Susan Boyle on his return from his first tour in Vietnam. She had been a sun-brown Manhattan Beach girl with sleek lines who was flying as a stewardess for American Airlines. She had had a leonine mane of hair and liked to laugh. He pictured her tall legginess and shoulder-length blonde hair, her wide smile and deep blue eyes, her magnificent breasts.

He fumbled on the low light by his bed and pulled her letter from the photo case he carried in his gear.

Got to see you, she wrote. *Too lonesome for words. Miss your kisses, your strong arms, your beautiful body, and your . . . oh, you know. Got some time off due and thought I'd use one of my hard-earned passes to come over your way and make some passes of my own. Oh Court, I miss you so much. I know this is kind of hurry-up, but please try to come down to Bangkok and see me. If you can't, maybe I can take the train or an elephant, or however they travel in Thailand, up to Ubon to see you. If I don't get bumped (Pan Am), I should arrive around the 23rd of October. Love, love, love, desperate to see you. Hope you don't mind the short notice. Your Susan.*

He had wired her to meet him at the Oriental Hotel in Bangkok, where he would arrange a suite. No, Babs Powers would not tempt him tonight.

He held the letter for a long time and thought about his sunny California girl with the long blonde hair and the deep blue eyes, who walked and talked with such special assurance and regal bearing. He studied her picture in the small brass folding case he carried. She stood poised and sleek on the foredeck of a large sailboat, holding the sheets with one hand and waving with the other, hair streaming in the wind, eyes alive and sparkling, her smile infectious and full. *To my very own,* was written on it, and the signature, *Your Susan.*

The last time they'd been together she had put him off when he'd pressed her to marry him. That had been in Singapore.

Had she changed her mind? What if she was here to say she was ready to get married? Now he wasn't certain if *he* would go through with it.

He knew he could get away from Ubon for a few days. He was the boss of his own outfit and they scheduled themselves as they desired and he was overdue for a break.

He crossed his legs and put his arms behind his head, thought of the song they'd sung when they were together in Singapore, *Gibraltar may tumble, the Rockies may fall . . . ,* and fell asleep.

"Oh, Wolfgang, you are so strong . . . ahh." She enfolded him, her strong legs gripping.

"Greta," Wolf said later, as the dawn broke.

"Yes, lover."

"I've been thinking."

"Yes, lover."

"That Swedish K that Perrit carried. The bolt clacks. The NVA and VC hears that in a firefight and knows only Americans use them. Don't you ever carry one. Get a clean AK-47, they won't know who you are.

"Yes, lover."

Jim Poulter got everybody out of bed at six in the morning by the simple expedient of frying bacon and eggs and turning Sousa marches up to maximum volume on his Akai stereo. One by one they dressed and stepped through the French doors onto the patio.

"The Beech for Ubon takes off at 0730 on the dot," he told them as he poured strong coffee. The brilliant sun promised to scorch the brick once it cleared the palm trees.

Wolf and Greta were quick to thank Jim for his hospitality. Greta had an unmistakable glow that had not been there the night before. Wolf was his usual bulky, quiet self. Court was not. He drew Polter aside.

"That was a setup, Jim."

"No – honestly. She was just checking you out. Little Babs can smell a new cock in town from a mile away."

"Good God, man, she's married! Does her husband know about her?"

"Can't help but know, but does nothing about it. I heard he spends his off-duty time at LuLu's."

"You sure you didn't aim her at me just to see what would happen?"

"No, I swear. Nothing happened?"

"Nothing."

"Historic first. It'll ruin her reputation."

"Pity."

2030 HOURS LOCAL, MONDAY 21 OCTOBER 1968
DOLLEY MADISON BOULEVARD
MCLEAN, VIRGINIA

The telephone rang and Sal answered. It was John Duchane, an old Army Air Corps chum of Whitey's who was now the owner and chief executive officer of the American Transport Company. He and Whitey belonged to a monthly poker group that Whitey rarely had time to attend.

"Heard you were retiring," Duchane said when Whitey got on the line. "Damn well time, too."

"And good to talk to you, John," Whitey said dryly. "Sorry I missed the game last week."

"That's not why I called. Since you will be without a job come fairly soon, I have a proposition for you."

In 1946, with $9,500 in squirrelled-away WW II poker winnings, a persuasive and compelling personality, and a $30,000 line of credit from the Bank of Southern Arizona, Duchane had started his company, ATC, with two surplus C-46 aircraft that he had bought for $8,500 each. By 1960, ATC and its subsidiary companies had a net worth of 4.25 million dollars. When the Vietnam war got in full swing in 1965, he was already supplying transportation and selling surplus airplanes back to the government.

He would not, however, sell back his beloved twin-engined B-26, *Excalibur,* upon which he had lavished $210,000 to turn it into a plush, fast, executive aircraft. He had deliberately left the warning placard on the modernised instrument panel that said DO NOT OPEN BOMB BAY DOORS ABOVE 425 KNOTS. (The bomb-bay doors were now welded shut to hold the flooring of what he called his executive suite.)

Duchane had approached Whitey with a job proposition five years earlier, when Whitey's time as a two-star general had been up. Generals were selected for three stars by being uniquely qualified for a specific three-star position. Nothing had existed for Albert G. Whisenand at that time, so he had been due to be involuntarily retired from the United States Air Force. His job had been to screen targets for air strikes emanating from the unwieldy chain of command for Vietnam. Then, in 1966, Lyndon Baines Johnson had picked him to serve as the Special Advisor for Air Support on LBJ's National Security Council.

With LBJ soon to be out of office, John Duchane was sure he could finally hire his old friend.

"Whitey, it's not like before, when I needed you to run ATC while I looked into expansions. Now I really need you to run the whole conglomerate while I run around the world and salvage old war birds. I'm sort of retiring. Those old planes are fun to fly, plus there's a lot of money to be made fixing them up and selling them. Listen, here's my offer: $200,000 per year, a staffed château on the Potomac, a limo with chauffeur, and you can fly *Excalibur* once in a while."

Whitey chuckled. "Make it $300,000, keep the château and the limo, let me fly *Excalibur* as much as I want, and I might be interested."

"Agreed," Duchane said without hesitation. He needed this man.

They set the timeline – early fall – when Whitey should know about his future in the United States Air Force, and hung up. Whitey returned to the couch and told Sal of the offer.

"A château on the Potomac? A chauffeured limousine? Why, my dear, you would make a fine country squire."

Whitey chuckled. "But we wouldn't own either. Further, I'd have to pay taxes on the use of both as if they were straight salary, and the IRS would calculate some astronomical sum that would drain my base pay. Maybe someday we'll buy our own château and limo. In the meantime I like this house and the Olds."

Sal sat forward, her eyes gleaming. "It would be nice for you to have a job where you would be home more. Are you seriously considering taking up John's offer? I do like him, you know."

Whitey sat back. "Yes, if things go the way I suspect, I would seriously consider taking the position." His eyes sparkled. "Mainly because I want to fly *Excalibur.*"

13

The white Mercedes limousine pulled up at the wide entrance of the old colonial hotel. A doorman clad in ancient Siamese warrior costume opened the door with a flourish and smiled as Court Bannister stepped out.

"Welcome, sir. May I help you with your baggage?" Court indicated the trunk that the uniformed driver had already opened.

The doorman went back and inspected with dismay the battered USAF B-4 bag Court used to carry what few civilian clothes he had. It wasn't what the doorman had expected from the plush-carpeted trunk of a new Mercedes limo. He noted with puzzlement that the Thai driver was remarkably obsequious to this tall *farang*, who must have paid much money in advance. He looked a bit rough, but he couldn't be an American military man. They didn't make enough money to stay at the Oriental. Maybe he was an oil worker from the Mideast come to Bangkok to throw his money around during a few weeks' vacation. Probably not. Those men usually stayed down around Patpong and hung around the dark noisy bars where all the naked girls danced. This big blond man might just be someone important after all. Maybe he actually owned a construction company.

The doorman was one of five men paid handsomely to greet the arriving guests in their best manner, but they made even more money from tips the *farangs so* lavishly passed out. He prided himself on being a good judge of character – who would tip well and who would not. This man would not. Therefore, he was surprised when the manager himself and the gracious lady from Public Relations greeted the *farang* with great deference and told him his friend was already in residence and waiting for him. The doorman turned the B-4 bag over to an elegantly dressed bellhop and resumed his post in front of the wide doors.

The manager personally escorted Court up the elevator to a suite on the top floor. The manager cited the cable he had received from Terry Holt of Bannister Enterprises in Hollywood, detailing Court's desires for a two-room suite with a view of the Chao Phya River and said he hoped the suite would suffice. A $10,000 wire transfer had been sent by Holt to ensure compliance. The bellhop followed, toting the battered bag.

Each room had its own terrace with trees and lounge tables and chairs that overlooked the bustling Chao Phya River. Long-nosed river taxis and fat boat-buses vied with barges piled high with goods as they plowed up and down the wide, sun-sparkling river, making it a broad street of aquatic commerce.

But Court paid no attention to the view. He had eyes only for Susan Boyle, in the middle of the suite, waiting for him. When they were alone, she threw her arms around him and they kissed and nuzzled and she murmured into his neck, "Oh Court, I can't believe we're finally together." His hands were firm and flat around her waist, and he pressed her close and hugged her. She smelled of girl and an elusive cologne.

They stood in the middle of her room. She skipped over to the door to the patio and drew the curtains and shed clothes on the way back. "Come on, oh come *on,* I've dreamed of this for so long. I just can't wait." He stripped and followed her to the bed. She tore the bed-clothing off and pulled him down on her and wrapped her arms around him for a long kiss. She had set in low music on the room radio in anticipation of his arrival.

When they finished making love, he fell asleep in her arms. She lay awake for long moments before falling into fitful sleep.

266

That evening they had drinks at the hotel bar and dinner on the candlelit wooden tables at Nick's Number One. They ate slowly and savored each bite. She stroked his hand.

"You're so quiet all of a sudden," she said.

"Memories. Some good ones and some bad." He had just had a momentary thought of the F-4 that had fallen in the night at Eagle Station. Then his face darkened and his eyes went frosty as he remembered another man who was close to him and was now in the living hell of a POW camp.

"Here's to Flak Apple," he said and held up his waterglass.

Algernon A. "Flak" Apple and Court had formed a friendship back at Edwards Air Force Base in California when Court had been a student in the test pilot school and Flak an instructor. Later they had flown against MiGs together from Ubon. They had been on the same mission when Flak had been blasted out of the air. Court had taken Flak's loss personally, thinking perhaps he could have done something to have prevented it. A few months later a confused and highly exploitive radio broadcast from an expatriate American living in Cuba had said that Major Apple was alive and in good shape, and although a war criminal of the worst type, he was being treated humanely by the Democratic Republic of Vietnam. That was the first anybody knew Flak was still alive.

They drank the water. If Flak and the other POWs couldn't have booze, then it was only fair to toast them with water.

Court shook his head. "Memories. Oh God. I need some new ones." He brightened. "And you're just the young lady to help me build some." They touched their wineglasses and drank deeply. "Let's press on," he said.

"Remember when we first met?" Susan asked.

"How can I forget? It was on the American Airlines MAC contract flight from Saigon to Los Angeles. You sat on my armrest. You smelled so good, I thought I'd attack you right there."

"I wish you would have."

"Oh yeah." Court laughed. "You couldn't even remember my name. You gave me that big line about simply adoring my movies."

"I did not," she said and flipped a piece of pineapple at him.

"Yes, you did. Then you said we'd meet at Donkin's for a beer sometime. We did, and here we are."

"Yes," she said, "here we are." She looked at him with troubled eyes that she quickly cleared up. She put her hand on top of his.

"Come on, fighter pilot," she said softly, "let's get on with it."

They roamed Bangkok in a rented Tuk-Tuk, an open-air three-wheeler with a two-stroke engine that made a nasal *tuk-tuk* sound. Their driver knew all the spots where Americans went for their night life. They danced first at the Cat's Eye, then the An An room, to the best brass bands and popular American and British singers the Philippines could imitate. They sweated and laughed as they danced the Monkey and the Frug and the Swim. She taught him the Mashed Potato and they inhaled all the tall gin drinks they could order. In the Tuk-Tuk, they sang verses of "Our Love Is Here to Stay" to each other as the driver careened over sidewalks and curbs to avoid the dense traffic roaming the street at two in the morning.

Exhausted and tight at three, they ate Chinese food at the open-air stalls near the hotel. They clowned with the awkward chopsticks and drank quarts of Singha beer. Toward the end of the meal he presented her with a tiny gold Risis horse that stood stately, head cocked and alert, into a breeze that fanned his golden mane. They called it Stately Horse. He had bought it earlier that evening from a vendor when she had been in the ladies' room at one of the clubs. Their Chinese waiter admired the exquisite horse. He liked the two happy Americans and joked with them and showed them how the right hand over the left was a Chinese sign for hello, but slapping the palm over a cupped hand was a vile insult.

Finally, just before dawn, they left the bar at the hotel, where they had been sipping plain iced tea both to cool down and sober up.

Arm in arm, they walked out as the Thai bartender gratefully shut the bar and pocketed the hundred dollars' worth of baht the *farang* had bribed him with to stay open. They strolled off, crooning about how the Rockies may crumble but their love was here to stay.

The next day was spent doing more touristing. The day after that, their last, was declared as health day. They ate well and exercised and swam lap after lap in the pool. They went to the Siam Intercontinental and played volleyball behind the west wing with some airline people and three Thud drivers down from Korat. He stood back and watched her walk across the lawn when they were through. Her stride was long and sturdy. She wore white shorts, no jewelry, and a vivid blue blouse that accentuated her striking blue eyes. In the early evening they lay together on the bed in his room, her head on his chest as the sun went down. The next day she had a late flight out, three in the afternoon; he had to catch the five PM C-130 courier to Ubon.

He deliberately hadn't talked of marriage as he had in Singapore. At that time he had had dreams of resigning from the Air Force, marrying Susan, and settling down. Not only had *she* seemed against the whole idea, but when he had been recalled to fight in the Tet Offensive, *he* could hardly wait to get back in the cockpit and resume combat. But that was then and this was now. He needed this girl the rest of his life. This was the one. All the rest were just practice: learning what was real inside himself and what was not. It was now time to talk, she judged.

"I'm glad you arranged to be here," he said, his voice deep and serious. "I've got to tell you something."

She was suddenly wary. "Shhh. This isn't the time to talk."

"Yes, it is. I've got to tell you a few things about me."

"Court . . ." She stood up.

He looked at her naked body. This handsome, lithe, and sleek female, this best of the very best. "God, but you are put together so well I can't believe you're mine now and forever. Our love is here to stay.

"Court, please . . ."

"Just listen, will you? No harm in that?" *What the devil is she so antsy about every time I try to talk serious with her?*

"Just listen. I think you know I'm not your basic nine-to-five kind of guy. I'm not the standard consumer with three kids, two cars, one wife, and a mortgage. I guess I'm still a kid who'll never grow up, a Peter Pan who really flies. I can't do the diapers-and-dentist, lawnmowing-and-retirement program for some airline. Once I thought that was what I wanted. But I'm a fighter pilot, and I know I wouldn't make it. I do what I do because it's difficult and challenging work and I thrive on it. When I do it good I feel a satisfaction no engineering or airline job could ever provide."

She kissed him briefly. "I know all that, silly."

"But I still want you to marry me . . ."

"Oh *damn*," she said and bolted out of the bed to stand by the sliding doors, clutching her arms around her body.

Outside, thunder riffed over the city and a warm rain fell. Sporadic gusts of wind brushed the trees and bushes on the patio and flung rain against the glass.

"What do you mean, 'Oh damn'?" He arose from the bed and put his arms around her. "That's a hell of a thing to say to a guy who's proposing to you."

She turned suddenly into his arms and kissed him, at first lightly, then deeply and hungrily, her hair streaming down her back. "Court, oh God, Court, I love you so much. Hold me." Her voice was husky and he could feel her body shaking. He stroked her back. "Hey there, hey now – I didn't mean to make you cry." He held her at arm's length and looked deep into her eyes. "You say you love me so much, but you won't marry me."

She looked away. "It would never work."

"Why?"

"I can't tell you. Just hold me, will you? Please?"

He picked up the perfect body and bore her to his bed.

Gray light outlined the drapes drawn over the patio doors as he awoke with a start. Something was wrong. He raised up, braced on his elbows. Her side was empty. There was an envelope lying on the pillow. He fumbled on the side table for his watch. It was eight-thirty. She must be packing. He quickly put on his pants and a shirt and ran across the living room to her bedroom. It was raining. Moisture was heavy on the windows. The hard rain drummed on the roof and plants. Her door was open, a maid's cart outside. He burst into the room.

"Susan," he called. "Susan!" The maid looked at him in surprise as he ran into the bathroom, then looked into the closet. It was empty. Her clothes were gone and the bathroom gleamed white, without a trace of her personal things. He stood in the center of the room for a long moment, then threw open the sliding doors to the patio and ran back to his room through the blowing rain. In his room he tore open the envelope on the bed. Her handwriting was even and large, with wide loops and whorls. The stationery was from the Oriental Hotel. It was dated at five o'clock that morning.

Beloved Court, My Forever Man, My Dearest Heart:

I know it isn't fair to do this to you, and I am the worst chicken fink in the world for running out on you. But I'll just have to tell you right up front so you won't holler for a taxi or steal a bike and try to pedal out to the airport. The truth is, I lied to you. Oh my dear, I just had to.

My plane doesn't leave at three in the afternoon, it leaves at eight in the morning. Maybe it's already taken off by the time you read this. I was so hoping you wouldn't do what you always say you do – double-check. But then, why should you double-check my takeoff time? You would take my word for it, wouldn't you? You old dear. Good old shambling trusting Court, the wonderful man I love so dearly and so deeply. The Supreme Court.

I can just hear you: "If she loves me so much, why the lie?"

And oh, my dear, our love is here to stay.

But I'm not here to stay. And that's why I lied. It seems there is this funny little thing that is running around inside of me. There are words like carcinoma and lymph glands involved. And nonoperative and terminal. Well, maybe it's not so little. It's in there, this black thing. I know it and I hate it. I thought I could exorcise it out of

271

existence by sheer willpower. If I hated it enough and loved you enough, it simply would cease to exist. The doctors tell me it doesn't work that way.

The doctors also tell me that with a sort of chemical therapy and maybe some radiation, I could hang around a bit longer.

"How much longer?" sez I.

"A couple of months. Maybe a year," sez they. "Of course your hair will fall out and your face will puff up and your arms swell from edema," they added.

"No, thank you," I said, and decided to make this last flight to Asia and be with you in this wonderful crazy place called Bangkok.

Oh Court, it was good, wasn't it? You were so good to me. And I was mean to you a few times, wasn't I? I had to be. I'm so sorry, but I had to be. You were getting too close to what I wanted to say only in this letter.

So now I'm doing what you always say a good fighter pilot does: he plans his course, double-checks, and presses on. I've planned my course and, oh, my dear, how do I say this — I must fly alone. You cannot come with me. And you can't follow me. You see, I told you another lie.

I'm not returning to work. Or to my apartment, I gave it up just before I left. I don't need it anymore. American Airlines is just great. They are footing the bill for a clinic, actually it's called a hospice, where people go to . . . to leave this mortal coil, I think is how the bard put it. (Mortal coil? Sounds like an odd type of mattress. I can still laugh, and so must you. Oh yes.) Anyhow, you cannot find out where I am. Oh, I suppose with your father's connections you could, but I beg you not to. I want to do this my way. Like Garbo, I vant to be alone.

So, my sweet man, there you have my little story. I thought about this so much, then I decided I simply could not tell you before. I wanted this, our last time, to be our best time. There is no second act, this was the whole play. You had all of me, the perfect me. No flaws, no . . . other

272

things. That's what I wanted. And it was good, wasn't it? And I am being a good fighter pilot, aren't I?

Fly high and fast, my beloved. And once in a while, when you see the right cloud, think of the girl who loves you so much,

Your Susan

He sat perfectly still, the paper clutched in his hand, then slowly doubled over onto the bed, where he could still smell her fragrance. He gathered the sheets and pillows into his arms and sank his head deep into them. At last he arose. He stood staring out at the rain, now streaming down the long panes and into the room where he had left the door open. He had to leave this place and leave it right now. There was too much here, too much. He quickly threw on his flight suit without showering or shaving, stuffed his civilian clothes into his B-4 bag, and walked into the bathroom for his Dop Kit. Next to it stood Stately Horse. His eyes stung as he carefully wrapped it in tissue and placed it in his kit. In the bedroom he held Susan's letter for a long time in his hand, then painstakingly folded it and put it into his pocket. The rain lashed the windows. He walked erect as a robot to the elevator and pressed the button. At the lobby desk he carefully checked out and engaged a hotel limousine to drive him to the military side of Don Muang, where he could catch the courier to Ubon.

Goodbye, my Susan. I loved you so much, more than I ever told you. I will need you for a long, long time. I will need you forever.

14

It was just past the peak of a sunny day, before the afternoon thunderstorm washed the Bangkok streets. Shawn Bannister and Richard Connert sat drinking gin and tonics at a table far to the rear in the cool dimness of the Bamboo Bar. They both wore tan safari suits and were on their third round of drinks.

From a distance, the two men were similar in appearance: blond hair, youthful faces, slender builds. Closer inspection showed Shawn Bannister's face to have more lines, and his shoulders and waist to be thicker than Connert's. They both looked to be in their mid- to late-twenties.

"I don't believe it," Connert said. "You went where? Brata what?"

"Bratislava," Shawn said. "In Czechoslovakia. And, later, in Cuba."

"How come you didn't tell any of us before we came here?"

Shawn leaned back with a superior look on his face. "Well, no one really had the need to know. Certain things had to be arranged, certain contacts made. Secrecy was the word. Didn't want the pigs to get on to what I was doing. We were" – he leaned forward – "working out ways to assist them in their war against the United States of Amerika, with a K."

"Oh, wow. That's really cool. And then there's *this* trip." Connert drained the rest of his glass and looked pointedly at

274

the waiter, who leaped to bring fresh drinks for the two men. Connert took a deep swallow. "Speaking of which, you said you were going to tell me more – why I'm here and all that."

Shawn leaned forward and spoke in a conspiratorial voice. "What would you say if I told you I arranged for the two of us to go to Hanoi?"

"To Hanoi? The *two* of us? Hey, that's terrific. I thought I was just coming to Bangkok to kind of introduce you to the Orient 'cause . . . you know . . . I'd sort of been here before and all that. The two of us? Groovy. Will we see the prisoners of war?"

"They're not prisoners, they're *criminals*, you got that? *Criminals.* You call them prisoners up there and we're both in trouble."

"Yeah, well, sure, but . . . but what am *I* supposed to do up there?"

"You were at George Air Force Base, weren't you?"

"Sure, you knew that."

"And you know all about F-4s, don't you." Shawn said it as a statement, not a question.

"Sure. I *flew* them, you know."

Shawn Bannister tried to keep the contempt from his face. *The only F4 this guy ever flew was that simulator thing.* But that was all right. It was useful to have Connert claim he had been a combat fighter pilot, even if it was a sham. He looked at his campaign manager.

"We're going to Hanoi to bring an F-4 pilot home, but we're not sure he really appreciates the opportunity he has. His name is Al Apple. He's an Air Force major."

"We? I thought nobody but you and me was in on this."

"Look, there are a few others. I didn't exactly go on those trips by myself, you know. We did meet some people."

Connert was wide-eyed with enthusiasm. "Yeah – now I got it! You and Bernadine and Tom were all gone at the same time."

Shawn leaned forward. "Listen," he said in a conspiratorial tone. "That stuff is real secret, like classified. We don't want just anybody to know about this trip. Like, the pigs might get on

275

to it, and maybe we're going places we're not supposed to."

"Okay, Shawn, okay. Whatever you say."

Shawn dug into his breast pocket. "Here, I got something for you. He pulled out two solid aluminum rings and handed one to Connert. It was lightweight and dull in appearance. "One for you, one for me."

Connert examined his ring. "What's this for?"

"A little gift from our friends up north. They're made from shot-down aircraft."

"Shot-down *American* aircraft?" Something flickered in Connert's eyes.

"Yeah, sure," Shawn said. "Are there any other kind doing the bombing up there? Here, put it on." He slid his own onto a finger of his left hand.

Connert tried the ring on several fingers. "It's too small," he said and slipped the ring into a pocket. He looked at Shawn with fathomless blue eyes. "Exactly what is it I can do for you up there?"

"What I want you to do is help me talk to Apple. You know about F-4s and pilots. Convince him that it's better for him to come home. He's a real patriotic guy and we want him to know he can serve his country a lot better in the good old USA than in some stinky prison in North Vietnam."

"Well, yeah, sure, but why us? I mean, what makes you think the North Viets will—"

"*Don't* call them *Viets*. They are Vietnamese or comrades – not Viets.

"Okay, sure. So what makes you think they will simply let a prisoner . . . unh, *criminal,* go away with us? What's so special about us?"

"That's why I was in Bratislava and Cuba, to hammer out those details. Look, I can't tell you everything, but leave it be that I and some other SDS-ers have a special deal with the Viet Cong and the big wheels up in Hanoi. They like us, they like *me*. I used to write great things about them. I used to write the truth."

"What do you mean, special deal?" Connert asked.

"The deal is that some of us can get visas to go up there and

276

see the criminals and try to bring them home. It's already happened. Just last August three Air Force criminals were released to one of our groups, three more before that in February."

The August group had included a USAF major, an Ace from Korea named Jim Low, who had told his captors right from the start that he didn't intend to go through any torture and would do whatever they wanted. He had been given an early release in what the POWs called the Fink Release Program.

"Wow, that's really cool," Connert said. "But I still don't know what you want me to do."

"It's easy. Like I said. You were in the Air Force, you know what fighter pilots think and how they talk. What you do is get Apple talking and tell him it's okay to come home, it's okay to leave the, ah, other people there. In fact, he'd be doing them a favor by coming home. You follow me?"

"Not exactly. How would he be doing them a favor?"

"By speaking out against the war. Then the war is over sooner and all the guys get to come home."

Connert looked thoughtful. "You really believe that?"

"Look, Richard. What difference does it make whether I believe it or not? The important thing is the Viet Cong and those people in Hanoi do. That's why we get to go up there."

"Yeah," Connert persisted. "If *you* don't believe it, why are you doing it, going up there and all that?"

Shawn fixed him with a steady gaze. "You want me to get elected, don't you?"

Connert nodded.

"Well, this is a big step. If it works I get lots of favorable publicity and that translates into votes. If it doesn't work, I still get lots of publicity. But we've got to move. We have to be in Hanoi by tomorrow—"

"Tomorrow?" Connert interrupted. "How come you didn't tell me?"

"Because, goddamm it, timing and secrecy are everything. This isn't just you and me going to Hanoi, you know. There are a lot more things tied into all of this. Other things have to happen also. We're after a big scoop, a big prize. One that'll not only help get me elected, but that'll help win the war."

277

"Win it? For whom?"

"For the Viet Cong. Who the hell do you think I mean?"

Connert looked at him, then suddenly dug his handkerchief from his pocket and sneezed.

1030 HOURS LOCAL, TUESDAY 29 OCTOBER 1968
WATTAY AIRPORT
VIENTIANE, ROYALTY OF LAOS

The two Laotians were waiting for them when Shawn Bannister and Richard Connert stepped down from the Thai Airways DC-3 twin-prop airliner.

"Welcome, Mister Gentlemen, to our poor country," said the taller of the two in French-accented English. "So pleased you could make this trip. You must be very tired. Come for refreshments before the next portion of your journey." The two Lao wore short-sleeved white shirts and baggy black pants. The two Americans wore safari suits. Each carried a small bag. Connert had the sniffles and kept using a handkerchief he carried in his hand.

They were led to a small, hot and stuffy room in a shed next to a nondescript hangar. The Americans accepted warm orange soda and sat on straight-backed chairs while the tall Lao told them of the importance of their trip and the fine cooperation between the Pathet Lao and the Democratic Republic of Vietnam. He explained that the next portion of their trip would be on an International Control Commission (ICC) airplane that would fly them directly to the Gia Lam Airport outside Hanoi. He kept up the one-sided dialogue until a Caucasian man entered the small room. The man carried a black bag from which he took a big Nikon 35mm camera and a tripod.

"If you please," the Lao said, "to stand up and everybody shake hands and smile. This is a very important event." He urged Shawn and Connert to stand between him and his companion while the Caucasian photographer took several photos with and without flash. He also took several close-ups of the two Americans.

"Who are you with?" Shawn asked with a smile and stuck out his hand as the photographer was stowing his equipment. When there was no answer he asked again, but the man mumbled something between a grunt and a hiccup and went out the door.

"Mister Gentlemen, it is time to go now. If you please." The Lao motioned to the door.

"Wait a minute," Connert said. "I thought we were going to get some publicity here. Who was that guy? Where are the other photographers and reporters?"

"Hold it, Richard. I don't know who that guy was either, but part of the deal is no publicity until a certain date. The second of November, I think."

"Why?" he asked into his handkerchief

"It just is. They have our trip and Apple's release tied in to something else, something important that's supposed to happen real soon. I'll get first crack at it, but they won't tell me anything in advance."

"Please to go now," the tall Lao insisted. "Your airplane is here."

"My God, I don't believe it," Connert said when they saw the ICC airplane taxiing across the apron to the small terminal building. It was a four-engined World War II B-17 bomber converted to carry passengers.

Minutes later the airplane was airborne, the gear slowly retracting into the nacelles beneath the inboard engines. Inside, small airline seats lining a narrow aisle held members of the ICC: a turbaned Sikh, a scowling Pole, and a smiling Canadian. Shawn and Connert spoke little as the B-17 climbed to 9,000 and set course northeast to Hanoi. The decrease in pressure bothered Connert and he kept sniffing and blotting with his handkerchief. It was worse on the letdown.

"Level off, level off," Connert screamed as the B-17 descended through 6,000 feet. "My ears. Oh God, make him level off."

"For God's sake, Richard, shut up!" Shawn said with great exasperation.

The Canadian went to the cockpit and spoke to the pilot, who leveled the big plane and sent his copilot back to see what was wrong. Connert told him it was an ear block.

"Here," the copilot, a big Canadian, said. "Shut your mouth, hold your nose – and blow. It's called the Valsalva maneuver."

Connert gave his thanks when his ears cleared, and the plane continued its descent into Gia Lam.

Thach met the two Americans as they walked into the shabby terminal that serviced Gia Lam International Airport. It was an attractive French design, but the concrete was now cracked and the flower beds were empty. It was as if the North Vietnamese communists didn't want to show a bright or cheery face to the world travelers who alighted at their only civilian airport in use. A group of thin Vietnamese came in from a Russian Aeroflot Ilyushin transport.

Thach walked up to them and spoke without preamble. "You may come with me, misters, there is no need," he said as he waved a hand at the customs and immigration counter. He offered a limp hand to Shawn.

"Mister Shawn, I am Thach." Shawn shook and introduced Richard Connert.

"Yes, misters. I am most pleased you are here and able to help us in our struggle." He led them to his Lada sedan.

Shawn and Connert were all eyes as Thach drove from the airport toward Hanoi. They drove by an abandoned church, then out to the main road, which was ragged and full of potholes that Thach said were called "hen's nests" in Vietnamese. People were busy in the fields harvesting rice. They would lay the grain sheaves in the roads, where what few vehicles there were ran over them, shucking the rice kernels from the husk. Some of the bundles were quite large, and the Lada bounced and swayed when Thach tried to avoid them. They crossed the Paul Doumer Bridge and drove into the main section of downtown Hanoi. Outside of wrecked rail yards the city looked shabby but untouched by what the protestors had called carpet-bombing.

The streets were lined with what looked like oversized manhole covers that rested on concrete cylinders buried upright in the ground. Thach said they were personal air raid shelters. He drove them to the Victory Hotel, where he took them directly to a small room overlooking the street. A ceiling fan stirred the air over the two small beds separated by a thin wooden nightstand. Upon a chest of drawers in front of a bust-sized smoky mirror hanging from a nail was a carafe of water and two glasses resting on a lacquer tray. A wooden chair was under a narrow desk, and a vinyl lounge chair was next to the window. Thach said the bath was down the hall to the right.

"We are very poor here, misters," Thach explained. "We conserve all our resources for the just struggle against the imperialists. We are very sorry, but electricity is not available from ten of the clock at night until six of the clock in the morning." By now Connert was sniffling and coughing. "Sorry," he said many times as Shawn looked at him in aggravation.

"We will have a small chat," Thach said, "before you see the criminal Apple."

"How is his attitude?" Shawn asked. "Does he want to go home?"

Thach regarded him through slitted eyes. "It is important that you and your friend convince him such a move is in his best interest."

Me? I thought you would have him ready. I thought we were only here to . . . to talk to him a little bit, then just accompany him home."

"Oh no, Mister Shawn. There is more. You must be very convincing. You and Mister Richard can do this thing, can you not? It will be very beneficial to you to do this thing."

"Beneficial? What do you mean by that?" Shawn said and shot a look of annoyance at Connert when he sneezed.

"You have an election process, do you not?" Thach reminded him. "A success here would give you much favorable publicity."

"Well, in any case I'm supposed to get a good story on something else up here too. I was promised."

"Promised, Mister Shawn?" Although Thach showed no

281

emotion on his face, his tone was an unmistakable combination of sarcastic disbelief and menace.

"Yes, promised by Huynh Va Ba when we met in Cuba."

"Mister Shawn, Huynh is a messenger, a courier. A man without stature. He cannot make promises. Here in Hanoi I can make you promises. If you convince the air criminal Apple to return with you, I will promise you to be the first witness to a very important event. Very important. An event that will show just how criminal the imperialists are in our neighboring country of Laos. You have but four days to accomplish this task, for you must be ready to leave with the air criminal on the second day of November."

"Wait a minute—" Shawn said in desperation.

"We have no minutes to spare. I suggest we go now to the hospital where the air criminal is receiving the most excellent of treatment. There you first will meet someone, then you will talk to him."

1745 HOURS LOCAL, TUESDAY 29 OCTOBER 1968
HANOI CITY HOSPITAL
HANOI, DEMOCRATIC REPUBLIC OF VIETNAM

Thach drove through pedestrian-clogged streets to the rear of the gray concrete Hanoi hospital and led them to the small doctors' lounge. Connert sneezed several times and blew his nose. Thach left them for a moment and returned with Co Dust.

"Tell these men," he ordered her, "of the air criminal Apple and what of his attitude to return with his countrymen."

Shawn noticed that even when she began to speak, Co Dust never looked up. He thought she looked very petite and attractive in her white uniform.

"He is a man who . . . who knows his own mind," she began in a low voice.

282

"What does that mean?" Shawn asked.

"It means he . . . he does not wish to . . . to leave just yet."

Thach rattled off some angry words in Vietnamese to her and yanked her by the arm out the door.

"God," Connert said, "what was that all about?"

"I think she's in big trouble," Shawn said, his face spoiled by a heavy frown.

Flak Apple was startled as the door to his room was flung open and crashed against the wall. Thach stomped into the room, dragging Co Dust by one arm. He spun her around to face Flak.

"There will be no more games," he raged. "Too much time has gone by – TOO MUCH." In a quick motion he lifted her long white skirt and pinched her genitals through her panties with clawlike fingers. She stifled a shriek and sank to her knees, sobbing. "You have accomplished NOTHING," Thach yelled and struck her face.

"You sonabitch, I'll *KILL* you," Flak screamed and struggled to sit up. He felt an incredible pain as his abrupt movement tore something within him. A slow red stain started in the wide bandages around his midsection.

"No," Thach spat as he reached down to punch Co Dust in the breast. "Only I kill here. And this one will die slow and hard and in front of you as you are chained to a wall unless you agree to cooperate." He sank his fingers into Co Dust's left breast and twisted until she screamed anew.

"Stop, stop," Flak cried and pounded the bed with his good hand, his agonized eyes on the sobbing Co Dust.

"You will cooperate, then?" Thach asked in a voice suddenly grown quiet.

"Yes, sonabitch," Flak gasped. "Just take your fucking hands off her." He hardly felt his own pain.

Thach helped Co Dust to her feet and led her gently to a chair by the window. She bit her lip and wouldn't look anywhere but out the window.

"Let us talk," Thach said to Flak as he approached the bed.

Twenty minutes later Thach returned to the lounge and apologized to Shawn and Connert.

"Things are difficult today. I do not believe that criminal Apple is well enough for a meeting. He needs, ah, continued medication. We will return soon. Perhaps tomorrow he will be ready to see you."

Thach pointed at the table. "Misters, please to have some soda." Thach bustled about pouring the sticky yellow orange soda into thick scarred glasses. "You perhaps will visit with me certain places here in Hanoi. I will show you where the hospitals are bombed and where the schools are bombed. I want to show you the museum where we celebrate the 5,000 airplanes of the imperialist air force we have shot down."

"Yes," Shawn said. "I would like that. Will the press be there?"

Thach thought quickly. "Yes, of course. Perhaps you would like to say a few words to them at the completion of your tour. A few words about what you have seen?"

"Yes, that will be fine."

"Fine, then, misters. I will take you to your hotel now."

15

"Eagle Station is becoming quite the hot spot, gentlemen," said Major Richard Hostettler. He stood in front of the 8th TFW Wing Commander, Colonel Stan Bryce, the four fighter squadron commanders, the commander and ops officer of the men flying the AC-130 Spectre gunship, the commander of the Wolf FACs, and Major Court Bannister, commander of the Phantom FACs. Each commander had his operations officer with him. Ken Tanaka, filling in for Howie Joseph, sat next to Court.

"This is about as unusual a frag as we are going to get in the war," Hostettler began. "It's about a raid that may never take place on a place that doesn't exist by people that aren't there. Ya got that?"

He pulled out a large map of Laos on a roller board from the wings of the stage and pointed to the high karst region west of Sam Neue. "We've got intelligence reports from sources so classified ya gotta burn them before ya read 'em. What they say is this: The bad guys want to snuff Eagle Station. It's a big thorn in the side of the Hanoi eastern air defense ring because it lets you guys in to Pack Six when the weather is real crappy and all that. They say the attack is imminent."

"What about evacuation of the American personnel?" Colonel Bryce asked. "Is that in the mill?"

"Funny you should ask that, Colonel. The way I hear it is that the Ambassador doesn't want to pull any of the troops out of there until the last minute. Seems the Agency guys say there are plenty of defenses, and there probably won't be a serious attack anyhow, so why get everybody all het up?"

"Then who says there is an attack coming?" Court asked. He noted Hostettler was not mentioning any of the other more classified reasons for why Eagle Station was the focus of such attention.

"Like I told ya, I can't tell ya. But 7th is impressed enough to order us to put some birds on alert and some on CAP for the next few days to see what develops. Ya know what *I* think – *I* think the AIRA up there said air power can save the day, and 7th is out to prove him right." Hostettler moved out from behind the podium and put his hands on his hips and let out a moderately loud fart. Life could be crude in a combat zone.

"Oh, come on, Dick," one of the squadron commanders said. "They don't have big guns up there yet. Or do they?"

Richard Hostettler, the famous chili-fart briefer, was barely warmed up.

"Not any AAA guns, because the Trail doesn't swing over that way, but we are starting to get reports of some artillery rounds impacting close to Eagle Station. You gentlemen will most likely be called upon to take them out."

He finished his briefing and gave way to the newly assigned weather officer, a young first lieutenant dressed in 1505 khakis who was clearly nervous on this, his first briefing. He assembled some notes, then pulled out a weather chart of Southeast Asia. He cleared his throat and spoke in a high-pitched nervous voice.

"The climate of Laos is primarily influenced by the monsoon winds that govern conditions in all of eastern Asia from India to Kamchatka in eastern Siberia. The monsoon cycle results from the changes in the seasonal flow of air over the vast Asian landmass and the oceans to the south and east. In winter, dry air over the continent becomes cold and dense, settles, and flows—"

"Okay, Stormy, that's just fine," Colonel Bryce said.

". . . and flows generally southward. From its prevailing

286

direction in the Indochinese peninsula, this winter airflow is called the North-east Monsoon. In summer, the situation is reversed. The continental air—"

"That will *do*," Bryce said, and stood up. "Thank you very much."

"But, sir, I'm not done yet."

"Oh, yes you are," Bryce said and looked at Hostettler. "You got anything more, Dick?"

"Yes, sir, the dry season is almost here but there are still some rotten weather days up at Eagle. In fact, rainfall averages sixty inches per year up there. I think we're going to have trouble maintaining a twenty-four-hour watch on that place."

"I think that's where we can help, Colonel," the commander of the AC-130 detachment said. "We fly almost entirely at night, and we have some bad-weather capability as long as the target is in a low-threat area. By that I mean we can tool around at 3 or 4,000 feet above the ground, but below a cloud layer that you men cannot dive-bomb through. We've got three Spectres here and operational now, and more coming. While we can't put one on dedicated alert for Eagle, we can divert easily enough from the Trail and send our alert bird out to replace the Trail bird. You'll actually get a faster response that way since the distance from the Trail to Eagle is shorter than from Ubon to Eagle." The Spectre detachment commander was a broad-shouldered lieutenant colonel named Spike Charles.

"Good, Spike," Stan Bryce said. "We'll integrate you into the plan." He turned to Gordie Breault, commander of the 497th Night Owl squadron. "I want your men to know that place like Patpong after dark."

"Ah, Colonel Bryce," Dick Hostettler said, "there is one other thing you should know." He continued when Bryce nodded. "The frag calls for a man on the ground to help self-FAC at Eagle."

"And just what are the qualifications for the man on the ground?"

"Well, that's just it. He has to be an F-4 driver who can FAC."

Bryce looked at Court Bannister, Breault, and B. J. Gierie,

the commander of the Wolf FACs. "Well, that leaves just you guys. Bannister, you've been there and set up Flaming Arrow, so you just volunteered. Get together with Hostettler for the details and work out the plans with Spike Charles, Breault, and Gierie to get Spectre, the Owls, and the Wolves into the system."

It was 2030 hours that night before the four men had made the plans to integrate the Mach 2 fighter with the 300-knot, four-engined gunship in night attacks. They planned altitudes, words to be used, radio procedures, roll-in tactics based on where the big gunship flew, and target-marking by both the fighter and the Spectre gunship. Spectre would lick the ground with 20mm tracers or throw out a device called a log that would burn cherry-bright for thirty minutes, then tell the fighters where to attack from that reference. They set up the procedures Court would use from the ground to talk to Spectre, and how he would call in their 20mm and 40mm firepower. Court explained about the Flaming Arrow and how to shoot beyond where it pointed.

"Here's a little something for you," Spike Charles said and handed a metallic device about half the size of a cigarette carton to Court. "If we lose all radio communication," he said, "you use this small built-in compass to align this thing to the north, then twist these dials to show the type of target and the distance. Our table nav gets all the info and feeds it to the pilot through the fire control system."

Etched on the metal face around one knob were stacked boxes to denote supplies, a truck, and stick figures to represent humans. The next knob dialed in the distance in meters. "You rotate the knobs to show the type of target and the distance. It operates off these dry batteries. It's kind of an electronic Flaming Arrow," Charles said. The batteries were flat and black and exactly the type used in the RT-10 survival radio. The case of the device was also from an RT-10.

"Solving the communications and rendezvous problems with the fighters is easy," Spike Charles said. "Alleycat or Moon-beam will code up the freqs each twenty-four-hour period and set up the rendezvous point off Eagle's Tacan."

"Better have a backup nav point in case Eagle gets blown off the air," Court said.

"Pessimist," Spike Charles said, "but you're right. We'll use Invert Radar and Udorn Tacan as backups."

Court had had a hard time concentrating on the briefing, but he was doing better than in the first week after his return from Bangkok. Pictures and slow-motion movies of Susan had kept entering his mind at wrong times. One minute he wanted to write his father and ask him to find Susan. Then he would change his mind and think he should respect Susan's wishes to be left alone. But did she really mean it? Could she really want to live her last moments by herself? He tried to imagine what it would be like: the tubes, the trays and bedpans, the helplessness, the losing of the body and the mind. Would he want anybody to see him like that? He decided he would not. So he did nothing and felt isolated and guilty. He snapped back to where he was.

"Hey, Dick," he said to Hostettler, "how am I supposed to get to Eagle Station?"

Hostettler checked the frag. "USAF courier to Udorn, Air America to the site. They want you up there by yesterday, so get hustling. Don't forget, wear civvies. The US doesn't have any combatants up there, doncha know."

2000 HOURS LOCAL, THURSDAY 31 OCTOBER 1968
RIVER SUITE, TWIN BRIDGES HOTEL
ARLINGTON, VIRGINIA

This is it, turn it on," John Duchane said to the four other poker players. "Whitey's former boss is going to give us the word." He put down his bourbon glass next to his chips in the rim tray of the green felt poker table. The men stopped the game to turn on the television for the speech of President Lyndon Baines

Johnson. "What will it be?" Duchane, a dark, swarthy man, asked Whitey Whisenand, who was soon to come to work for him.

Whitey took a short sip from his waterglass. "Could be any number of things," he said reluctantly. No longer privy to happenings in the White House, he had been closing out his office in preparation for his retirement, which was scheduled for the 31st of November at Bolling Air Force Base, across the Potomac from Washington. Soon after, he hoped to be flying the beautiful B-26 *Excalibur*.

There had been many messages back and forth, Whitey knew, between Johnson and his emissaries in Paris and Saigon regarding the peace talks with the North Vietnamese which were to begin the second day of November. Consensus had it that Saigon felt sold out by the United States because they thought the US had done anything it could to get the communist North to the tables in Paris to discuss peace in Vietnam. Saigon's biggest complaint was that the US was allowing the Viet Cong's National Liberation Front a seat at the tables, with status equal to the United States, Saigon, and Hanoi. Tonight President Johnson was to brief the nation about the latest agreements on those peace talks.

The poker players were solid Republicans who had contributed heavily to the Richard Milhous Nixon presidential campaign against Hubert Horatio Humphrey. Nixon was now crossing the nation with his plea for unity among the divisive, law and order for the unruly, and peace for all. He said he had a secret plan to end the war and win the peace, but did not want to divulge details for fear of disturbing the ongoing negotiations. He had been so successful against Humphrey's dismal campaign (that didn't even have the full backing of the Democratic party) that the polls had showed Humphrey trailing Nixon 43 to 28 percent in September, with but five weeks to go before the vote was taken. Now it was the end of October, and the voting would begin in four days, on Monday the fourth of November.

Whitey remembered his talk with LBJ the day two weeks before, when LBJ had fired him. The President had said he would stop *all* air strikes in North Vietnam. Whitey had been met with disbelief when he had told this to the Chief of Staff of the United States Air Force. "Good God," the Chief had said. "He wouldn't dare." The Chief had also offered Whitey his condolences for being fired. Whitey had said he had lasted longer than he had originally thought he would, and that hopefully he had done some good.

The poker players settled down to watch as Johnson faced the American people with a heavily lined face and a hoarse voice. He spoke of the tasks he had taken on as the President and of the horrors of the Vietnam war. He made no reference to the upcoming election. Finally he licked his lips and read without emotion from the Tele-PrompTer:

> "I have now ordered that all air, naval, and artillery bombard-
> ment of North Vietnam cease as of 8:00 AM Washington time,
> Friday morning the first of November. I have reached this
> decision on the basis of the developments in the Paris talks.
> And I have reached it in the belief that this action can lead
> to progress toward a peaceful settlement of the Vietnamese
> war.

"My God," one of the men said. "There goes the war for us and there goes the election for Nixon. All those middle-of-the-road voters will take to this ploy."

"What do you think, Whitey?" Duchane asked. "Did he do this because he really thinks it'll help the peace talks or is it only a grandstand play to get more people to vote for the Democrats?"

Whitey rubbed his jaw. "Can't really say," he admitted finally. *Oh, Whisenand, you liar you. You know damn good and well you suspect LBJ of trying to swing the election by this call.*

"We're in for some tough times if Humphrey gets it. He has absolutely no plan for Vietnam, but here at home he wants to give away the store."

"Well, he did say he'd crawl to Hanoi on his knees to get the POWs released."

"Damn liberals," another man growled. "Deal."

291

By ten o'clock the next morning the public opinion polls showed Humphrey had made a phenomenal jump and that Nixon had lost a lot of ground and was ahead by only 5 points. By two in the afternoon Nixon had only a 3-point lead, and was predicted to lose that slim margin very soon, particularly if a major event occurred that signaled the end of the Vietnam war. The Democrats were in office, the Republicans were not. Incumbent President Johnson could make an immediate and hopeful action to end the war; presidential hopeful Nixon could only make promises.

One of Whitey's longtime friends called him and asked if they could meet for a quick talk about an important subject dear to Whitey's heart. Whitey told him they could meet at O'Tooles in McLean.

They took their coffee to the farthest corner booth in the bar. The place was frequented by CIA officials, who found it delightful not only because it had no sign advertising its presence, but because everybody that came there was associated with the intelligence community in one way or another, so it was fairly safe to talk almost on a classified level.

"What's up?" Whitey asked Dick Murnane, an Air Force chum who had as much time in the intelligence business as Whitey.

"I just want you to know," the silver-headed Murnane said over his cup, "that Dancer was accepted and has gone in."

Whitey made a delighted smile. "And Dipper has no idea."

"None. At least now we're fairly sure some of them will get the messages."

"Damn, but that's good news. What have you heard about the big propaganda coup they want to pull off up there? Any tie-in?"

"We're a bit blind there. We do know they've assembled a lot of East Bloc and North Korean writers and photographers in Hanoi and Vientiane. In Hanoi, we think it's for a big splash, like an early release or at least an anti-American speech or concession of some kind from a live POW."

"It's great to have Dancer on the scene."

292

"Right, but we can't get a handle on what the other part might be. All we know is they have some plan or gimmick called Brave Fight or Valiant Struggle. Something like that. In Vientiane we've got so many people watching those commie newsmen they're stumbling over each other's cloaks."

"No penetration?"

"None.

"Dick, I appreciate your keeping me current even if you have to sneak around to do it."

"Only fair. After all, you're the man who dreamed up Combat Dancer."

"Yeah, but I never thought he'd wind up in Hanoi."

0900 HOURS LOCAL, FRIDAY 1 NOVEMBER 1968
HANOI CITY HOSPITAL
HANOI, DEMOCRATIC REPUBLIC OF VIETNAM

Thach ushered Shawn Bannister and Richard Connert into the same doctors' lounge they had been in two days before. During the wait Thach had taken them to the makeshift museum, which contained the remains of no more than three or four airplanes and some piles of scrap that seemed to be from the pile next to it, although labeled as a different airplane. Shawn had proudly displayed his ring made of shot-down American aircraft, but Connert mumbled he had lost his.

The room had been freshly whitewashed and a square table covered with a blue cloth stood next to one wall. On the table were two bowls full of rice wafers and bananas.

"You will see him before his press conference. You will talk to him. He will be here soon. Sit, please to sit." Thach pointed to two chairs placed in front of a low stool to form a triangle.

"No, thank you," Shawn said, prowling the room, looking out the window, eyeing the fruit. Connert's cold was worse and

293

he was constantly coughing and sneezing. Shawn gave him a look of disgust after one particularly loud sneeze.

"Christ, Connert," he said, "can't you do anything about that?"

Connert shook his head in mute apology while blotting his nose with a big wad of tissue.

The door opened and Co Dust entered, helping a shambling Flak Apple. Maroon-and-gray-striped pajamas hung on his emaciated frame like rags on a weather-beaten ebony fencepost. His face was lined and strained as he peered at the two Americans through black eyes sunken deep into his skull. He knew now why they were here. The weeks of sustained pressure and torture of Co Dust had proven these Americans weren't here to help him. It was another propaganda session. But so what? Maybe they wouldn't help, but he *would* escape his surroundings – one way or another.

"Well, well," said Thach with false gaiety. "Look who we have here." He turned to Shawn and Connert. "Misters, this is Algernon Apple. He is very glad to see you." Thach ignored Co Dust, who was as pale as her uniform.

Shawn and Connert stared in shock at the apparition in front of them.

"How – how do you do?" Shawn stammered and put out his hand.

Flak Apple looked at it as if he didn't know what it was or what he was supposed to do with it. After an awkward moment Shawn withdrew his hand and asked Thach if they could sit.

"Please, misters, take some fruit. See, we give our prisoners good care, we give them good food." He snatched up two bananas and handed one to Shawn and one to Connert, who took it and sniffled and coughed heavily. "If they have medicine problems, we take care of them," Thach continued, eyeing Connert.

Flak Apple didn't want the two Americans to see the hate he felt for them and kept his eyes down. *Goddamm these bastards. Can't they see I've been tortured? Can't they see this is a setup? What kind of Americans are they?* A moan escaped his lips as he sat down. *Oh God, help me. I hurt so bad.*

Shawn leaned forward. "I'm Shawn Bannister and this is Richard Connert. We're here to help you." Connert had a sneezing fit.

Flak's eyes blinked in surprise but he didn't answer. *Bannister, for God's sake. This is Court's dipshit brother. It wouldn't take much to spit in his face. Christ, that Connert is almost spitting in mine with all that hacking and sniffling.*

Thach looked at Flak with barely concealed menace in his eyes and surreptitiously motioned with his head at Co Dust.

"I am Major Algernon A. Apple, United States Air Force. Please tell my mother I am alive and . . . and well." He stopped talking, to see what would happen next.

"Oh, Major Apple—" Shawn blurted.

"There are no ranks here," Thach interrupted.

"Algernon," Shawn continued, "would you like to go home with us? You can, you know. You would be doing your country a great service if you did."

Flak looked up. *Doing my country a great service? In a pig's ass. Doing you and these commies a great service. God, that Connert has some trouble . . .* "What do you mean, 'go home'?"

Shawn licked his lips. "Well – I mean you can walk out of here with us and get on an airplane and fly back to the United States with us."

"Can all of the POWs leave with me?" *That Connert is some . . . oh my God, oh my God . . . he's flashing code at me.* Flak felt as if an electric shock were surging through his body, and he suddenly got goose bumps as thrill after thrill went up his spine. He had to restrain himself from shouting. He tried to collect his thoughts and listen carefully to the sniffles and coughs that Connert was wheezing into his tissue and handkerchief. He watched Connert's body motions as well as he could without attracting attention to what he was doing.

HI FLAC U OLD CELL RAT . . . HOW THEY HANGING . . . YOUR DOG QUEENIE MISSES U AND THE SKINS ARE DOING TERRIBLE THIS YEAR . . . FLAC . . . FLAC . . . U READ . . .

Flak suddenly lowered his head, as he knew his face was

lighting up, and tears of joy sprang to his eyes. He didn't want Thach to catch on. *Oh dear God. Right in front of these commie bastards. He's real, he's from home, he knows about Queenie and the Skins.*

Every combat aircrewman had to write out for the Intelligence people an authentication file with a few easily remembered facts known only to them. These could then be used to authenticate the crewman to determine if he had been compromised in a rescue situation. They would usually list a favorite car or dog or sports team. *I've got to keep this conversation going – I've got to stall. Can this guy Connert read my flash?* He raised his head and started to talk.

"Go home, you say – yes, well, let's talk about that." As Flak spoke he nervously started to rub his face and massage his fingers.

YES YES YES I READ, he flashed.

Shawn shot a triumphant smile at Thach. "What we can do," he said to Flak, "is walk out of here anytime we want."

"You mean I can get up and go out the door with you whenever we want to go out the door?"

"Yes, yes, that's exactly what I mean."

"Right out that door over there?" DO YOU READ ME, he flashed.

"Yes, yes. That very door."

"Well, do I get any clothes to wear? I can't very well go out like this, can I?"

"Yes, goddammit, you'll get clothes." *This guy is so* thick, Shawn said to himself

"Well, what *kind* of clothes?" DO YOU READ ME.

"Clothes clothes. How the fuck would I know?" Shawn turned to Thach. "For God's sake, you got clothes, don't you?"

"Yes, I have clothes for Algernon Apple when he is ready to go." Thach beamed as much as a man who never smiles can beam, and said, "I will have the press conference for him now."

"Good, good," Shawn said and fluffed out his hair with his fingers and wished he'd thought to bring a pocket mirror. You never know when someone will take a picture.

"You will prepare to read this statement," Thach said as he handed a piece of paper to Flak and walked to the open door. Flak took the paper and read the words to himself:

"I Algernon Apple of the United States Air Force confess to indiscriminately bombing the peaceful peasants and children of the Democratic Republic of Vietnam. I am very sorry for my crimes and I repent my awful crimes. I ask for my release under the humane and lenient policy of Ho Chi Minh."

Three heavyset Caucasian men came in the room at Thach's bidding. Two carried still cameras and tape recorders, the third held an electric newsreel camera plugged into a battery pack on his belt. They set up their gear and Flak heard the camera whir and the shutters click as the men warmed up their equipment.

I READ YOU, Connert flashed.

STALL. WHEN THEY ROLL FILM U TRY FLASH CODE ON FILM . . . NAME N TORTURE . . . WE TRY GET FILM FOR OUR USE . . .

Flak didn't know why Connert wanted him to do it, but he flashed AA APPLE and the words TORTURED TO BE HERE over and over as he stalled the proceedings with inane talk.

"You sure you got enough light in here? Maybe I should stand over by the window? You want me to stand by the window? Where you guys from, anyway? You speak English? Hi, what's your name?" Flak wondered what the hell he meant by "for our own use" as he babbled on and on.

SORRY YUR ESCAPE WENT SOUR, Connert flashed.

THEY BEAT THE SHIT OUT OF ME . . . CILLED FREDERIC I THINC, Flak answered as the cameras clicked and whirred, totally oblivious to the coded conversation taking place. A *C* replaced a *K* in the code matrix.

Shawn Bannister looked at Flak in amazement and decided he needed to get in the footage too. After all, this was just a ploy to get some good voter-grabbing material, he told himself. But what is with this Apple idiot? First he wouldn't talk at all, now he won't shut up.

HOW YUR PHYSICAL CONDITION, Connert asked.

THEY GAVE ME SUNDAY SPECIAL . . . DAMN NEAR
DIED . . . THEN PUT GIRL TO GET ME GO HOME OR
AT LEAST GO FRONT OF CAMERA BY TWO NOV TO
DENOUNCE WAR . . .

Shawn stepped over and grabbed Flak's hand and shook it.
"On behalf of the United States of America," he said, "I am
very proud to congratulate you on your momentous decision
to return home to help win the war."

THEY TELL U WHAT SO IMPORT BOUT TWO NOV . . .

NO . . . WHO THE L R U ANYHOW . . . HOW U NO
HOW TO FLASH . . .

Flak deftly pulled from Shawn's hand and mumbled something Thach couldn't hear.

IM A BLUE MAILMAN . . . Connert flashed.

Flak was so excited he had to work hard not to leap about
the room in spasms of joy. All his pains and aches disappeared
under the rush of adrenaline from contact with a real live
American military man. After one of his survival schools
had been completed, Flak had stayed on for a special course
taught to aircrew who were going into combat where the
danger of being shot down was high. The men had been
taught they might receive clandestine communications from
select persons who would identify themselves as mailmen.
As an extra identifier, a color code was added to denote the
mailman's service: blue for Air Force, green for Army, gold
for the Navy, and red for the Marines. Civilian mailmen were
white. Flak was taught that mailmen were strictly communi-
cators, but package carriers were guides and rescuers who
were trained to get a prisoner out under the worst possible
conditions.

U GOT A CALLSIGN . . .

DANCER . . .

U GOT ANY MAIL . . .

MUCH . . .

"Excuse me, what did you say?" Shawn asked Flak.

"Eat shit, hippie prick," Flak mumbled under his breath.

WHO FOR . . .

EVERYBODY BUT MOST IMPORTANT FOR SROS . . .

SROs were the senior ranking officers in each of the compounds. They had the duty and responsibility to take command the best way they could. If they were slammed into solitary – which they often were – the next man would step up to take his place in the clandestine POW command network.

"I am *not* a hippie. We need to discuss what you must do," Shawn said to Flak.

When Flak continued fidgeting but did not answer, Thach spoke up from behind the photographers. "Perhaps Algernon Apple's nurse can help to sit down and relax." He thrust Co Dust forward. She took Flak by the hand and led him back to his chair.

SHE TRIES HELP ME, Flak flashed. I WANT ESCAPE . . . CAN U HELP . . .

NO . . . U CANT ESCAPE . . . NOT NOW . . . U MUST DELIVER MY MESSAGES . . .

WHAT SHOULD I DO RIGHT NOW . . .

STALL . . . I GOT MESSAGES TO PASS . . .

Flak took the paper with his prepared speech and spent long moments smoothing it out. He found his motions a fine way to flash to Connert. "Unh, this is what you want me to read?" he said to Thach.

Embarrassed, Thach said, "Of course, they are *your* words."

Flak continued to smooth the paper.

R . . . GO AHEAD WITH MSGS . . . he flashed. R was POW shorthand for Roger, meaning yes or go ahead.

NO ESCAPE ATTEMPTS WITHOUT PERMISSION FROM SRO

R . . .

DESIRED BUT NOT MANDATORY THAT NO ESCAPES ATTEMPTED WITHOUT OUTSIDE HELP . . . SRO TO USE THIS AS DECISION FACTOR

R . . .

ONE SONIC BOOM WHEN NO STRICE ON MEANS RESCUE ATTEMPT WITHIN WEEC AT CAMP THAT GETS THREE BURNER BANGS DURING NEXT STRICE

R . . . Flak was so thrilled over the news he almost dropped the paper. To his knowledge there had been no outside

299

communication ever before on the subject of a rescue attempt. His fingers trembled on the paper so much that Thach glared at him. "Okay," Flak said when he settled himself down. "Here's what I have to say."

EVERYONE ON FLOOR WHEN RESCUE IN EFFECT . . . NO MOVE TIL HEAR AMERICAN VOICE . . . R . . .

GIVE FOLLOWING TO MORALE OFFICER . . . EVERY MAN PROMOTED HIS DUE DATE . . .

WHAT ABOUT LEAVES N PASSES . . .

HA HA . . . U GOT ALL THIS . . .

YEAH BUT GOT TO TALC NOW . . . Flak pretended to read from the paper. "I am United States Air Force Major Algernon A. Apple and I want to tell you—"

DONT PO EM . . . U R ONLY CONTACT . . . U GOT TO DELIVER THE MAIL . . .

". . . and I want to tell you . . . to tell you that we receive food here and . . . and we receive—"

CAREFUL . . .

". . . and we receive, unh, food and goodies and, unh, Ho Chi Minh is the leader here."

One of the photographers said something in a language that Flak did not understand, and all three men laughed.

"Well," Shawn said, "is that *all* you have to say? What are your views on the war, Algernon?"

My views on the war, you hippie prick, are that we should shoot you, nuke Hanoi, and make a parking lot out of Moscow. And nobody calls me Algernon and gets away with it.

CAREFUL . . . U R ONLY GUY TO DELIVER MAIL . . .

"It is a long and dangerous war and I hope it will be over soon and I am sorry so many people have died. I really am sorry." Flak almost bit his tongue off.

"Do you have a message for the American people?" Shawn asked.

You bet I do. Tell them to get off their dead ass and invade this place. "I think the American people should take the appropriate action to end this dreadful conflict."

"What exactly do you mean by 'appropriate action,' Algernon?"

Nukes, invasion, the usual, you prick. "Prayer. Yes, prayer. The American people should go to church and pray for peace."

Connert made some frantic flashes. HEY I NEED MORE . . . STALL . . . I GOT QUESTIONS FOR YOU . . .

Thach rose and stood in front of Flak. "That is enough," he said with barely concealed rage. The interview had not gone the way his superiors had told him it must go, and he was angry and worried about his future. He needed a favorable event by tomorrow, the 2nd of November. He nodded to Co Dust and told her in Vietnamese to take Flak to his room.

"Wait," Flak said. "I have more to say." Thach turned and studied Flak, a wary look on his face.

WE NEED . . . Connert started.

While he spoke, Flak tried to keep his concentration on Connert's coughs and sniffles and his hand movements without appearing to. "I want everyone to know, to be aware of what I feel." The newsmen had puzzled looks on their faces.

. . . TO NO ALL CAMP LOCATIONS AND ALL POW NAMES . . .

IMPOSSIBLE . . . Flak flashed. Like many of the POWs, Flak had spent time memorizing name, rank, and service of as many POWs as were in the collective memory of those about him. As prisoners returned from various camps, they fed into the POW memory where they had been. The different camps had names based on the first prisoner's impressions: in Hanoi was the Plantation, the Zoo, Alcatraz, and Hoa Lo Prison, known as the Hanoi Hilton. Up and down the Red River were scattered six other camps. It was rumored there might be a camp up on the border between North Vietnam and Red China, but if there was, no one had returned from it.

DO BEST U CAN . . .

GOT TO THINC . . . WRITE IT DOWN . . . PASS TO U . . .

Flak tried another meaningless statement. "I feel this is a long war that should come to a satisfactory conclusion." He noticed Thach had a look of impatience that would soon erupt.

DO WHAT U CAN . . . ARRANGE MEETING TOMOR-ROW . . .

Flak let his knees buckle and staggered to a chair. "I'm not well. Maybe I should go home."

Shawn shot a look of triumph at Connert.

"Tomorrow," Flak said. "We'll talk tomorrow." He looked up at Thach. "You will let these journalists back in tomorrow, won't you?" Co Dust went to his side.

Thach bit his lip. His gaze flicked to the newsmen. His indecision whether or not he could trust Flak Apple was clear on his face. "Yes," he said finally. He thanked the photographers stiffly and suggested they come back tomorrow at the same time. He again told Co Dust to take Flak to his room. When they were gone, he turned to Shawn and Connert.

"He was not himself today," he said.

"Will you actually bring him back tomorrow?" Shawn asked.

"He will be here."

"Did you hear what he said? Do you think he really will depart with us?"

Thach hesitated. "It would be a very good thing," he said slowly. "Come, I will take you to your hotel." He wondered at the strange look on the face of the man called Connert. It was almost exultation. He held the door for them.

"By God," Shawn said to Connert as they walked out, "there was no point in bringing you along. You never did talk to Apple."

"No," Connert said and sneezed, "I guess I didn't."

"Jesus," Shawn said, "can't you do something about that fucking cold?"

Connert shrugged his shoulders. "No, I guess I can't."

After she helped him into bed, Flak grabbed the wrist of Co Dust. "I need paper and a pen," he whispered into her ear.

"Maybe I can bring those things in a few days," she said.

"No, today. I must have them as soon as possible. Immediately." All thoughts of escape were out of his mind now. He had a mission to perform.

She returned as quickly as she could. Her footsteps were noiseless on the bare concrete as moans and other horrid sounds echoed through the rough halls. Her gray cotton uniform matched those of the other nurses, who tried desperately to work in the crowded conditions while hopelessly understaffed. Those close to her station eyed her with mistrust because her only duty now was to be with the black American. She rounded the last corner to the American's room and gasped in surprise as Thach appeared from nowhere.

"Where have you been, wretch? And what have you there?" He grabbed the coarse notebook and pen from her trembling hands.

"It . . . they are for him. He – he wants to write."

"A confession?"

"Yes, that's it. A confession. He did not like the one you gave him."

"I will go with you." He pulled her along the hall and into Flak's room, startling him.

"You want to write a confession?" Thach said in an even voice.

Flak quickly glanced at the writing materials in Co Dust's hands and understood the anguish in her dark eyes. "Yes," he said.

"Write then. I will wait. You can read it tomorrow at the news conference.

"I don't know what to say."

"You know exactly what to say. We have discussed it many times," Thach flared, then got hold of himself. "It is an easy task," he said in a soft voice. "Make it natural, like a conversation. Start from the beginning. You do not have to say you always had these repentant thoughts. Tell them it was only after your leader King was killed that you—"

"King? Martin Luther King? Killed? *What do you mean?*" Flak's face was filled with disbelief

"He was murdered by Johnson's killers."

Flak relaxed. "Well, that's so much bullshit." LBJ might do insane things about the war, Flak thought, but he didn't run about murdering people.

"Your Martin Luther King was assassinated in Memphis in the state of Tennessee on the fourth day of April this year. He was shot by a white man."

303

Flak's whole body flamed. "You're lying. This is a trick. That could never happen."

Thach realized this man had been out of contact from all news, even camp propaganda broadcasts, since his escape attempt last March. "And Robert Kennedy was shot to death in Los Angeles two months later," Thach said with mock sorrow.

Flak frantically looked to Co Dust for confirmation. "It's not true, is it? Ah, God, tell me it's not true," he said, his voice torn with an anguish deeper than anything he had ever experienced.

Co Dust looked up and into his pain-filled eyes and nodded slowly.

Flak clenched his fists. *Oh Jesus, oh Jesus, it's true. My country, oh God. What's happening there? What? What? What?* He took a deep breath and struggled to control himself He stared at the ceiling a long time before he spoke. "Okay, give me the pen and paper. I'll write. But you have to leave the room. You make me too nervous."

Thach stood up. "Are you sure you will write a confession?"

"I will write a confession," Flak said through clenched teeth.

Thach strode up to Co Dust, grabbed the paper and pen, and threw them at Flak. Then he slapped the stunned girl's face with a loud crack and said over his shoulder, "You must write confession for tomorrow or you know what will happen to her." He went out the door.

She stood by his bed, head bowed, hands limp at her sides. Flak reached for her hand and caressed it, a look of anguish on his face.

"He is an animal, a crazy animal," he said. She didn't speak. He squeezed her hands. "Princess, is it true? Is it really true?"

"Yes, they are dead." He could barely hear her words. "They are both dead. You Americans . . ."

Flak lay back and put his hands over his face. "Ah God," he sobbed. "Why? Why? Ah God." He rocked from side to side. "It doesn't get any worse than this." His voice cracked with emotion.

She went down the hall for a wet cloth and put it on his forehead. After a few moments he calmed and sat up.

"Okay, I'll write. You bet I'll write. Give me that paper." He struggled to sit up and she helped him position himself to write and gave him the pad and pen. He started. After a few minutes he swore and changed positions. It still didn't work. His bent arms and shoulders didn't allow his hands and fingers to manipulate the pen.

"Here," he said, and handed her the tablet and pen. "You write for me. I'll dictate. But write real small, as small as you can."

She wondered why but did as he asked as he started dictating in a strained voice.

0930 HOURS LOCAL, FRIDAY 1 NOVEMBER 1968
EAGLE STATION AT LIMA SITE 85
ROYALTY OF LAOS

The pilot dodged among the wispy clouds, plopped his high-winged Porter down on the short strip, and reversed pitch on his big propeller, blowing huge clouds of dust forward of the plane. He taxied over to where Mister Sam and Wolf Lochert stood by the operations shack. The ceiling was low, heat and humidity high. Dust devils swirled across the short strip as a birthing thunderstorm to the west sent out exploratory winds.

"You always draw the shit details?" Mister Sam said as he shook hands with Court Bannister.

"No bad remarks," Wolf growled. "This man is a warrior."

"I'm not complaining," Mister Sam said. "Glad to have you back, Bannister." All three wore safari suits. Court wore his green survival vest over his.

"We've got other visitors," Mister Sam said as they trudged up the hill to Pearson's office shack in the Eagle Station complex, "but they're being picked up this afternoon by a Company helicopter. This place is a regular Grand Central Station."

Armed and grinning Hmoungs stood outside the door like palace guards. They made head bobs in salute as the men entered the small wooden building.

Bob Pearson and Al Verbell greeted them and watched as Court pulled maps from his B-4 bag. "Never thought we'd see you here again, Major," Pearson said as he helped Court spread them out.

"I admit I'd rather defend this place from the air than from the ground," Court said. "Here's what I've got. The intell people think this place is going to be hit within days if not hours. They think Hanoi has had it with your Tacan, but mostly because of the bombing directions your radar provides. Now, for some reason they have indications this site is going to be struck by a main-force outfit and captured soon – very soon, maybe tomorrow." He held up his hand at the exclamations. "Not everybody believes that, but because our intell officer, Dick Hostettler, does, then I do." Court went on to explain about the ground self-FACing that was to be done at the site and that he, Court, would handle the radio with the fighters.

"Between the Wolf FACs in the day and Spectre and the Phantom FACs at night I think we've got it covered," he finished.

"Well, shit," Pearson said. "If I had thought the bad guys were going to get so pissed off, I'd of stayed in Poughkeepsie." He made a face. "Ah well, some guys just can't take a joke." He got up. "Come out here, there's something I want to show you." They followed him out to the steep cliff. "Look at this," he said and stepped into a small notch in the cliff hidden behind scrub bushes. Hammered deep into the rock were spikes that had a half dozen heavy nylon straps attached to them. Each strap was neatly coiled and attached to a parachute harness.

"These are 3,000-pound test straps. They are just the right length to let us over the cliff to hang under the outcropping and then swing into a limestone cave. It's kind of our last-ditch defensive maneuver. A place to hide. I've got provisions and a radio down there."

"Let's hope we don't have to use it," Court said.

"Roger that," Pearson said. He led them through the rest of the radar and radio compound. He finished the tour at a newly constructed bunker sunk well into the ground and covered with heavy logs and layers of dirt. "There's radios and food and water in there," Pearson said with pride. "Had a hell of a time getting those logs cut and carried up the trail."

"All my recommendations were followed, I see," Wolf said as he looked with pleasure at the bunker and mortar pits, the machine gun sites, and the carefully laid-out positions with clear and interlocking fields of fire. Court noted with approval that the two separate Flaming Arrow pits he had helped build had fresh oil-soaked rags in the cans.

"It's damn near impossible for anybody to scale those cliffs and get up here," Mister Sam said. "We've got trip wires, booby traps, and flares on all the scalable trails."

"What about Bunth and Touby down below?" Wolf asked.

"They act pretty military these days and draw their rations without giving us any problems. I think you shook them up bad," Mister Sam said.

"Maybe so, but how are their defenses? Can the PL or the NVA get through their perimeter?"

"Probably a concentrated force could, but I've been too short-handed to check. I don't have anyone to send down there, and your report is as current as I'm going to get. That's why I've concentrated in keeping the approaches up the karst to this place so heavily guarded. If things really turn to shit, all we need is enough time to put the evacuation plan in effect and get the technicians out of here. The equipment is expendable, nothing classified about it. The plan is just to leave for a while if we can't hold the station, then return when the bad guys go away. But don't sweat it. They can surround the base but they can't climb this mountain."

In the distance they could see a rainsquall rapidly approaching the site. They walked across to the village of Poo Pah Tee, perched on top of the karst. Several of the women were washing clothes in tin tubs, a gift of the USAF; others were tending gardens. Chickens lazily clucked and pecked the bare earth for the minutiae of the bug world. Men wearing parts of camouflaged fatigues made their way up and down the dirt paths and between the thatched huts on errands only they knew.

"What about these tribesmen?" Wolf asked as they walked down the dirt paths between the thatch huts. "Would they be evacuated also?"

"Well, there's no plan for that at this time," Mister Sam said.

"Why the hell not?" Court asked. "If they're here to defend you, seems to me they should get the same protection you do."

"Doesn't work that way, Major," said Jerome Powers as he stepped out of the door of the village supply hut. "These people are well paid to stay here and defend their own property . . . property they would lose if we didn't give them the means to defend it."

"You mean property nobody would want if we didn't have military equipment up here," Wolf said. "What are you doing here, Powers?"

"He's part of the visiting team," Mister Sam said.

"And I'm the other half," Barbara Powers said as she stepped from the supply hut. She wore a nicely tailored green jumpsuit and carried a large tan over-the-shoulder bag. "And a cheery hello to you, Major Courtland Bannister."

"Team for *what*?" Wolf snapped.

"Basically, it was sort of a last-minute thing," Babs said. "I got this fabulous idea that since I am married to one of the important men in the Embassy, and since I work in the Embassy, I should get out and see what's going on in the villages. Jerome was a perfect darling and agreed to show me around."

Perfect darling squirmed and made deprecating motions with his hands. "Well, actually I had a supply run to make and no reason why . . . I mean, there was a seat open on the helicopter."

Court thought perfect darling looked like a man caught with his fly open in a girls' school. "Do you normally take your wife on a field trip?" he asked.

"Well, unh, no. You see—"

Wolf Lochert looked at Powers with contempt. "You better

get your butts out of here right now before this place gets hit. Didn't you get the warning? This place is due for imminent attack. Call up your bird, get it in here early, get moving."

"Just a minute there, Colonel," Powers said. "You can't talk like that to me, I'm a civilian with a higher rank than you—"

"You're a civilian *Scheisskopf* who's out here on a boondoggle—" Wolf never finished his sentence because the first bomb impacted with a blast that sent dirt and rocks flying over the south end of Poo Pah Tee and the concussion smashed into their eardrums. Within seconds the moan of a hand-cranked siren split the moisture-laden air. The male villagers scurried about grabbing their weapons and running to their fighting positions; the women scooped up their children and ran into their flimsy huts.

"Back to the bunker," Wolf yelled.

"What is it?" Powers yelled as he ran.

There had been no characteristic express-train sound from an in-coming artillery shell before the blast. Court heard the sound of a piston engine overhead and looked up to see an airplane he had seen only a few times in an aircraft recognition book. It was a six-passenger single-engined biplane that looked like a DeHavilland Beaver with two wings.

"We're being *bombed*," Court said in surprise as they darted into the bunker, "by one of the oldest airplanes in the Soviet inventory."

16

"What the hell is it?" Powers demanded.

"A Colt, the AN-2," Court replied. "It's got fabric control surfaces," he said in amused wonder. He stood in the doorway and watched the ancient airplane come around for another pass. Soon an object split from the airplane and fell dartlike toward the radar dome.

"That's no bomb," Wolf said. "It's too small."

"Looks more like a shell," Mister Sam said as the projectile hit the ground and exploded too far away from the radar dome to cause any damage. Court saw that the clouds were so low where the plane was turning to come in for another pass that it would have to clear a ridgeline at less than 100 feet.

"You got any automatic weapons in here?" he asked Mister Sam as he moved away from the doorway. "Let's get em out. I think we can hose that bastard from the ridge."

Mister Sam rushed inside and back out with three AK-47 assault rifles. He gave one to Court and one to Wolf as they ran up the hill.

"Hey, how about me?" Powers yelled. "I wanna shoot, too, you know.

"Guard the women and children, asshole," Mister Sam yelled over his shoulder. Mister Sam flung Wolf and Court a bandolier as they flopped down on the shale and rocks of the ridge. "These have tracers," Mister Sam said. The tip of every fifth round was

310

green in the Russian style and made of a material that would burn bright green as it flew through the air. Snicks and clacks sounded as they charged their weapons.

"The only way he can make it back here," Court said, "is between those two clouds – and they're moving in fast and low."

The biplane made a right turn and headed toward the ridge. They lined up their guns and waited till it drew closer.

"Almost zero deflection," Court said. They did not have to calculate a long and difficult angle by which to lead the aircraft as they fired.

"Hot shit. He'll be lower than fifty feet if he wants to stay out of those clouds," Mister Sam said with glee. "I don't think he even sees us."

The plane bored in on a line that would place it a few feet to one side. The three men had nothing to fear. The plane didn't carry any guns with which to strafe them, and the bombing with whatever they dropped had been pitiful. Its top speed was no more than 120 knots. They opened up when the Colt was 100 feet in front and to their left.

At first the tracers were behind, then quickly converged on the brown-painted plane. As it flew closer they could see the goggled pilot stare out at them in surprise when the tracers swarmed all over the cockpit. The engine coughed and belched a fireball, then the plane trailed black smoke as the left wing went down, and with a loud thump the aircraft crashed into a small rise. There was no fire.

The men and the villagers ran to the wreckage. There were two men pinned in the torn metal. One was obviously dead.

"This guy might be alive," Wolf said as he tore pieces of the airplane from the man's body. He pulled the small figure out and wiped away the blood.

"Viet," he exclaimed. *What are you doing here? Where are you from?* he asked in Vietnamese.

The man's face was a twisted mask of pain and incomprehension. His eyes were wandering, with huge pupils. He repeated words over and over through a nearly crushed throat. He spasmed, and as he did so, blood erupted from his mouth and he went slack.

311

"What did he say?" Mister Sam asked.

"Sounded like he said 'Brave Fight' or 'Valiant Struggle,' as if it were the name of some operation," Wolf said as he sat back and wiped his hands on a bandana he jerked from a rear pocket.

"Guess he thought he was a hero," Mister Sam said. "What's written on here?" He pulled a paper from a clip attached to the right thigh of the pilot's coveralls.

"It's a pilot's flight card," Court said, recognizing the general format. "The numbers and headings show he came from some place in North Vietnam." He examined the map. "About five klicks over the border."

Wolf studied the paper. "And these letters mean he was scouting for artillery placement. He was only supposed to be a forward artillery observer, to place shells as they landed. I guess he wanted to get in on the act and drop something of his own. Cost him a lot."

Court poked around the wreckage. "Look at this," he said. "That tube out of the bottom of the aircraft. It's crushed, but those are 120mm mortar shells in a rack next to it. They were trying to bomb us by sliding shells down the tube."

The sound of a rushing express train filled the air. "Incoming," Wolf yelled. "Take cover." The three men flung themselves to the ground as an explosion from the tiny airstrip shot red dirt and debris high into the air.

"Let's make it for the bunker," Wolf yelled. "Those are 133mm high-explosive shells." They got up and dashed into the low, sandbagged structure.

The bunker was small but complete. Pearson had set up phone lines and a Motorola radio circuit with the radar van. A Mark 128 radio pallet rested on a wooden table. The diverse radios provided long-range contact with Vientiane and 7th Air Force commanders, and local contact with ground troops and airplanes overhead. An outside generator provided power for the radios and the lights. Fans in hidden ventilators moved the air.

"Where's Pearson?" Court asked.

"Gone back to the radar van," Barbara Powers answered, her face flushed. "Said for me to stay here. Said I'd be safer."

Her eyes were bright and her pupils enlarged. She licked her lips. "What a lark. We're being shelled, aren't we?" She clutched her large shoulder purse under one arm. Her green jumpsuit was wrinkled and smudged.

Another crash sounded from outside.

"Yeah," Wolf said with disgust.

Court couldn't tell whether it was disgust at Barbara being at Eagle Station or at the incoming shells. He decided it was both.

Mister Sam called Pearson on the landline and switched on the voice box so the others could hear the report. "Eagle, this is Maple. What's your situation?"

"Small problem here," Pearson's voice crackled from the box. "Our radar and the TACAN are okay but we've lost our radios. Can't talk to anybody. Guess you'll have to take over from down there. Call Cricket and tell them what's happening and get some fighters in here." Two loud explosions punctuated his words. "What about that airplane that was dropping bombs? Think there will be another one?" Pearson asked.

"Can't say," Mister Sam said. "You got the radar, you tell us if one is inbound. I think this guy was supposed to be an artillery spotter."

"Glad he couldn't make it," Pearson said. "So what do we do now? Even if no one is spotting, those are real shells dropping on us. Even randomly, one could connect."

"I'll call Victor Tango to get the evacuation plan cranked up," Mister Sam said, "but I don't think we'll need it. I'll get reports from Hak and Bunth and see if they have any ground contact. Meanwhile I'll put Bannister in touch with Cricket and let him find out what the fighter and weather situation is." He rang off and handed Court the microphone for the UHF radio.

Court pressed the mike button. Cricket, Phantom Zero One on Primary. "Primary" was aviation shorthand for the major frequency of the day.

"Phantom Zero One, Cricket, gotcha loud and clear," the voice came back promptly. "Didn't know you were airborne."

"I'm not, I'm on the ground at Eagle Station. We're under artillery attack and there'll probably be a ground attack later tonight. What's the fighter and Spectre status?" A shell blasted in the distance.

"Phantom, we've got plenty of fighters, and Spectre can be overhead in thirty minutes, but we've had reports of a solid overcast covering your position. Best we can do until it clears is use the fighters on Skyspot and maybe Spectre on a beacon." He meant the fighters could drop on the directions from the Eagle Station Skyspot radar and Court could direct Spectre to fire through the overcast using his hand-held beacon.

"Good idea, Cricket," Court said into the microphone, "but right now we don't know where the big gun is that's lobbing the shells on us. Once we get a fix we'll let you know and put some ordnance in." A crash sounded closer to the bunker. "We'd better find it damn quick."

He signed off.

"I just got Bunth and Hak on the horn," Mister Sam said. "Here's the situation. Bunth says his men are spread out on a circular perimeter that radiates out twelve kilometers from here. Unfortunately, the gun has a firing range of 15 klicks. He says that his men in the east quadrant know the gun is somewhere out there because they hear the boom and then the sound of the shell as it goes overhead. They calculate it's somewhere between 080 degrees and 100 degrees from us."

Court looked at his map. There were heavy karst ridges and jungle in that direction. "Depending on the weather, I can get Spectre down there after dark to look for muzzle flashes. In the meantime can they get a better location on the gun? Maybe even mount a ground attack?"

"Okay, set the Spectre support up," Mister Sam said. "I'll see if I can goose Bunth into a more active search mode, but I doubt he'll attack anything more dangerous than a wounded water buffalo. I talked to Major Hak. His men are all primed and cocked for movement up the trail. They're ready to fight. As yet they haven't seen or heard a thing except the artillery."

The shells were falling at two-minute intervals and so far had not hit anything vital.

"I made contact with Victor Tango, Mister Sam said to Jerome and Barbara Powers. "Your helicopter is inbound to pick

314

you up. Should be here in thirty minutes or so." He looked pointedly at Powers. "They said they had never authorized your wife on this trip and never would under any circumstances."

Barbara Powers looked at her husband. "Well, duckie, you lied to me, didn't you? Big man, said you could do anything you wanted. God." She threw her hands up in disgust. "Anybody got a drink around this dump?" Jerome Powers grabbed her roughly by an arm. "Shut up. Just shut up." She shook loose and walked back to a corner, where she dug into her large bag.

Mister Sam glanced after her and rolled his eyes. He said to Court and Wolf, "You guys want to haul ass, now's your chance."

"After you," Wolf said with mock gravity.

"I wouldn't miss this for anything," Court replied.

"Well, you know *I'd* love to stay," Powers said, "but there's no one to run the office, so I've got to get back." Babs made a disparaging sound from her corner.

"Last chance, gentlemen," Mister Sam continued. "Victor Tango told me the Ambassador is not actuating the evacuation plan, because he doesn't think the threat is high enough. He does promise to have the standard Jolly Green alert bird at Lima Site 36 keep a listening watch on HF for us in case we need him."

"Fair enough," Court said.

"Well, nobody has asked *me* whether or not *I* want to go," Babs Powers said as she walked over to the group. "And the answer is – I don't want to. This is the most excitement I've had in years." Her breath had the faintly sweet smell of a good gin.

"You have no choice, Mrs. Powers," Wolf Lochert said in soothing tones that surprised everyone.

"Oh, yes I do, Colonel. You can't order me around."

"Can't order you, but I can lift and toss you into the helicopter," Wolf said as smoothly as before.

"We'll see about *that*," she snapped.

"You can't talk to my wife like that," Jerome Powers said in a high-pitched voice.

Wolf gave him a withering glance and Powers took his wife back to the corner.

Court looked around the bunker and found a PRC-25 FM radio. "I'm going out and take a look."

"*We'll* go out and take a look," Wolf said, grabbing his AK-47.

"Keep us informed," Mister Sam said. Another shell impacted in the distance.

"Court," Barbara Powers said as she walked up to him, "take care of that magnificent body." She swayed slightly and put her hands on the lapels of his safari suit.

"Madam," he said, and pulled her hands away, "you have the wrong man."

"*I'm* not a madam," she exclaimed.

"To me you are," Court said.

"By God, you'll pay for that," Jerome Powers said. "When we get back I'll have you up on charges."

Court ignored him and followed a chuckling Wolf Lochert out the door.

Outside, they found themselves in dense fog that had rolled in. "This karst sticks up so high we're in the clouds," Court said. "I wonder what the ceiling is down below."

They jogged at an easy pace through the mist around the complex, checking damages and the fighting positions of Hak's men. At two-minute intervals they heard the express-train rush of another shell and took cover.

"Those shells are not very effective with only one tube and no one to spot for them," Wolf said. They crossed to the village of Poo Pah Tee, where the people were out walking, unconcerned, about their business. They found Major Hak at one of his mortar pits that doubled as a forward observation post looking out over the surrounding jungle to the east. The mist was an impenetrable wall.

Major Hak greeted them with a broad smile. "We can see nothing, they can see nothing." A shell crashed into the eastern hill well below them. Then the sound of machine gun fire came up from the northern side, where the trail from the jungle floor rose up to Poo Pah Tee. Immediately after the shooting, some rapid-fire Hmoung syllables sounded on Hak's radio. He listened intently and snapped a few comments in return.

"They say enemy soldiers come up trail, they fight now," he said calmly.

The battle sounds of shots and bursts of automatic weapons were muted in the mist and fog. Several explosions that Wolf said were hand grenades rolled up heavy and thick from below. A 133mm shell crashed behind them toward the radar site.

"Hey," Mister Sam said on Court's radio, "that was pretty close. Pearson said fragments sprayed the radar van. I'm telling him to shut down and move his men in here."

Firing started from a section of the trail leading to the village. Hak took the report on his radio and said his troops were engaging another attacking force. He turned and gave information to the mortar crew. They rotated and cranked the barrel to a predetermined elevation and started dropping mortar shells into it. The *whumpf* of their departure was followed seconds later by the muffled bang of their impact. Court and Wolf stayed a few more minutes while Hak fed the corrections he received on his radio to the mortar men. Soon he grinned at a report coming back from them and said, "We kill *mak-mak* bad guy down trail."

Court and Wolf headed back to the command bunker. It was hot and crowded. "Man," Pearson said, "this is a twelve-man bunker. It isn't geared for all" – he counted rapidly – "twenty-three of us." The technicians from the radar site sat on the dirt floor with their backs to the walls. There wasn't another inch of wall space available. Jerome and Barbara Powers had a section to themselves. Court saw her return a silver flask to her bag.

Wolf checked about the sandbagged room and noted that Mister Sam had done a professional job in setting up the facility.

"I've got food and water for all of us for a week," the CIA man said, "and more ammo than we can possibly use, mainly because there aren't any gunports to fire from."

A loud boom sounded close by, jarring sand loose from the roof.

"Where *is* our helicopter?" Powers said to no one in particular. Babs shot him a contemptuous glance.

317

Mister Sam turned from his HF radio. "Just talked to Victor Tango. They say no pickup helicopter. Weather is too sour and it'll be dark out there damn quick." Another crash outside dislodged a cascade from the roof.

"That's twice in a row they came close," Mister Sam said. "That's not coincidence. I think somebody's spotting for them now."

"So do I," Wolf said. "Bannister, let's go take a look."

For the second time both men went out the door. In addition to his PRC-25 radio, Court carried one of Mister Sam's AK-47s and ammo and grenades. Wolf was equally armed.

"First thing we do," Wolf said over his shoulder as he ran in a crouch to the closest underbrush, "we get away from the lucrative targets."

Court followed him until they both lay prone under scrub bushes next to a rock formation. The two-minute interval between the shells remained the same, but they were landing with more accuracy. Court eased up the side of the largest rock to look at the airstrip. The cloud-fog had lifted.

"Can't get anything in there but a helicopter until we fix those holes," he said. A roaring noise sounded and he ducked down. The shell landed near the radar bubble, puncturing it with tiny holes from rock splinters.

Wolf rose next to him. "We need to find the highest place a spotter can be to see where the shells land." He looked around. "Over there." He nudged Court and pointed to a pile of shale and karst 500 feet away at the far end of the plateau, away from the village and the radar site.

"Oh, damn – look," Court said, pointing at the command bunker. Babs Powers had come out the door and was walking in weaving strides across the open area to where Court and Wolf were crouched. Her bag was clutched under her arm. Court checked his watch. Another shell was due any second. He stood up. "Go back, go back," he shouted.

She smiled and waved. "Wondered where you were," she said gaily. "Whee, isn't this *fun*?"

The rush of the express train started and, without trying to call or wave, because she probably wouldn't respond in time,

Court sprinted out and scooped her up and ran back to the rock basin where he and Wolf had crouched. He was barely two feet short of the sanctuary when the shell impacted where she had been standing and the concussion blew them in a heap at Wolf's feet. They sat up and brushed off.

"So thaaaat's what it's like to be shelled," Babs said after a moment in that falsely gay voice one usually gets the first time one has just escaped death on a battlefield.

Court and Wolf ignored her and gazed intently at the rock pile.

"I think he's in there," Wolf said. The ground was flat and open on their left side back to the command bunker and the radar complex. To the right was scrub and rock formations. He grabbed his AK and said, "I'll try to flank him. You shoot at him, keep his head down. Won't be able to spot the shells very good if you do that and maybe I can sneak up on him." With a wave he was gone.

Court lay prone at the base of the rocks and sighted his rifle around the right side. He fired off a three-round burst and watched with satisfaction the dust spurt high from the rocks at the position of the spotter. *Not bad for 500 feet,* he told himself.

Babs lay behind the rocks at his feet. "Hey," she said and tugged at his pant leg. "What's going on? What are you shooting at? May I look? May I?" She had the open flask in one hand.

"God *damn,*" Court said and shook his leg as if at a pesky fly as he fired another burst. "Missed." He turned his head back to look at her. "Goddamn it, woman, keep your hands off me. This is real, not some Embassy movie." He snatched the flask from her and threw it under a bush.

With his head bent, he didn't see the quick movement from the rock pile as a figure in camouflage clothing darted down from the rocks into the scrub on the side away from where Wolf Lochert would appear. When Court turned back he fired another burst at the top of the rocks. He watched for Wolf to appear at the base, and planned to fire many bursts at the top as Wolf started to climb.

319

He saw a cautious movement where he expected Wolf to appear, and quickly fired several bursts into the rocks as a signal to Wolf to begin his ascent. Wolf crept from the brush and started up the incline, climbing easily, AK at the ready in his right hand. In a movement almost too quick for Court to catch, the camouflaged figure to the right of the rocks stood up and shot Wolf in the right side as he climbed, and just as quickly dropped down again into the bush. Nearly too surprised to shoot, Court managed to get off the rest of the magazine of the AK as he sprang to his feet and ran in a zigzag pattern toward the rock pile, then punched off the empty magazine as he ran and clawed out another from a pouch and rammed it into position. As he ran, he fired three- and four-round bursts from the hip at the last place in the bush he had seen the figure. He swept his eyes up to the limp form of Wolf, who had slid down into the dust at the base of the pile. He looked back to where the figure had been. He kept up the constant bursts – too angry at himself to do anything but attack and kill the one who had shot Wolf.

It was his fault. He was so enraged at the girl that if she were to somehow show herself in front of him, he would have shot her too. Now he was in grenade range, and he clawed for one from his vest, but it was too hard to dislodge, then he was almost on top of the position, and before he could think of what else to do, he was there and at his feet convulsing and bleeding from the mouth was a small bare-chested man wearing tiger suit pants. The man looked up through eyes squinted in pain and blood from a head wound that dripped into the channel made by the scar on his left cheek. It was Touby the Curer. Around his neck was a strap holding the binoculars he used to spot artillery. At his side was an ancient Chinese radio on which he called in corrections.

In a rage, Court shot him in the forehead and ran up to Wolf's body at the foot of the rock pile as another shell thundered in. He flung himself over the inert man and shielded him from falling dirt and rocks. He lay stunned for a second in the following silence.

"Get your knee out of my back," Wolf said in a voice muffled by Court's body.

"Oh God, you're okay," Court said and rolled off.

"And don't swear, either." The two men sat up. "You get him?" Wolf asked.

"Yeah. It was Touby."

"Figures."

"Where are you hit?" Court asked.

"I'm not. That guy was so close I had to fake being hit until I could figure something out. The fall stunned me for a while." He examined his body. "Gimme a hand and we'll get back to the bunker."

"We've got about thirty seconds," Court said, checking his watch.

"What about the girl?" Wolf asked.

"Leave her out here. She's the one got you shot." Court almost meant what he said. He pulled one of Wolf's arms around his shoulders and helped him hobble across the compound.

"How so?"

"Got me looking at her when I should have been looking at you." They drew near the brush pile and rocks where Court had left Babs. "Move it," he yelled as they passed by. "Let's go." There was no answer. "Oh hell," Court said.

Mister Sam opened the door of the bunker and Court passed the groggy Wolf off to him. "Where's that dipshit broad?" Mister Sam asked.

"I got to go back. I think she's been hit," Court said.

"You got about two seconds," the CIA man warned over his shoulder as he helped Wolf into the dark mouth of the bunker.

Court sprinted to the brush and flung himself flat next to the rocks as the next shell arrived with a bang that shredded the mist. Babs lay as if asleep at the base of the rocks. When the dirt and rocks from the explosion subsided, he rose to his knees and looked at her body for wounds. She was covered with fine dust, but there was no blood. He shook her shoulder.

"Babs? Babs? You okay?" When she didn't answer he put his arms under her body and scooped her up and poised himself ready to run to the bunker. She opened an eye.

"Don't be in such a hurry, lover," she said, her breath sour. "Why don't we just stay like this for a year or two?"

In answer Court sprinted the distance to the bunker and all but threw her into the door held open by Mister Sam. She caught her balance and stopped next to the radio table. Court pointed his finger at her and said, "Goddamm it, stay away from me." He felt his face flame when several of Pearson's men snickered. He turned to Mister Sam and asked, "What's the latest?"

"Notwithstanding that Bunth's man was calling in artillery on us or that Bunth himself no longer answers our radio calls, we have good reports from all over, namely good old Major Hak. He says none of the bad guys are making it up the karst."

A voice crackled on the UHF loudspeaker. "Eagle Station, this is Spectre Two Two, you copy?"

Court answered the call. "Spectre, this is Eagle Station. Glad you could make the party. The weather's clobbered for the moment here at the site. I don't know how it is to the east. Check that for us, will you? We got a big gun over there and we want you to kill it. Copy?" All activity ceased in the bunker as the words crackled through the air.

"Spec Two Two copies. Go secure and give me some numbers."

Court switched in the voice scrambler and gave Spectre 22 the estimated azimuth and range of the gun. Spectre called back in a few minutes.

"Eagle, I think we can do you some good. There are plenty of clear areas in the clouds over here. We'll just drive around and keep an eye out for muzzle flashes."

"Roger. They're firing about every two minutes." A heavy boom outside sifted dirt from the bunker roof "They're still at it," Court said.

A few minutes later Spectre came back on the air. "Ho, ho, and ho. Think we got a fix on your little problem. We got to stay to the east of them so they don't know we're here and stop firing. Will keep you advised."

There was silence in the bunker as they listened to the running report from the man called the table navigator on board the big C-130 Spectre gunship. He was an Air Force navigator who sat at a console and coordinated all the external sensor inputs with the fire control system to present the pilot with the best firing data available. Inputs included infrared, low-light-level TV (LLLTV), radar, and a device called Black Crow that detected the ignition coils from piston engines. He also handled communications with the ground commanders.

"Looking good, here, loooking gooood. I think we've got a fix. Firing now, firing. Loooking goood." There was a pause, then, "Got him, oh boy, look at him cook off. Hey, Eagle, scratch one big gun. What did you say? 133 mil? Well, you can just take that tube from the NVA inventory. Man, is it cooking off. Beautiful."

Court told the listeners that "cooking off" referred to the ammunition that exploded in the heat of whatever fire Spectre had started.

"Let old Spectre know if you have any more problems. The wheels say we're to be on station just for you guys until relieved by another Spec. Copy?"

Court said he copied, then relayed the good news to Cricket.

"Roger, Eagle Station. Be advised, we have launched the pickup helicopter. Have your passengers standing by in four zero minutes."

"Sounds good, let's move it," Mister Sam said. He got up from the table where he had been working the radio, talking to Major Hak. He stretched and yawned. "Hak says he's not having any trouble with the PL that are trying to climb the trail. Been knocking them off like flies. Says his own casualties are very light. Looks like we've cleaned house today. Maybe now they'll leave us alone."

Thirty minutes later Court and Wolf, carrying AK-47s, escorted Powers and his wife to the helio pad. There had been no shell impacts on Eagle Station since Spectre Two Two had reported knocking out the gun. The firing from Hak's defenders down the side of the karst had grown sporadic and finally quit. The radar station was fully manned and back on the air. The weather had improved.

They stood in a group and heard the *whop-whop* of the approaching Huey HU-1B helicopter. Court estimated visibility was now up to five miles and the cloud ceiling over their heads at about 200 feet. It was growing dark. He looked at his watch. Official sunset was in fifteen minutes, but the thick low clouds overhead prevented the last rays of the sun from reaching the top of the karst. He looked down at the approaching Air America helicopter. It flew in the clear below the level of the clouds and below the level of the helipad.

"Well, really, genil . . . gentlemen," Babs Powers slurred, "I don't want you to feel I am running out on you. Unlike duckie here, I'd love to stay."

Both Court and Wolf remained silent, and Jerome Powers took a step to one side as if to distance himself from his wife. As the helicopter came closer, Court ignited a smoke grenade and threw it by the helipad to help the pilot determine wind direction. The red smoke rose almost straight up in the still air. The blade sound changed slightly at a half-mile distance as the helicopter pilot started the climb for the landing site. When it was at 100 feet above the helipad and 1,000 feet horizontal from the steep edge of the karst, Court could make out the forms of the pilot and copilot staring at the landing site as they prepared to touch down.

Suddenly a *whoosh* sounded and a small rocket trailing red fire and thick gray smoke rose from below the edge of the karst and struck the helicopter directly in the big exhaust tube that extended from the engine mounted on top. Instantly, the turbine exploded and the helicopter broke in half in a ball of flame and pieces plummeted to the ground 5,000 feet below the lip of the karst. The big overhead blades had torn loose and spun off at crazy angles. Forward momentum carried larger pieces of the helicopter smashing into the top of the karst short of the helipad.

"Oh my God," Jerome Powers said, his face a twisted mask. "Oh God, what *happened?* Why did it blow up? What's going to happen to us?"

Court and Wolf unslung their rifles and ran past the helipad to the edge of the karst and climbed out to an overhang to try to look down at the fallen wreckage.

"I've never seen any missiles like that," Court said in shocked but professional tones to Wolf.

"I think I know what it was," Wolf replied. "Don't get out too far, there's somebody down there that doesn't like us. We got some real problems coming up from whoever fired that rocket. I don't think they're out there just to shoot down helicopters."

They stopped near the edge of the downward-sloping rock outcropping the size of a tennis court, which was covered with loose shale and rugged bushes growing from the cracks. "Go back to the bunker," Wolf said. "Tell them what's going on. Take those civilians with you. Get Mister Sam to rally Hak and some men and get a perimeter set up around the Station. Get hold of Cricket, tell 'em we got a problem and we'll tell more once we know more. Then you grab a couple Prick 25s plus all the ammo, grenades, and Claymores you can carry and come on back. I'll stay here and try to dope out what the force level is down there and who it is."

"Who do you think is down there?"

"Don't want to get you all upset, but I think they speak Russian."

1400 HOURS LOCAL, FRIDAY 1 NOVEMBER 1968
SUB-COMMITTEE OF THE CENTRAL WAR PLANNING COMMITTEE
HANOI, DEMOCRATIC REPUBLIC OF VIETNAM

The Chairman spoke to the GRU man in passable Russian. He did not know the GRU man spoke flawless Vietnamese.

"Our reports are that the attack for the capture and display of the Americans at that Eagle Station in Laos goes well. Valiant Struggle is advancing to culmination as we have planned."

"I beg to differ, Comrade Chairman," the GRU man said in brisk tones. "My sources have just this day told me the attack on the radar site is not going well at all. They tell me that one of your pilots, instead of directing artillery, was

325

playing at attacking the site himself. And that your men attacking the site are easily being thrown back. Is it that you are quite sure your plan will succeed?"

The Chairman stared slightly to the left of the GRU man, with expressionless eyes, and did not answer.

"I have a *Spetsnaz* team standing by. They await only my command to have that site securely in our hands within one hour of their arrival. This can be done easily by the time you originally desired."

The Chairman swung his head to regard the speaker with hooded eyes. "We are succeeding. There is no need for what you suggest." He turned to his aide and nodded. The aide walked to the wooden door, opened it, and beckoned to the man outside. Thach entered and took the one chair across the table from the committee members. With a small sound the Chairman cleared his throat and spoke.

"Comrade Thach, this is our final coordination meeting for Valiant Struggle. Everything we have planned must happen tomorrow. You assured us of a successful news conference for tomorrow. What have you to report?" The Committee Chairman quizzed Thach in a thin voice that cut to the marrow of Thach's confidence. The other members remained silent and frozen-faced. The GRU man sat in his place at the far end. No one was smoking.

Thach saw on the table in front of the Chairman the most dreaded article used to ensure quavering fear in the core of the most stalwart Party member. It was a worn khaki canvas pouch with four cylindrical compartments. It was worn slung over a soldier's shoulder and was used to carry four large mortar shells in the field. First, as a warning, any committee member who did not uphold communist party standards or who committed any transgression would be shown the pouch. Then, if he made no improvement, he would be silently handed the pouch. The guilty one knew he was then to report to a certain section of the 559th Transportation Battalion, where he would be issued four mortar shells and a pair of sandals made from old truck tires and be told to join the next supply column walking down the Ho Chi Minh

Trail. Of those who had set out on the journey, none had returned.

"Comrade Chairman, today went very well."

"I heard there was confusion."

"Comrade Chairman, there was some. I am not certain he will depart with the Americans tomorrow."

The Chairman remained silent as he stared at Thach. "Then tell me exactly what will happen tomorrow." His voice was a razor blade drawn across steel.

"Comrade Chairman, the criminal Apple will read a confession in front of the cameras that he deliberately bombed innocent people and hospitals."

"He was to read the confession today and depart tomorrow."

"I realize that. He did not. But he is now in possession of information that is quite detrimental to his country and to his spirit. He assures me he will read a confession tomorrow. He even wants to write it himself. In it he may ask for leniency."

"Is he rational? Is he unmarked? Is he ill?"

"Comrade Chairman, he is in presentable health. We have told the American delegation he has suffered injuries from his crashed aircraft."

"Do they believe you?"

"It is of little consequence. They desire to believe and that is sufficient. The cameramen are from our sister countries and realize what the situation requires."

The Chairman looked around the table. "I will attend the press conference tomorrow. I want to be present when he reads his confession. If he asks for leniency, I want to be there to grant it to him in front of the cameras." He flicked his hand. "You are dismissed, Comrade Thach."

As Thach walked out, a man from the War Office, wearing the red tabs of a colonel on his thin khaki uniform, entered clutching a folder to his chest. He had obviously been waiting and looked harassed and nervous. He stared at the Chairman, who tilted his chin in signal to approach. The colonel bent and whispered into his ear.

"It does not go well," he said.

The Chairman looked up and caught the eye of the GRU man, who did not look away in time. The Chairman saw a fleeting look of smug satisfaction on the Russian's face.

1730 HOURS LOCAL, FRIDAY 1 NOVEMBER 1968
SUB-COMMITTEE OF THE CENTRAL
WAR PLANNING COMMITTEE
HANOI, DEMOCRATIC REPUBLIC OF VIETNAM

The phone on the Chairman's desk rang once with shrill insistence. It was French style, black and old-fashioned. The Chairman picked up the receiver and listened to a hurried message from the colonel in the War Office. With a hiss of exasperation he hung up, dialed the Russian Embassy, waited an interminable time to be connected, and made an immediate appointment with the GRU man. Moments later, he sat in the rear as the driver of the black Peugeot sedan threaded through the bicycle and foot traffic toward the diplomatic area of Hanoi. The afternoon sun was hidden behind clouds and the heat was not as crushing as it had been earlier in the day. He had heard Americans had air conditioners in their cars but he did not believe it possible. The units were simply too big and cumbersome and required too much electricity. He sometimes wished he had one in his office, but no one else did, not even Ho Chi Minh.

They drove down the tree-lined streets, where the only villas being kept up were those of the diplomats. They pulled up at the high green wall topped with barbed wire that surrounded the Russian Embassy, where the Chairman was admitted through the thick gate by an armed Russian in baggy civilian clothes. He walked under a huge willow tree thrusting up through the gravel that covered the entire walled-in complex. He was met at the door to the villa, which was tightly shuttered, and led to a small meeting room. *They never take you to their offices,* he thought

328

to himself *but then we do not either.* The room had a small table and four chairs. The man who led him in turned on the overhead light, then punched a big button on a ceramic circuit breaker, and an air conditioner started to wheeze from high on the wall. It was rusty, but he recognized some letters he believed to be Czech. His intelligence specialists had told him the Russians were not authorized air conditioners but got them by trading cases of vodka with members of the Eastern Bloc embassies.

The GRU man made him wait five minutes before he walked in with the air of a harassed official forced to deal with petty problems. It hadn't always been this way. This was only the second time the Chairman had had to visit the Embassy, and how different this time was from the first. Then they had wanted a mutual treaty signed and he had been given all honors. Now he was treated like an unwelcome supplicant. These Russians were like all foreigners; no, they were worse. They were overbearing and ponderously arrogant, as if only they had all the answers.

"You are here because of the attack on the American radar station," the GRU man began. "There is little to be gained talking about it, comrade. Your forces were not up to the task. Mine are. As you probably now know, I instructed my *Spetsnaz* to finish the task. What did you wish to see me about?"

The Chairman steeled himself not to get up and walk out. "I must have your assurance that your men are instructed not only to capture as many Americans alive as possible, but to bring them here immediately."

The GRU man regarded the Vietnamese with barely concealed dislike. *Alive and in Hanoi,* he thought to himself. *Now, that is a joke. Bring them here, then someone from the other side who knows* Spetsnaz *was in there will be exhibited to journalists, maybe even Western journalists. This cannot be allowed to happen. Once our men have the Klystron tube, they will kill all survivors and depart. If they decide one is an engineer and knows the electronics of the tube, and if all goes well, they will take him alive, but certainly not deliver him to Hanoi and these monkeys. He will be taken to that special camp in Siberia where the other engineers were.* He leaned forward and tried to assume an earnest expression as he recited his lie.

"Of course we will bring them here. It is what was agreed for your forces to accomplish. We are proud to help our allies in their struggle." *Allies, hah. Inscrutable savages.*

The Vietnamese had no expression. "Tell me, what went wrong? We had carefully conditioned two men from the other side. Were they found out?" It was a question the Chairman preferred not to ask, but he had to have this man's response for the Committee. It would be interesting to see how it compared with what his informers had told him.

The GRU man almost laughed. *What went wrong,* he said to himself, *was exactly what we planned to go wrong. Those Bunth and Touby idiots did just what we knew they would do — just as we had programmed them to do. They were not fighters, they were grasping dope peddlers who paid allegiance only to themselves.* "We have no reports as yet," he replied solemnly.

"Yes," the Chairman said. "I understand." *I understand you have lied to me,* the Chairman thought. He arose and they went through the departure amenities.

The GRU man watched him go. *We will have our Klystron tube,* he said to himself as he returned to his tiny cubicle of an office, *and no one will be the wiser. At least we left them their dope production and delivery channels.*

He tapped his tooth as he thought about the possible capture of a radar engineer from the site. The GRU man was well versed on American POWs. And detainees — as they called the hundreds of World War II American airmen who had crash-landed in Soviet territory. Those men were held incommunicado in Kazakhstan until the end of the war. These days, because Kazakhstan was too well known, the special POWs from Korea and Vietnam were in a highly secure camp in Siberia where they could be exploited at leisure. Unlike the detainees, the POWs would never be released. But they had to be highly skilled before being selected for the camp. Merely piloting an airplane was not enough. A candidate had to have had special electronic warfare or nuclear delivery and targeting experience. *Too bad the Strategic Air Command B-52s only fly over South Vietnam, where we cannot get at them,* he thought. *They have special crewmen who would be highly useful to the technicians in the Siberian camp.* He nodded to himself. Few within the USSR government éven knew such a place existed. The GRU man felt content. His plan was working.

The Chairman's driver opened the door of the ancient French sedan for him. He climbed in, barely aware of the surroundings as he thought of the conversation he had just had. *Those fools do not lie well. We have accomplished our goals. The radar site is shut down, we will soon have three captured Americans, our poppy production is untouched. The Soviets will now be blamed if anything goes wrong, and we have photographs of Soviet men in uniform in Laos. Clandestine release of those pictures to the Western press would cause great condemnation to fall upon the Russians. Unless they agree to providing us with better weaponry for our struggle, such a thing will happen.*

17

Court Bannister climbed back to where Jerome and Babs Powers were huddled next to Mister Sam's wooden operation shack. This was ground combat, something he wasn't trained for, but he knew he had the best man in the business running the show, and he would do anything Wolf told him.

"What's going on?" Powers yelled. "Why didn't you stay here with us? We don't have any guns."

"Get a move on," Court said. "Back to the bunker."

"But what about our helicopter?" Powers said, on the verge of hysteria. "We're supposed to leave. Maybe there's another."

"Maybe," Court said, "but not for a while. Let's go now."

"Come *on*, Jer. Do like the man says," Babs Powers said and walked to where Court stood in the gathering darkness. Slowly, as if reluctant to leave a place of known safety, Jerome Powers joined them. Court urged them into a trot up to the bunker.

"What in hell is going on?" Mister Sam said as they entered. Quickly Court briefed him on what had happened, then grabbed the microphone and, using his Phantom call sign, called Cricket, who answered on the first call, and they went secure-voice.

"Cricket, we got a big problem down here. An unknown force is on the south face of the karst. They just shot down the Air America helicopter with some kind of a surface-to-air missile. No survivors. One of our guys is down there now trying to

332

get a line on who's doing the shooting. He thinks they're Russian. We need Spectre ASAP and have the Phantom FACs standing by for cover tonight. Copy?"

Cricket said they copied and asked Court for the eight-digit map coordinates of the enemy force. Court read off the numbers, then asked what the weather report for the night was.

"Not too good, Phantom. We've got buildups to 35,000 feet, scattered thunderstorms, ceiling running about 5 to 6,000 feet, visibility zip when it's dark." Although the ceiling was a mile above the jungle surrounding the karst, Eagle Station once again jutted into the low clouds.

"We can give you some Skyspot birds," Cricket said over the loudspeaker, "if you can keep your radar on the air. And we just got word from 7th we can give you Spectre coverage all night."

"Sounds good," Court transmitted.

"Ah, Phantom, there is a bit of a problem. We can't clear any birds in until we have permission from Victor Tango, and if we get it then we have to pass that through 7th for final approval."

"What do you mean, 'if' we get the approval?"

"Well, sometimes it has been denied because of friendlies in the area."

"How the hell does *he* know?" Court asked.

Mister Sam walked over. "Let it go," he said. "I'll explain it to you."

"Okay," Court said into the microphone, "do what you can as fast as you can. Meanwhile I'm taking a Fox Mike radio and going back out to the attack site. I'll call you from there and tell you what's going on." Cricket gave Court the primary and secondary FM frequencies and they signed off.

"What the hell is all that 'permission' stuff?" Court all but yelled at Mister Sam.

"Take it easy. We've got some pretty tough rules of engagement out here and—"

Court cut him off with an impatient gesture. "Okay, okay. I gotta get back to Wolf. Do what you can." He made hasty communications arrangements with Mister Sam and put Pearson and Verbell to work helping him pack ammunition, radios, and the other equipment that Wolf wanted into canvas bags. He set both radios to the frequency Mister Sam had given him for contact, using the call sign of "Maple."

"I want to go with you," Pearson said.

"You got any infantry training?" Court asked as he strapped on water canteens and shouldered the bags.

"Not any more than you."

Court gave him an appreciative glance. "Look, you guys stay here. Do what Mister Sam tells you. I have a hunch you'll get your chance."

"I've got some of Hak's men waiting for you," Mister Sam said. "Lead them back to where Wolf is."

Court went out the bunker door and found a squad of Hak's men, with M-16s, crouched to the side of the structure. He could barely see them in the gloom. Heavy firing and the crump of mortars came from the helipad. Court handed each of two men a sack of ammo, waved for them and the others to follow, and moved as quickly as he could toward where he had left Wolf.

He tried to stay low in the grass as he neared the spot, but had trouble in the dark and had to feel his way. He stood up to get his bearings and a burst from his left sent him diving for cover. A man behind him cried out and dropped like an empty sack. Court jerked when a loud burst of answering fire from Hak's men cracked over his head. He rolled over on his back and wiped the sweat from his face on the bandana he pulled from his safari suit. He could barely make out the forms of Hak's men crouched behind him. He saw two of them crawling and dragging a body back to the rear. In minutes it would be pitch black and he knew he had to get the radio and supplies to Wolf before that or he would never find him. Another burst of fire from the helipad snapped over their heads. This was not a situation for which the Air Force had prepared him.

"Any of you speak English?" he asked in a low voice.

The only answer he got was a few words of Hmoung.

"Spread out," he said, and waved his arms to each side. "Move forward, find" – he remembered the Hmoung words – "find *Animal-Man*." He repeated the name twice more and pointed with his finger in the direction he thought Wolf to be. He kept one sack by himself and pointed to the other, then forward while repeating *Animal-Man.* A tribesman Court guessed was in charge seemed to understand. He rattled off a few words and three of his remaining six men scrambled forward into the darkness, one of them dragging the sack of supplies and a radio. The firing became sporadic as the area became pitch black.

Court lay on his side and slapped at a bug crawling on his face. He felt sticky and sweat-soaked. Now there was no noise toward the helipad. By feel he pulled the radio from the bag and turned it on. He cupped the telephone-like headset to his mouth.

"Maple," he said in a voice barely above a whisper, "this is Phantom. Do you read? *Maybe I'm not trained for this,* he thought as he wished for a reply, *but I damn near enjoy it. If I wasn't a fighter pilot I'd probably be in Special Forces.*

"Phantom, this is Maple. What the situation?"

Another burst went over Court's head. He heard a rustling in the grass at his feet and a Hmoung crawled next to him and said a few words he could not understand. Court keyed the radio.

"The situation is we haven't made contact with Wolf yet and we're pinned down. I've got a guy here I don't understand. Get someone to start talking Hmoung and I'll hand him the headset. Have him ask my guy what he's trying to say, then relay to me." He gave the handset to the Hmoung. There was much talking back and forth, then Mister Sam spoke to Court.

"Ah, now don't get all pissed about this, but, heh heh, they say you are not a soldier. That you go through the bushes like a three-legged water buffalo and would you please return to the bunker so they can get about their business."

"They said all *that*?" Court asked in chagrin. *Me? Special Forces?*

"Actually, a bit more, but best we let it go."

"Well, hell. I'm staying here. I already sent out some of them with the supplies and radio for Wolf, and I haven't heard from him yet. So tell them to go ahead out there and find where the supplies are and get them to Wolf." *All right, so I'm only a fighter pilot, but I'll do what we do best – press on.*

Mister Sam acknowledged, spoke a few words to the Hmoung, and came back on to Court.

"No word from Victor Tango yet. They said they are studying the problem but feel we can handle it ourselves. They say there are absolutely no Russians around here and quit trying to make things worse by saying there are. So, ah, sorry 'bout that."

"Who the hell is the real enemy around here?" Court shot back and signed off. He checked his area and realized with a start that all the Hmoung were gone. It also occurred to him he had been doing a lot of talking on the radio and that his voice had been rather loud.

I better get my ass out of here, he said to himself and started crawling in the direction of the helipad. A burst of fire passed over the area he had just vacated. It was awkward moving with his AK-47, radio, and bag of water and ammunition. He crawled as quietly as he could until he came to an area where the grass stopped. He flattened to look around but it was pitch black and he saw nothing. He reached out to touch the clear area and felt what he guessed was the dirt surface of the helipad. His mouth felt dry and he took the canteen from his belt and swallowed several times. He heard the *whump* of a mortar, then, with a loud pop, a small parachute opened and a mortar flare illuminated the battle area in a sickly yellow light as it drifted earthward trailing a thick stream of smoke. It oscillated in its parachute, causing shadows on the ground to move black fingers to and fro.

He saw two figures at the far end of the helipad who were dressed differently and much larger than the Hmoung. They moved swiftly and he could see they would be upon him in seconds if they stayed moving in the same direction. He eased the AK forward, fumbled the big safety lever to what he hoped was full auto and carefully sighted along the barrel at the moving men. They wore dark camouflaged clothes, had thin packs on their backs, and carried what he thought to be AK-47s at port arms as they ran. They had small caps on their heads and wore some kind of mask or goggles. His heart started thudding. There was no doubt they would be upon him, and he pulled the trigger as the flare hit the ground. He saw one man go down, then all went black as the flares burned out.

Then he was so stunned by the terrific light given off by the muzzle flash of his weapon that he released the trigger. Instantly, the man fired back and Court realized he had compromised his position. He scuttled backwards in the grass, then got to his feet and started running what he hoped was parallel to the edge of the pad. He quickly slowed because it was so black he was afraid he might slam into a rock or fall into a hole. He slowed, then stopped and crouched down. It was only then he realized he had left behind the bag with the extra ammunition and the radio. He flattened himself on the ground and tried to think.

Okay, okay, calm down. He rolled over on his back and realized a light drizzle had begun. The adrenaline surge through his body was decreasing and he felt his heart slow its heavy thumping. The picture of the two men he had seen impressed itself in his mind. One man had definitely gone down, but the other had been still running. With a shock he realized what the goggles they wore meant: they had to be night-vision devices. With them, the wearer could see in the dark if there was any faint light to be gathered and amplified. Court looked about. He figured the overcast prevented starlight and the fine mist would coat the lenses. For the moment they were as blind as he was.

He jerked as a shriek pierced the blackness. It came, Court thought, from the area he had just fled, or beyond, maybe across the helipad. He was disoriented and wasn't sure. The shriek sounded again. He felt his stomach contract and a spasm in his bowels as the shriek became a hoarse scream and died off in a burbling groan. He thought he heard Hmoung syllables in the groan. Then several shots sounded and he heard a man yelling guttural words that he knew were not Hmoung. Another flare popped over the helipad and was so absorbed in the mist the light was as dim as in the hour before dawn. But it was adequate for Court to get oriented. He lay on his back in the tall wet grass and raised his head just enough to look around.

He could barely make out some of the antennas and Mister Sam's shack, but was able to triangulate his position as away

337

from the helipad and in a grassy area that butted up to a
shale pile. He could see he had curved away from the open
area as he had run. There were figures by Mister Sam's
shack and a strange form against the wall of the shack. There
was a struggle among the standing figures, then they pushed
something else against the wall. Another loud shriek split the
air and Court realized what was happening. The camouflaged
men had thrown ropes around the feet of two Hmoung they had
captured and were hanging them upside down from the bamboo
rafters that protruded from under the roof. One figure was still.
As he watched, two of the men worked over the second figure
with something in their hands and he heard the man shriek
again and again. As he did, several of the big soldiers faced
outward, weapons at the ready. In seconds they began firing
at small figures, Hmoung, Court knew, that ran towards them,
screaming like madmen and firing weapons from the hip. Just
before the flare died, Court saw all of the Hmoung cut down
and he realized what the camouflaged men had done. They
had baited a trap with screams and goaded Hak's men into an
uncoordinated wild charge that had ended in death.

It was black again, but in the brief light Court knew where
he was and where his radio and ammunition were hidden. He
wondered if Wolf had received his supplies before the Hmoung
had been cut down or captured. He wasn't sure whether to try
to make it back to the bunker or find his supplies and look for
Wolf.

A panicked voice inside said to go back to the bunker.
*Nothing you can do out here – you aren't trained for this.
Get back there and call in some air support. That's what you
do best. Get back to the bunker.* He took a deep breath and
tried to rationalize what he really should do. The other voice
in his mind said he was a fighter pilot and fighter pilots don't
quit and that the hardest decision was invariably the correct
decision. Thoughts tumbled through his mind.

*Oh shit, I don t want any part of this, now I know what scared
truly is. Wolf's dead. If not, he can take care of himself. I'll
never find those supplies in the dark, or those other guys will
find me and I'll wind up hanging on the wall. Maybe I should*

just stay here and wait for daylight. Maybe this will be all over by then. Yeah, and turn my wings in while I'm at it. Bannister, don't be an asshole. Maybe I'm not infantry-trained, but I am a fucking combat pilot – and this is combat, so I ain't got no excuse. Press the fuck on.

He fixed in his mind where the supplies were and started to crawl in that direction. Dragging his rifle was awkward. Then, clear as a movie in his mind, he saw a training film demonstrating that a crawling soldier was supposed to cradle the gun in his arms. He shifted the weapon and resumed his crawl. It occurred to him there had been no shots and no sounds since the Hmoungs had been cut down. He figured the invading force was headed for the radar site and would probably leave a holding force at or around the helipad. He moved as slowly as he could to avoid noise. The wet grass slid across his face and had a sharp vinegary smell. He moved several feet, then stopped to listen. He repeated that several times until he came to the edge of the grass and realized he had veered back to the helipad. He thought about the man he had shot. Maybe he was still out there and had a pair of the night goggles. Then he dismissed the thought. These were obviously elite forces, and they would never leave a known wounded or dead companion just to lie there. He would be brought to a central point. The thought struck him that maybe the helipad was the central point. Maybe a helicopter would come in to lift the force out when their job was done. He crawled toward the center.

He estimated he was halfway to where the body should be when the thought struck him that if a mortar flare went off now he would be as obvious as a mouse on a billiard table. He scuttled faster along the ground and then realized he didn't have a good fix on the body. Then he realized he no longer had a fix on the edge of the pad where his gear was located. He stifled an urge to jump to his feet and start running, running in any direction. Then he smelled something. It was an odd mixture . . . then he knew he smelled the dead man. It was a mixture of excrement and blood and came from close by. He swung his head back and forth until he had the strongest scent and started in that direction. The smell got worse and

339

then he realized he was within a few feet of the corpse. For an instant it was as if he could feel the warmth of the body on his cheek. He put his hand out and felt a booted foot.

Lying flat, his rifle on the ground next to him, Court fumbled with the body, feeling clothes and belts, and a harness, then he realized his hand had come away sticky with blood, and the stench from the man's voided bowels was overpowering, and he was afraid he would retch and throw up but he held on and continued working his way up the corpse. He got to the face and found that the goggles had slid up the man's forehead. He reached to take the goggles and almost cried out loud as a hand grasped his wrist in a grip of iron.

He snorted in desperate fear and rolled away and the hand let go, then he heard a gagging noise that sounded terribly loud in the night air. His heart had resumed its chest-thudding gallop and he was afraid the man would scream and his companions would come and find him and kill him. Without a conscious decision, Court's survival instincts took control and he rolled over, found the man's neck, and strangled him.

When it was over he lay panting for an instant next to the body of the man he just killed. With a surge he rolled back, fumbled in the dark, and snatched the heavy goggles and tried to slide them over his head and found they were attached by a wire to what he surmised was a battery pack. He freed the battery from the man's harness, pulled the eyepieces into place, and saw absolutely nothing. He slowly moved his head to see all around his position, and found if he tilted his head back he could see a faint greenish glow in one direction. He dropped the goggles to his neck and looked in that direction. The drizzle had stopped and the best he could tell was that there was a slight break in the low overcast and faint starlight was causing some illumination. He pulled the goggles into place and by craning his neck and looking almost sideways, he could just make out the edge of the helipad where he thought Wolf Lochert had gone. Then he heard the cough of a mortar leaving its tube and knew he had scant seconds to clear the pad before the flare opened

340

up. He sprang to his feet and took off in the direction of the green glow. When he reached the tall grass he ran in several feet, then flung himself to the ground just as the pop of the opening flare sounded and the yellow light flooded the area.

Court lay still for a moment, then rolled over on his back. It was then he realized he had left his gun at the side of the dead man. *Not trained isn't the word,* he said to himself. *Dumb. Stupid mother-fucker is more like it.* He lay back and felt a terrible lethargy start to creep over his body as if some foreign substance were replacing his blood. His legs felt like lead and he knew he couldn't raise his arms. His brain fogged and he thought he would just sleep for a little while and he would feel much better. He mused over whether the lethargy was caused by the let down after the adrenaline high or the realization that he was doomed and might as well accept the inevitable. He closed his eyes for an instant, then snapped wildly awake as he heard the hissing of the burning magnesium in the flare. He looked up and saw that the flare dangling under its parachute would drop right on top of him if he stayed where he was. *Is this where I am to die? Some obscure dot on a map in a country few people have even heard of? Someplace where I have no control?* Used to the positiveness of flying an aircraft that always had something functioning a pilot could use, Court felt totally helpless. He felt like a bug in the bottom of a bowl that someone was toying with. Some absurd being was letting him climb up the sides to freedom, then shaking the bowl so he would slide back to the bottom.

He almost laughed.

The flare grew larger.

Christ, man, get hold of yourself.

Okay, fighter pilot, move it, move it. There's always one last trick, one last maneuver, one last hope. Move it. He grew alert again, galvanized, and crawled off in the grass, still toward the direction in which he thought Wolf Lochert had gone. When he was sure he was clear of the flare, he stopped and hastily pulled the goggles up to his eyes to get a fast look around before the flare went out. He sat up and cautiously raised his head. He looked slowly in all directions. Seeing through the lenses was like looking at a murky green world through two long tubes. There was no depth of field and no peripheral vision. The two forms were still dangling by Mister Sam's shack, and he could see green blobs making their way up the path toward the radar buildings. He swung his head farther toward the rock pile and saw a green blob near the top that appeared to move. With a thud and a hiss in the wet grass, the flare fell to the ground behind him and the night was black once more.

He kept his eyes in the direction of the rock pile and saw the faintest of a green gauze blob that could possibly be a man. He noticed the man never fired a weapon. If he had, his goggles would have lit up with an unholy green light caused by the muzzle flash. He crept slowly toward the area, then realized there was no way he could approach Wolf – if the blob was Wolf – without his head being shot off as a potential attacker.

Firing broke out toward the radar huts. Court swung his head around and by the light generated by the muzzle flashes he could see several of the armed intruders dashing toward the bunker. *Nothing I can do from here,* he said to himself and pushed on toward the man he hoped was Wolf. The firing created enough noise so that he didn't have to move as cautiously and was able to cover ground faster. He sensed the mass of the rock pile the same time he saw it in his goggles and took refuge in a crevice between two rocks.

It was now or never. He took a deep breath and cupped a hand around his mouth.

"Wolf," he called softly. "Wolf. Do you hear me?"

There was no answer. The rocks prevented him from seeing up to where he thought his friend was crouched.

He waited a few more seconds and was ready to try again when his world suddenly turned upside down and he was on the ground with a hand over his mouth and an arm around his throat. He was pinned so quickly and so expertly he couldn't cry for help or move an arm or hand to get at the attacker behind him. The goggles were ripped from his head in the struggle. He braced his feet against the rock and tried to buck and shove backwards to bash the man who had him against the other rock. The man was braced, and it was like trying to move the rock itself. Then he became aware that the man was talking very quietly in his ear. He lay slack and gasping through fingers that slowly released pressure so he could gulp in more air.

"Hey, that's better, jet jockey. Maybe now you quit squirming we can get on with it."

"Oh God – Wolf."

"You said that so nice I think it was more a prayer than a swear," Wolf whispered and released him completely. They stayed in the shelter of the rocks but could not see each other.

"How did you know I was here? How did you know it was me?" Court asked.

"I smelled you."

"What? How?"

"Your soap, your after-shave."

"How could you smell me from up there?"

"Up where?"

"Up on the rocks. That's where you were, weren't you?"

"No," Wolf said and tensed. "How did you know someone is up there?"

"These," Court said and fumbled around until he found the night vision goggles. He found the wire had separated from the battery. "They won't work now, the wire is broken. I can maybe fix it if we need them."

"How did you get them?"

"From one of the attackers."

"How?"

In a whispery voice Court told him the story of the man he had wounded then strangled.

"Umph. Tough duty . . . for a jet jockey. Do you know you just killed one of the Russian *Spetsnaz* troops? If they ever find you and know you did, you would not have an enjoyable

343

episode." Wolf moved. "These glass things, they any good?"

"Only if there is some residual light. Starlight is enough." Court looked around. To the west the break in the overcast had increased, causing the faintest of glow to his naked eye. "The light is a bit better. We can use these now."

"If you could see what you thought was me up there, and those guys all have these glasses, then he could probably see you."

Court felt his blood run cold. "Then he knows we're here." In the dark he started tracing the wire from the set and from the battery to where they had broken.

"Yeah," Wolf said "He's probably a stay-behind with a radio to keep an eye on his buddies' rear.

"And on the helipad, maybe." Court used his teeth and thumbnail in an attempt to strip the wires by feel, without much luck.

"Any of those Hmoung find you?" Court asked. "You get the radio or ammo?"

"Never saw 'em."

The shooting up the hill near the radar buildings and bunker stopped.

"You think they've overrun the place?" Court asked in the darkness.

Wolf didn't answer. Instead he grabbed Court's shoulder and whispered in his ear. "Get that thing fixed in a hurry. I think we've got company."

Court heard a faint scrape of equipment against a rock. His fingers trembled and he tried to steady them to pick at the wires.

"He's close, very close," Wolf whispered in his ear. "And I can't see." He felt around. "Where's your gun?"

"Out there with that guy I killed." He had an idea. "Give me your knife."

"You're nuts," Wolf whispered. "I wouldn't turn you loose against that guy with a howitzer, much less a knife."

"Very funny. Give it to me. I need to strip the wires."

Wolf moved very slowly and by feel handed him his knife. Court placed a wire against the blade and rubbed back and

344

forth. He heard the sound again. "He can't see us from the angle I last saw him," he whispered.

"I know," Wolf replied. "That's why he's out looking for you. Probably doesn't know there's two of us. Probably only spotted you as you dove into these rocks. That's why he didn't shoot earlier."

A loud explosion ripped the night with concussion and noise. It was muffled and contained by large rocks to one side of their position.

"Hurry," Wolf said. "That was a grenade. He's probing by fire."

Court felt what he hoped was the bare copper strands on both wires. "Put them on," he told Wolf. "I'll have them bare in a second, but I need to be next to you to hold them together. No time to splice."

Court felt Wolf grab the goggles and fumble them on his head. "Everything will look green," he told him and pressed the wires together. Instantly Wolf rose to a crouch. The wires tugged in Court's hand and he rose with him. He felt Wolf rear back and heave something over the rocks with his left hand. As soon as what he had tossed clattered off to the side, Wolf stood all the way up, swung his head from side to side like a searching radar beam, then suddenly fired a burst from his AK. Court heard a cry and the crash of a heavily loaded body falling among the rocks.

"Come on, easy now," Wolf said, and led Court to where the fallen soldier lay. Court let go of Wolf's wires and felt around in the dark until he found the man's goggles and battery pack and put them on. When he could see, he said, "This isn't where I first saw him. He was higher up. Maybe he's got some equipment up there we can use."

By touch alone, Wolf started to strip the man's body of grenades and AK-47 ammo pouches. He felt around the field pack and found a sharp-edged folding shovel, which he pulled loose and tucked under his belt in the small of his back. "Okay," he said, "you got the eyeballs. Go up there and bring down whatever we can use."

The clearing to the west still provided enough light as Court edged his way along the rocks and carefully climbed to where he thought the man had come from. As he gained the location, heavy firing broke out up at the site. He found some tins of water, what he thought was a radio in a backpack, more ammunition, and a bundle of what seemed like tent and camouflage material. He gathered everything up except the tenting and carefully worked his way down the rocks to Wolf.

"Here's our first order of business," he said to Wolf, handing him a water tin. By feel alone Wolf produced his Randall stiletto and punctured the tin and both men drank heavily.

"Look what I found while you were gone," Wolf said. He produced a small radio that Court could tell by feel was an RT-10 survival radio. "Was in one of his pockets. Probably the one Perrit had," Wolf continued.

Court was ecstatic. He snapped out the antenna and turned the set knob by feel to Transmit/Receive, the only operable frequency used for emergencies by aircrewmen.

"Eagle, Eagle," he transmitted, "this is Phantom. You read?"

There was no answer, and Court tried again. This time Moonbeam, the ABCCC C-130 on night orbit, answered.

"Phantom, this is Moonbeam. Got you weak but clear. What's going on down there? We're working Eagle on Fox Mike, said all his UHF and VHF antennas were blown down. He said you all are under attack and that you were missing, along with some Army guy. He's inside some kind of a bunker and doesn't know who's doing what."

"Moonbeam," Court transmitted, "the site is under attack by Caucasians who speak Russian. Now you tell that to MACV. Tell them we need air support, and if we can't have any, we need to be gotten out of here. We won't have any kind of a count until daylight, but I think we've been hit bad."

Court asked Wolf what he thought was going on, while they waited for an answer from 7th Air Force in Saigon.

"What's going on is exactly what I told those *Scheisskopfs* in Vientiane would go on: the bloody *Spetsnaz* are working us over and in a very professional way. No handful of Hak's men

346

are going to stop these guys. We need outside help, big outside help."

"Phantom, Moonbeam."

"Go ahead."

"Yes, sir. Ah, 7th said that given the weather circumstances he'd rather not risk any aircraft in your area, at least not before daylight. You copy?"

"Moonbeam, Phantom copies. Moonbeam, you in contact with any Phantom FACs right now?"

"As a matter of fact we are, Phantom Leader," the Moonbeam controller said with conspiratorial pride in his voice.

"Phantom Leader," a new voice broke in on Guard Channel, "this is Phantom Zero Three. We're holding over Delta 36 at this time. We read you weak but clear." Delta was the coded reference for a geographical area in Laos.

All US military and civilian aircraft have a second receiver to monitor the emergency channels of 243.0 on UHF and 121.5 on VHF and can switch their transmitters to talk on that frequency. Phantom Zero Three, although on another mission, could hear the traffic between Court on the ground and the controller airborne in the ABCCC. Every other plane within the 200-mile radio range monitoring Guard Channel could also hear the transmissions. Normally, emergency transmissions were soon switched to another channel once contact was made, to leave Guard Channel free for other problems. Court could not do this because his survival radio had only the one emergency channel.

Court recognized the voice of Phantom Zero Three as that of Ken Tanaka. Normally Phantoms did not hold over Delta 36. Their mission was to patrol the Ho Chi Minh Trail at night for trucks and guns.

"Hey, Zero Three," Court transmitted, "what's your mission?"

"Night Rescap escort," Tanaka said.

Wolf was listening to the exchange. "What's that?" he asked.

"Something is going on over North Vietnam, and we have some Jolly Green rescue helicopters on alert at Lima 36. The Phantoms will be initial escort in case they have to go in after a shootdown." Delta 36 and Lima 36 were the same place.

"We need a little Rescap here ourselves," Wolf grunted.

"Copy," Court said to Tanaka. "You got to stay where you are. Any other Phantom up tonight?"

"Roger, boss," a new voice came up on the radio. "This is Zero Two. Just happen to be in your local area with nothing to do. Weather is delta sierra on the Trail." Phantom Zero Two was Howie Joseph, Court's Operations Officer, the number two man in the Phantom FACs. Delta sierra was pilot talk for "dog shit."

"How much playtime you got, Zero Two?" Court asked how much fuel the pilot had, translated into flying time.

"About an hour, then off to the tank." The Phantom FACs would aerial-refuel from KC-135 tankers orbiting just across the fence in Thai airspace.

"Keep monitoring this freq, Zero Two. I may have something for you." He turned the radio off and put it in his pocket. The firing was heavier from the bunker complex.

"We gotta get your Prick-25," Wolf said. "We gotta talk to the bunker."

Court pulled the goggles up. "I can see the general area well enough to go get it."

"Go ahead, I'll cover you."

"How? You can't see."

"Simple, anybody shoots at you, I shoot at the muzzle flash, then move my position."

"Oh, good deal." Court adjusted the glasses and crawled off into the grass. He found it quicker to skirt the edge of the helipad, and in seconds was picking up his radio and the bag of ammunition. As an afterthought he detoured out to the middle of the pad to get the rifle he had left by the dead man. When he arrived where he was sure the man had gone down, he found nothing: no body, no gun. He had a terrible feeling of being watched. He kept the radio and the bag and moved quickly back to the rock sanctuary where he had left Wolf and slid in between the two boulders. Wolf wasn't there.

18

Wolf was missing. Court drew back as if struck by a snake. The two events could only mean one thing: some *Spetsnaz* had returned for whatever reason, and, wearing the goggles, had found their dead companion and somehow found Wolf. They were probably still in the area. His stomach gave a half-twist as he remembered Wolf's words about what they would do to a man who killed one of their own. His mouth went dry and he desperately wished he had never, ever gone out of the safety of the bunker into the night. He backed up from that and wished he had never, ever accepted the TDY to Eagle Station; but maybe he never should have joined the military. He almost grinned at the absurdity of this line of reasoning. He had had it before and recognized it for what it was: his body's attempt to tell his brain that he was in serious trouble and that if he had only done something different at an earlier time this terrible situation would not have arisen.

Even in the split second these thoughts were flashing through Court's mind, he knew he had to get away from the position. He looked up the rock pile and decided that was the best place to be: take the high ground. At least that's what all the movie lines said to do. *Oh God, if only this were a movie.* He felt around for the water tin, which he had decided he'd better have, and found it near the folding shovel. He stuffed both in the bag, shouldered the radio, and started the laborious

349

slow climb to the top, trying to shake off the feeling of doom that was weighing him down.

As he worked his way up, he remembered that Wolf had pulled the shovel from the second dead man's pack and, he was sure, had tucked it into his belt behind his back. Finding it now, he reasoned, meant that Wolf had felt or seen what was coming and had slowly eased the shovel from his belt into a rudimentary hiding place. Maybe Wolf wasn't dead, he thought.

Once on top he lay flat and scanned the area through the goggles. He saw movement near Mister Sam's hut and saw what he interpreted to be two men doing something to a third. *Oh God, that's Wolf,* he thought. *They've got him and they're going to do the same thing they did to the Hmoung. I've got to help him – but how without a gun?*

Court rummaged through the bag and found what felt like hand grenades, the water tin, and a few flares. There were boxes of what he was sure was ammunition for the AKs and nothing else. Hand grenades and a shovel. How to do this? In the dark, he picked up the shovel and hefted it. It felt balanced and menacing in his hand as if it were an ancient warrior's weapon and not just a tool with which to dig dirt. He took stock. With the goggles he had night vision, with the grenades he had a relatively long-distance weapon, and with the shovel he had a close-in fighting tool.

His tongue felt thick and he realized he was terribly thirsty. His own sweat was now so much a part of him that he had almost forgotten he was soaked. He used the shovel to open the water tin and was surprised how easily the sharp steel of the blade cut the metal. He took long swallows, paused for breath, and took more. Then he rechecked the goggles, shoved grenades in his pockets, and started back down the rock pile. He had to keep swinging his head to keep oriented as he peered through the tubes. He plotted his course so as to not be seen by anyone farther up the path toward the radar complex.

The firing was intermittent up the hill, and he tried to use the noise to mask his footsteps and movements over the rocks. Soon he was in the grass and had to lie flat to crawl up to the hut. He found he could not quietly drag the radio with him and had to

350

leave it behind. Then, as he got closer, he could see what was going on among the three blobs. Two of them were shoving and pummeling a third. Court guessed the two *Spetsnaz* men, who wore their goggles, were toying with Wolf, who could not see. At one point Wolf caught hold of one man's arm when he came too close, but the other circled behind and banged something off Wolf's head. The goggle resolution wasn't good enough to see what they were hitting him with, but Court could hear the smacks and Wolf's grunts as the blows landed.

Jesus Christ. I can't just jump in there swinging a shovel. These guys are masters at this.

Then he had an idea. A sudden flash of light amplified through the goggles might blind them enough so that he could step in and jerk their battery wires out. Then he would be the man with sight in the kingdom of the blind. He reached into his pocket and pulled out two grenades. He couldn't remember the timing interval between releasing the spoon and the detonation, thought the hell with it, put one in each hand, held them to his mouth one after the other, and pulled the pins with his teeth. He flung one to the left of the three men and one to the right and lay flat on the ground and closed his eyes.

When the explosions sounded, he leapt to his feet, held his goggles in place with his left hand and the shovel in his right, and ran to the area. He was astounded by the residual light left from the burning powder and bits of sparkle that clung to the grass where the grenades had detonated. The increased light made the resolution very clear, but all he could see was one figure, bent over, the bulk of which made him sure it was Wolf. He knew he had about a half a second to find the men and disable them when he saw they had each dropped to the ground and were pulling sidearms from their holsters. The resolution was now so good he could see the lines of the goggles and the wires running down their backs to the battery pack. One man had pulled his off. Court made it to the man who still wore his and chopped wildly with his shovel at wires on his back. The shovel buried itself in the man's back with a chopping grinding sound and wedged tight in his spinal structure. Court couldn't pull it loose. The man gave a hoarse scream and bent back like a bow.

351

Court heard the blast of a pistol close behind and dropped to the ground. As he hit, his night goggles jarred loose and he couldn't see. From the direction of the shot he realized it was probably the second *Spetsnaz,* shooting at sound only. As he fumbled the goggles back on he heard a rushing of steps across the earth, then a heavy thump, and regained vision in time to see Wolf Lochert fling himself on a man in the grass holding a pistol. Court scrambled over to help, but as he did he saw Wolf's hands close on the pistol and force it to the man's stomach and squeeze so hard the gun went off and the man went limp.

"Oh my God, Wolf, you're okay," Court gasped out as he slid to the earth next to the two men.

"Christ almighty," Wolf said between pants and gasps. "I've told you not to swear." He sat up and felt the man's throat. "He's dead. What about the other one?"

"I chopped him in the back with the shovel. I couldn't get it out."

"See if he's alive."

Court went to the body. "He's dead," he said in a voice far too even.

"Get his guns," Wolf ordered. *Got to keep this guy from thinking too much,* he told himself. "Hell, man – you done great," he said. "I guess you got your eyeballs on. Let's get the radios, get under cover, and find out what the hell is going on." He searched the man by feel for weapons, found his pistol, and put it in his pocket. Then he stripped the rucksack from the body.

"Wolf you're swearing.

"I am *not,* goddammit. Give me the bag."

Court handed it to him and saw him place the contents, along with a heavy device, into the Russian rucksack. "It's a Russian mine," he explained. When he was finished he said, "Okay, lead me – and move it. Back to the high ground."

Using the goggles, Court got them back to the top of the rock pile. He gave them to Wolf to look around while he got on the FM radio and called the bunker.

"Eagle, Phantom, you read on Fox Mike?"

"Do we ever. Thought you'd had it."

"What's the situation?" Court asked. He recognized Pearson's voice.

"They're hammering on the door but we ain't opening. All our antennas are down and I think the radar station is gone. We haven't heard a word from the guys up there for the last thirty minutes. Hak's men are holding but he says they're being whittled down pretty fast. Says these guys can see in the dark. Know anything about that?"

"Yeah. They got night vision goggles." Court was speaking as quietly as he could into the headset.

"God help us. Anything we can do about getting some airpower in here?"

Court almost chuckled. Here he was with two radios and the blackest night he'd ever experienced. "Pilots don't have goggles, and you said your radar is down. Doesn't look good until daylight. Anyhow, the ceiling and visibility are zip." He thought for a moment. "You say you got contact with Hak. Can you relay some instructions for me?"

There was a pause. "Mister Sam says affirmative. What you got in mind?"

"Might just try some Flaming Arrow. Who knows what Spectre or the Phantom FACs can do if I light one."

"You got a map? I'll give you some cords."

"Negative," Court said. "We've got to assume the bad guys are monitoring our transmissions, anyhow. Get the info from Hak where the bad guys are relative to the arrows and I'll see what I can do. Get his guys to talk in slang Hmoung or very fast so the bad guys can't catch it."

"Rog. We'll get right on it." The radio went dead.

"Here's how I see it," Wolf said. "There's twenty-five, maybe thirty guys here. There's no doubt in my mind they are *Spetsnaz*. Although I couldn't see their faces, I felt their bodies and heard them talk. They definitely were Caucasians and they were speaking Russian. They're not advisers, because there is no way advisers could come up that cliff, then be able to fight so well. These guys are in peak condition and well trained. There has to be some cosmic reason why they want to take this site

353

to risk being caught here. It's my feeling they want to grab this place intact. Notice there are no big satchel charge explosions. Just small arms and a grenade or two. They can't be here just to take out the site. Too much of an international risk. The PL can put this place off the air sooner or later if they really worked at it. Maybe these guys want prisoners or the equipment."

"The equipment is pretty run-of-the-mill," Court said. "Nothing very high-powered or classified about it. They have comparable stuff, so there's no reason to try to capture ours."

"Then they must be after prisoners . . . but there isn't anybody special here."

"Mister Sam is special. But the Agency has their guys at many places. Then there are the technicians and radar operators – but if the equipment isn't classified, why capture them?"

Wolf chuckled. "Well, there's you and me."

"And Powers and his wife, for that matter. But this thing was set up long before anyone knew we'd be here."

"Yeah. Well," Wolf said, "on to business before we wind up with a case of dead or an extended TDY to a gulag. Here's the situation. This rock pile, the helipad, and the bunker form a lopsided triangle, with the bunker being at the north end of the triangle. A trail leads north from the bunker to Hak's village. One arrow is outside the bunker, the other is by Hak's village and sort of guards where the easy trail from below tops out. One of the *Spetsnaz* units is up the trail from the helipad toward the bunker. From what I can tell by the goggles, they seem to be moving freely in the radar site compound but are still attacking the bunker. I hear other firing farther away toward the village, but I don't know what the situation is. See if Eagle has any info yet."

Court made contact with Eagle, who handed the mike over to Maple. "Here's what I have from Hak," Mister Sam said. "He reports a blocking force on the trail that keeps him and his men pinned in the village. They don't seem to be advancing, but he can't get his men out to come down here to relieve us. He thinks he could point the north arrow at them and light it off. Best I can tell about the guys outside our door is that they are south of us. Our arrow is between this bunker and them,

354

but we can't get out of here to light it off. Any suggestions?"

"Stand by," Court said. "You heard all this," he said to Wolf. "What's your thought?"

"More convinced than ever they want prisoners. If not, they'd try to take Hak's village as well as blow up the bunker."

"If that's the case, they probably would want to extract everyone at daylight."

"By helicopter right from this pad," Wolf said.

"So the guy up here and those below were supposed to hold the pad."

"Exactly. And they are dead and not checking in on their radio net, so maybe we'll get some visitors to see what went wrong."

Court could feel Wolf swing around and survey the area toward the bunker. "Ay-yup," Wolf said, "and here some of them come this very minute."

"How many?"

"Four. Let's get busy."

"Busy? One gun, one pistol, one set of goggles, a few grenades, outnumbered two-to-one and you want to get busy? Wake me when it's over."

"I have an equalizer," Wolf said. "Found it with those two guys we took out at the hut."

"I'm awake and ready to play."

"You're getting pretty smartass for a guy who was coming apart a little while ago," Wolf said with approval.

"Just your basic fighter pilot," Court said.

"Okay, basic fighter pilot, here's what I want us to do. We gotta take out those four guys, then hit the guys attacking the bunker."

"Supposing," Court said, "we bypass those guys, flank the baddies at the bunker, and light up the arrow."

"Great," Wolf said, "but what good will a lit-up arrow do? We ain't got no air."

"If I can get Spectre on the radio and get him to go into orbit overhead, maybe his infrared detectors can pick up the arrow."

"Say, what about that hand-held beacon you were so proud of?" Wolf asked.

"It's back at the bunker."

"Get them to use it."

"Can't. The antenna has to be in the clear, and they can't exactly stick it out a window."

"Okay, let's see if you can contact Spectre before we move," Wolf said.

Court pulled out the RT-10. "Spectre, this is Phantom Zero One on Guard. If you read, come up four and a half bucks on Fox Mike." Court used the simple dollars and cents slang code to tell the orbiting gunship to call on 45.0 megacycles, which Court could receive on his PRC-25.

"Well, hello down there, Zero One. This is your friendly Spectre Two Four on station. Two Two has RTBed. How you read?" The deep voice of the table navigator was reassuring to Court. He felt like he was among his own once more.

"Your Item Roger and NOD all tweaked up?" Court asked. The infrared and the NOD Night Observation Device were sensors Spectre used to gather all available heat on the infrared band to locate targets.

"Big fat roger on that. What you got?"

"Do you think you can pick up a flaming arrow through the clouds?"

"If you mean what I think you mean," the deep voice said, "we probably can get some sort of a trace if the clouds aren't too thick and if there isn't any rain. Lousy resolution, though."

"Roger, Spec. Stand by this frequency and we'll try to get a fire going for you."

"What we need now is to get to the arrow, swing it into position, and light it," Wolf said.

"Simple enough. I'll just stroll over and do that little thing. Got a match?"

"You're coming along, Bannister. Might make a Special Forces man out of you yet. And you have a point. We need something to light the rags. All I have is a thermite grenade. You got matches or a lighter?"

Court patted his pockets. "Yes," he said in relief when he felt his rubberband-covered Zippo in his right pocket. He silently thanked his SF buddy Joe Lopez who had taught him the trick at Bien Hoa so his lighter wouldn't slip out of his pocket.

"Thought you quit smoking," Wolf said.

"I did, but I still carry something to light ladies' cigarettes."

"Will it work first time?"

"It better. With all those guys out there I won't get much of a second chance."

"We won't have much of a first chance unless we get those guys in the bunker to help us. We need a diversion. Anything to keep the attention of the *Spetsnaz* while we sneak by and get to the arrow. Once the arrow's lit, that ship has to fire within seconds or we'll be shot up and overrun."

"Diversion," Court mused. He looked up. "Notice you can see better? Take those goggles off and look around. That break in the clouds to the west is bigger. I may be able to bring in one hell of a diversion." He pulled out the RT-10.

"Phantom Zero Two, Phantom Leader on Guard," Court transmitted to Captain Howie Joseph. "You still on station?"

"Roger, boss, but I've only got twenty minutes more of playtime. Less if I have to let down."

Court knew what he meant. As long as Joseph kept the big jet at altitude in an orbit with its engines throttled back, he saved fuel. If he had to come down to low level, the engines would gulp much more fuel and he would have to break off earlier.

"What I need won't take much, but you will have to come down."

"Well, I *am* assigned to a Rescap. Can't really break away."

A new voice cut in: "Phantom Zero Two, this is Moonbeam. I'll get your replacement up so you can go off station ten mikes early, copy?"

"Roger, roger," Howie Joseph said with glee in his voice. "You heard the man, boss," he transmitted to Court. "Tell me what you want and I'll do it in ten."

"I'll need some of your rockets and maybe some strafe. You got a fix on my location?"

"Same place you said you were going?"

"That's affirm. When I call, I'll want it high up on the west face, near the top but not over the top. Under no circumstances over the top. Copy?"

"West face, high but not on top. What's the weather like down there?"

"Lousy everywhere but to the west. There's a sucker hole over there that I hope will stay open until we need you. Note that Spectre will be orbiting east."

"How about ground fire?"

"Don't want to scare you, but a hand-held missile of some kind shot down a helicopter a few hours back. I think it was IRguided, so just pull up into the clouds after you fire." The moist clouds would throw off the missile's heat-seeking guidance system by diffusing the heat from the attacking jet's tailpipe.

"Roger, copy. Standing by." If Howie Joseph had any fear of a missile, it didn't appear in his voice.

"Ah, Phantom Zero One, this is Moonbeam. Can you come up Fox Mike?"

Court changed radios and called back. Moonbeam answered.

"Didn't want to clutter up Guard any more than we had to. Got a question for you from Seventh. Sorry 'bout that, know you're busy. They want to know who are the attackers and what is their Order of Battle?"

Court told them it was thirty or so *Spetsnaz*.

"Spet-who?"

Court spelled it out phonetically. There was a pause, then Moonbeam came back on. "Unh, Phantom, we got a phone patch for you from Seventh. Some, ah, Oh Seven wants to talk to you." Oh Seven was part of a numbering system denoting an officer's rank. Oh One was a second lieutenant, six grades higher was a brigadier general: an Oh Seven.

"Go," Court said.

A very faint and garbled voice came through the headset. "Phantom, this is Blue Chip. Do you read?" Blue Chip was the call sign for the air support command post run by 7th Air Force.

On instinct Court did not answer. Blue Chip called twice more, then said, "Phantom, this is Blue Chip transmitting in the blind. You are not to engage foreign nationals, repeat, you are not to engage foreign nationals. Under no circumstances are you to engage or cause casualties to foreign nationals. This is Blue Chip at 2015 Zulu Hours, 2 November 1968." Foreign nationals was the current euphemism for, Court guessed, Russians.

Wolf gave a low whistle. "Is that how your generals operate a war?" Even in the humid night, Court felt his face flame. He couldn't tell if it was from anger or embarrassment. A little of each, he decided. He realized he had to make some response, then decided no response was best, as if he had not received the message.

"Phantom, this is Moonbeam. Did you copy the message?"

"It was pretty garbled, Moonbeam," Court waffled.

"Blue Chip wants to know if you copied or not."

"Tell them . . . tell them I copied but will act as required to save the mission."

There was a pause, then Moonbeam came back on. "They want your initials, Phantom."

"Charley Baker."

Another pause. "They're happy now."

"What was that all about?" Wolf asked.

"A little game of CYA – Cover Your Ass. Some brigadier will sleep better tonight knowing he's carrying out regulations."

Wolf made a faint snort. "Okay," he said, "time to go. It'll take us at least ten minutes to get up to those guys. It's critical for you to get the noise in to their west so we can slip by on their east."

Although the faint starlight from the cloud break to the west gave overall form, it was much too dark to make out substance. Wolf kept the night goggles on and led Court down the side of the rock pile. He carried his AK-47 and wore the rucksack he had taken from the dead Russian. They walked in a crouch, Court's hands on the pack on Wolf's back. Each step was done almost in cadence, to help Court put his feet where Wolf had put his and to avoid noise. Court carried the PRC-25 on his back and the RT-10 in his pocket. They kept the firing to their left and stayed off the path as they headed north. Twice Wolf eased them to a halt and they crouched down and waited for a movement to their left to subside.

When they were almost abreast of the firing, Wolf veered behind a limestone outcropping.

"Now," he said, "put your man to work."

Court pulled out the RT-10 and called Phantom Zero Two. "Okay," he told him, "put four Willy Petes below the ridge, west side."

For his night mission Howie Joseph had turned all the instrument lights off in the front cockpit of the big F-4D Phantom jet he was flying. The lights were simply too bright even when turned to "dim," and destroyed the pilot's night vision. Howie had the red-filtered cockpit lamp attached to a swivel over his right elbow at its lowest setting. The soft glow barely illuminated the attitude indicator that showed Howie the position of his airplane relative to the horizon: diving, climbing, banking. He could not read his airspeed or altitude. He relied on his GIB – Guy in Back – for that information. He reached around the control stick to a panel and by feel selected the proper switches to fire his Willy Pete rockets. Willy Pete was pilot slang for the white phosphorus head of the rocket that exploded in a blinding white flash and issued huge volumes of thick smoke to mark targets for fighters to strike. His GIB was First Lieutenant John Martin.

"Got that Eagle Station on your scope, John?" Howie was asking if Martin had broken out the mile-high karst on his ground radar screen. Howie had a repeater scope up front but kept it off to protect his night vision.

"Got it. One o'clock for ten."

They were ten miles south of the karst. Howie turned northwest until he was in position to roll in west to east and fire his rockets at the west face. They were three miles above the ground in the night sky, flitting in and out of clouds that were black shadows against starlight made dim by a high, thin overcast.

"Thirty-degree dive," Howie alerted Martin on the intercom. "I'll pickle at eight thou." "Pickle" was slang left over from World War II bombardiers, meaning to push the button that released the ordnance. A good bombardier, it was said, could put a bomb in a pickle barrel.

"Rodg," Martin answered. His job now was to monitor the situation and call out the dive angle, airspeed, and altitudes as his frontseater made his pass.

"Zero Two's in, west to east, rockets," Howie transmitted to Court in the stylized cadence of a combat pilot. "Wish I could say 'FAC in sight,'" he added. That was a normal call for a day-strike pilot to let his FAC know he wouldn't be overrun. Tonight it was Howie's attempt at humor, for he knew his boss was in deep shit without a stepladder.

He heard the two clicks in his headset as Court punched his mike button in the standard abbreviated response that meant "I understand."

"Altitude 12 thou, airspeed 425 and increasing, dive angle 25 and increasing."

"Unh, huh." Howie Joseph concentrated on trying to pierce the black night in front of him, to break out the bulk of the huge karst piece into which he wanted to slam his rockets.

"Going through 10, you got 450 and 30 degrees. Looking good."

"Unh, huh." Howie strained against his harness as his plane plunged through the black clouds, now in a cloud, now in the clear. *"God-DAMN,"* he said to himself. *Where is that frapping mountain?* Something niggled in his mind. He had forgotten something. This was not the normal sequence for him to strike a target. Normally he was either the FAC or the strike pilot. Tonight he was a little of each, but something had been left out of the ritual. Some piece of information.

"Eight thou," John Martin said. "Pickle and pull, pickle and pull."

"Shit – don't see it yet," Howie Joseph breathed into his mask. He held the dive. "Give me another 500." Those were his last words. His last thought in the split second when the black karst appeared in front of his airplane and when he reflexively jerked the stick full back in his lap was the absolutely clear revelation that they had never gotten an altimeter setting for their descent below orbit altitude.

The 50,000-pound airplane slammed into the karst in a nose-high attitude, driving the white-hot engines into the remaining

8,000 pounds of JP-4 fuel, causing a blinding flash and a rolling, boiling red fireball that lit up the entire karst ridge as it climbed skyward borne on its own heat. The high tail section of the F-4 broke off at impact and whistled and spun though the air up the slope and over the top and cracked into the rock surface in the radar compound.

"Oh GOD," Court Bannister yowled in agony.

"Move it," Wolf barked and grabbed Court by the sleeve and pulled him running and stumbling to the safety of the sandbagged Flaming Arrow pit. He had jerked the goggles down to his neck the instant they had bloomed in the green incandescence caused by the fireball which lit the terrain for the time Wolf needed to make the run. He had had time to note the position of several of the *Spetsnaz* troops as he ran behind them while they all looked up to the horrid rising sun in the west. As the fireball climbed and faded, Wolf had time to swing the arrow toward the enemy, pull an oil-soaked rag from the nearest can, tear it in two, hand half to Court, and say, "Time to light up."

Almost in a trance, Court put down the radio he had clutched in his hand and reached in his pocket and pulled out the lighter. Darkness lit only by the fire down the slope settled on the pit, but he still saw in his mind the roaring flame that meant the death of two of his men. Mechanically he held the lighter out, flipped open the top, and was about to spin the wheel when he stopped. Reality had suddenly replaced tragedy.

"Wait," he said to Wolf. "No point in lighting this thing and calling attention to ourselves until we get Spectre set up." He had his mind back on business.

"Right – do it," Wolf said over his shoulder. Court could just make out Wolf's form as he lay prone behind the sandbags, aiming his rifle in the direction of the firing. Flames below the lip of the cliff illuminated the low clouds to the west, which acted as a soft backdrop to the scene. "We don't have much time. I think they're getting ready to rush the bunker," Wolf called.

Court unslung the PRC-25 radio from his back, turned it on, and called Spectre 24.

"My God, man, what happened down there?" the table nav responded." I've got more IR light than Times Square."

"Spectre, relay to Moonbeam that Phantom Zero Two impacted with the ground at 0315 hours local with no survivors."

"Wilco," a sober voice acknowledged.

"And, Spectre, have you got a clear read on the easternmost fire?" Court had put the crash of Phantom 02 out of his mind and dealt with the problems at hand.

"Affirmative, but it's not consistent."

"That's okay. I'm going to light a Flaming Arrow about 200 meters east of that flame. Hose down the area from fifty meters in front of the Arrow westerly to the other flame. Copy?"

"Roger," Spectre said. "Good copy." He repeated the instructions.

"I'll have the arrow lit in two secs," Court said and flicked a flame to his lighter and torched off the rag he held. He could easily see the whole arrow as he moved quickly from can to can, igniting the rags within. He heard Wolf fire three shots.

"They're on to us now," he called out. "Get those guys shooting, *schnell.*"

"Okay, Spectre, have at it. We'll take all you got."

Before he could reply, a new voice cut in. "Phantom, Spectre, this is Moonbeam senior controller, do not fire. Repeat, do not fire. You are not cleared by Blue Chip."

19

0330 HOURS LOCAL, SATURDAY 2 NOVEMBER 1968
EAGLE STATION AT LIMA SITE 85
ROYALTY OF LAOS

"What's going on? Wolf yelled back to Court. We need that fire-power *now*."

"What do you mean?" Court roared into the handset to the Moonbeam controller. "Not cleared? Jesus Christ, man, we're under attack here. Give us Spectre or we're dead meat."

"You got to answer some questions," the senior controller said, his voice less certain. "It's for the ROE. Do you have a TIC?"

"ROE, TIC. Jesus Christ, YES, for Gods sake, yes."

There was a man in the Blue Chip command post, it was theorized whose sole job it was to conjure up acronyms. ROE for Rules of Engagement and TIC for Troops in Contact were a couple he had done just for warmup one day before breakfast.

"Are American lives and/or property in danger?"

"Jesus Christ, YES, you numbnuts. Will you give Spectre permission to shoot?"

"What are your initials?"

Wolf was firing steadily now. Court had to duck down as bullets whistled over the rim of the pit. He had the crazy urge to run about and put out the telltale flames in the cans with his hands. If Spectre couldn't shoot, the flaming arrow worked in reverse, putting him and Wolf under fire from *Spetznaz*.

"Shoot, goddamm it, shoot."

"Your initials?"

364

"Charlie Baker, you asshole," Court thundered into the handset.

"Stand by."

"Get that thing from the ruck," Wolf yelled. "The mine. Open it up. Hurry."

Court tore into the rucksack and jerked out a black metal container the size of four cigarette cartons. He fumbled until he found a key like a Spam can and peeled back the top, which opened with a hiss of air. He took out a convex plastic device, some wire, and a small plunger. The plunger spun a tiny generator to send a charge of electricity down the wire to detonate the mine.

"Hook up the wires, then hold the plunger and give me the mine," Wolf said between bursts.

Court did as he was told in the flickering light. Wolf took the mine, yelled at Court to hold tight to the plunger while the wires unwound, fired a long burst, then heaved the mine in the direction of the enemy. "Push on that thing when I tell you," he yelled at Court. He leaned back to his AK-47 and fired a long burst. *"Scheiss,"* he yelled. "Here they come. Push the plunger." The flickering flames from the arrow accentuated the sweat and grime on his face and the deep furrows of his brow. "Push it NOW," he bellowed.

"Phantom, this is Moonbeam senior controller relaying for Blue Chip, do you read?"

Court ducked as more bullets flew over the edge of the pit and jammed down on the plunger. Nothing happened. He frantically pulled it up and slammed it down twice more. There was no answering explosion. He checked that he had wound the wires correctly around the posts. He had.

"Phantom, do you read Moonbeam?"

"Yes, yes, goddamm it. Tell Spectre to fire." Court snatched at the handset, his voice ragged with tension and frustration.

"Spectre, do you read Moonbeam?"

"Jesus Christ, YES. Can we shoot or not?"

"Spectre, this is the Moonbeam senior controller. Blue Chip clears you to—"

Court didn't hear another word as the 20 and 40mm rounds

moaned down through the clouds and thudded and hammered and exploded in the terrain where the *Spetsnaz* attacking the bunker were hidden.

Court heard faint screams and yells through the pandemonium, then the sound of Wolf's weapon firing burst after burst. He crawled to the edge of the pit and peered over the sandbag edge. Backlit by the flames of the burning Phantom and the reflecting clouds, it looked like a scene from Dante's *Inferno* as the smaller 20mm cannon shells detonated in white sparkles and the larger 40mm shells boomed and exploded into three-foot orange fireballs. Figures and pieces of figures were jumbling and tumbling in the air along with pieces of rock and earth as the sweeping guns churned men and dirt into red-brown clots.

"Beautiful," Court shouted into the handset. "You're right on them, Spec, keep it coming. Beautiful." His blood was pumping and he felt an exhilarated rush as his body and mind came together in the exuberant realization they might just escape annihilation on this Laotian mountaintop. And he had successfully put the crashing death of his two men out of his mind. For five more minutes the torrent of death washed the enemy enclave.

Wolf fired out and inserted a fresh magazine into his AK-47. He sighted down the barrel but didn't fire. He got slowly to his knees, sighting carefully beyond the sandbags, then sat back on his heels. "All right," he said, "all right. That's enough. Turn it off."

"Hold fire," Court ordered Spectre. "Hold high and dry. You guys done good, real good," he said, falling into the ungrammatical phrases combat men use to congratulate each other.

"This is Gunship Charley, at your service," a new voice said on Court's radio. "You ask, we bash. You call fast, we haul ass. Have guns, will travel. We got lots of playtime and we'll just hang around till daylight."

Court thanked what he suspected was the aircraft commander of the huge four-engined plane. Prior to this, neither he nor Court had ever seen what incredible destruction and death their weapons caused below their flight path. This was Court's first time to see war from the ground.

Through slitted eyes Wolf saw the elation on Court's face

in the flickering light. He wondered how long it would last as they made their way through the carnage to the bunker. "Come on," he said. "Let's move it." They climbed out of the pit and stood on the rim, quite safe now. Silence hung humid and heavy over the area that moments ago had yielded thunder and screams in the crescendo of battle. There were no moans, for there were no intact throats. Throats and lungs were long separated and shredded. The cans on the flaming arrow behind them made small pops and clicks as the heat source in each slowly burned out. The flames from Howie Joseph and John Martin's funeral pyre were lowering.

They picked their way to the bunker door. Court saw here an arm, there a leg draped in looping wetness, a headless bulk in a shredded uniform blouse, broken weapons, smoking holes. He felt the headiness of victorious battle drain quickly. *It's so quiet, so silent.*

Inside the bunker was pandemonium: hoarse yells and hysterical laughs as the men surrounded Court and Wolf and pounded them on the back, spouting half-sentences of relief and joy. "We were dead . . . God, what noise . . . what took you so long . . . helluva job . . . heard the whole thing on our Fox Mike . . . Who *are* those people out here? Are there any more?"

"Take it easy, guys," Pearson said, drawing his men back. Wolf and Court stood with the two Powers. Mister Sam drew them back to a corner, where they grouped around the edge of the rough wooden table that held the radios. Babs Powers looked bright-eyed, almost feverish, Court thought, and wondered if all the action had sobered her up. He made his report to Moonbeam on the bunker's Fox Mike. When he gave the details of Phantom 02's crash, they promised that Phantom 03 would be on call when his Rescap orbit time was completed over Lima Site 36.

"There's more out there, aren't there?" Powers said, facing Court and Wolf preempting anything Mister Sam might want to say. "Why didn't you get them all? What's the matter, chicken?"

"Jesus Christ," Mister Sam said, "these guys were out there

getting the fucking job done and you were in here drinking coffee."

Powers whirled on him. "How *dare* you talk that way to me? Listen, you, I'm the ranking civilian in here and your job is to protect us—"

"You're the ranking idiot, who's got no business even *being* here," Mister Sam said.

"Jer, do shut up," Babs Powers said in a weary voice.

"He's right on one thing," Court said, trying to be conciliatory. "There are more out there."

"That's what I'm trying to tell you," Powers said scornfully as he turned to Court and tapped his chest with a forefinger. "And where is our mighty Air Force now? Why, one of you dummies flew right into this mountain. A little higher and he'd have killed us all."

In a flash of red rage, Court became suddenly and irreversibly involved. He slammed his right fist into Jerome Powers' mouth, knocking him back against the table, where he slipped to the floor.

There was shocked silence in the bunker. Enlisted men – whether or not they are sheep-dipped and called technicians – were not used to seeing an Air Force officer deck a civilian wheel, even if the wheel was the all-time asshole of the universe. One hidden-in-the-crowd man found his voice.

"Good on ya, mate," he said in a phony Australian accent, "served the little bugger right."

"You're going to pay for this, Bannister, oh, how you're going to pay," Powers said from his position on the floor. He found a handkerchief and dabbed at the blood from his cut lip. Babs knelt next to him and took the handkerchief away and blotted the blood for him. "Next time, ducks," she said, "use your brains, not your balls." She helped him to his feet. He eyed Court as if planning to punch him but didn't move.

"Let's figure out what to do next," Mister Sam said with a barely concealed grin on his face. "All is not lost."

Bob Pearson joined the group. "Is it clear enough out there for me to get back to the radar van to see what happened? We haven't had contact with them for a while. Verbell would have checked in by now."

"You got maybe five minutes," Wolf said, "before the part of the contingent that held Hak's troops away will be here. They're going to want to know what happened to their buddies."

"We'll be back in two," Pearson said, nodded at a buck sergeant, and they slipped out the bunker door.

"Here's how I see it," Wolf said. "I'd say there's fifteen or so more of those guys by Hak's village, and they are going to come back here to open this place up like a Spam can when they see what happened to their buddies." He looked at Mister Sam. "Does Hak have any men left who can engage?"

Mister Sam shook his head. "We're lucky he can still talk on the radio. He said the bad guys pinned them all in the village, then hosed off a round or two every few seconds to keep their heads down. He has maybe ten effectives. They're armed but low on ammo."

"How about the men on the north slope trail? They still holding off the PL from below?"

"Negative. Hak said the PL withdrew when that Phantom crashed."

"I don't suppose there's any reason to think Bunth might send some people up to help us."

"Wolf, you've got to be an incurable optimist even to *ask* that question. Forget it. He won't even answer us on the radio.

Wolf turned to Court. "Okay, flyboy, what you got for us?"

"Once we get the word from Pearson about who or what's left in the radar van, I say use Spectre all night. If this bunker is as well-built as Wolf wanted, we can take 20mm and 40mm hits without any damage. Use Spec to shoot until daylight, then get some strike flights in here and an evac bird to get the Powers out of here." Court did not look at either Jerome or Babs Powers when he spoke. He referred to them as if they were merely cargo that needed to be transported from one location to another.

"You might consult us about that," Jerome Powers said, a petulant look on his face.

"You want to stay here?" Mister Sam asked.

"Well, under the circumstances I think not. But you should check with me first before making any plans."

"Consider yourself checked," Mister Sam said.

Men near the bunker door opened it at Pearson's signal. He and the buck sergeant came in looking tense and worried. Their USAF fatigues were dirty and torn. Court noticed almost with amusement that they wore steel helmets. It seemed the Air Force sometimes found it necessary to issue steel helmets and sometimes even flak vests and M-16s to its people, but never really trained them in how to use them properly in combat.

"We didn't find either one of them," Bob Pearson said. "But I think I know what happened and where they are." His face looked drawn. Mister Sam handed him a water bottle and he drank deeply. "The *Spetsnaz,* or whoever, broke in there by blowing the door off its hinges, not by blowing the van up, which would have been easy from underneath. When I got there, nobody was inside, no bodies, no blood, no fired rounds or bullet holes – nothing except this."

He took out a radar operator's plastic card with a compass imprinted on it. It was called a "handy-dandy" and was used to help track blips on his scope. The word "straps" was scrawled on it in grease pencil, as if written in haste.

"I think," Pearson said, "Verbell knew they were coming and knew he couldn't get back here. I think he took Evans to the slings and they let themselves down to the caves."

"Nothing we can do about them now," Wolf said. "We'll go after them in the morning."

"No," Pearson said in agitation. "I've got to go look for them now. I think they're in the straps and need some help." Before anyone could stop him, he grabbed an M-16 and bolted out the door.

Court jumped to his feet to go after him. "Hold on," Wolf said. "Just hold on. We'll go out together real soon, once it's first light. No sense in everybody running around in the dark around those cliffs."

Court sat back. Thirty minutes passed as he and Wolf tried to relax. The other men settled down and tried to sleep. The

Powers retired to a corner. Then the bunker shook as a blast sounded at the barricaded front door.

"They're here," Wolf said, opening his eyes.

"God, what about Pearson?" Court asked.

Wolf shrugged. "He was a good man, went out after his troops. Get Spectre to fire on us, otherwise those guys are going to blast in here and we'll all be wiped out."

Court tried to put Pearson out of his mind as he picked up the handset and made contact with Spectre on the PRC-25.

"Fire on your position?" the table nav said. "No sweat, I've got it in the computer, but you gotta be crazy . . . or want the Medal." Spectre's black humor came from the unwritten law that if you fell on an enemy grenade or called in artillery or air upon yourself then you were a candidate for a Medal of Honor. A posthumous presentation was almost always guaranteed.

Court saw Pearson again and again in his mind as the young surfer who had met their plane in what seemed a long time ago. He snapped back to what he had to do.

"Neither. Shoot, goddammit. We're overrun and well protected. It would take a direct hit by a 1,000-pound bomb to blow us away."

Spectre was quick. Court wasn't through talking before the 20 and 40mm cannon shells rained on the earth and rock covering the buried bunker and the immediate area. The rapid sharp detonations of the 20mm shells made it sound as if they were in the middle of a giant popcorn machine, and the sharp *wham, wham, wham* of the 40s rattled everyone's teeth and caused dirt to fall from the wooden shoring above their heads. The concussion made them feel as if little puffs of air were slamming into their bodies. Soon the smell of cordite permeated the air. No one spoke, and they all sat on the floor with their mouths slightly open to absorb the concussion.

After two minutes the heavy fire stopped and the voice of the table navigator came over the loudspeaker.

"Phantom, this is Spectre. It's not that we're out of ammo, but can you tell us if we are doing any good out there? Are we hitting where you want? Are there any more left? Can you

371

give us a quick recce?" Wolf nodded and Court told Spectre to stand by while they went out to look around.

He and Wolf stood by the door and listened for outside sounds. "You sure you want to go back out there, flyboy?" Wolf asked. "This is way out of your MOS." MOS was the Army's acronym for Military Occupational Specialty. JOB would have worked just as well.

"No, I don't *want* to go out there, but you can't go by yourself." Court grabbed the RT-10 survival radio and the Spectre hand beacon and stuffed them into his pockets.

"You're a real walking command post," Wolf said. He punched Court lightly on the arm, nodded to the two airmen handling the door, and the two of them stepped into the light lock, closed the door, then opened the outer door and crept into the night. They carried AK-47s and Wolf had a PRC-25 on his back.

After they were gone, Mister Sam arose, lit a Coleman stove, and put a tin can full of water on the surface. "Coffee, anyone?"

Jerome Powers sat as if in a trance. His mouth hung open, eyes unfocused. Babs sat next to him, not touching him, hugging her drawn-up knees to her chest. Her eyes drooped in fatigue as the effects of the liquor wore off. She stirred and rubbed her eyes. They felt grainy and red. She bet she looked a mess. She felt in her purse, then remembered that Court had thrown her flask away. She pulled out a comb and a compact mirror and gave her hair a swipe. In the dim light of the kerosene lantern she saw some of the troops look at her with what she hoped was sexual desire, but down deep, in the cellar of her mind, she was afraid their glances were more of curiosity or even dislike.

She thought about Court Bannister. *Play your hand cautiously,* she thought. He would come around. She had never had trouble getting a man to do what she wanted before, and he was no different. A sharp explosion outside snapped her eyes open.

"Does that answer your question?" Wolf said as he and Court

peered into a smoking depression where Wolf had just flung a hand grenade.

"Yeah. Now I know what probe by fire means."

"So there was no one in there. Next time there might be."

The fires were out, but first light put a vague gray behind the black masses that made up the Eagle Station complex. They made a quick check of the radar van and found it empty, as Pearson had said.

"Where did he go?" Court asked the dawn sky.

"Let's check the straps," Wolf said and started toward the top of the cliff face where the lowering straps were concealed. "Maybe we can find something out." They reached the spot and saw the straps were unreeled and hanging over the edge.

"Something wrong," Wolf said. "There's no tension on them." He pulled at one and it came up easily in his hands. The line had been cleanly severed. Court pulled up the other two lines and found the same thing. Wolf looked at the tracks in the dirt near the cliff and by the rocks, where the straps were secure.

"Somebody's got those guys," he said, pointing at the strange boot patterns. "I think the bad guys just got themselves a couple new POWs. Maybe Pearson is alive." He turned. "C'mon, we don't have time to look further. We better get back."

They hadn't gone three steps when the sudden yammering of a Kalashnikov assault rifle up the trail toward Hak's village split the dawn quiet. There were shouts and more shots, then a rapid exchange of automatic weapon fire. Some of the bullets zinged down the trail and smacked into rocks and bushes by them.

"Well, somebody's still alive up there," Wolf said as they flung themselves behind a rock. He pulled the handset from its holder and asked Maple what he had heard from Hak.

"He said the enemy had not fully disengaged. When he started down the trail to us, a rear guard or something like that opened up on him. He doesn't have a count of how many. And he hasn't heard from his troops guarding the climbing trail on the north face, but he heard some shooting down there."

"I think there are Spets still alive up here and maybe more coming up the trail," Wolf told him. "Any contact with Bunth?"

"Nothing," Mister Sam radioed back.

Wolf handed the handset to Court. "Get Spectre on this. Have them zero in but stand by till we sort it out."

"Spectre 24, this is Phantom. We got another fire mission for you."

"Stand by, Phantom," the worried voice of the table nav said. "I think we're under attack by a MiG."

20

Court didn't waste a second when he heard Spectre say their big gunship was under MiG attack. He pulled out his survival radio and called Phantom 03, who he knew was orbiting over Lima Site 36. Ken Tanaka answered.

"Phantom Leader, this is Zero Three, go."

"You want a MiG, get on over here."

"Hey, hey, on my way. Orbit time is over, the mission was scrubbed. Me and the Jollys have been released."

Wolf looked up from his prone position behind a rock and pushed his floppy hat back. There was enough light for Court to see his craggy features. "A MiG? Is that all you flyboys think of, shooting down MiGs?"

"If you beetle-crunchers want nothing but friendlies overhead, somebody's gotta get the MiGs. That's what we do." A short burst cracked over their heads. "I think they're headed our way," Court said and ducked.

"A real Dick Tracy," Wolf said and cackled spasmodically in a sound that reminded Court of a stick being dragged along a wooden fence. They had both been up for many hours and were getting giddy.

Court thought about what Tanaka had said about there being no current mission for the Jolly Greens. He called Moonbeam.

"Go ahead, Phantom," Moonbeam replied.

"Understand you got a spare Jolly at Lima 36 – that affirm?"

"Yes. But listen, Phantom, you're not a command post down there. You can't be running this show, you know."

"Moonbeam, in case you've forgotten, this is Eagle Station, and I am the commander and we have self-FAC, Skyspot, and on-orbit authority at all times. You copy that?"

Court was reaching and he knew it. He was the ranking Air Force officer on Eagle Station, but that didn't mean he was in command. Further, although the station had self-FAC and Skyspot authority, that was in effect only when the airplanes were fragged to them by Blue Chip, the 7th Air Force command post. The men at Eagle Station could not generate the assets, and certainly not the targets for the Skyspot missions. And "on-orbit-authority" was a phrase he had pulled from his test-pilot days at Edwards Air Force Base. It had no basis in reality here, but Court hoped to keep the ABCCC at bay until he could get the job done from the ground.

"I'll have to check with Blue Chip," the controller said, "and the Rescue Control Center."

"You have a Mayday situation down there, don't you?" Ken Tanaka transmitted his question.

"That's affirmative," Court answered. "MiGs in the air, bad guys on the ground, and two evacuees to be pulled out."

"I'll relay that to the Jolly Green that's just lifting off to return to its home base. It's fully mission-capable. We'll see what he can do. Meanwhile I'm one mike from your position. I'm going over to Spectre Primary."

It was light now at 35,000 feet, where Ken Tanaka flew. The bright sun was above the horizon, shining bright new rays down on the jumbled cloud pattern that covered the green jungle and karst mountains of Laos. He lowered the nose of his F-4D Phantom fighter and told Matt Henry, his GIB, to sweep ahead with his radar. As the plane gained airspeed he switched to the proper frequency and contacted Spectre. "You sure you're under MiG attack?" Tanaka asked. There had been only a half-dozen cases in the last three years of MiGs attacking US aircraft over Laos. For whatever their reasons, North Vietnamese policy was to leave the airspace free.

376

"Listen," Gunship Charlie, the Spectre pilot, panted to Tanaka, "the delta-winged sumbitch has already made one pass using guns, and if it ain't a MiG I'll kiss your radome. He made the mistake of making a highside pass at me from the port and I threw my left wing up and fired everything I had at him. Didn't hit shit, but the muzzle flashes must have scared him off, but now he's behind someplace and I ain't got no tail gunner." In fact, he did. Staff Sergeant Bill Beddor, a scanner, was at that very moment in the prone position with an M-16 on the open rear ramp door, quite determined to be the first Spectre crew member to shoot down a MiG. He was attached to the gunship by a long strap from his parachute harness.

"Contact, twelve o' clock low for six," Matt Henry, Tanaka's GIB, said from the backseat. Ken Tanaka looked down at his repeater scope and saw the large and small blips that could only be the AC-130 gunship and the smaller fighter.

"You sure he was shooting?" Tanaka asked the Spectre pilot. It could be a Navy or Marine A-4 fighter buzzing the gunship. A dumb but not unheard-of maneuver.

"Well, if he wasn't shooting, he's got headlights that spit cherry balls that me and all my crew saw," Gunship Charlie rasped back. As the aircraft commander he had to make all the split-second decisions, and this was no time to use his table nav as a go-between. The table nav's detection and fire control devices were air-to-ground-oriented, hence useless against MiGs anyway. He kept his ship in a right-hand orbit to keep his guns on the side the MiG might attack. "I'm at base plus three," he added. The base altitude code for the day was 5,000 feet, which meant the gunship was holding 8,000 feet.

Tanaka looked up and saw the silver MiG hang in the sky far above the orbiting AC-130 gunship. "Has he got a wingman?" he asked Spectre.

"Not that I can see, but my visibility isn't all that good."

Ken Tanaka scanned the sky. It would be very strange if that MiG was out here without a wingman. At minimum, it was standard fighter doctrine always to travel in pairs.

"You got any other paints?" he asked Matt Henry.

"Negatron," Henry said, elated at the prospect of being the first GIB to be in on a MiG kill over Laos – or, for himself to get a MiG under any circumstance. "Got a lock on," he said. "You're cleared for missiles. "

"Negative," Tanaka said. "They're too close. This has got to be guns." Tanaka's airplane carried an assortment of radar-guided and heat-seeking missiles, either of which could lock on to the big four-engined AC-130 a lot easier than the tiny MiG. Tanaka intended to use the 20mm cannon slung under the belly of his fighter to ensure there was no mistake. He was excited. This was every fighter pilot's dream: fight a MiG and shoot him down. Especially good if with guns.

As Tanaka's fighter screamed on down and passed through 25,000 feet at a speed of 600 knots, he assessed the situation. He was coming in at the rear of the MiG, which he estimated was two miles beneath him at 15,000 feet, ready to make another pass at Spectre in his orbit at 8,000. Tanaka had to slow down or he would overshoot the MiG. He throttled back to decrease airspeed. He was surprised the MiG didn't have a wingman, and he knew North Vietnamese radar coverage did not extend this far west into Laos.

"Strange, strange," he said to Henry. "But I'm not going to look a gift bear in the mouth." His gunsight pipper was on the MiG, and the electronic range ring circling the pipper said he was at 6,000 feet from the tail of the enemy plane.

"Six thou range and 100 knots overtake," Henry said.

"Boards coming out." Tanaka pushed the button on his throttle that extended the two huge metal speed brakes, also called speed boards in the early F-86 days, into the slip-stream. In less than two seconds, fifty knots bled off and Tanaka pulled the boards back up.

"Piece of cake," Tanaka hummed as he settled in to apply all his thousands of hours of study and flying time learning and teaching fighter tactics to this one pass. "Piece a fucking cake."

At 1,200 feet the MiG loomed in his sights and he started firing his cannon and saw a few sparkles on the empennage of the silver fighter as the API (Armor Piercing Incendiary)

378

shells impacted. Immediately the MiG rolled into a vertical left bank and pulled so many Gs in his turn into Tanaka that white streamers of water condensation trailed back from his wingtips. The turn was an attempt to force Tanaka to overshoot so the MiG pilot could then reverse his turn and be on Tanaka's tail. But two things were working against him. For one, Tanaka was a highly experienced fighter pilot who instantly converted his speed into altitude and prepared for another pass; for another, the MiG had sustained hits in the engine that suddenly reduced his speed. A thin line of smoke trailed from the tailpipe.

The MiG pilot, Duy Ui Tran Van Quoc, was an experienced captain who had been told his mission was so important that he had to go without a wingman. And it was strongly hinted that he was not to come back unless the Yankee gunship was down in flames. He looked down at his engine instruments and saw the temperature and pressure gauges that said his engine would soon quit or explode. Quoc tilted his head over his shoulder and saw the Phantom fighter poised against the high clouds, ready to roll in for the kill. Then he looked over and saw the giant black four-engined gunship and knew what he had to do. He had been trained in Russia, where the ram tactic was known and taught. It had not been taught to Soviet pilots since the Great Patriotic War, but had been taught to third-world pilots who passed through the Russian schools.

"Look out, Spec, he's making a direct pass at you from your nine," Tanaka warned as he rolled in. The MiG was boring in on Spectre directly from his nine o'clock position.

"Yeah, and his headlights are blinking at me," Gunship Charlie said. Charles L. Branski was a burly man, and he hauled back on the big control yoke with ease as he kept his head turned left, staring at the attacking MiG. He handled the bank angle while his copilot used the rudders to keep the turn coordinated.

"He's smoking, he's slowing down," Tanaka said. "I think he's gonna ram and I can't get to him in time."

Still in the left turn, Gunship Charlie pushed the nose of the big ship down, and the MiG followed. He pulled back on the yoke to raise the nose, and the MiG had enough forward speed to do the same. There was no doubt, the MiG had the residual momentum, even if its engine quit, to ram Spectre.

"All guns on the line," Gunship Charlie Branski yelled on the intercom, and rolled out of his turn for a second, giving the MiG an easy shot at them. Two of the MiG's 27mm shells ripped through the top of the fuselage of the gunship, sending slivers into the pressurization lines and the delicate computer. Ignoring the impacts, Branski rolled in right aileron to raise the left wing and pushed left rudder to keep the big nose from swinging to the right and, in this cross-controlled position, fired everything he had at the approaching MiG.

The steady roar of the 20mm Gatling guns combined with the *slam-slam* of the twin 40mm cannon created a din in the aft cabin of the big gunship the crewmen were used to. What they were not used to was the guns firing in anything but a left bank. Gunship Charlie Branski had to keep the left wing up, not down, to fire at the approaching MiG. The Fire Control System he used was not equipped to solve the geometry of an approaching fighter, nor the calculus of the changing speeds. Empty casings spewed out of the guns in such a way as soon to cause a jam. The gunners had to brace themselves in an entirely new manner. One fell backwards and shattered his elbow. Staff Sergeant Bill Beddor grabbed his M-16 and wedged himself into position and hammered away at the approaching fighter. The table nav told Branski there were no injuries from the 27mm shell impacts and, as far as he could tell, no system damage.

Tanaka put in his burners and streaked toward the attacking MiG. He could see the first bit of flame from the enemy's tail, but it was obvious there was no damage to the flight control system, and forward momentum would carry the North Vietnamese plane into the side of the gunship. He saw the MiG was not firing: either out of ammunition or the engine damage was enough to take out the system that enabled the guns to shoot.

Looking through the gunsight superimposed on his left-hand window, Gunship Charlie Branski saw the tracers of his guns converge far behind the MiG that loomed larger in size each second. The guns were harmonized far beyond the 1,000 feet through which the fighter was now flying. Branski had about three seconds in which to do something, and he did it. He sawed and yanked the rudder pedals and control yoke in an abrupt and rough gyration that made the nose of the giant plane describe a figure eight in the air. Performing that violent maneuver forced the guns on the left side to depart from the neat lines of fire and spray a wild pattern of shells directly into the path of the MiG. At 200 feet from the AC-130, Duy Ui Tran Van Quoc and his MiG-21PF became a giant fireball, raining parts that instantly slid from view behind the AC-130.

"I got him, I got him!" Beddor screamed into the intercom.

"My God," Ken Tanaka said in awe as he yanked his Phantom out of the way of the MiG parts.

"What's going on up there?" Court Bannister asked on FM from beneath the thin cloud layer over his position. "When you gentlemen are through playing around, I would appreciate some firepower down here."

"Glad to oblige, Phantom," Gunship Charlie Branski said, trying to keep his voice as deep and cool as possible considering he was the only C-130 pilot in the world who had ever shot a MiG down with his airplane. "Just tell us where you need the lead."

Court pulled out the hand-held beacon and turned it on. "You got my flash on your scope?" He asked. The table nav said he had the plume loud and clear on his scope.

"Good," Court said. "Stand by while I get things sorted out down here." He pointed the nose of the beacon down the trail from which the shooting had come. "What's their distance from us?" he asked Wolf.

"Try 200 meters. Don't want to fire into Hak's village."

Court dialed in 200 meters, moved a knob to the position that indicated troops, and cleared Spectre to shoot. Instantly a dozen shells rained down. Suddenly a voice from the impact area screamed, "Don't shoot, God almighty, we're friendly!" The accent was pure Midwest American. Before Court could react and tell Spectre to hold fire, the guns stopped shooting and the table nav came on the line.

"Phantom, Spectre Two Four. Got some bad news. Our computer just went tits up. We can't shoot another round. Pilot says we will have a replacement Spectre but not for another hour or so."

"Okay, okay, Spec," Court said.

"Hey," Ken Tanaka transmitted, I've got Willy Petes and 20 mike-mike if need be, and I can call in all the fighters you need."

Court scanned the weather. Dawn gray had given way to a sullen overcast that had few breaks. "Just go on high orbit and throttle back," he told Tanaka. "The weather is Delta Sierra. Call me when you find out about getting a Jolly Green in here." He turned his attention to Wolf who was sighting down the trail over the muzzle of his AK-47.

"Hey, thanks," the hidden voice said. "Don't shoot me, now. I'm coming along the trail."

"Who are you?" Wolf bellowed in the sudden jungle silence.

"Lieutenant John Green, Air Force. I just escaped. I need help. Don't shoot.

"Advance slowly – very slowly," Wolf yelled at the disembodied voice.

The morning air hung cool and humid. Court saw a figure detach itself from the shadows of the bushes along the path and with careful steps advance toward where they lay. He wore a USAF flight suit and had his hands up. "Hey, gosh, where are you?" he asked in a boyish voice. "Boy, am I glad you're here." Court could see him clearly now: young, clean-cut face, shock of blond hair, wary but pleased look on his face. Court was about to speak to him when Wolf shot him between the eyes.

"Wolf – what in hell—"

"What in hell, nothing," Wolf snarled back. "That man was *Spetsnaz.* The flight suit was *clean,* his face was *clean,* and he was wearing *boots.* No POW is allowed to keep his boots. And look at that thing strapped to his back. Court saw something on the back of the fallen man. "Watch this," Wolf said and fired a round into the pack, which exploded with an enormous roar.

There was a shocked silence, then a furious hail of fire came down the trail to smack into the rocks and zing off in moaning ricochets. A loud explosion against the rocks in front sent chips and dirt flying into the air.

"RPG," Wolf mumbled, meaning they were firing rocket-propelled grenades at them. He leaned around the rock to fire a burst up the trail. Another RPG burst behind them and one farther back by the bunker. "We gotta move back," Wolf said. "We've got problems. Get that fighter in here with whatever he's got." He fired another burst and drew back. "Let's move it," he said, rising to a crouch.

Behind the protection of the rocks, a stunned Court Bannister followed him to the mouth of the protective area in front of the bunker, where they flopped down behind the sandbags. He still had trouble believing what he had seen.

"We're in trouble now," Wolf said. "Get that fighter in here and tell him to call for more." As he spoke, the outer door of the bunker opened and Mister Sam ran out carrying an AK and threw himself next to the two men.

"Bad news. That dumb broad stuck her head out the door, I guess to see what you guys were doing, and a fragment caught her in the leg. She's got a piece of bone sticking out and is bleeding bad from an artery. We've stopped the flow, but she's got to be evacced immediately."

Court put the image of the round dot appearing between the blond man's eyes and his body evaporating in the explosion out of his mind and called Tanaka on the RT.

"Got to have that Jolly in here immediately," he said to him. "Fighters as soon as you can get them, and rockets and strafe now – right now."

"The Jolly's inbound, Boss, and I've got fighters on call, but I'll tell you the weather is bad-bad. Low ceiling in layers up to five thou, one or two miles viz, but there are a few sucker holes. I can maybe slip in down there and see what I can do." Tanaka's voice was calm.

"There, shoot up there," Wolf said, pointing up the trail to figures crouching and running. Both Court and Mister Sam blasted away with their AKs. The figures slowed, melted off to one side, then started a steady cadence of fire at the bunker. "They're sending out flankers and there's nothing we can do about it," Wolf said. "What about Hak's men?" he asked Mister Sam.

"We lost contact about the time you guys went out. I think he's been overrun."

"Eagle Station, Eagle Station – this is Jolly Green Three Two on Fox Mike. Do you read?"

"Jolly Green, this is Phantom Zero One at Eagle Station. Read you loud and clear. We've got two to go, one badly wounded and bleeding.

"How's the weather and is there any ground fire?"

"Inbound weather reported bad. You've got Phantom Zero Three overhead for a pilot report. The helipad is clear down here – no ground fire yet – but the approaches are clobbered."

"Hate to say this, Eagle, but we might just not be able to get to you guys."

21

It was dawn by the time he had finished dictating to her. It had been painful and he had had to stop and rest and think it through many times. He was exhausted and wasn't sure how he would present himself at the press conference. Finally, he had fallen into a nightmare-ridden sleep and had awakened covered in sweat, trembling. The girl had fallen asleep in the wooden chair in the far corner. He looked at her troubled face. Even in sleep, when her face should be relaxed as a child's, she wore a wary look as if any moment something terrible would happen and she would have to wake and face it. He cringed inwardly as the awful realization of what he had heard yesterday about King and Kennedy surfaced in his memory. He didn't know what hurt more, his body or his spirit. He decided his body would heal someday, but he wasn't sure about his spirit.

He looked down at himself. His hospital garb, a thin gray poncho-like garment, given to him fresh yesterday before the conference, was now damp with his sweat and stained with yellow and red liquid that oozed from sores in his body. He pictured the awful comparison between this room and a cell at Hoa Lo. As backward and dirty and rough as this hospital room was, it was heaven compared to the sweat and stink and fear of solitary in black cells where rats and cockroaches slipped through the ooze and feasted on human flesh. He knew he would not be returning to this room and this bed ever again. He remembered then what she had done and turned suddenly and pulled the papers she had written for him from beneath the tick-filled mattress. He admired the neat small printing she had made with the curlicues and extra lines of a European hand. He folded them nervously, again and again. When he was done, he looked over at her.

"Princess," he called softly. "Hey, Princess." Her eyes opened and she had a momentary look of terror until she realized where she was and who was calling to her. She arose silently and went to his side.

He gave her the papers. "You must get this to one of the Americans." He described Connert. "Put them in your hand. I will get him to shake hands with you. Give it to him then. Be very careful."

"Yes," she said so softly he had to strain to hear her words. She tried to conceal the papers in her right hand. "They are too thick." She looked up and made a tiny smile at the crestfallen look on Flak's face. "But I know what to do." She rose. "Wait," she said and ghosted out the door. In a moment she returned holding a glossy magazine called *Soviet Life*. "They give them to us. I like to read English."

"Do you believe what you read?"

"Russia is a beautiful country. I would like to visit someday."

"So is America."

"We see such bad pictures. It does not look nice."

"They only show you the bad parts. Come visit us someday."

"You could show me your country. That would be nice." She smoothed the pages and put them in the magazine.

He leaned on her to get up from the bed. "There is one last thing," he said as he took her hands and kissed the palms. "I wish we had made love."

Her hands folded around his face. "Yes, my black king, *mon roi noir,* I too wish we had made love."

They kissed, tentatively at first, then deep and thrusting. Finally they pushed apart.

"I . . . have never kissed like that before," she said. "I only heard about it . . . in France."

386

He held her close for a moment before he spoke. "I think it's time."

She glanced at the position of the sun through the window. "Yes, it is time." She looked almost serene.

"It is going to be very bad for you when they take me away."

She nodded and looked up from her normal downcast view and gave him a small smile. "I am not afraid. It will be worse for you."

"If only I could get you away from here," he said.

She put her fingers to his lips. "That is not to be. What is to be is now. We must go." She put her arm around his waist and he hobbled through the door.

Richard Connert arched his back and tried to keep his hands from trembling. God, he had worked so hard to get to this point. He had literally sacrificed his Air Force career to get to Hanoi and communicate with the POWs. There had been long sessions in the Air Force intelligence community, trying to decide the best way to get messages to and from them. Originally, crude codes had been used in family letters to the men and they had tried the same in return. The method was excruciatingly slow, as few words could be incorporated in each short letter and there was no assurance it reached the POW. The Navy had used a simple invisible ink to one of its men, Stockdale, and in broad hints in the letter from his wife, Sybil, he had been told about it and how to bring it out.

In joint sessions with the other services they had thought of ejecting a man in from the backseat of a fighter during a raid to carry in messages. But what kind of messages do you carry in? "Hang on, guys"? What was needed was a two-way street: messages in and messages out. When the ejection idea had been rejected as too risky and pointless, the Marines had said they thought it was nifty and they would probably do just that. Connert had heard no more about that project. He didn't know if the Marines, acting on their own, had done it or not. Then the joint committee had buckled down and started teaching Project Mailman in special adjuncts to survival schools. That at least was a method of teaching aircrew how to identify mailmen, but no one had any idea how to get a mailman in and back out. Finally someone had talked about the peace groups going to Hanoi. If we could just get a guy in and out with them, he had said. So Project Combat Dancer began. *Combat* was a prefix word used before a mission-title word.

Richard Connert and eight other men from the OSI had been identified as likely prospects and given a chance to volunteer. Like the others, he had been trained and filtered back into the Air Force to develop the legend he had invented in training. Each man had had to develop his own legend to include how he would get out of the service and infiltrate the organization he thought stood a good chance of getting to Hanoi. Once submitted for approval, the legend would be accepted, rejected, or modified by a board in the basement of the Pentagon.

Connert's had been as a F-4 simulator instructor – he had actually served in that capacity for a few months at George Air Force Base – who would be transferred to Vietnam, where he would go visibly bonkers. Connert used to grin a lot to himself after his discharge. He had had a ball discomforting his frontseater on some missions in South Vietnam. After great study, he had picked Shawn Bannister as the star protestor to which he would hook his red wagon and, by an interesting turn, it was Shawn's half-brother, Courtland, with whom he had flown. It hadn't been planned that way, but when the opportunity had presented itself at Tan Son Nhut during the Tet Offensive, Connert couldn't resist the irony of the situation. Court had needed a back-seater for a few days, and Connert was available. He had done things in the rear cockpit just short of disastrous, but enough to drive Court Bannister to ground him and find out he was, according to his legend, a non-rated man acting as a pilot. That had earned him the discharge and notoriety he had sought. Though not an Air Force-rated pilot, Connert *had* flown with the base Aero Club as a hobby and earned a private pilot's rating. That experience plus his training in the F-4 simulator had allowed him to pretend to be a lot more dangerous than he really had been in the backseat of the F-4. His pilot's license had also given him the edge over all the other volunteers.

He had not had much trouble getting into Shawn Bannister's campaign headquarters. Once out of the Air Force, he had grown a beard, joined the Vietnam Veterans Against the War, and been loud and vociferous in the front ranks of protest groups. With those credentials and a real college degree he had easily been accepted into Bannister's group. His roommate, Michael LaNew, had tried another method, but so far had been unsuccessful in getting to Vietnam in any capacity.

Connert put his hand in his pocket and touched the ring made from a shot-down American airplane. *We'll get 'em for you, buddy. We'll get the motherfuckers.* He looked at Flak Apple on the stage. *God, what that man has been through,* he thought as he began flashing.

The bright lights on tripods were powered from the operating room circuit. They blinded Flak when he stood next to the raised platform Thach had caused to be constructed. He decided not to shield his eyes, but to appear unmoved by the lights. There was a curtain forming a wing where he could see Thach standing next to Co Dust but those in the audience could not. In front, he saw, there were more journalists and photographers than before. They were standing around, waiting, he supposed, for someone to tell them to be seated on the rows of folding chairs. Flak stood as straight and tall as he could without the pain doubling him over. He searched for and finally found Dancer, the Blue Mailman. He watched Dancer's hand and fingers and listened to his coughs. It would be hard. He would have to use blinks and nods in addition to his hands. He wasn't sure Dancer would be able to read him.

WHAT R U GOING TO DO . . . Dancer asked.
IS CING DEAD . . .
YES . . .
AND CENNEDY . . .
YES . . . WHAT R U GOING TO DO . . .
READ MY CONFESSION . . .

389

DO U HAVE THE LIST . . .
GET MAGAZINE FROM GIRL . . .

Connert could see no girl. Perhaps she was behind the curtain and would be whisked out at the completion of the interview.

Shawn Bannister sat down impatiently, muttering about how soon was the show going to start. Connert remained standing and suddenly spoke out.

"Say, what's behind that curtain? How do we know he isn't going to be signaled from back there?"

"You crazy?" Shawn hissed out of the corner of his mouth. All the newsmen ignored him, except the Japanese, who put their camera on him. The East Bloc people had been admonished to film only what was acceptable propaganda. Although the Japanese had been warned to do that and follow the Party line, they nonetheless did exactly as they wished.

"I think we should be allowed to see what is behind the curtain," Connert said to the audience in general. All but one ignored him. This was not supposed to be part of the program.

"Sit *down*," Shawn said and tugged at his pant leg.

"Yes," the Japanese newsman said. "What is back there, please?" Connert sat down.

There was a fluttering of the curtain, then it was pulled back on the wire from which it hung. Trying to appear calm, Thach spoke.

"All we have here is the nurse for the patient Apple. He is a sick man and the lenient and humane policy of Ho Chi Minh provides him with a nurse when even our own people are suffering."

Co Dust stood straight and tried not to blink in the light. She nervously twisted a rolled-up magazine in her hands.

Connert walked rapidly toward her as he pulled a steno notebook and a pencil from his pocket and started a series of rapid-fire questions he hoped would complicate and confuse the situation.

"Do you speak English? Are you his nurse? How do you feel about having to attend an American war criminal? What are you reading? It's in English. Is it an American magazine? He took the magazine quickly from her nerveless fingers and rapidly glanced at the cover. "Oh, this is about Russia. Is it good? I must read this!" He covered it with his notebook.

"Please, Mister." Thach inserted himself between Connert and Co Dust. "Please to be seated. We must begin." Connert allowed himself to be led off and returned to sit next to Shawn Bannister, who rattled off words in a low and furious voice.

"Goddamm it, Connert, you're crazy! Give that to me." He snatched the magazine from Connert's hands. "I'll give it back to them so they don't think we're completely nuts." He looked up as Thach led Flak Apple to the stage. Connert's face drained as he realized Shawn Bannister would probably open the magazine and discover the list.

The Committee Chairman sat motionless and took in the lights and cameras. He studied the black man who stood before them. He allowed himself one small movement of his upper lip in satisfaction. It was going just as had been planned in Bratislava. It had taken hard work and some anxious moments, but it was working out. Valiant Struggle, as conceived by the American in Bratislava and put into effect by his men, was proving worth the effort. The resultant publicity and photos of a black American imperialist renouncing his country in Hanoi, coupled with the fall of the clandestine site exposing the American military imperialists in Laos, would, he had been told by the American, assure election of the proper man in the United States. He did not understand, he admitted to himself how these elections worked. They seemed such a waste of effort to attain a dubious outcome. Better to know what is best for the people and give it to them by force, if necessary, until they are reeducated about their duties to the State. The proper man, that Hom-free, needed help against that reactionary Nik-shun. That man Hom-free had said he would crawl on his knees to Hanoi to free the air pirate prisoners. He almost smiled. He would give him that chance.

* * *

391

Flak tried not to look at Connert and the magazine. He had heard that the young seaman Doug Hegdahl had been ordered out on early release by SRO Navy Commander Dick Stratton with the POW names, but so far hadn't made it, so maybe here was the chance for this vital information to reach America.

He looked out over the assembled newsmen. He saw several that looked East Bloc and some Japanese. One smiling man he knew to be Wilfred Burchett, a card-carrying communist from Australia. He was not popular among his countrymen. The POWs called him Willful Bullshit because he frequently broadcast propaganda to them and sometimes met with them in an effort to get them to do the same.

Flak flash/fidgeted as long as he could and figured he'd better start talking. He had done all that he could. It was up to Dancer to get the magazine to the proper people.

Thach led Flak by the arm and mounted the stage and told the audience to be seated. After the cameras were readied and coughs and scraping of chairs died, he said, "The man Apple has something he wishes to confess to you." The cameras quickly rotated a few degrees back to Flak, who stood as straight as he could.

"Yes. I wish to confess," he said.

The Chairman shifted imperceptibly in his chair. This was what he had been waiting for. The first half of Valiant Struggle was about to culminate.

0730 HOURS LOCAL, SATURDAY 2 NOVEMBER 1968
EAGLE STATION AT LIMA SITE 85
ROYALTY OF LAOS

Aboard Jolly Green 32, Joe Kelly turned to his copilot, a new captain from Udorn. "Doesn't look good, does it?" he said on the intercom.

"No."

"Wanna try it?"

"Sure, if the rest of the crew does."

"How 'bout it, guys?" Kelly said to the two PJs and the crew chief. They exchanged a few words, then said in unison, "Press on, oh learless feeder."

Kelly smiled at their new malapropism, took a bearing on the Udorn Tacan, and started to descend. His hands and feet were busy as he spiraled the big ship down through the clouds two miles west of the Eagle karst. At two thousand feet he broke out in the clear beneath the clouds and flew back to the Eagle karst. It thrust up into the clouds like the top of a skyscraper on a bad day in New York. He circled the karst. There were no breaks.

"Phantom, this is Jolly. Can you bring your survivors down the karst? It's clear down here and we can make an easy pickup."

"Negative, Jolly," Court replied. "We're under fire from the side where the down trail is located."

"Phantom, this is Spectre," Gunship Charlie Branski broke in. "Maybe we can help. If you put that beacon on minimum distance and lay it in the middle of the helipad, we can maybe vector the Jolly down on top of it. Our fire control system is out but our radar is okay. You copy?"

"Roger, can do," Court said.

"We're game," Joe Kelly answered.

"Get on with it, then," Branski said.

"I've got to get the beacon to the helipad," Court said to Wolf, who was busy shooting.

"I heard."

"Can you cover me?"

"They've got that pad zeroed in like they got us zeroed in. We need some air support in here or we're dead." He said it so calmly, Court asked him if he was sure.

"Dead sure. They're gonna charge any time and we're gone."

Court looked around and spotted the Flaming Arrow pit. "You have any thermite grenades?" he asked Mister Sam, who said he did. "Spectre, Phantom. If I light up the Arrow, can you vector Phantom Zero Three in for a napalm run?"

393

There was a pause while Branski checked with his crew. "Roger that," he answered. The infrared detection system still worked.

"I need at least five," Court said to Mister Sam.

"Got 'em," Mister Sam said, patting his ammo satchel.

"Zero Three, you ready for a napalm run?" Court asked Tanaka.

"Sure. Only one small problem. Ain't got no napalm and there's no way I can put a strike fighter in there."

"You got Willy Petes and fuel in your drop tanks?"

"Affirmative . . . ah ha, good boy. Can do," Tanaka said with obvious excitement in his voice. He realized Court wanted him to fire his white phosphorous marking rockets to provide hot flames to ignite the fuel from the drop tanks that would burst when they smashed into the ground.

"You're Flaming Arrow-qualified, aren't you?" a voice from the ABCCC broke in.

"I will be on my first pass," Tanaka replied.

Court raised up and looked at the Flaming Arrow platform. It hung askew, shredded and torn by fragments. He lay flat and said to Wolf and Mister Sam, "We gotta toss these out to make a V pointing at those guys. I'm in the middle, I'll throw long, you throw short." They agreed and each man took a grenade.

Court checked that the Spectre table nav and Tanaka were ready, and on his count they pulled the pins and tossed the grenades. They roared and threw up great flashes of illumination and white smoke.

In seconds Tanaka's jet flashed across the karst. Eight loud bangs sounded on top of each other as he rippled off his remaining rockets. From under his wings the two fuel tanks tumbled to the ground, and a burst of fire erupted from the 20mm gun he carried under the belly of the airplane. In a roar of engines, he was gone in the clouds. They could smell the diesel fumes of the JP-4 jet fuel.

Nothing happened. The shooting had slackened slightly as the jet roared overhead, then resumed. Court thought he saw figures gathering for a charge.

"Here they come!" Mister Sam yelled.

"What's going on down there?" Joe Kelly yelled on the radio. Court was too busy shooting to answer. Then a wisp of black smoke appeared at one edge of the jungle, then another, and a third, then with a gigantic whoosh the entire jungle went up in red flames that boiled hundreds of feet into the air, burning into the clouds. The reflected heat made the three men press into the earth, gasping and covering their heads. There were loud screams from the inferno that died off immediately. Two human torches staggered out and fell in ghastly heaps. The wet jungle could not sustain the blaze, but it had been enough. There was nothing living where the fuel had sprayed and ignited. They lay still for several minutes as it burned out.

The three men climbed to their feet, too awed at what they saw to speak. Although the heavier leaves and palm fronds were too wet to burn, the heat had dried and curled them and all the small underbrush and grass was blackened cinders. What had been a green and impenetrable jungle was now a black and brown shriveled horror. On the far side they saw Hak's men start toward them, pointing their rifles and sweeping aside the cinders, looking for survivors. There were none. Mister Sam went to the bunker to get the two Powers. Court called Tanaka.

"It worked – my God, but it worked!"

"Shit hot," Tanaka said. "But now I got to make it to the tank before I flame out. I don't want to see how far I can fly on no fuel."

Joe Kelly came up on the radio. "Tanaka, is that you, you sorry son of a bitch?"

"Kelly, you bastard, I've saved your dumb ass again. Remember, green sparrows never wear pants. Red-Tagged Bastards Hang Together. Ta ta, off to the tank." And he was gone.

Court put the beacon in the helipad and called Spectre, who said they had a good fix. Minutes later Jolly Green 32 clattered out of the sky and touched down with a great whir and buzzing. One PJ jumped out while the other and the crew chief manned the guns.

Court turned to help Mister Sam and Wolf carry Babs Powers on an improvised poncho litter. She looked pale and thin. Her

395

leg was bound with blood-soaked bandages. Jerome Powers looked pale and distraught and seemingly oblivious to his wife's presence and condition. The PJ ran up and helped them steer the litter to the door of the big helicopter. He was dressed in camouflaged fatigues and wore a dark helmet with boom mike. He stooped to take a quick look at the patient. Court saw his face twist in sudden comprehension and pain. On his helmet was painted his name: Dominguez.

"Barbara, oh Barbara," Dominguez breathed to himself so low no one heard him in the noise of the helicopter. He carefully took her hand in his and looked at her with anguished devotion. He had removed her picture from his wallet and started carrying it in a plastic case in the flight-suit pocket over his heart. This was the young Barbara Westin he saw now.

"You the helicopter guy?" she shrieked, not recognizing Dominguez. "Goddammit, what took you so long? Get me out of this shit hole." She jerked her hand free.

"Come on, get a move on,' Jerome Powers yelled. Dominguez looked up in sudden recognition and was flooded for an instant with the conflicting memories of a teenager seriously in love. But only for an instant.

"Shut up and get out of the way," Dominguez ordered. Powers did not get a clear view of his face.

"See here . . ." Powers started, but Court cut him off and gave him an impatient push. "Get a move on, asshole."

They moved the stretcher to the door of the helicopter, where PJ Two and crew chief Dan Bernick reached down to bring it aboard. Powers fussed and climbed in after his wife.

Manuel Dominguez turned to Court and Wolf. He had a dazed look on his face, and an odd half-smile. *Her face has changed. That's no longer the girl in the photo.*

"You okay?" Court asked.

"Yeah. Yeah, as a matter of fact, I am." His dazed look was rapidly changing to amusement. "I just saw what I used to think was the most beautiful girl in the world," he said wryly.

He started to laugh as he swung aboard, and was roaring

above the noise of the blades when the helicopter lifted off. Soon, bits of a torn-up photograph fluttered from the door.

0830 HOURS LOCAL, SATURDAY a NOVEMBER 1968
HANOI CITY HOSPITAL
HANOI, DEMOCRATIC REPUBLIC OF VIETNAM

Flak Apple ignored the hot pokers of pain as he straightened his back and stood tall in front of the newsmen. It was all over now. He had done what he could for his fellow POWs. Dancer had to take it from there. Now it was his time, time for his feelings and thoughts. The tension and strain of his prisoner predicament was being overridden by his sickness over the killing of King and Kennedy. He blinked in the lights and tried to focus on the faces of the newsmen, to make eye contact, but no one outside of the Japanese and Connert would hold his gaze. The Japanese looked friendly, even sympathetic. Connert looked like a man about to explode.

"Yes, I have a confession," he began as cameras whirred and shutters clicked. "I confess to being a black man brought up in the United States. I confess to seeing and hearing some people say black men cannot function well and black men cannot contribute to the United States. I confess to a pain that penetrates deeper than I ever thought possible when I heard Reverend Martin Luther King had been shot and killed by a white man. I have seen the news articles from American papers presented to us that show pictures of American students and professors and congressmen waving the Viet Cong flag and saying this is a bad war and the United States is wrong and Ho Chi Minh is right. I confess to thinking long and deep about those things right here in Hanoi."

Things were going so well that Thach risked a glance at the Chairman, who sat in the back row. His earlier frown had disappeared. The Chairman's normally inscrutable expression

397

was almost benign. Behind him, Thach noticed the Chairman's aide from the war office entering. Far from inscrutable, he looked to be bursting with information.

"And I have one final confession – the most important confession of all," Flak continued.

Connert suddenly had a suspicion of what was to come and jumped to his feet.

"Just a minute!" he shouted. "Just a minute. How are you going to protect this man? How do we know he will remain alive after his confession? He looks very sick. You said yourselves he has a nurse. He is, after all, one of your most important prisoners. Can you guarantee after this confession that he will be alive a year from now? Alive and available for us to meet with him a year from now? The whole world is watching. Can you guarantee this?"

Thach looked at the Chairman, who nodded almost imperceptibly. "Yes, we can guarantee that. He is, after all, departing with you," Thach said. When Connert sat down, he deftly pulled the magazine from the hands of the speechless Shawn Bannister. At last he had the POW list.

Flak looked almost pained at the exchange. This was something he had not expected. He had made up his mind during the night about what he was going to say, and was quite prepared to take the consequences by himself. Help from any quarter was a surprise. He continued as he had planned.

"I have been told I can leave Hanoi for the United States if I make a sincere confession. Therefore, my final and most important confession is . . . that I am an American fighting man and I believe in God and my country and that if America has ills we will cure them by ourselves. I will not leave Hanoi without my fellow American prisoners."

There was shocked silence. Connert resisted the impulse to stand up and cheer. He worked very hard at keeping his face straight. "Well, Jee-sus," was all Shawn Bannister said. He and Connert were immediately hustled out of the room.

When the room was cleared, the Chairman threw the mortar pouch in Thach's face and signaled to an aide, who marched him out the door. Thach's biggest regret was that he could not ravage that Co Dust whore and leave her dying in her own treacherous blood. The Chairman then told the guards to return the criminal Apple to a cell in Hoa Lo and to allow the nurse Co Dust to return to her duties.

The colonel with the War Office finally approached the Chairman. "It has failed. Our troops, the troops of our Laotian comrades, and the special forces of the Soviets have all failed. We have no prisoners. The site the Americans call Eagle Station remains in their hands." In silence, the Chairman departed the hospital.

The Chairman sat back in his Peugeot as the driver fought the hen's nest potholes. He was well satisfied. That idiot Thach was finally removed. It was obvious, the Chairman knew, that the black man would never do in public what they had to beat out of him in private. Thach should have known that. No matter, the film of the black man boasting would never get out. All the journalists present were sympathetic to the cause of freedom in North Vietnam and would not release anything that would jeopardize that concept. And the Chairman was satisfied that the arrogant GRU man had been shown that his vaunted *Spetsnaz* was not as invincible as he had boasted. The Chairman did not care about the radar site. The bombing was over. That long-nosed pig Johnson had assured the world of that. It would have been interesting to capture Americans for display in Laos, but that was not to be.

The most important event of all had occurred exactly as he had planned. That idiot Touby had been killed, as he had hoped. Now Bunth could run all the poppy products down to the American pigs in South Vietnam without that grasping Touby taking nearly half for himself. He almost smiled. Every American GI who gave in to his product was one less his forces had to face.

The Chairman thought about the American election. His sources assured him that man Hum-free would be elected. That would be nice. The Chairman would like to see him crawl on his knees to Hanoi.

22

It had been a hectic weekend. Political pundits had never seen such dramatic events. On Friday, Americans were convinced peace was at hand. On Saturday, South Vietnam backed out of the peace negotiations. Sunday was a quiet day of reflection. Then Monday had dawned on the United States, with the astounding poll results taken by Louis Harris that Hubert Horatio Humphrey was ahead of Richard Milhous Nixon by 43 to 40. Less than two weeks before, the same Harris poll had placed Nixon over Humphrey by 8 points, at 44 to 36.

But today was election day and polls meant nothing. Gut feelings would out when the curtain was drawn at the polling booth and 73,000,000 Americans pulled the handle for the man of their choice. When it was all over, Richard Nixon had beat Hubert Humphrey by a mere 500,000 votes, 43.4 percent to 42.7 percent. Yet that was four times as much as the 112,881 votes by which Jack Kennedy had beat Nixon for president in 1960. George Wallace, with ex-SAC General Curtis LeMay as his running mate, had garnered nearly 14 percent of the votes. Despite the intense controversy, only 61 percent of the voting public had turned out.

Nixon remained in Suite 35H of the Waldorf in New York until 11:30 Wednesday morning, when Humphrey telephoned to concede defeat. That evening he telephoned Whitey Whisenand.

*　　*　　*

400

"It's for you," Sal said. "Do you know a Chapin, Dwight Chapin?"

Whitey took the call on the extension in the library. He and Sal had been pleased with the election results, and the idea of having a Republican Commander in Chief for at least the next four years.

"General Whisenand – good evening, sir. I am Dwight Chapin, one of the president-elect's aides. Mister Nixon would like to speak to you, sir."

Whitey decided it was no joke and waited for Nixon to come on the line.

"Are you there?" Chapin asked.

"Yes. Put him on."

"Ah, no. I mean he wants to speak to you here in New York. Would you come up here at your earliest convenience, say, tomorrow?"

Though taken aback, Whitey agreed and was told to show himself at the security desk at the president-elect's transition headquarters at the Hotel Pierre in New York.

Clean-cut young men monitored security cameras in the reception area just off the elevator on the 39th floor. One of the most clean-cut and youngest greeted Whitey and said he was Dwight Chapin. He looked as if he wanted to ask Whitey to bare the contents of his old leather briefcase, then decided against it. He escorted Whitey to a living room in the suite overlooking Fifth Avenue and brought him coffee. After ten minutes Richard Nixon walked in. He wore a dark suit and appeared to Whitey to have just shaved. His face was clear and jovial. He carried a yellow legal pad with many scribbled notes.

"Ah, General, what a pleasure, sir. Be seated, be seated." Chapin brought coffee without being asked. Nixon sat on a silk sofa with his back to a window.

"I am," he said, "preparing to build a new government. I want to be perfectly frank with you. We met only briefly when I was vice-president for General Eisenhower, but I remember quite well your insistence with General Ridgeway we not involve American forces on the ground with the French at Dien Bien

401

Phu. I am aware also of how you stood up to Johnson and McNamara to stop them from picking air-strike targets in North Vietnam at their Tuesday lunches And I know why you have resigned from the Air Force. You are a man of integrity." He sipped his coffee incessantly. He continued.

"Now, I want you to know how I feel, and what my aims and goals are. I have little or no confidence in the State Department. The Foreign Service didn't see fit to include me in their briefings when I was vice president. Unlike Johnson, I intend to run foreign policy from the White House. And I do not intend to let those Ivy League liberals from the CIA figure in my plans for foreign policy. Also, unlike Johnson, I do not intend to ignore the military while making tactical decisions for them. I do intend to rely on your experience and what you have to say." He wet his lips. "Now then, my plan for the Vietnam war is threefold. First, I want the military to turn over combat responsibility to the South Vietnamese. There must be a training, a phase-in period, to accomplish this. During this time I want us to provide air and logistical support. In the second phase, I want us to help the South Vietnamese develop their own support capabilities, factories and the like, with our training. Lastly, US forces would revert to only an advisory role, as when we started over there in 1961. Throughout this plan, which Mel Laird calls Vietnamization, I will gradually reduce the amount of our forces in Southeast Asia." He regarded Whitey. "If you are at odds with these ideas, I wish to hear you say so now. For if you are, I would like for you to take a few days and tell me what it might be you would change."

Whitey leaned back. "Mister President, I am no longer in the Air Force, hence not privy to inner council happenings. I am not qualified to say one way or another on Vietnamization except perhaps to ask if you have consulted the Vietnamese."

"Not to the extent I will once in office."

"Mister President, there is something of the utmost importance I wish to bring to your attention. You did not mention it in your campaign, therefore I feel you must be made aware of a most serious problem."

Nixon looked puzzled and waved him to continue. Whitey dug into his briefcase and produced his most current "blackboard."

	MIA/KIA	POW	AIRCRAFT
USAF	452	240	1054
USN	253	132	448
USMC	81	20	247
USA	179	59	544 (Helios)
TOTAL	965	451	2293

Nixon frowned an instant, then lit up. "Oh, yes, I've heard about your famous board and how you won't let the Commander in Chief forget his men for an instant. Very commendable. I shall want you to keep that up for me."

"I beg your pardon, sir, but I no longer work for the government."

Nixon gave a short laugh. "I have already spoken to our mutual friend John Duchane, and he informs me he will be happy to see you once more in government service and will certainly hold your job for you should you decide to return to the military."

Nixon leaned forward. "I would like to recall you as a lieutenant general, effective my Inaugural Day the twentieth of next January."

At that moment one of the men Whitey had noticed earlier in the hall entered the room without knocking. Whitey guessed he was in response to a pressed button.

"Oh, yes, General," Nixon said in his deep halting voice, "this is Bob Haldeman." A green-eyed slender man with a crew cut stood before them.

Whitey had read up on Nixon's aides and future chief of staff. H. R. "Bob" Haldeman, a former very tough Los

Angeles advertising executive, was the keeper of the gates. He controlled all access to the president-elect. He had said in private to close friends that he was Nixon's "no-man," that Nixon had to have an SOB in his entourage, and he was it. He was going to be a very important staffer in the White House. Staffers did not require Senate approval, nor did they have to answer to Congress, as did presidential Cabinet appointees.

"Bob, this is the Air Force officer I told you about. The one who stood up to, ah, Johnson about his targeting missions, and McNamara about the Stennis Committee."

Haldeman shook hands with a firm, dry grasp.

"Sir," Haldeman said to Nixon, your call to Henry Kissinger is ready now."

"I'll take it in the other room," Nixon said and rose and said to Whitey, "I'll be back. I have something for you to do. In the meantime Bob here will tell you how we do things around here. And Bob, fix the General up with a direct phone line from, ah, his house to my office here, will you?" He walked out the door.

"Here is the deal," Haldeman said without warmth or preamble. "I don't want any end runs."

Whitey raised an eyebrow without answering.

"No end runs," Haldeman continued in a crisp voice. "That means no papers go to the President without passing through a staffer, and no conversations with the President without a staffer present."

"Staffer?" Whitey said, thinking that this young man was rather full of himself and wondering if this was his personal policy or if he had been so advised by Nixon himself.

"I am the chief of staff. There are others. Dwight Chapin works for me. John Ehrlichman, he, ah, works here too. But not *for* me. *With* me, actually, even though I am the one who brought him on board." He pronounced the words with some asperity. "There are others. You will get to know them." He got up from the edge of his desk and sat on the leather chair behind it. "Now, I'm not sure just what your job was over there," Haldeman continued. "Special assistant to the NSC for air power or special assistant to the President for air

404

power, or something like that. Here you will be *assistant* to the President, no *special* attached."

"*If* I accept," Whitey said.

"*If?* You mean there is some doubt?"

Whitey looked at him. *Work with a man like this?* "Most definitely there is some doubt."

"Even if you are promoted?" Haldeman looked startled.

"Even if I am promoted."

The President walked back in. "Kissinger will be here tomorrow," he said to Haldeman, who nodded and left the room.

"Now, then," Nixon said. "I would like you to perform almost the same duties for me as you have for President Johnson. That is, you will be my special liaison with the Department of Defense. And I have a first task for you."

Whitey took a deep breath, ready to say "no." He had made up his mind. There was nothing Richard Nixon could offer him that would induce him to return to active duty. Of course, the President could always recall him involuntarily, but he doubted if Nixon would do that. There was nothing he could offer to induce him to return. He already saw himself at the controls of *Excalibur*. Nixon spoke.

"I want you to devote your time to determining how we can rescue American prisoners of war."

23

Court Bannister and Wolf Lochert climbed down from the Pilatus Porter and reached in for their equipment bags and AK-47s. They were both dirty, bloody, caked with old sweat, and staggering from lack of sleep. They shouldered the bags and silently walked to the Air America flight operations shack. Their pilot, red-haired Dave Little, gunned the big turbo and taxied down the ramp to load for another run, his eighth of the day.

Inside the ops shack they dropped their gear and got a Coke and a beer from the makeshift snack bar, then stood in front of the floor fan to cool off. Court drained his beer, got another, and finished half before he spoke.

"I don't get it. How can we win and still lose at the same time?"

Wolf grunted. They walked to a small wooden table and sat down. "I don't know how they pulled it off unless all that fighting at the top was a cover for it." He thought for a few minutes, then told Court about the *Spetsnaz* code. "They will die just to die," he said. "Their training goes on forever. It is so brutal and dangerous that it changes the man from whatever he was before to a highly trained animal, contemptuous of life. They don't die for *Rodina*, the motherland, or for communism, or for *any* way of life. They don't even sacrifice themselves for each other. They have no friends and form no friendships. When they die, they die to show their contempt for whatever is around them. They use death to prove they don't care about existence."

"Whatever the reason, they got away with three of our men and that big radar tube."

After the battle was over and the Jolly Green had lifted off with the Powers, Mister Sam had gathered together the survivors for roll call and to determine the extent of the damage. Pearson, Verbell, and a young technician were missing. When they had gone to the rocks where the severed harness straps hung and had had more time to look around, they had found strange rappelling gear hidden next to the rocks. They had lowered themselves down to the limestone caves and found footprints mixed with blood scuffled in the dirt. More rappelling gear hung from the cave down the side of the cliff to a wide ledge several hundred feet below.

"They made the snatch here and were picked up by a helicopter down there," Wolf had reasoned.

When they had returned to the radar van, the technicians had said the big Klystron tube had been taken from the TSQ-81 radar set, and that was really strange, because there was nothing special about the tube. They were even available on the surplus market in the States.

Court and Wolf drank in silence. Jim Polter was scheduled to pick them up in a few minutes. Court was struggling to subdue thoughts both ugly and lonely. He had just shot and strangled men, chopped one with a shovel, lost the girl he loved to cancer and his operations officer to a karst mountain. Wolf, with a warrior's consummate wisdom, surmised what Court was going through. He looked at him with gentle eyes, knowing what he was going to say, while true, was not enough. "Time, my friend, time."

Shawn Bannister and Richard Connert stepped down from the ICC plane with several East Bloc journalists and were taken to the one-story cement civilian terminal. The trip had been very hot and extremely bumpy. They had been whisked from the disastrous interview with Flak Apple and held almost under guard for three days until the ICC plane was due out. Whatever the big event was they had promised Shawn he could

407

cover was never mentioned. And they never saw Thach again, but some thin-faced Vietnamese had taken them once more to the shoot-down museum and to several sites they said American air pirates had wantonly destroyed. Outside of a five-minute propaganda broadcast he had made for Radio Hanoi, Shawn had shown no interest, and Connert was desperate to get to US soil with the magazine from Flak. Both men elbowed their way to the Thai Airways counter to purchase tickets for Bangkok and were told they would depart in a few hours. The two men bought beers and sat under the slowly turning ceiling fan.

"I'm still not sure you did the right thing, Connert," Shawn said for the tenth time on the trip. "Pushing those guys so hard for another visit to that awful place." Shawn had made up his mind never to go back to Hanoi.

"I had to make it look real, didn't I? After all, we had a lot of cameras focused on us. As the only Americans, we had to show some concern for one of our countrymen, particularly a black one. You are going after votes, you know, and black votes count just as much as white."

"I suppose you're right." Shawn had never really thought about the hundreds of Americans held in Hanoi.

"And it might just guarantee us a trip back next year."

"Hmmm, maybe." Shawn Bannister had no intention of ever returning to this hell hole of Southeast Asia for any reason, votes or no votes. He stood up and paced in anxiety and boredom. "Look, I can't stand this. Let's get a rickshaw or whatever they have for a ride into the town. I hear Vilay Phone's is a good place to buy gold."

Jim Polter picked up Court and Wolf in his jeep and headed for town, saying he had to make one stop, then they would go to his villa for some refreshments. He said he had been told the Powerses were in Bangkok, where Babs was being attended to in the 5th Field Hospital. He had been well briefed by Mister Sam's radio report, but listened with awe to Wolf and Court's detailed report.

"Hell of a deal," he said when they were finished. He drove down the road toward Vientiane. The air was cool and humid under an overcast. The smell of the sewage by the road was pronounced. "Now let me tell you about a certain broadcast from Hanoi," he said. "Better bite down on something, Court – your half-bro really did a number on the United States. Here's a transcript." He produced a paper from a breast pocket that Court took and read as they bounced along.

"I am Shawn Bannister, broadcasting to you from war-torn but courageous Hanoi in the Democratic Republic of Vietnam. As an American, I am ashamed of what my so-called countrymen are doing to this small defenseless nation in an attempt to take over and exploit Vietnam, just as the colonialist French did. American Navy, Air Force, and Marine flyers are making deliberate terror raids on hospitals and schools in a genocidal attempt to subdue these gentle people. If you are an American soldier in South Vietnam or a sailor at sea or an airman, lay down your arms and convince your officers that what they are doing is criminal and they will be held accountable. I and the peace-loving people of the Democratic Republic of Vietnam urge you to accept peace as your goal. This is Shawn Bannister, speaking to you from Hanoi in the Democratic Republic of Vietnam."

Court's face flamed red when he finished reading, and he crumpled the paper in his fist.

"Hang on," Polter said as he spun the wheel of the jeep. "I got to pick up something at the jewelers." He wheeled in front of Vilay Phone's and stopped, as Shawn Bannister and Richard Connert, arms laden with gifts wrapped in brown paper, walked from the shop.

Totally forgetting his legend, Connert's face lit up as he recognized Court Bannister. Connert had just returned from an extremely hazardous combat mission and was ready for the accolades of his warrior contemporaries. But it was not to be, of course.

Court, his face a raging mask, shouldered by him and grabbed his half-brother, sending his packages flying. Before Shawn

409

could say a word, Court had him in a headlock and jammed the wadded-up Hanoi broadcast into his mouth. Connert stood by, helpless to move. He wanted to cheer, but couldn't make a sound.

"Here, you sorry son of a bitch," Court said, and twisted quickly and flung Shawn into Connert, who staggered back into the wall, regained his balance, and eased Shawn to his feet.

Polter led a furious Court to the jeep, saying he'd pick up his package some other time. Wolf Lochert sat there shaking his head as they drove off.

Connert watched them go. For the first time it truly dawned on him how much he had given up to infiltrate the Movement. He would never, ever forget the look of scorn on Court Bannister's face. He tried to compose a look of concern as he turned to Shawn Bannister. Maybe someday he would be able to tell both Bannisters what his true mission had been. He would like to see Court's expression change, see the recognition on his face of a fellow warrior. And Shawn's face, too. Oh yes, that would be priceless.

Meanwhile Connert knew he would have to continue in his role, content with the expression on another man's face: the one instantaneous look of pure joy he had received from Flak Apple, when Apple realized his country had sent someone in to contact him and his fellow POWs. And he knew that expression made it all worthwhile.

Whistling silently to himself, he took Shawn's arm, nodded agreement to whatever Shawn was muttering, and walked off down the street.

MARK BERENT

PHANTOM LEADER

Vietnam, January 1968: the full fury of the Tet offensive is about to burst. While politics and inter-service rivalries add to the confusion, the Viet Cong attack in force, catching a handful of men in the very heart of the conflict.

USAF spotter pilot Toby Parker – shot from the skies and trapped in the jungle – among the North Vietnamese tanks the top brass said couldn't be there ...

Major 'Flak' Apple – parachuting from his burning F-4 Phantom jet he is captured, tortured and finally imprisoned in Hanoi's infamous Hoa Lo Prison ...

And USAF Major Court Bannister – facing a choice that could make him Vietnam's first air ace – or end his military career altogether ...

PHANTOM LEADER is a searingly authentic story of air combat, written by a much-decorated three-tour Vietnam veteran who portrays the reality of the war as few others can.

HODDER AND STOUGHTON PAPERBACKS

BOB MAYER

DRAGON SIM-13

DRAGON SIM-13. Just another computer-simulated war game.

SCENARIO: a long range Special Forces strike.

TARGET: a strategically vital pipe line.

LOCATION: mainland China, close to the Soviet and North Korean borders.

The top brass in the underground ops room were impressed with the realism.

But then they didn't know that someone had changed the rules. That somewhere in the interior of a China in turmoil, a crack team of Green Berets was in action for real.

And that the computer plan was about to go very wrong indeed.

'A nail-biter in the best tradition of adventure fiction'
Publisher's Weekly

HODDER AND STOUGHTON PAPERBACKS

BOB MAYER

EYES OF THE HAMMER

The jungles of Colombia harbour a deadly secret: cocaine-producing laboratories, market – the United States.

Dave Riley, leading a team of U.S. Green Berets, is tasked to seek out, infiltrate and, with the aid of the heavy weaponry aboard the AC-130 Spectre Gunships, destroy the labs. With the Green Machine team is CIA liaison officer, Kate Westland, one of the few people aware that this is a 'deniable' project – one even the politicians don't know about.

The operation starts well. The first target is taken out with minimal interference and loss; but the special forces team isn't aware that they are being used in a large political game, and their true enemy – Colombia's most lethal drugs baron – is about to make his move. A move that leaves Kate and Dave facing the Ring Man and his henchmen alone . . .

'The climax will have the reader yearning for more nails to bite . . . not to be missed'.
Library Journal

'If you enjoy a good technothriller, this one will leave you spellbound'
Book Ends

'A scorcher of a novel'
Stephen Coonts

HODDER AND STOUGHTON PAPERBACKS

RICHARD HERMAN JNR

FIREBREAK

Lt Matt Pontowski, USAF, just might have wrecked his career. A brilliant flyer but wild. No respect for authority. He could turn an F-15E into a demon from hell and disregard proper procedure like a spoilt kid. Well-connected and good looking, he had a knack of making enemies.

But when the 45th Tactical Fighter Wing find themselves in the eye of a Middle Eastern hurricane, tasked to fly the most dangerous mission of their careers, Matt Pontowski has to grow up fast.

The vengeful Iraqis have developed a new nerve gas and a missile system that can deliver it to the heart of Israel. The Israelis are preparing to go nuclear in response. Only the destruction of the Iraqi chemical plant can avert total war.

The politicians and the military analysts are powerless. Now the issue will be decided by Matt's squadron in the most dangerous skies and over the most unfriendly terrain in the world . . .

HODDER AND STOUGHTON PAPERBACKS